BIRDS IN THE BELFRY

Harry the milkman loses his boots in *Ben Hur* and falls in love. Unfortunately he also falls down the *Ladies* and meets a policeman called Fred. Ob the assistant though unemployed taxidermist tangles with Red and meets Nemesis halfway down a tunnel. Red of course is Boy Blue's *bête noire* and not unnaturally the whole thing reaches its climax at the Fair.

Being set in England's green and pleasant land the climate of the story is meteorologically unsettled—to say the least.

Comedy, crime and unheard-of-situations are the ingredients of Laurence Payne's latest and most addle-pated novel.

By the same author

THE NOSE ON MY FACE
TOO SMALL FOR HIS SHOES
DEEP AND CRISP AND EVEN

BIRDS IN THE BELFRY

by

LAURENCE PAYNE

HODDER AND STOUGHTON

THE CHARACTERS IN THIS BOOK ARE ENTIRELY IMAGINARY AND BEAR NO RELATION TO ANY LIVING PERSON

First printed 1966

PRINTED IN GREAT BRITAIN FOR HODDER AND STOUGHTON LIMITED, ST. PAUL'S HOUSE, WARWICK LANE, LONDON, E.C.4 BY C. TINLING AND CO. LIMITED, LIVERPOOL, LONDON AND PRESCOT

For

BERYL and WINSTON

'I count myself in nothing else so happy
As in a soul remembering my good friends.'

Richard II

PART ONE

CHAPTER ONE

WITH a pint of milk in one hand and a small carton of raspberry-flavoured yoghurt in the other Harry stood straddle-legged in the kitchen doorway and stared at the litter of shavings and sawdust surrounding the bath with mounting apprehension.

'Now what?'

Ob waved a welcoming hammer and mumbled something through a mouthful of nails.

'What?'

Ob spat the nails inexpertly into a grimy palm.

'Making a bath-cover.'

'A what?'

'A bath-cover . . . a cover for the bath.'

'What for?'

'To cover the bath with.'

'Why?'

Only for a moment did Ob hesitate then he said with a certain amount of class, 'If *you* don't mind eating in the bath-room, I *do*!'

'This is the kitchen.'

'With a bath in it.'

It was true enough. There it was, this bath, for all the world to see, a depth to be plumbed and a height to be scaled and over the years Harry had plumbed it and scaled it and come to an understanding, as it were, with its square, uncompromising contours, chipped, yellowing paint and enormous brass taps.

'Why suddenly?' he demanded.

'Suddenly?'

'Why suddenly? All of a sudden you want to cover in the bath. Why?'

'It hasn't been all that sudden; I've been thinking about it for some time.'

Harry wandered disconsolately over to where the table used to be only to discover that it wasn't there any longer. He turned in silence and regarded the bath-cover intently. Even from where he stood he could make out the familiar pattern of the cigarette burns and the place where he had carved his initials into the well-scrubbed wood of the table top. His eyes met Ob's.

Ob waved his hammer encouragingly. 'I only had to tack on a small bit. Now we've got a lot more room.'

'Where,' asked Harry, 'are we going to eat?'

'Off the bath-cover.'

There was a moment of brooding melancholy during which Harry dumped his milk and yoghurt on the floor and seated himself gingerly on one of the two kitchen chairs. He placed his hands on his knees, braced his arms, hunched his shoulders and stared about him for a second or two with ostentatious deliberation.

When he was ready he came back to Ob's friendly brown eyes.

'You,' he said softly and succinctly, 'are a nut.'

Ob didn't mind whether he was a nut or not and said, 'At least it's given us more room. And we don't have to look at that terrible old bath any more.'

'Nut!' repeated Harry. 'Nutcase. The nuttiest nutcase of all the nutcases. Supposing,' he reared up suddenly as another thought struck him, 'Supposing I want to have a bath when you're having your dinner.'

Ob frowned. 'What for?'

'What do you mean "what for?" why shouldn't I have a bath when you're having your dinner?'

'You never have done before.'

'But supposing . . .'

'All right then. I've thought of that.'

'I don't believe it.'

Ob crossed confidently to the bath. He had made a good job of it—even Harry had to admit that; the whole thing had been boxed in with panels of hardboard; the cover had been hinged on to the adjacent wall so that it fitted neatly over the yawning emptiness of the bath like a lid. Only the brass taps, thrusting their slightly obscene, pot-bellied shapes up into the light of day, together with an amazing complication of water pipes, indicated the presence of anything other than a vast, hideous, seven-foot-by-three-foot unenchanting wooden sarcophagus.

Ob raised one end of the lid and looked at Harry to see how he was taking it. Harry didn't move. Ob raised another section —then another—three in all—one after the other. Harry remained unperturbed.

'There,' declared Ob in triumph, 'You can lie in your bath with the top bit open so that your head sticks out and have your dinner at the same time as me.'

Harry groaned deeply and shook his head. 'You're fuller of crackpot ideas than a banana-skin is full of banana.'

'I thought you'd go for it.'

'Okay, so we've got a bath-cover—I go for it. I'll miss the table for a bit, I suppose, but I'll get used to it in time. The trouble with you is that you're so unexpected. I never know what I'm going to find when I get home of a night—especially Friday nights when you know I'm going to be late. There's no stopping you on a Friday, is there?'

'Improving the property, that's all I try to do.'

'My Aunt Fanny! Wish to God you'd get a job. Why don't you get a job and go out all day so's I don't have all this worry. What happened today? Nothing, I suppose.'

Ob looked vacant. 'I signed on; they were very nice; nothing happened.'

'Did you ask about National Assistance?'

'They wouldn't give me National Assistance.'

'I know they wouldn't, but if you never ask you'll never get will you? How do you know there might not be another nit sitting behind the desk who might think you were deserving. Not that I'm surprised, mind you. Who the hell would want an assistant taxidermist? An *assistant* taxidermist, that's the bit I like.'

'I can't help it, can I? I don't want to stuff poor dead animals any more'n you do; I don't know anything else.'

'You don't know much about that either according to you.'

'Dad never taught me properly, that's all. How was I to know he was going to get up and die like he did? Even he didn't know—probably got a bigger shock than I did. One minute there he was stuffing this eagle, next minute he was off—gone. And you know—I couldn't even finish that eagle. By the time I'd done with it the bloody thing looked like a parrot.'

Harry had heard it all before so he was filling in the time by staring at the wood-encased bath. 'Do you know what that thing looks like?' he said, suddenly interrupting Ob in full spate. 'It looks like one of those things in the British Museum with an Egyptian mummy inside it . . .'

'A sargophacus.'

'What?'

'A sargophacus.'

Both decided to let go of it for a bit. Harry sat brooding like an old hen on his kitchen chair whilst Ob collected up his tools and swept the shavings and rubbish into a corner. He paused once by the bath and ran his fingers along the smooth wood. 'Don't you like it, then?'

'What?' Harry roused himself. 'Yes, sure, it's all right. Spot of paint on it, bit of polish on the taps, and we won't know where we are.'

He looked bleakly around the room with its shiny pink and green check wallpaper and its brown patternless lino; he took in the hideous built-in dresser groaning beneath a gallimaufry of different-sized and multicoloured cups, mugs, plates and dishes, tins of soup and loaves of bread, sardines, jam pots, marmalade jars, cornflakes, milk bottles, kitchen scales, a gramophone record, a ball of string and a hard-boiled egg that had been sitting there almost as long as he could remember. Everything you wanted was there on that dresser. And more, he thought, as he watched Ob push aside the boiled egg and gramophone record to make room for a tenon saw, a hammer, a pair of pincers and three ounces of nails.

Then there was the comic gas stove which had been examined and studied by every gas man in the district and was regarded by most of them as a novelty. Nobody knew why it roasted its joint every Sunday to the accompaniment of a high-pitched inhuman scream. Men in cloth caps had sucked and blown, tapped and probed, squinted and listened, and stared at it with glass-eyed frustration. Uniformed inspectors with shiny peaks to their caps had come to peer at it and ask questions, and once a young perky sales manager with a sheaf of coloured brochures tucked under his arm had arrived to inform them that the thing was highly dangerous and should be removed if only for the sake of the adjacent community.

'Right,' Ob had told him. 'Take it away and give us another. But nobody's paying for a new one.'

Since then nothing had happened and the thing screamed

at them mercilessly, burnt their joints, and filled the kitchen with carbon monoxide fumes.

The refrigerator was all right. It hummed and rumbled periodically and the whole place shook with its frenzied ice-making but it worked splendidly, and if the weather ever cheered up it was nice to think that they would be able to keep drinks and things cold.

Harry stared glumly at his aching feet. He had donned his high-heeled elastic-sided Beatle boots that morning to cheer himself up and had regretted it ever since. Once during the lunch hour when he had driven his milk van into the quiet cul-de-sac where he usually took a short nap he had struggled out of them to give his feet a rest and a bit of an airing; it had taken him ten minutes to get them on again.

He regarded Ob's spiky black hair with affection.

'Help us off with my boots will you? I ricked myself today getting into them. Bloody things.'

Ob laid hold of the left one and prepared to take the strain. 'Don't know why you ever bought them. It's not even as though you're mad about the Beatles.'

'I thought I might get to a dance or two, meet a couple of birds p'raps, eh?'

The pain was excruciating as the boot came away but it seemed to hurt Ob more than it did Harry.

'They'll cripple your feet.'

'My feet have always been crippled. That's the best hammer toe on the waterfront.'

The other foot came out with an explosive pop, and settled itself down to a quiet moment of ecstatic expansion.

'How about a cup of tea, then?' enquired Ob.

'Let's do that. What's for supper?'

'Bangers.'

'I don't believe it.'

'I thought you liked bangers?'

'At one time I thought I did too—'

'There's eggs.'

'No, bangers'll do. Take no notice. I'm having one of my turns.'

He rose to his feet, gathered up the milk and yoghurt and padded across to the refrigerator. He stared down at the nearby bath.

'It looks all right. You're a clever old nit, even though you are a nut.' He grinned reminiscently. 'Remember the night I carved those initials?'

'No.'

'Yes you do. What was her name? . . . Nelly? Fanny? What was it?'

'Elsie.'

'No,' Harry was derisive. 'Elsie was the one with the . . . she was the one that creaked all the time—the stays one. This was a blonde kid. Picked her up on the pier if I remember rightly. Now what did she do for a living? She was in a shop . . . or was she a shorthand-typist? . . . She was quite a bird, whatever she was. Her father was a . . . no, he wasn't—he was a shoe salesman—kinky boots and that sort of thing, don't you remember? You remember, she was wearing those high-heeled boots—white, they were—white leather . . .'

'Sandra,' said Ob.

'Sandra! That's who it was. Sandra! Well, well, fancy forgetting her. Sandra. Well, I never. Wonder whatever became of her?'

'She was a toffee-nose; didn't go for you being a milkman. Quite nice though—if you like toffee. So then you carved your initials on the table . . .'

'I did.'

'Why was that? I don't remember why that was.'

Harry stared at him for a moment, then opening the refrigerator he deposited the milk and yoghurt into its grumbling interior, slammed the door, looked obliquely at his initials carved on the bath-cover and finally resumed his perusal of Ob.

'Do you know something?'

'You don't remember either.'

Harry nodded. 'You'd have thought I'd have remembered a thing like that wouldn't you, but I don't. I remember sitting there carving away as if it was only yesterday—in a state about something I was. Makes you think though, doesn't it?'

'Oh, ah.'

'The way we forget. When it's happening it's like hell on earth. One day you wake up and bingo! It's gone, all gone . . .'cept for your initials carved on the table top.'

Ob was filling the kettle at the sink. 'Go and park your feet, I'll get tea.'

'Polly put the kettle on . . .!'

'I must have a hole in my head waiting on you like I do.'
'I'll miss you when you've gone.'
'Where am I going?'
Harry made a face. 'One of these days you'll go.'
'Where?'
'How the hell do I know? You'll meet up with a bird or someone and settle down, I shouldn't wonder.'
'You're joking.'
'We can't stay like this for the rest of our lives, can we?'
'Why not?'
'Come off it. Who's happy? Are you happy?'
Ob was busy swilling tea-leaves down the waste pipe.
'Why shouldn't I be?'
'Well, are you?'
'Of course I am. Aren't you?'
'Sure,' grunted Harry, going through into the sitting-room, 'Sure,' he said, flinging himself down in a despondent heap on the sofa, 'Sure I'm happy.'
He stared sullenly at the stuffed seagull rooted on the mantelpiece. 'You happy?' he asked it. Its bright yellow bead of an eye stared back at him without a blink.
'What?' said Ob from the kitchen.
'What?'
'Thought you said something.'
'No,' said Harry, 'I didn't say anything.'

In the darkness the clock ticked away his lifetime.
He had a headache, his throat was dry, his eyes itched and he was sweating slightly.
For three hours he had lain awake conscious of the shifting, sifting turmoil of his own thoughts.
From the other side of the room came the rhythmic snores of Ob, sprawled on his back with his mouth open. Less than a mile away—turn left outside the front door, left at the traffic lights, right at the next crossing and straight on until you can't go any further—the sea, black and sinister in the darkness, thudded upon the beaches, hissed among the stones, and sucked and gathered itself back into the silence from which the next onslaught would be born.
Between Ob and the sea an occasional car sped through the town; a motor-cycle thundered along the coast road from Oak-

haven, tearing the night in two; a lonely drunk muttered and stumbled his way through a haze of alcoholic uncertainty.

Only once when a girl had giggled suddenly and sensually outside had Harry stirred; the sound had cut off abruptly—as if a hand had been slapped quickly across her mouth ... or another mouth ... His head twisted on the pillow, his eyes, flickering restlessly, sought out the green, glowing hands of the clock. They were just coming up to three o'clock ... another two hours and he'd have to be up and about ...

Ob's breathing grew heavier. His snores were like groans.

'Ob!' said Harry sharply.

Silence fell like an iron curtain. Ob's bed twanged as its burden changed position, then there was silence again, but it wouldn't last long ... it never did ...

Swearing quietly to himself Harry fought his way into a sitting position, struck out at his pillows, and after a moment of intense meditation delivered himself of a well-rounded belch; the satisfaction thus achieved was dulled only by the fact that Ob slumbered on unmoved.

Snapping on his bedside lamp and screwing up his eyes against its glare Harry peered through narrow slits at the untidy recumbent figure. Ob's face was half-buried in the pillow, his hair, black and spiky, stood taut and alert like the bristles on a wire brush. Nothing, it seemed, would ever disturb him again.

Desolate in his frustration, Harry hunched himself into a disgruntled heap and stared gloomily about the room. What he saw did nothing at all to relieve him of his melancholia. He might just as well be sleeping in the kitchen for all the change of atmosphere and organised thought there was about him; there were two beds and no refrigerator in this room, that was about the only difference—and no gas stove, of course, but whoever heard of a gas stove in the bedroom? Jack What's-his-name used to have a gas stove in his bedroom, but then Jack's bedroom was Jack's kitchen and sitting-room all rolled into one. He wondered whatever had become of Jack. During the long winter evenings Jack used to sit watching the television with his bare feet stuck in the gas oven for warmth. Jack was a postman. Jack, he remembered, had been bitten in the calf by a pug dog. Jack was going to sue—everyone had told him to sue, but the owner of the pug dog turned out to be an attractive bird by the name of Gabby, and Jack and Gabby had gone steady for a couple of weeks until the wound in his calf had healed up. By that time he was ready to bite *her* in the calf and they had parted with no regrets . . . Jack had certainly had a gas stove in his bedroom . . .

Harry resumed the contemplation of his own environment; the brown wallpaper, threadbare carpet, marble-topped wash-stand—Jack hadn't had one of those—a wicker chair, a decadent *pouffe* and, over the fireplace, a heavily-framed colour print of a Spanish lady with a red rose clamped between her yellowing teeth. The mantelpiece was littered with the sort of masculine bric-a-brac calculated to strike despondency into the bosom of any female worthy of the name. There were pipes which neither of them smoked, and several cigarettes which both of them had; bottle-openers, old corks, letters, postcards, a Coca Cola bottle with ink in it, the Three Wise Monkeys, an ashtray shaped like a death's head, purporting to be all that was left of Fred who smoked in bed, a bag of sweets, a box of biscuits, some nutshells and two empty glasses. There was also a clock which hadn't worked for five years—and a transistor radio which *had* worked quite well until the ever-curious Ob, having taken the thing apart in a frenzy of well-meaning enquiry, had lost not only his nerve but one or two of the more essential components.

'I wish,' said Harry in a sepulchral voice, 'I wish I was dead.'

'Why is that, then?' asked Ob.

'Oh,' said Harry, '*you've* surfaced.'

'Why do you wish you was dead?'

'Why don't you go back to sleep and mind your own business? You've been snoring the place down all night long, and now when I'm trying to have a few quiet moments you wake up and start asking questions.'

'Pardon me.'

'Go to sleep.'

'Put the light out then.'

'No.'

Harry clambered stiffly out of bed and tried out a couple of painful stretches.

'You too,' he told Ob, feeling guilty about his ill-humour, 'could have a body like mine.'

'You,' returned the ungrateful Ob, 'can keep it.'

Harry flung open the window, hung precipitously out of it and breathed the raw damp air of the imminent dawn deep into his lungs.

Ob stared at him horrified. 'You'll catch something if you're not careful.'

Harry snorted. 'We don't have enough fresh air in this room, that's our trouble. When I get up in the morning the place smells like a frowsy brothel.'

'Wish it was.'

'What?'

'A frowsy brothel.'

'You're disgusting.'

Remembering, he peered down into the street from which the shadows were just beginning to lift. 'There was a bird giggling down there earlier on. Wonder what she was up to?'

'On her own, was she?'

'Why would she giggle if she was on her own?'

'Then we know what she was up to, don't we?'

Harry slammed down the window and came and stared down at Ob from a great height.

'You've got a one-track mind.'

'I used to be all right. It's the company I keep, I expect.'

Harry slumped down on to his bed.

'Look at the time . . . four o'clock. I don't know if I'm going to be able to stand this much longer.'

'Stand what?'

'All this . . . this . . .' Harry waved a desperate hand.

'Why don't you try and get some sleep?'

'What do you think I've been doing for the last three hours?'

'Cup of tea, then?'

Harry shook his head.

Ob was silent for a long time, then he said, 'You want to move out of here, don't you?'

After a moment Harry sighed heavily and lifted his shoulders. 'It's not much cop, is it?'

'It's cheap.'

'You can say that again.'

'Where would we go?'

Harry said nothing.

Ob said, 'You want to be on your own?'

Harry bit into his lower lip then looked directly at Ob. 'Can't imagine what it would be like without you.'

Ob grinned. 'Nights would be quieter.'

Harry returned the grin. 'I might even get some sleep.' He wandered glumly through his thoughts. 'I don't want to break anything up. We get on all right together. I just wish sometimes . . .'

'What?'

'I just wish sometimes you was a nice bird, that's all.'

CHAPTER TWO

ANOTHER brain-child of the resourceful Ob was the 'alarm-clock system'. Since, however, the alarm clock in question invariably refused to fall off the bedside table, and since this particular occurrence was absolutely essential to the smooth accomplishment of the remainder of the plan, it will be readily understood that the word 'system' is used only in its most far-flung interpretation.

The whole thing was really quite simple but was, unfortunately, neither reliable nor foolproof; indeed, had there ever been any question of its coming under consideration for a Certificate of Good Housekeeping, Ob himself would have been the first to demonstrate its shortcomings.

Six mornings out of seven, for fifty weeks of fifty-two, Harry's alarm clock, a monumental example of unbreakable and imperishable pre-war clockwork surmounted by two enormous dissonant bells, had juddered itself off the bedside table on to the floor, where it had squirmed and shook and screamed its rousing message to whomever it concerned—and several others whom it did not.

Four mornings out of every six it had required the added impetus of a shriek from Ob and a shower of random objects to get Harry on the move.

Ob had therefore applied himself to the problem.

If, he argued, the impetus and weight of the falling clock could be harnessed to power, the answer was in sight.

He therefore tied one end of a long piece of string to the clock, passed the other through a pulley which he had screwed into the ceiling immediately above the bedside table, ran the length of the string down the wall and completed the circuit by fixing it firmly to the power-switch which, as luck and clever planning would have it, was situated in the wainscot at just that point. He had previously inverted the switch so that 'Up' was 'on' and 'Down' was 'Off'. The gravitating clock would therefore switch on the power; it would also switch on, according to Ob's whim, a lamp, an electric fire, an electric iron, the gramophone, the radio—or whatever happened to be plugged in when the moment of truth arrived. What was usually plugged in was Ob's tape-recorder—a survival of his palmier days with which he obstinately refused to part—which, with all its knobs turned to the 'On' and 'Go' positions, required nothing more than two hundred and forty volts to launch itself into a repertoire as extensive and varied as the mind could desire; there were seagulls screaming outside the kitchen window and a talk by Ob on the Childhood of Ob; there was *Juke-Box Jury,* several mornings of *Housewives' Choice* and the complete second act of *Tosca* sung by Maria Callas and Tito Gobbi. Such was the entertainment liable to be thrust upon an unsuspecting and sleeping world at five-thirty in the morning to continue non-stop if need be until eight-thirty—at any rate until such time as Harry had aroused himself sufficiently to reach out of bed and under the table and turn the thing off.

In theory foolproof, in practice falling a little short of 'completely unreliable'.

The first time Ob tried it out the weight of the clock brought down the pulley and a considerable portion of the ceiling, an event which proved to be not altogether unrewarding, for it revealed a sturdy crossbeam into which Ob, with an eye on posterity, immediately rescrewed his pulley.

The second time the string broke, the third time the clock refused to judder itself off the table, the fourth time the clock refused to judder itself off the table ... in fact, had Ob set himself the task of curing the clock of its habit of juddering itself off the table, success would now have been staring him in the face. From that moment onwards the two stumpy brass feet of the clock appeared to develop a faculty for suction second only to the acorn barnacle. If he tipped the table at an angle of forty-five degrees the clock slid off splendidly and the whole thing worked like a charm—but who needed a table with an angle of forty-five degrees?

Ob lost interest. Neither Harry nor he dismantled the 'system'; it was just left to look after itself—sometimes it worked, more often it did not. Ob continued to shriek and hurl handy objects at the slumbering Harry.

But on the morning in question, of course, it worked.

To say that the sleep which had overtaken Harry at about five o'clock was a deep sleep would be like saying that Rip Van

Winkle fell into a doze. The depths to which he finally plunged were unplumbed and unsounded—certainly unoccupied; he lay sprawled like a starfish on the bottom of the Bottomless Pit which was just one station beyond the Primordial Deep.

Imagine, then, his astonishment when, in the space of two seconds, he found himself staggering to an upright position in a small, sordid room on the South Coast of England, with a great blasting of trumpets and crashing of gunfire resounding in his deafened ears; an alarm bell was ringing, someone was shrieking at him and there were heavy thumpings on the ceiling above his head. A shoe hit him in the stomach and with a wail of agonised confusion rising to his lips he collapsed back on to the bed.

'Turn it off! ... turn it off! ...' shouted a voice.

It was Ob, hair on end, eyes popping, bolt upright in the bed opposite. Every one of Harry's outraged senses stopped and stared at him uncomprehendingly.

'The Thing!' yelled Ob, struggling to extricate himself from his mummy-like wrappings.

The sound of artillery shook the room, five brass bands and three full orchestras hurtled their way relentlessly through the Russian Imperial Anthem, every bell that had ever been cast clanged and chimed ... Still only half conscious of what he was doing Harry flung himself at the tape-recorder, grappling with knobs and tugging blindly at wires. A reel of tape came away in his hands—the machinery snapped and whirred angrily. He hit out at a switch. There came an ugly *clump* and everything suddenly went quiet. Breathless and confused, his heart doing its best to clamber out of his aching chest, he clutched the reel of tape to his stomach and sank low on the floor like a Buddhist monk worshipping a tape-recorder.

It had become so quiet that they could hear the gentle rhythmic straining of the string as the clock swung slowly to and fro from its pulley in the ceiling.

Ob, his nether limbs still incapacitated by their swathing of sheets, sat on the edge of his bed swaying wordlessly; Harry, kneeling on the floor, nodded and moaned at his devotions; against the window the wind blew a swift scurry of rain.

It was some time before life began to seep back into their limbs, and when it did it was Harry who finally ventured to break the silence.

'What in the name of God was that?' he demanded in a hoarse whisper.

Ob looked at him soberly. 'I didn't even know it was on there.'

'What? What was it, for God's sake?'

'The 1812 Overture.'

'What, all that banging and shooting and trumpets ... sounded like the end of the bloody world!'

'I didn't know it was even on there. It's just supposed to be a recording of *Housewives' Choice;* I must have been out of the room when they played that one.'

'You must have been out of the country if you didn't hear that lot. I'll never be the same again. And old mother Bagwash upstairs'll do her nut.'

He clambered slowly to his feet, winding the loose tape on to the reel he was still clutching.

'I've bust your tape.'

'It'll mend.'

'I had to stop it, didn't I? Sorry I bust it.'

'Doesn't matter. Quite easy to mend.'

Harry stood scratching his head. 'Blimey, I still can't get over it—I'm all of a quiver.'

He caught the clock by the string and peered at it in the half-light. 'I've been asleep for twenty-five minutes.' He let the clock go and watched it swinging for a moment. He squinted up at the pulley in the ceiling. 'It's no good, this thing of yours, is it? I mean it doesn't work, does it? Sometimes it works—like this morning—but more often than not it doesn't, does it?'

'No,' said Ob.

'Quite a good idea, of course—if it worked. Pity it doesn't.'

'Mind you—' said Ob.

'What?'

Ob pursed his lips thoughtfully. 'It just struck me ... probably wouldn't work either ... still, no reason why we shouldn't try, is there?'

Harry stood over him, resplendent though threatening in scarlet woollen pyjamas. 'Do me a favour?'

'What's that?'

'Forget it.'

'As I say, it probably wouldn't work, anyway.'

'Well, don't let's try, eh?'

'Wouldn't take a minute ...'

'Ob, listen ...'

'If I could just jack up that table ...'

'For crying out loud! You'll get us chucked out of this place. It's crummy enough as it is, God knows, without you messing about with it.'

'I'm only trying to improve it.'

'No. How many more times do I have to tell you? No!'

Harry stalked out into the kitchen and banged the kettle on. It wasn't that he didn't sympathise with Ob, he did; in fact he could see his point of view quite clearly, but Ob had to be made to understand that whether he, Ob, considered that the removal of an odd wall or two would improve property or not, it wasn't his, Ob's, sacrosanct duty to remove that wall with his own two hands.

Whilst he waited at the sink for the water to run hot enough for him to shave Ob came and loitered at the kitchen door and watched him. Harry ignored him for a bit then said reasonably, 'It's not as if it's our house. You can't just dig up the floor whenever you feel like it. We're only tenants ... we pay rent ...'

'*You* pay rent ...'

'Well, *I* pay rent, then. You pay it when you can. I like it that way. But if we get chucked out ...'

'We won't.'

'If, I said ...'

'I won't mess about any more.'

'Good.'

'Not unless we both agree that something should be done.'

'That,' said Harry emphatically, 'will never be.'

Ob shuffled off but was back a minute later swathed in his second-best raincoat, which served as a dressing-gown.

Harry looked at him uneasily. 'Why don't you go back to bed?'

'Now I'm up, I might as well stay up.'

'I hope that doesn't mean you've got a busy day in front of you.'

'Doing nothing, as far as I know. What about you? What are you going to do?'

'Work.'

'After that, though.'

Harry turned on the light over the steamy mirror and lathered his chin. 'If I'm through by two I thought I might have a bash at *Ben Hur*.'

Ob's face fell open. 'What for?'

'Five,' said Harry rudely.

'What?'

'Pot!' said Harry. He scrubbed irritably at the mirror then turned and looked steadily at Ob for a second. 'What, might I ask, is wrong with *Ben Hur*?'

Ob thought for a moment then said, 'It's six hours long.'

'Four.'

'It's one of those epic things—ten thousand in the cast and all that.'

'So, what's wrong with that? At least you get your money's worth. Anyway, I like epics with ten thousand in the cast.'

'That's right,' said Ob remembering and nodding. 'You always go to them, now I think of it.'

Harry snorted. 'Damn sight better than all them mucky old foreign pictures you're always going to that don't have any beginning or any end and then go and break in the middle. I'll never forget that last one you made me see.'

'You didn't have to come. Which was that?'

'The sewer one ... the one in the sewer ... the one that all happened in the sewer. It was so bloody dark nobody could see what was going on. 'Bout the only thing I saw all evening was the sub-titles—and I didn't even understand them.'

'Shall I make the tea?'

'What?'

'Tea.'

'Yes, if you want to. Why don't you go back to bed? Not used to seeing you prowling about at this time of night.'

'I'm up now.'

'You going to cook me some breakfast as well, then?'

'What do you want?'

'Bacon and fried bread.'

'I can't say I don't miss the old table,' said Harry, pulling his chair up to the bath.

'We'll get used to it.'

'It's sitting beside each other like this that seems funny. I liked you better when you were over the way.' He stared dismally at the mess of prunes, yoghurt and All-Bran in Ob's bowl and felt queasy. 'I also couldn't see what you were eating. That stuff'd do me an injury.'

Ob stirred the mixture with a disinterested spoon. 'I don't like it much either, but it's good for me.'

'Bunk.'

'You can laugh, you don't know what it's like.'

'And I don't want to neither.'

'No, I mean you don't know what it's like not to be regular.'

'I try not to think about it,' said Harry unsympathetically. 'So you won't come to *Ben Hur,* then?'

'No.'

'P'raps I won't go then. I hate going alone.'

'Find someone to go with you.'

'For instance?'

'Some bird you know.'

'Like who?'

Ob addressed himself to his prunes and yoghurt for a thoughtful moment or two. He ejected a prune-stone into the bowl of his spoon and stared at it solemnly. 'You never see anything of Ada Lewis nowadays, do you? You used to chat her up quite a bit at one time. Don't you ever see her now?'

Harry made a derogatory noise. 'She's not interested in me any more. What can *I* give her? She met up with that singer-bloke—*singer*! Don't make me laugh—the one with the haircut and the banjo, used to do his stuff at the *Bull* down the road 'til the telly discovered him—'*discovered*'! They couldn't very well have missed him the way he used to throw himself under their wheels.' He raised a finger at Ob. 'If,' he added wisely, 'he'd *got* any talent they'd have missed him by miles, you take my word for it.'

The profundity of this remark startled them both into a silence which was broken only by the bumble of the refrigerator and the steady downpour of rain outside.

Breakfast over, Harry rose, burped and peered disconsolately through the window.

'Who'd be a poor, bloody milkman?' he muttered.

'There's Elsie West, what about her?' Ob's brain was still concerned with match-making. 'There's always Elsie West.'

Harry said, 'There always *was* Elsie West, you mean. She's

gone. Hopped it. Her firm went off to London, don't you remember? And she went with them.'

'Myra Hacket?' suggested Ob.

'B.O.'

'Polly Hardcastle?'

'You're joking.'

'Freda Frazer—Fred—How about Fred Frazer? She was quite a dish in her own small way.'

Harry stared at him wearily. 'Fred Frazer married a policeman two years ago and went to live in Worthing. Now shut up about it, will you? If I want a bird to go out with I'll find one on my own without your help, thank you very much. I know you mean well but I'm quite capable of running my own love life—and all that.'

'What's the matter with Polly Hardcastle?'

'Polly Hardcastle,' growled Harry, 'has got a moustache.'

They both laughed a bit over that, but Harry soon sobered up as he struggled manfully into his gumboots. He shrugged on his shiny black oilskin and stood for a moment still glooming out of the window.

'Who wants a bloody milkman, anyway?'

'Don't keep saying that.'

'Well, who does? You tell me.'

'Lots of women are married to milkmen.'

'What have I got to offer, eh? What have I got to offer anybody? I'm not even a *positive* milkman.'

'A what?' Ob looked startled.

'A Positive Milkman. There are two sorts of milkmen—so they tell us down at the depot. Up on the wall down there they've stuck a damn great picture—the Positive Milkman and the Negative Milkman. The first one's a silly bugger and wears his uniform all the time and carries a loaded crate of milk bottles and smiles at all the customers like an idiot. The negative milkman doesn't do any of those things. He doesn't wear his cap, *or* his little white jacket, and he bangs about with a hundred and thirty milk bottles bunged under his arm—and what's more, he doesn't smile at anybody. That's me—the negative one, and don't think I'm not proud of it!'

'You're a rebel.'

'That's me. The Rebel Milkmaid.' Picking up the kitchen clock which lay on its face on a shelf over the sink—the only position in which it would work at all—he peered at it closely. 'I'm going to be late. Standing about here gassing with you ... like a couple of old hens ...'

Halfway down the passage he paused and came slowly back to the kitchen door. Ob, who had been doing nothing at all, looked guilty. 'Don't get up to anything while I'm away, will you?' warned Harry in a level threatening tone. 'Building things and sawing things up and the like ... all right?'

Ob grinned and shrugged. 'You know me.'

Harry nodded. 'That's why I thought I'd just mention it.'

CHAPTER THREE

On the corner the small, drenched boy waited patiently.

As the van drew alongside he stepped solemnly aboard and took his place on the long seat beside Harry.

The van whined softly and the bottles jingled.

'Hi,' said Harry.

'Hi,' said the boy.

On their right the sky and the sea merged into a dull flat nothingness of grey; the tyres hissed on the wet road.

'Didn't think you'd turn out on a morning like this,' said Harry.

'Said I would, didn't I?' answered the boy, brushing the long sweep of wet black hair out of his eyes.

'Lots of people *say* they're going to do things and then don't do them.'

'Not me,' said the boy shortly.

Harry glanced at him. 'No, not you.'

The boy was sickly-looking, underfed, and could do with a whole new outfit—the clothes he was wearing were just about falling off him; the jeans and the shirt and the grubby sweater—all of them should have gone into the rag-bag long ago; the short Wellingtons were all right at the moment but wouldn't be for long.

'Haven't you got a coat or something?' asked Harry.

'No.'

'You'll catch your death of cold wandering about on a day like this without any coat.'

The boy said nothing. There was an air of secretiveness about him and a self-sufficiency which was vaguely disturbing in one so young.

'How old are you?' asked Harry.

'Thirteen.'

'Bit young, aren't you?'

'What for?'

'Don't know as I'm really allowed to take on a bloke as young as you.'

'You did last week.'
'I know I did last week. But I didn't know then, did I?'
The boy looked at him. 'I'd have told you if you'd asked.'
Harry shrugged. 'I don't make the rules. As far as I'm concerned it's okay—so long as you do the job. It's what they say up at the depot that counts.' He made a face down at the boy. 'If anyone wants to know, you're fifteen, right?'
'Right.'
'Now we've got that settled, what do they call you?'
'Who?'
'Anybody. What's your name?'
'Ben.'
Harry thought for a moment. 'You're the first Ben I've ever met in my whole life.'
'Go on?'
'Ben what? Hur?'
'Hart.'
'You can call me Harry, if you want to.'
The boy didn't seem to be in any hurry to call him Harry. He was occupying himself with an attempt to dry out the knees of his wet jeans; the heat of his body was making them steam.
Harry said, 'Haven't you got a mack or anything at home?'
'Never had a mack in my life.'
Harry grinned. 'No Rolls-Royces either, I suppose? Or yachts and things?'
'I had a yacht once,' said Ben solemnly, 'got stuck in the weeds and when I went to get the park keeper to get it out for me someone must have waded in and pinched it. I never found out who it was. Will you let me come with you every week?'
'Er—sure, yes, if you think you're going to like it. The chap I used to have packed it in a couple of weeks back to go and play football on Saturdays, so you just came along at the right moment, didn't you?'
'Sundays too?'
'If you want to.'
'Okay.'
'And you're fifteen if anybody wants to know.'
'Right.'
Ben suddenly smiled. It was a good smile and lit up the whole of his face.

'This is my first job—ever.'

'Well, don't flip your lid, it's nothing to write home about.'

'My mum says it isn't the job what counts but what you make of it.'

'Your mum,' said Harry, 'sounds like a wise lady.'

The morning went quite well. Twelve o'clock found them parked by the war memorial opposite the pier. Harry had bought a couple of bars of chocolate and they were helping it down with a pint of milk.

'When's dinner-time?' Harry asked.

'My dinner-time?' Ben shrugged. 'When I get it.'

'We'll be through in half an hour once we get going again.'

With the shrewd eye of a connoisseur he followed the progress of a pert young lady picking her way carefully through the puddles like a chicken; her skirt was too tight, so that the necessity of stepping across a wide puddle usually finished up with her standing in the middle of it. The legs were quite good, he thought, though the ankles erred a bit on the thick side, nice hips and narrow waist, a splendid pair of Bristols—aided and abetted though they obviously were by artificial means—and he craned his neck as she tapped busily past, a very nice, very smart, and very dainty little bottom. It was just the face he hadn't cared for—the face and the ankles ... otherwise ...

'Why do you look at all the girls like that?' asked Ben.

'Pardon?'

'You look at 'em all like that.'

'No extra charge, is there?'

'Why, though? I want to know.'

'You're too young. Don't ask questions.'

Ben smirked. 'There's not much about girls I don't know.'

Harry raised his eyebrows. 'How old did you say you were?'

'Thirteen.'

'Blimey.'

'What did you think about that one?'

'I didn't exactly go a bundle on her face.'

'Why not?'

'Didn't appeal, that's why not.'

'Do they have to be pretty?'

Harry glanced at him warily. 'It helps.'

'Why?'

'Thought you said you knew all about it.'

'So I do. That's why I want to know why it matters if they're pretty or not.'

Harry cleared his throat uneasily.

'Do you like this place?' he asked. 'Funny old dump, isn't it?'

'It's all right,' said Ben. 'My sister's quite pretty.'

'You always lived here?'

'I was born here. It's all right. I liked it better when I was young. Playing on the beach and up on the cliffs at Oakhaven.'

'How old is she?'

'Who?'

'Your sister.'

'Older than me.'

'You're kidding.'

Ben pursed his lips. 'I think she's older than she says she is.'

'How old,' asked Harry, 'does she say she is?'

Ben looked at him shrewdly. 'She *says* she's twenty.'

Harry took a long thoughtful gulp of milk. Ben turned a vacant gaze in the direction of the grey sea.

'Er . . .' said Harry tentatively.

'She goes out with a bloke but she don't like him much,' said Ben. 'Why? Haven't you got a girl of your own?'

Harry was startled. 'Course I have—plenty—two or three as a matter of fact . . .'

Ben gave a secret smile. 'I thought you was married at first.'

'What made you think that?'

'The way you looked at girls . . . they usually do that when they're married . . .'

Harry leaned back and stared at the boy with growing respect. 'Your mum's not the only wise old bird in your family, is she? You got a girl, I suppose?'

Ben made a rude noise. 'Don't make me laugh! Girls!' Another rude noise followed the first. The whole sentence had been on one long note of quite startling derision, opened and closed by a pair of unusually vocalised inverted commas.

Harry said, 'Sounds as if you don't like girls.'

Ben shrugged. 'Oh, I like them all right, I just haven't got much time for them.' He looked airily at a passing female and snapped off a piece of chocolate with an expressive gesture. 'I think they always try too hard.'

Harry's jaw sagged.

'Tell me . . .' he said.

'What?'
'What's your sister's name?'
'Betty.'
'Elizabeth?'
'No, Betty.'
'Betty.'
'That's right.'
Harry drained his bottle of milk, sat for a couple of indecisive moments smacking his lips, then said, 'Wonder what she'd think of me . . . your sister . . . Betty . . .'
Ben looked at him seriously but said nothing.
'. . . I mean, if she doesn't like this bloke she's going out with . . .'
'I thought you said you had two or three girls.'
Harry's laugh sounded a bit empty. 'So why shouldn't I have?—safety in numbers. Would she mind me being a milkman?'
'Why should she?'
'I don't know.'
'What's wrong with being a milkman?' Ben was fervent in defence of his newly-acquired occupation. 'I wouldn't mind being a milkman!'
Harry's head was whirling. 'What? It's all right—yes, but . . . well, girls don't go for it . . . some of 'em.'
'Why not?'
'I don't know why not!' Harry was becoming petulant. 'You ask too many questions. How do I know why they don't like milkmen. At least, I don't say they *don't* like them, but they don't like them like they like, say . . . oh, I don't know. You're getting me all mixed up—I don't know what I'm talking about any more. Shut up, will you, and let's get on with the job.'
When, half an hour later, he dropped the boy off at the corner and the van had drawn away from the kerb, he glanced curiously at the reflection in his driving-mirror. The boy, with both hands thrust into his trouser-pockets, was standing in a self-assured straddle in the middle of the pavement staring after the receding vehicle.
'He's an old man,' muttered Harry in a not altogether distressed tone. The thought set him on to wondering whether he himself at the age of thirteen had even been aware that there was any intrinsic difference between boys and girls, other than the usual things of girls not being able to throw straight and

C

boys being more knowledgeable. He could certainly remember his open-mouthed scepticism when, loitering one wet night on a corner beneath a lamp-post, the difference had been succinctly pointed out by a worldly cynic some six months younger than he. He even remembered what the cynic looked like, after all these years. Jack Havergal—a peculiarly apt name under the circumstances but one which, in the light of subsequent events, proved quite unsuitable.

As far as he could recollect the knowledge had done little to alter the course of his life; he did ask one girl to prove the whole thing to him, but she had not taken kindly to the request and went home and told her mother, who then came and told *his* mother and there was a fair bit of unpleasantness about it.

He slowed down at a pedestrian crossing to allow the passage of a pretty young thing in tartan trews across his bows, his admiration of her lines almost bringing to grief a large lady with a flat green hat and two heavy shopping baskets who was floundering and tacking in the wake of the trim little vessel. The large lady stopped in the middle of the road and stared at him wordlessly through her round gold-rimmed glasses. She looked a bit like his mother. He stuck his head out into the cold wind.

'Sorry, lady,' he said.

She shook her head at him. 'You're all the same—no eyes for anyone who hasn't got a pretty face.'

She went on her way and as the van glided forward he felt guilty.

He was an unconscionable time trying to make up his mind about his Beatle boots; they squatted, like evil things, in the silence of the hearth behind the fender and eyed him narrowly. Resplendent in his light grey flannel, white shirt and scarlet tie he sat in morose contemplation of them, weighing up their pros and cons.

Ob looked in curiously. 'Thought you were going to have a bite of something before your orgy.'

'So I am, down at the caff.'

'If you go on thinking about it much longer *Ben Hur* will be dead and buried and over with.'

'What's the time, then?'

'Past one.'

Harry blew down his nose. 'What am I going to do about my boots?'

Ob wrinkled his nose; they'd had this conversation before. 'What,' he asked dutifully, 'do you want to do about them?'

'I don't know whether to wear them or not.'

'They're your boots.'

'They're also my feet.'

'If they hurt that much I shouldn't wear them.'

'The other black ones let in the water, that's the trouble.'

'You've got three pairs of brown ones in the cupboard.'

Harry looked disdainful. 'Brown with grey?'

Ob made a face. 'Used to be all the rage at one time—brown with grey.' He watched Harry for a second, then said, 'You're putting them on, then?'

Harry grunted as he struggled grimly into the boots. 'It's the blokes down at the caff; you know what they are. I'd never live down brown boots.'

Ob leaned up against the doorpost and shook his head sadly. 'Dirty old jeans, crummy leather jackets and cut-down gumboots is what they go in for.'

'You've never seen 'em geared up.'

Ob shrugged and lounged away. 'They're your feet.'

When he got to the café there was only a handful of the boys there; most of them on the pin-tables, three others were huddled together in a story-telling conclave at the far end of the coffee-bar. One of them, a broad-shouldered redhead in a multi-studded leather jacket, looked round, stared hard at Harry for a moment then said, 'Hi, Flash.'

'Hi,' said Harry. The greeting, whilst according certain satisfaction, caused him also to throw a furtive glance at his reflection in the long mirror behind the bar. Normally he wouldn't have been worried by the remark—might even have been flattered, but the fact that he had never seen the redhead in his life before made him wonder whether perhaps there hadn't been something the slightest bit derogatory about it.

He humped himself up on to a high stool and grinned at Fat Doris as she lumbered up behind the bar.

'Hello, luv,' she said, 'What's it going to be?'

'Couple of 'burgers, Doris, please.'

'Onion?'

'What?'

'Onion.'

He shrugged. 'What have I got to lose?'

Doris clattered about behind the counter for a bit humming something unrecognisable beneath her breath. Harry tried to ease his feet inside his boots. A raucous gale of laughter came from the direction of the pin-tables. The redhead at the end of the bar looked up and caught Harry's eye in the mirror; they stared at each other levelly for a moment, then the redhead craned his neck and regarded his contestant without the aid of the mirror. Harry grinned and nodded companionably.

'Hi, Flash,' said the redhead again.

Harry set his jaw.

'Hi, Red.'

The redhead's little eyes narrowed with suspicion, 'Do I know you?'

'You keep talking to me.'

'How do you know my name?'

Harry shrugged modestly. 'How did you know mine?'

'Flash? Is that your name?'

Harry grinned. 'What else?'

Red's eyes ran over him once again. 'You're right,' he said in a vaguely puzzled tone, 'What else? Good for you, Flash.'

Red's two companions were following events in the mirror and when Red finally turned back to them one of them, a gaunt young man with thinning hair and a drip on his nose, said in a loud *sotto voice*, 'Who's that then, Red?'

'Ask him,' said Red.

While Harry chewed his way stubbornly through the two hamburgers which did nothing at all for him other than make him feel like an over-inflated rubber mattress, the café's Saturday afternoon business began to boom considerably, most of the excitement being brought about by the crowding-in of honest, masculine, football types in parti-coloured woollen scarves and carefree knitted hats who jostled and elbowed and yelled their various ways to and fro and up and down the narrow confines of the premises, hurtling good-natured abuse at one another and whirling their earsplitting rattles playfully above their heads.

With an outward stoicism which belied his inner feelings Harry munched at his onions and stared unenthusiastically at the whole thing in the mirror behind the bar.

His attention was suddenly diverted by the fact that the multi-studded leather jacket with the red hair was showing signs of imminent departure. His two henchmen—the other one was a short, spotty-faced boy with a Beatle hairdo which had to be seen to be believed—the two of them all but withdrew the stool from beneath the tight-jeaned posterior of their rufous-headed leader as he rose augustly to his feet. At least, it was fairly august until he reached ground level then one realised that he had not really risen at all—as he forsook the temporary advantage of the stool he also shed several inches. Harry decided that without the two-inch heels on the richly-tooled cowboy boots he would stand no more than a mere five feet six in his stockinged feet.

Harry stared down boldly at the thinning red crown.

'See you, Red,' he said.

The whites of Red's eyes glowed a little pinkly as he flicked them sidelong at Harry.

'In church, Flash,' he growled in a surly voice.

Like a small sturdy fleet of ice-breakers they elbowed their way through the throng; nobody noticed their departure.

Fat Doris floundered up and spreading her ample bosom over the counter leaned confidentially in Harry's direction.

'What did you tell him your name was Flash for, Harry?'

'I didn't tell him.'

'I don't notice you arguing about it.'

'Who is he? Never seen any of 'em before, have I?'

Doris shrugged and rolled her popping blue eyes. 'They've been in a couple of times; come from over Oakhaven way, I believe. They behave 'emselves all right, but up to no good I'll be bound.'

She went off to replenish somebody's teacup. Harry, looking around, could see no one he knew. None of the regulars seemed to be there. Even if they were it wasn't likely that any of them would feel inclined to accompany him to *Ben Hur*.

Doris was back. 'Enjoy your 'burgers?'

Harry burped gently. 'Bit fat-making, but otherwise all right.'

'Fat-making!' Doris crowed with laughter and dealt him a hefty blow on the shoulder with an iron fist. 'You can talk! Look at me! When you're as fat as me you can talk.'

When I'm as fat as you, thought Harry to himself, I doubt whether I shall be able to talk.

'Still,' she spread herself even more fulsomely over the counter, 'it's glands with me, you know.'

'Go on,' said Harry.

'Thyroid.'

'Really?'

'That's why my eyes pop a bit, haven't you noticed that?'

'What?'

'That my eyes pop a bit.'

'No,' lied Harry. 'Do they? isn't there anything they can do about that sort of thing, then? Like taking something for it?

Doris thought for a moment then said. 'I think I could have it out if I wanted to.'

'Have what out?'

'Whatever it is. I don't know what they call it. The thyroid, I suppose, how do I know?'

'Is your clock right?'

'Five minutes fast.'

'I've got to go.' He added sagely, 'you can have most things out nowadays.'

'At a price.'

'On the National Health.'

Doris opened her eyes wider than anyone would have thought possible. 'I wouldn't let none of them National Health doctors touch *me*. Now they don't get paid for it they don't care *what* they take out. First thing they see when they open you up, out it comes. You off to the match?'

'No, pictures.'

'On a lovely afternoon like this?'

Harry stared at the opaque steamy windows. 'It's raining cats and dogs.'

'Well I never!' said Doris. 'You'd never know in here, would you?'

It wasn't raining cats and dogs, as a matter of fact—it wasn't raining at all—so Harry decided to walk to the cinema rather than take a bus—the film didn't start until two-fifteen and it wasn't two yet.

A brisk, gusty breeze blowing in off the sea caused him to tug irritably at his collar, which action caused him in turn to wish that the designers of the latest trend in masculine rainwear had not dictated that the collar and lapels of his new white shortie had to be quite so narrow thus affording no shelter and warmth for his suffering ears. But nowadays, of course, you didn't pay for comfort and warmth, you paid for 'line' and new materials and fibres, all of which, you could rest assured, would be out of date in another few months.

His undiminished depression clung to him like a damp towel. He watched the pointed toes of his Beatle boots carrying him forward along life's road and wondered where the hell they were taking him—and why the hell they had to hurt so much while they were doing it. No comfort, no warmth, and out of date in a couple of months—typical! Still, at least they didn't let in the water like his others did, so he walked through all the puddles just to prove it.

A smart, glossy little black mackintosh with knee-length patent leather boots to go with it gave him what he interpreted to be a glad eye as it swished invitingly on its way towards Headington and, dismissing for the moment all thought of *Ben Hur* from his adaptable mind, he turned and splashed off in dutiful pursuit. The pace set was quite considerable and after he had been at it for a couple of minutes he was breathing quite heavily and wondering whether the whole thing was going to be worth it. Then, quite suddenly, without any warning at all, the mackintosh stepped off the pavement on to a bus which was just pulling away from the kerb. He stopped in his tracks and watched the patent leather boots ascend primly to the upper deck. Through the rear window of the bus he caught the red-lipped curl of a mocking smile.

He shrugged good-humouredly, turned, and once again set his helm for Ancient Rome and the Holy Land.

CHAPTER FOUR

HALFWAY through the chariot race he lost his boots.

It was his own fault. With considerable fortitude he had tolerated an hour and a half of foot-destroying agony until it seemed to him, wallowing in the bitter waters of masochistic submission, that amputation would have been preferable to the further endurance of the torture inflicted upon him by that pair of cobbler's misfits. To the accompaniment therefore of a great deal of straining and heavy breathing on his part, and a fair amount of uneasy speculation on the part of those in his immediate vicinity, he had removed the offending footwear and placing them carefully, almost reverently, beneath his seat, had indulged himself in the rapturous relief only to be appreciated by those who have assumed, worn and shed ankle-high Beatle boots two sizes too small for them.

By the time the interval arrived Harry, already identifying himself with the tall, craggy, blue-eyed Ben Hur, could only sit back in a preoccupied Biblical daze and toy half-heartedly with an ice cream and a small bag of assorted nuts.

It was not until the nuts had gone and the polythene bag consigned to outer space with a dexterous flick of the forefinger that he recalled that his boots had not been the only distraction during the first half of the film. Several moments of uneasy concern had been caused him by the heavy wafting of perfume liberally exuded by the female on his left, so that he had found himself peering obliquely and vainly through the gloom in an attempt to ascertain whether any suits pressed in that direction would be likely to yield a beneficial return or two. Now that the lights were up and it was possible to take a more objective view of the matter he was glad that his instinct had adhered to its own particular maxim, that discretion is the better part of bird-watching, for the bird in question was well past middle age, blue-jowled and masculine, and met his eye with a predatory gleam which would have put a lesser man off his food for a week. She also wore some twelve or thirteen bangles on her right forearm which clanged and clattered alarmingly at her slightest move. Harry found himself regarding them in the light of a kind of life insurance policy.

On his right a man with a protruding lower lip and an undeniable partiality for Indian curry returned Harry's stare with a stony indifference which would have been rude if Harry hadn't started it.

Most people were smoking, and there was an air of damp depression about the place which made Harry slump down in his seat and long for the resumption of the entertainment. Apart from a dame, he thought, there is nothing quite like a wet Saturday afternoon in an English cinema. He frowned. That sounded as though a dame was like a wet Saturday afternoon in an English cinema—which wasn't what he meant at all. It was the song from *South Pacific* ... how did it go? *There is nothing like a dame ... nothing ... nothing in the world ... that is anything like a dame ...* A jangle of bracelets on his left brought him down to earth again with the realisation that his feat of memory had been in the process of becoming vocal; a man and woman sitting in the row in front had turned and were looking at him.

He made a face. 'Enjoying it?' he asked. They turned away quickly.

If I, thought Harry with a certain amount of complacence, had a face like that one there—meaning the man who had turned and looked at him—I would take jolly good care that no one else knew about it. Fancy being married to a face like that—living with it—seeing it every morning in the shaving-mirror. Fancy owning it! *Mirror, mirror on the wall, who is the fairest of us all? Well, not you, mate, for a start, I'll tell you that for nothing* ... He gave the lady on the left a surreptitious side glance and wondered how she got on when she shaved. Perhaps she was a man dressed up as a woman. *Excuse me, madam, but are you a man? ... Pardon me for asking, sir, but are you a madam?*

He suddenly wished he was Ben Hur—not in the painful uncomfortable bits like the galley-slave bit, but the noble bits ... all those heroics—fighting for his rights and that and being nobly sullen when he couldn't get them. Of course, now that he had saved Jack Hawkins' life things had taken a turn for the better. Oh yes, things were going to be better for Hur from now on ... it should be Him really ... Ben Him ... *Pardon me for asking, sir* . . . shouldn't joke about things like that—Hur was probably a good old Jewish name . . . Things were going to be all right for him now—except that he didn't know yet about his mum and kid sister—about them both having a touch of the leprosies. That would give him a nasty turn—bound to, stands to reason, your own flesh and blood a couple of lepers—But not half such a nasty turn as it would give his one-time Roman mate, Messala, when they had it out at the end of the picture. He wouldn't care to be in Messala's sandals when they had it out at the end of the picture. Funny, really, the way they had been such mates at the beginning and then turned on each other like a couple of raving lunatics. It all went to show that even in those days you couldn't trust anyone—not even your best pal—least of all your best pal. He wondered about Ob. Even with Ob it was true, in a way. He couldn't *really* trust Ob—not *trust* him; the moment his back was turned there was Ob sawing things down or nailing things up . . . still, they didn't throw javelins at each other. Ob's heart was in the right place; in all the big things he would trust Ob.

As he began to wonder what Ob was doing at that moment the lights, mercifully, began to fade.

It was halfway through the chariot race that he lost his boots. The excitement of the race was too much for the man immediately behind Harry—watching it was not enough for him, he had to take an active part in it. Cries of 'Come on Ben! Attaboy, Ben! . . .' rent the air every now and again, and at the precise moment that Hur's horses leapt at full gallop over the wrecked chariot of a less successful contestant and Ben himself was flung half in and half out of his own chariot, the man behind, in a frenzy of emotion, completely lost control of himself and lashed out in all directions. His flaying feet, falling foul of Harry's boots nestling beneath the seat, dispatched them at two entirely different points of the compass with the speed and lethal accuracy of a couple of guided missiles. Even above the general uproar Harry heard a muffled female scream six rows away as one of them struck home; he even saw the recipient rise a foot or two from her seat in pain and, he imagined, not a little surprise, since it is not every day that one is struck on the ankle by a footloose boot. However, it was only a glancing blow, the flying boot had gone on, and the lady's companion was finding it next to impossible to explain that he had not deliberately kicked her on the shins. Of the progress of the other boot there was no sign.

In abject and horror-bound misery Harry sat rigid. To be bootless on a wet Saturday afternoon in an English cinema was an experience new even to him. What could he do? Sit there until the programme was through, or pad up and down the aisle in his stockinged feet asking if the kind people would mind passing his boots along to him? He could imagine the reception he would get. The situation being what it was at present, with emotions running high and Messala being towed behind his own chariot in a welter of blood and sand, it was highly likely that he would be lynched on the spot. No, sit tight until it was all over and wait until everyone had left the cinema—that was the best thing to do. He knew more or less the direction taken by the left boot, but could only surmise the possible whereabouts of the other. The latter had actually glanced off his right ankle-bone as it had shot past—that's how he had become aware of the disaster at all—so perhaps it hadn't gone all that far, perhaps it was even within reach.

He waited until Ben Hur had ground his chariot to a triumphant standstill, then, under cover of the frenzied acclamations of the rest of the cast, Harry bent low in his seat and groped hopefully in the nether darkness. His hand touched a boot, and with a sigh of relief he had seized upon it and raised it a good ten inches off the floor before he realised that it was crammed full of somebody else's foot—the foot, in fact, of the Indian curry-fancier next door. Harry dropped the foot as though it had suddenly become afflicted with bubonic plague, the man grunted inarticulately and after a moment of stunned surprise began to lean with purposeful pugnacity in his direction.

'What the flaming 'ell you up to?' he growled.

'Sorry mate,' hissed Harry hastily, 'sorry. Thought it was mine.' Even to Harry it sounded a bit far-fetched.

'You keep your 'ands to your bleeding self,' the man went on in a voice two or three tones too loud. Harry felt his ears begin to burn as the bangles on his left clanked expressively. He remembered the man's protruding lower lip and empty cod-like eye.

'Blimey,' he said, 'you must think I'm bloody hard up for it!'

'You keep your 'ands to yourself, I'm telling you, or I'll settle with you outside.'

'You and who else?'

'I've 'eard of the likes of you,' grated the man in a venomous voice.

Harry's ears flamed. I'll kill him, he thought, I'll stand him up against a wall and kill him.

The bangles jangled in his left ear. He twisted his neck into a hairpin bend and glared at her. Even in the darkness he could see the prim set of the over-made-up mouth. I hate people, he thought, it's just people I hate. She pulled herself tightly into herself, wriggled a little, and stared over-intently at the screen. If she wasn't a woman, thought Harry, I'd bash her one right on the nose—a bunch of fives right up her bracket . . . but perhaps she wasn't a woman, perhaps she was a man dressed up . . .

Harry took a hold on himself. Silly old cow, what did it matter what she thought? Or old cod's-eyes on his right if it came to that. Blimey, he had a hope! You'd have to be pretty hard up before you went groping after someone like him. He had to be joking, of course. Nobody in his right senses, looking as he did, could ever begin to think that it was all happening to him.

Only by dint of a great deal of self-discipline did Harry finally simmer down into a state of being quietly though dangerously on the boil. When he was able, once again, to pay attention to the screen Messala was busy dying and there was a great deal of blood about and Harry felt that he just didn't want to watch any more. The film had been spoilt for him. He speculated sadly upon the whereabouts of his boots and wished to God he had never worn the bloody things—never even bought them. He made up his mind to give them away. He'd find someone deserving enough for them—they'd have to be pretty deserving to endure the kind of torture he'd been through. Pity young Ben wasn't big enough to wear them—he could really have done with them. Young Ben. Funny that. He'd said this morning that he'd never met a Ben in his life and yet here he was watching the life story of another one, Ben Hur. Ben Hur and Ben Hart. Funny . . .

His feet were beginning to feel very cold; he wrapped his raincoat around them and while he was doing so, needless to say, everybody started looking at him again. How he hated people.

That was supposed to be Jesus up there on the screen about to give his sermon on the mount—you couldn't see His face, they weren't allowed to show His face. He wondered why? Was it because no one was good enough to act the part? Or just good enough! Now there was someone who ought to have hated people and didn't. Perhaps it was easier for Him because he was supposed to be the Son of God. Harry wondered what He would have done if He had lost his boots in a cinema on a Saturday afternoon, and people had looked at Him as they had just looked at Harry. Harry suddenly felt sick. They hadn't only looked at Him, they had beaten Him up and hung Him on a cross.

Almost without thinking Harry unwrapped his feet, stood up and began pushing his way roughly out into the aisle. With his raincoat trailing behind him he walked slowly up the ramped aisle.

At the back he leaned over the wooden barrier. He felt better, more able to breathe.

'You all right, sir?'

A little usherette stood at his elbow looking up at him.

'Yes, sure, I'm all right.'

'I just wondered. Saw you come up. Thought p'raps you might not be feeling very well.'

'I'm okay.' He smiled at her.

As she turned to move off he said, 'Where are you going?'

'Pardon?' She looked surprised.

'Stay for a bit? You don't have to go, do you?'

He saw her peer up and down the dim passageways.

'Manager doesn't like us talking to people.'

For some reason he took her hand in his; it was soft and firm. 'Just stay a minute—only a minute. There's no need to talk.' He suddenly realised that he was near to tears, his voice was trembling and he couldn't have gone on talking even if he'd wanted to. What the hell was the matter with him? He looked down at the girl. She was small, the top of her head hardly reaching his shoulder, and in the dim light seemed to be quite pretty. He clutched hold of her hand as if it were a lifeline. What had got into him? What was going on?

Her hand returned the pressure of his, a little uncertainly.

After a long moment he said softly, 'Sorry, I didn't mean anything . . . it was just . . . I don't know what came over me . . .'

She stared forthrightly at the screen.

'It's all right, I don't mind.' She suddenly looked up at him. 'I really don't mind.'

He became aware that his heart was doing overtime. His right arm with his raincoat thrown over it was resting on the barrier in front of him. He pressed his face against it. The dampness of the raincoat was cool against his skin.

'You sure you're all right?' queried the girl.

He nodded. 'Bit hot, that's all. I'm not ill or anything, honest.'

They stood there like that, hand in hand, for a long time, watching the film.

She whispered. 'Smashing film isn't it? Do you like it?'

'Yes, sure, it's good. Been a bit spoilt for me though.'

'Why?'

He lowered his head so that his mouth was close to her ear. 'I've been and lost my boots.'

She tilted her face and looked up into his. 'Your what? Boots? Did you say "boots"?'

He tickled one of her ankles with his left sock; she jerked away, a broad smile lighting up her face.

'Where? Where did you lose them?'

His gesture encompassed the entire auditorium. 'Out there somewhere. They were under the seat and some silly . . . nit kicked them.'

She suddenly began to giggle into her hand.

'No, don't laugh,' he whispered at her, 'it's nothing to laugh about. How would you like to go home on a day like this without any boots?' He was laughing now. 'No, shut up, you only make it worse by laughing about it.'

Somebody hidden by the barrier in front of them hissed irritably. She pulled him towards the rear exit and they passed through into a silent deeply-carpeted corridor. As the door swung to with an asthmatic wheeze their laughter for a moment was unrestricted, and when it was over she said seriously, 'We'd better go and find them.'

He looked startled. 'No, not now. We can't go in there now, we'd get slaughtered. No, let's wait 'til it's all over and everybody's gone.'

'Supposing somebody goes off with them?'

He grinned. 'Then I'll have to borrow a pair of yours.'

She was tiny; small-boned and slim, she moved with the grace, thought Harry, of a fairy. Her little elf-like face was round rather than long, and the light brown hair which framed it, cut in the urchin style, straggled with deliberate dissarray over her finely-marked eyebrows and did its best to conceal her tiny ears which stuck out of the side of her head at right-angles. The eyes, hazel in colour, sparkled like stars when she laughed.

'What's your name?'

'Jenny, Jennifer. And yours?'

'Harry ... Harold ...' He just stood there looking at her. '... Stillwater ...'

'Pardon?'

'Stillwater ... that's my other name ... Stillwater ... run deep and all that ... funny old name, isn't it?'

'Harry Stillwater.' It sounded better when she said it.

'What's yours?'

'Oh dear ...'

'Pardon?'

'Love.'

'Love?'

'Jennifer Love, yes. Talk about really soppy names!'

'I don't think that's soppy at all, it's nice ... Jennifer Love ... that's a nice name—trade you mine any day—suits you too ...'

She coloured slightly and said, 'Don't keep looking at me like that.' Confused, he dropped his eyes abruptly and she went on at a rush as though afraid she had offended him.

'It's my ears isn't it—the way they stick out? My mother ought to have stuck them under the brim of my hat when I was little, but she didn't, so they grew out sideways—like jug-handles.'

He laughed again, they both laughed. He said, 'It's the nicest jug I've seen in a long time.'

'Ah,' she smiled gently. 'Thank you.'

'No I mean that, honest. I didn't mean it as a line.'

'I know you didn't.'

At the far end of the lobby one of the doors opening into the auditorium was swung open and a tall gangling usherette with a great deal of lank flaxen hair stood peering in their direction.

'Jen? Is that you, Jen?'

When Jenny said it was the newcomer wobbled forward on

very high heels staring vacantly at Harry with wide baby-blue eyes. 'I was wondering where you'd got to,' she said, and her gaze was so fixed that Harry felt quite sure that she meant him.

Jenny said, 'This gentleman's lost his boots.' Disbelief took the place of vacancy in the wide blue eyes but before it had time to translate itself into words Jenny added for Harry's information, 'This is Maisie, a friend of mine.'

Harry nodded. 'Hi, Maisie.'

'Lost your boots?'

'That's right. They're busy kicking them all over the theatre right now.'

'Who is?'

'Search me, I don't know.'

'Well!' Maisie advanced another couple of paces to take a closer peer at him, 'That's a new one on me.' She stared at him unblinkingly for a long moment as though he were something under glass in the British Museum, then smiled and nodded comfortably at Jenny as though he weren't there. 'He's not bad, I suppose, if you like that type.' She looked at him sharply as though he had just come back from wherever he had been. 'You really lost your boots?'

Jenny said, 'Well, he's not wearing any, is he?'

'Some of 'em'd try anything to chat a girl up—not even a by your leave. I must say, though, getting rid of your boots seems a funny way of doing it.'

'Why don't you shut up for a minute?' put in Harry mildly, 'and let me say something.'

'That's right, Maisie,' nodded Jenny. 'Shut up and let him say something.'

'Go on then.' Maisie narrowed her eyes at Harry. 'Have a go.'

'You sound like you was her keeper.'

'Somebody's got to look after her. If I don't keep an eye on her who will?'

'I will.'

Maisie made a face at Jenny. 'He's not slow, is he? Sorry I spoke, I'm sure. Do you want me to go, now?'

'Don't be silly,' said Jenny.

'Not wanted on the voyage, that's the story of my life.' She stared vacantly in Harry's direction. 'I'll come and help you look for your boots if you like—when all this is over.' The expressive jerk of her head in the general direction of the auditorium seemed to indicate that orgies unmentionable were in progress. 'I don't mind it but it don't half go on, it's like having your inside out twice a day.' She set an uncertain course over the thick carpeting for the door through which she had made her appearance. Fumbling for the door-handle she turned and stared at a point somewhere between them. 'Don't do anything I wouldn't do, will you?' she whispered hoarsely, then slapping her thigh vigorously she disappeared with a hiss of compressed air.

'Well,' said Harry, 'She's a laugh, I must say.'

'Poor old Maise, she's as blind as a bat; she's got glasses but won't wear them.'

'Don't blame her.'

'It's so silly, though, she doesn't look bad in them. When she was at school she had to wear those thick lenses and all the girls used to laugh at her and call her "Goggles" and "Four-eyes"—and the boys wouldn't even look at her—so when she started work she stopped wearing them. Says she'd sooner be blind than ugly. Poor old Maise.'

'She a good friend of yours?'

'I was at school with her.'

'You laughed at her too, did you?'

'What do you take me for?'

He said, 'How about me? Can I be a friend of yours too?'

He realised as he asked the question how much the answer would mean to him, and almost fearful of it, added clumsily, 'I suppose you've got a boy friend—someone to go 'round with; you've only got to say so—I mean, all that's just the luck of the game, isn't it?—You've only got to say so and—well—that'll be the end of me, won't it? It was nice while it lasted...'

He trailed off into silence, sniffed apologetically and stared with self-conscious intensity at his stockinged feet.

'Have you finished?' asked Jenny.

'What? ... Yes, sure, I've finished. It's just that—well, you know—it's better that I get ... that we ... I mean ...'

'You don't know what you mean, do you?'

He raised his eyes and looked at her. 'I know exactly what I mean ... only ...'

She looked back at him, a ghost of a smile hovering in the depths of her hazel eyes. 'Go on then, tell me ... what do you mean?'

For a long moment they stood staring at each other, as though each were willing the other to make a first move, each knowing that the decision of this moment was one which neither of them wished to make lightly, each hoping that perhaps it was the one which would alter the course of their entire lives, each knowing that such decisions had been taken before with disastrous results.

He held out a hand. 'Come here.' She stood close to him. 'I don't know why,' he went on, 'but this seems right, somehow —I didn't know you ten minutes ago—and yet it seems right to me . . .'

She smiled. 'If it's wrong we'll soon know . . .'

She was so small he had to lift her off her feet to kiss her.

CHAPTER FIVE

When Harry finally arrived home Ob was closely closeted with *Dixon of Dock Green* on the television. He looked into the sitting-room, said 'Hi', and when Ob made no reply looked out again and wandered off to the kitchen where he sat down in a dream by the bath, stared aimlessly at the wall opposite and wondered whether he should make himself a pot of tea. He was in no fit state to do anything other than just sit and stare so that's what he did for about twenty minutes until Ob came out to see what had happened to him.

'Hi,' said Ob. It was Harry this time who turned a deaf ear, so Ob came up behind him and waved an experimental hand in front of his eyes. Harry stared up at him glassily and blinked. 'Ah,' commented Ob. 'Thought you'd dropped off. What's up, then?'

'What?'

'Yes.'

'You want a cup of tea?'

'I was just thinking of nipping out for a noggin.'

'Where?'

'I'm not particular. One place is as good as another. Coming?'

He took his raincoat from the hook on the back of the door and shrugged himself into it.

'Where are you off to?' asked Harry.

Ob stopped what he was doing and went and stood at the end of the bath where he had a better view of his friend.

'You all right?'

'Course I'm all right. What's up with you?'

'We've just had a long conversation about going out for a drink.'

'Go on?'

'Don't you remember?'

'I thought we said something about having a cup of tea?'

'Blimey, if this is what going to *Ben Hur* does for you I'm glad I stayed away. What's the matter with you?'

Harry said after a pause, 'Ob . . .'

Ob said, 'Yes . . .' and waited. Since nothing else appeared for the moment to be forthcoming he settled himself on the edge of the bath-cover and regarded Harry with the professional air of a doctor about to make an expensive preliminary diagnosis. 'All right. I know. You don't even have to tell me.'

Harry looked at him. 'Go on then, you tell me. Give you three guesses.'

'You've met a bird.'

'Don't call her a "bird".'

Ob sat back resignedly. 'Oh mate,' he muttered half to himself, 'I hope we're not going through all that again. Go on.'

'Pardon?'

'What happened? Who is she? Where did you pick her up?'

Harry stared at him tolerantly. 'You're vulgar.'

'Who is she?'

'Her name's Jenny.'

'Where?'

'Down at the pictures.'

'How?'

Harry widened his eyes as his mind went back. 'It all started with me taking my boots off . . .'

'Blimey, that's a new one . . .'

'Now don't you start! That's what Maisie said.'

'Who's Maisie?'

'Jenny's friend.'

Ob brightened visibly. 'What's *she* like?'

'Blind as a bat.'

'I'm not *against* blind girls.'

Harry looked at Ob speculatively. 'Wonder if she'd go for you?'

'What's she like, then, apart from being blind.'

Harry pursed his lips. "Tall, blonde, blue-eyed . . Skinny, double-jointed and will soon be a cripple if she goes on wearing three-inch heels.'

'I don't mind high heels either.'

'You're a pervert.'

'When are you meeting them again?'

'I'm not meeting *them* anywhere.'

'Well, Jenny then. When?'

'I'm picking her up after the pictures tonight.'

He launched into a fully-detailed account of all that had gone on during the course of the afternoon, how he had lost his boots and met Jenny and Maisie, and how practically the entire staff of the cinema had combed the empty theatre for the missing boots to find one of them wedged beneath a radiator, and the other, oddly enough, perched high on a shelf in the Gents' toilet with a lavatory brush growing out of it like a hyacinth and a note attached explaining to those interested that it was a *Botanical lavatorius* and very rare. He finished up by saying that he had fixed up with Jenny to meet her at the stage door immediately after the late showing.

When the recital had come to an end Ob went off into a lengthy prowl. Harry watched him apprehensively as he brooded aimlessly about the kitchen, pulling thoughtfully on his lower lip and humming with a dismal lack of tunesmanship beneath his breath. He straightened a mat that wasn't crooked and peered inquisitively into an empty saucepan; he turned on the tap, waited until the water ran hot, then turned it off again with a satisfied grunt and squirted a couple of spurts of washing-up liquid into the sink. He wiped the steam off the mirror and surveyed himself with an alarming lack of enthusiasm; he bared his teeth, examined his tongue, pulled down the lower lid of his right eye and had a look at the red bit like the doctors do, looked stern, joyful and romantic in quick succession, then, becoming suddenly aware that he was under observation, cleared his throat, screwed up his eyes at an uncertain point somewhere above Harry's head and said, 'By the way . . .'

'What?'

'I didn't tell you . . .' Harry gave him no encouragement. 'I've found out how the stripes come out in the toothpaste.'

Harry said 'No,' in disbelief.

'I took the tube to pieces and it's all in the top and there are four little slots and it all comes out there.'

'What does?'

'The red stuff—the mouthwash—the stripes. Quite clever really . . .'

'Fancy.'

Ob looked nonchalantly knowing. 'Interesting, though, isn't it, when you come to think of it?'

'Very,' said Harry again. 'Well done.'

Ob turned again to the mirror and with his fingers began combing his hair downwards on to his forehead until it sat there in an obscene-looking bang. The effect was disastrous and not a little frightening.

'Sexy old bugger,' commented Harry.

'I was just wondering . . .'

Harry shook his head. 'It's not you.'

Ob pushed his hair back roughly into its original spikes. 'You can laugh.'

'Why can I laugh?' echoed Harry. 'What have I done?'

Ob made a face. 'You wouldn't understand even if I told you.'

'Try.'

'You wouldn't.'

'Oh come off it! You want to meet Maisie, don't you? That's it, isn't it?'

'Maisie?'

'All that prinking and tarting about in front of the mirror. What was all that in aid of? Who was that for? Me?' Ob opened his mouth to say something but Harry ploughed on. 'If you want to meet her, meet her, I'm not stopping you.'

'You wouldn't mind?'

'Mind? Why should I mind? What's it got to do with me? That will be Maisie's funeral, not mine . . . I don't know what's the matter with you, honestly I don't. Standing there waggling your hips in the glass. Do you think I don't know exactly what's going on in that thick head of yours. "Who the hell would want me?" That's what you've been thinking, isn't it? "Nobody but an ugly middle-aged cow would ever look at me twice." That's what you're thinking, isn't it?'

Ob lowered himself unhappily on to the edge of the bath.

'I'm not exactly God's gift, am I?'

Harry groaned, got up and went over and stood in front of him. 'You really are a stupid old nit, aren't you? You said I wouldn't understand—well, you're dead right, I don't understand.'

Ob said, 'Well, look at me.'

'I'm looking at you. What in hell's name is wrong with you? You talk as if you'd got a couple of heads, a hump on your back and a pair of cloven hooves. I don't see anything wrong with you . . . I never have . . .'

'You're not a bird.'

'For crying out loud! Look, I may not be a bird, and thanks very much for noticing it, but I've seen some of the things that birds knock around with—so have you—and if you can't hold your end up with that lot . . . well, mate! . . .'

There was a pregnant silence, then Ob summoned up a pale grin. 'We've been through all this before, haven't we?'

'You're dead right we have, several times.'

'It's just that . . . well, I don't seem to be able to . . .'

'What?'

'I don't know . . . I just don't seem to be able to chat 'em up like you do . . . I haven't got the confidence . . . comes natural to you, it doesn't to me . . .'

'Balls.'

'I couldn't pick up a bird if my life depended on it.'

'How about that piece you brought back here from the Pavilion a couple of weeks back? Alice somebody . . . Crumpet . . .'

'Crump. She picked me up. She sat next to me at the concert and dropped her flaming chocolates. I couldn't get rid of her. She was like one of those squid things—all arms and legs—all through the rest of the concert. I only brought her back because I thought you might be interested in her and all you did was bugger off to the pictures.'

'Well, don't blame me. That's the arrangement, isn't it? If one of us comes back with a likely bird the other buggers off. How the hell was I to know you didn't want her? You should have told me.'

'I couldn't get rid of her long enough to tell you.'

'She looked all right to me.'

'I had to beat her off.'

'Well, there you are then. You must have something. I've never had to beat a bird off in my life.'

Ob shook his head. 'You're just not listening. She was a bird of prey, a vulture . . . a man-eater . . .'

Harry made a face. 'Sounds like you should have stuffed her and stuck her on the wall.'

They both thought that was fairly funny and laughed about it for a second or two then Harry suddenly brought his hand down on the bath-cover with a dull boom. 'I don't know why the hell we're discussing *your* love life. I've just met the only girl who has ever meant anything to me, I come home here drooling at the mouth expecting a bit of comfort and sympathy from—God help me—my best friend, and all I get is a lot of chat about her mate. If you want to meet her, meet her, for God's sake—how many more times do I have to tell you. Come with me tonight and see if she's around. If she isn't Jenny'll be able to tell you about her and where you can find her, but don't, and I'm telling you straight, don't hang around and get under *my* feet. I'm going to have quite enough on my plate without having to keep a weather eye on you all the evening.'

They stared at each other for a couple of minutes in silence. They could hear old Mrs. Thing's television upstairs screaming out advertisements. Ob said, 'You coming in to watch the television?'

'I think I'll have a bite to eat first.'

'Being in love is supposed to put you off all that.'

'What is there?'

He went over and peered into the throbbing depths of the refrigerator.

'Cold bangers,' suggested Ob.

'What did you have?'

'Cold bangers.'

'And what?'

'Bread and butter.'

Harry straightened up and looked at him. 'I'm right, you know, it's time *both* of us got married. Cold bangers and bread and butter. One of these days we'll be found dead with nothing inside us but cold bangers and bread and butter. Haven't we got any eggs?'

'There's one.'

'Right, I'll fry it.'

Ob watched him silently as he bustled about the kitchen making a great deal more noise than was necessary. The egg was spitting and crackling in the pan when Harry finally turned almost petulantly on his friend.

'Why don't you go and watch the television?'

Ob said slowly, 'You're serious about all this, aren't you?'

'All what?'

'Marrying and that.'

'Why shouldn't I be?'

Ob shrugged. 'Doesn't seem to have worried you much in the past. But suddenly, all at once, as if something had come down out of the blue and hit you over the head, you want to get married and settle down with a bird. Why?'

'I don't know. Why not? I'm fed up, I suppose, cheesed off

with living like this. Probably because I'm the marrying type. And don't get all down in the dumps about it. It's not your fault.'

'It's the spring, I expect.'

'What is?'

'Spring. April. Young man's fancy and all that.'

Harry ladled his egg on to a piece of fried bread and plastered the whole thing over a cold plate.

'Well, I don't know what's the cause of it, all I know is that it's here and I'm stuck with it, and somehow I've got to do something about it.' He stared morosely at the congealing fat on the plate. 'Look at that! It's cold already.'

'You should have warmed the plate.'

'If I was married, *she'd* have warmed it.'

'She'd also have cooked it.'

'That's what I'm saying! Life would be so much more worthwhile. There's no doubt about it, it'd be lovely to have a woman about the place cooking and mending and smartening the place up. Look at all that muck on the dresser—that wouldn't be there if there was a woman about.'

'She might be a bigger muck than you are.'

Harry was indignant. 'Most of that muck's yours, not mine. You never put anything away when you've done with it.'

'That's not my gramophone record.'

'Maybe not. It's *your* saw and *your* hammer and *your* packet of nails, not to mention *your* hard-boiled egg what's been there for the last two months. Throw it away, why don't you? It won't do anything for anybody after two months except kill 'em. Let's see you throw it away now, right now, while the spirit's with us. You throw that egg away and move your tools and I'll put my record in the box. Go on, let's see if we can do it.'

Ob moved impressively to the dresser and stood thoughtfully with the egg between his finger and thumb. 'It's a pity, you know, to have wasted an egg. Could have been a two months' old chicken by now.'

'Get on with it.'

Ob tramped lustily on the plastic pedal of the Jolly-Molly, the lid of which flipped back to reveal an already over-crowded interior; a crumpled sugar packet and a number of corn flakes slid sordidly to the floor. The two eyed each other bleakly.

Ob said, 'It's going to be an uphill battle.'

'Open the window,' instructed Harry with his mouth full of egg.
'What for?'
'Open it.'
Ob opened the window and looked enquiringly at his friend.
'Now bung it out.'
'Bung what out?'
'The egg. See if you can get it into old Mother Johnson's water-butt.'
Ob stared into the darkness for a few moments until his eyes became accustomed to it, then with a sharp lobbing movement the egg shot across the nextdoor neighbour's fence. Even from where he was sitting Harry heard the splosh as it struck its watery target.
'Well done, that man.'
Ob hung out of the window. 'It's floating.'
'Come in and close the window.'
'I'd have thought it would have gone straight to the bottom.'
'Come in and pull the blind down before anyone comes out to see what's going on.'
Ob grinned at him. 'Wonder where they'll think it came from.'
'They'll know damn well where it came from, but they won't be able to prove it.'
'Fancy waking up one morning and finding a hard-boiled egg floating in your water-butt. It's not something that's likely to happen every day. *The Day of the Egg* they'll call it.'
Harry grinned. 'You're still a nut. Why don't you go and watch the television?'
'Have you finished eating?'
Harry stared at him. 'What else is there?'
'There's a tin of pineapple.'
Harry shooed him off to the sitting-room and busied himself with the tin-opener. He couldn't be bothered to tip the pineapple into a bowl or on to a plate so he ate it out of the tin with a pickle fork.

CHAPTER SIX

THEY were early so they propped themselves up against a sandbin outside the stage door and waited. An under-sized policeman in an over-sized helmet, attracted no doubt by their lack of industry, came and had a look at them. They nodded cheerily at him and wished him 'Good night', but his eye was as blank as a whitewashed wall; he passed on, crossed the road and lurked gloomily in a dark doorway hoping for something to happen.

Ob said, 'Let's write something rude on the wall.'

Harry asked him to shut up.

Ob raised his voice and cried discreetly, 'Lily Law!'

'Belt up, for God's sake.'

'What's the time?'

'I don't know.'

'You've got a watch.'

A church clock struck the quarter. 'A quarter past. Satisfied?'

Ob sauntered off and stuck his ear up against the stage door.

'Music, I can hear music.'

'Why tell me? You should go and talk to a doctor.'

'Oh mate,' said Ob. 'Ha! ha!' He listened again. 'Sounds like an opera.'

Harry came to and began smoothing down his hair.

'That's the end, I expect.'

'I hope it is—nothing could follow that. Except of course the National Anthem. There's always the dear old National Anthem.' Ob's favourite occupation was knocking the National Anthem. 'The worst piece of music ever written, bar none . . .'

'Don't start all that.'

'It's only my personal opinion; you don't have to write in and complain.'

'God, you are a bore about the National Anthem.'

'Two hates I've got—Transport workers and the National Anthem.'

Harry stared at him in the dim light. 'You don't have to be so nervous, you know, she won't eat you.'

'Eh?'

'You heard.'

The cacophony of clashing push-bars interrupted them and a monstrous army of half-blind maniacs pushing and shoving and clambering into coats surged out on to the pavement; above the chatter of voices and the shuffling and stamping of feet, the slamming of car doors and the revving-up of countless cold engines came the over-abundant tones of the National Anthem.

'There you are,' shouted Ob over the din, cowering up against the door and prodding Harry in the ribs. 'There it goes! And look at the respect they've got for it. If you want to empty a theatre in thirty seconds flat put the Anthem on; they're trampling each other into the aisles before the drum-roll's over.'

At that moment the stage door hit him smartly in the small of the back and a square man in a cloth cap and thick glasses came out and peered at them with no curiosity.

'Ah,' he said.

'Sorry,' said Ob.

'Pardon?'

'I was in the way.'

The square man nodded. 'Cleared up now, though, hasn't it?'

They watched him lose himself in the crowd.

'Wonder what he does,' queried Harry.

'So long as he's not the projectionist!'

'Hello Harry,' said someone he didn't recognise. 'All right for Thursday?'

'Yes, sure, okay,' returned Harry, as the shadowy figure moved on.

'Who was that?'

'No idea.'

'What's Thursday?'

'There must be other Harrys.'

They went back to their sandbin now that the crowd had begun to thin out. Harry pulled his collar closer.

'Seems to be getting colder.'

'I'm sweating,' said Ob. 'Hold it! Lily Law's back.'

The under-sized policeman glanced up at them under the over-hang of his large helmet. Harry thought he caught the vestige of a smile in his eye as it encountered Ob. They watched him in silence until he had turned the corner.

'I think he fancies you,' observed Harry.

Ob shrugged. 'I couldn't go for that big hat. Perhaps he's lovely underneath.'

Two girls swept out of the stage door and giggled off without a glance in their direction.

The street was suddenly quiet. A small boyish figure shining in a raincoat of scarlet P.V.C. stood in the shadowy doorway.

'Harry? Is that you?'

'Hi, Jenny.'

'Sorry if I kept you waiting. Some woman lost her gloves.'

' 'S all right, we haven't been waiting long.'

'We?' Jenny's eyes sought out Ob.

'Oh—er—yes, this is a friend of mine, er, Ob is his name—er—is what's-her-name about? you know . . . Mildred . . .'

'Maisie.'

'That's right, yes, Maisie, I was telling Ob about her—Maisie, and he thought, well, he said that if it was all right with me—you—Ob, this is Jenny, Jenny, Ob . . .'

They nodded at each other in silence, then they all stood around wondering what to do next. It was Maisie herself who broke it up. She peered through the door, caught sight of Jennifer on the step, said, 'Haven't you gone yet? He hasn't come has he? I knew he wouldn't! They're all the same! Men!' and was about to retreat when Jennifer seized her by the arm and dragged her in amongst them.

'This is Ob, Maisie . . . Harry you know.'

'Pardon?' asked Maisie, rustling, as Ob remarked later, in her pale-coloured mackintosh like a surprised stick of tall celery.

Jumping in to re-introduce them and explain matters more thoroughly Harry found that Maisie was understanding the situation very well indeed. She and Ob were nose to nose peering closely at each other and looking as though they were both enjoying it.

'Ob?' murmured Maisie voluptuously, 'What a funny name.'

'He's a funny boy,' said Harry jocularly.

'Ob what?'

'Hobson Harvey,' aspirated Ob, 'but I'm always called "Ob" without the "H".'

'Why?'

'Er . . .'

Harry said, 'Because he's always called Ob.'

'Oh,' said Maisie, 'I see.'

She, thought Harry, is a ripe one; Ob will like her! He'll go for her like he would go for a hole in the head.

But oddly enough he did like her, or appeared to, for it took him no time at all to forget, or deliberately ignore, Harry's warning about not hanging around and queering everybody else's pitch; he plunged Maisie's arm possessively through his own, blinked brightly at the assembled company and said 'Where shall we all go then?'

Harry could cheerfully have killed him on the spot and when Maisie followed the question up with, 'Who's got any money?' he could have done away with her too, just as cheerfully. He didn't have to be reminded that Ob possessed about one and sixpence in his pocket and the clothes he stood up in; it was not surprising therefore he felt it incumbent upon him to admit that what little he had was at their service.

He felt Jennifer's hand on his arm. 'What do you want to do?'

He shrugged. 'Not much doing at all at this time of night. If you want to drink and dance there's only *The Elbow Room* left now.'

'And they close at twelve,' said Ob.

Harry asked Jennifer, 'What time do you have to be home?'

She grinned. 'When you get me there.'

Maisie muttered fervently, 'Oh dear, I do hope it's not going to be one of those nights. My feet are killing me.'

The Elbow Room was a cross between Calcutta's Black Hole and the engine-room of a no longer seaworthy submarine—and not much bigger than either of them. Whilst it would have been quite impossible at any given time to estimate the number of people present, because of an almost complete lack of illumination, it may be said that progress across what was hilariously known as the 'floor' would have been more appreciable, if not more spectacular, by resorting to the expedient of walking on the heads and shoulders of the clientele rather than attempting, at ground level, a more orthodox passage through a semi-static wall of intertwined human bodies—a process fraught with danger and possible misunderstandings and one to be achieved only by the adroit application of elbows, knees and the occasional well-judged toe of a pointed boot.

For the regulars this was all just part of the fun and the frequent outbreak of wordy skirmishes which accompanied such behaviour earned little or no attention from those not immediately concerned. Only when the words were accompanied by blows did the general interest quicken, to flag abruptly as soon as one of the contestants had staggered off into the surrounding gloom to lick his wounds and mutter darkly about the future of his more successful adversary.

Soft drinks, coffee and tea were to be had at a price from a bar of sorts at the far end of the place, in the close vicinity of which long tables and wooden benches sprawled uninvitingly. A baffling display of murals, multi-coloured, grotesque and mercifully indeterminate, staring down from the walls for those with eyes to see, had been executed and presented free of charge by a sad young artist who had been obliged to leave them uncompleted upon being removed to prison.

Rhythm and 'the Beat' were supplied by a trio of long-haired, black-leathered, highly untalented young gentleman who loomed at fitful intervals through the smoke-laden atmosphere lunging, wrestling and screaming imprecations at their instruments and crying hoarsely into the wilderness of frustration and unrequited genius.

Nothing of all this however was immediately apparent upon entering the establishment. Only the gradual re-orientation of one's entire being finally brought the picture fully into focus, and even then the eyesight lagged reluctantly and drew alongside the other senses only when they had been reduced to a state of near pulverisation. If you could live with it for three-quarters of an hour you survived, if not you would find yourself back on the streets seeking quieter climes.

Whilst Harry and Jennifer hovered for a moment or two at the head of the stone steps to get their bearings, Ob and Maisie plunged precipitously into the abyss, Maisie screaming above the din, 'I love this place, don't you?'

Jennifer grinned at Harry. 'Do you come here often?'

'Only when the spirit moves me,' he replied with care.

By the time they had reached the bar Ob and Maisie were nowhere to be seen, so they collected a couple of coffees and some crisps from the shadowy bar-tender-owner of the joint whose name was Eugene—'Jeannie-with-the-light-brown-hair' for short because he was as bald as an ostrich egg—cleared a space at one of the tables and sat and watched the weaving darkness for a moment or two. Now suddenly for the first time their proximity and awareness of each other created a shyness between them; they were almost grateful for the shattering barrier of noise which made conversation difficult. They stirred their coffee, sipped it and grinned stupidly over the rims of their cups at each other. A girl on Harry's left voiced a plaintive, 'No, don't do that, Jack, get off 'ome, you'll mess my hair up.' Harry watched fascinated whilst she extricated herself carefully from beneath the heavy sailor who had been lying on top of her along one of the benches. She clambered into an upright position, found herself face to face with Harry, giggled breathlessly, crimped her hair, which was looking terrible, and said, 'Aren't they awful, these Navy boys?'

'I don't know,' said Harry truthfully, 'I've never had one.'

The sailor craned his head round and took a long look at him and grinned slowly. 'You should try one some day, boyo, you'd never be the same again.' Then seizing the girl around the shoulders like an all-in wrestler he bore her down once again upon the bench and got on with whatever it was he had been doing. There was only the faintest whinney of protest from the girl.

Harry took a quick look at Jennifer, who was peering over his shoulder in an effort to see what was going on. Their eyes met.

'I was in the Air Force,' Harry told her.

She held his eyes for a moment; 'Pity,' she said.

A writhing body lurched against the table and their coffee slopped over into the saucers.

'Want to dance?'

'Not unless you do.'

'D'you like dancing?'

'Not much. Do you?'

'Not much. Not very good at it.'

He poured the slopped coffee back into his cup.

She said, 'How're your feet now?'

'Pardon?'

'Your feet? How are they?'

'Oh better. I left those boots at home. I'm going to give them away.'

'Good thing too.'

'What?'
She put her lips to his ear. 'I said a good thing too.'
He turned his head quickly and touched her lips with his.
'It's too noisy in here, don't you think? Want to go somewhere else?'
She peered into the darkness. 'Wonder where Maisie has got to?'
'I thought she was supposed to be looking after you.'
'She's a fine one to talk! She needs more looking after than a cartload of monkeys. There they are.' Harry couldn't see them. 'They seem to be enjoying themselves. Let's stay for a bit.' She took his hand gently in hers. 'Your friend seems quite nice.'
'Ob? He's all right, bit of a dope, but he's all right.'
'I like his hair.'
'His what?'
'Hair. It's like spikes.'
'Like a loo-brush.'
She smacked his hand.
He leaned closer to her. 'I'll tell you something else about him, too.'
'What's that?'
'He's an assistant taxidermist.'
'A what?'
'An assistant taxidermist.'
'What's that?'
'He stuffs things.' She looked startled. 'Animals and things—he stuffs them . . . birds and animals . . . and things.'
She still looked startled. 'What an awful thing to do.'
'They're dead first.'
'I realise that, silly, but I still think it's an awful thing to do.'
'Why?'
'I don't know. It just doesn't seem right somehow. When a thing is dead it's dead . . . you don't want to keep looking at it when it doesn't have any life left in it, doesn't matter how fond you were of it.'
Harry thought it was time he told her that Ob hadn't done any stuffing for three years, and what was more, hadn't done anything—period—for four months.
'I think he's probably given it up. He wasn't very good at it anyhow. Says he made an eagle look like a parrot once.'

She laughed a lot at that. He loved it when she laughed. He had heard it said on the television or at the pictures that there was a certain type of idiot who liked it when a woman was tearing a strip off in a rage; but not him—he couldn't stand seeing anyone in a temper—he ran a mile if a bird got into a tizzy about something. He thought he must be a bit soppier than most men—he liked to see them laughing; he liked the way their heads went back and the shape of their necks and throats. Funny, they never seemed to have an Adam's apple ...

'Why don't girls have Adam's apples?'

'Perhaps Eve was too clever to swallow it.'

'Or maybe it just got stuck in his throat because he had more conscience.'

She had another try at her coffee and made a face. 'Not very nice coffee.'

'Have a Coke.'

She shook her head. 'What do *you* do?'

'Pardon?'

'What sort of work do you do? Or are you out of work too?'

'Not me. I work like a slave.'

'Doing what?'

He thought for a moment. 'I'm a dairyman.'

'What's that?'

He thought for a moment. 'A milkman.'

A broad smile spread itself over her face. 'A dairyman!'

He shrugged resignedly. 'Well ...' He added after a second, 'Do you mind?'

'Why should I mind?'

'Some girls do ... er ... people do sometimes ...'

'Why?'

'I don't know. They seem to think it's a bit ... you know ...'

'What's wrong with being a milkman? Somebody's got to do it. Like being a dustman—where would we be if there weren't any dustmen?'

He was not sure he quite understood what dustmen had to do with it so he said, 'Refuse collectors,' just to remind her, if she didn't already know, that even dustmen had girls, got married and multiplied.

'That means you have to get up early, doesn't it?'

'Five o'clock.'

'Never!'

'Five o'clock.'

Her forehead puckered a little. 'Our milkman doesn't come till four o'clock in the afternoon.'

'You want to change your milkman.'

'You can't change your milkman. There's one dairy for each district and if you don't like it you've got to lump it.'

He squeezed her hand. 'Why are we talking about milkmen?'

'All right then.' She tickled his palm disturbingly. 'Let's just talk about one milkman. Where were you born . . . and when? And why don't you take your mack off instead of sitting there looking as if you're not staying.'

He struggled out of his raincoat, rolled it up into a small ball, and was looking around for somewhere to put it when the music, which for some time had been working itself up into a lather of cacophony, came to an end. Everyone present with the exception of Harry and Jennifer and possibly Jeannie-with-the-light-brown-hair behind the bar screamed and shrieked at the breathless trio and with one accord stampeded towards the bar where only the strongest survived. Harry, his rolled-up raincoat held before him like a rugger-ball, found himself face to face with Eugene at the bar wondering how he had got there. He managed to grab four Cokes from an ice-bucket full of warm water, counted some money into Eugene's hot palm and fought his way back the way he had come.

'Where did you get to?' enquired Jennifer mildly.

Ob had appeared with a panting Maisie clutched possessively under one arm. Her round blue eyes fixed on the Coke bottles.

'I hope to God one of them's for me,' she breathed, and wrestling one from Harry's grasp she spread herself out on the bench, threw back her head and poured threequarters of the bottle's contents down her throat—the rest went down the front of her jumper. The others just stood and watched. When it was all over she planted the bottle firmly on the table, stared at it short-sightedly as though hoping it might replenish itself, then with a genteel burp she closed her eyes, breathed heavily for a moment, leaned back against the wall and appeared to fall asleep.

'Have fun?' asked Jennifer of Ob.

Ob's face shone, his hair stood alert and upright, his eyes rolled expressively at the unconscious Maisie. 'Cor!' he said.

Harry was puzzled. 'What have you two been up to?'

'What do you think we've been up to?'

'You look as if you've both just run round the world.'

'Ah,' said Ob, and eyed Maisie with sober intenseness. 'She looks like she's dead.'

'I am,' said Maisie.

'I was just saying you looked as if you were dead.'

Maisie opened her eyes and stared blankly in his direction. 'You didn't hear what I said, did you?' Then, turning to Jennifer who was nearer and therefore in focus, she confided solemnly, 'Dancing with him is like dancing with an electrified octopus. Wow! ... I'll never be the same again, I just know I won't. I'm crippled for life.'

'It's those shoes,' murmured Ob.

'I suppose I finished that Coke, didn't I?'

Ob gave her the rest of his and she swallowed every drop of it. Ob said, 'I didn't want any more, anyway.'

Maisie was regarding him with a pale speculative eye. 'What was that remark about my shoes?'

'They're too high, the heels are too high. You'll break your ankle one of these days.'

Maisie said loudly to Harry, 'I didn't know your friend half an hour ago and he's already telling me what to wear.' A sudden strange quiet had fallen on the room. Maisie stirred uneasily. 'What's up? What have I said?'

'I think,' said Ob quietly, 'there's going to be a spot of trouble.'

Halfway across the floor and heading towards the bar limped a youth in his late teens; tall, fair and good looking he wore the uniform of a Rocker—zipped black leather jacket, bleached blue jeans, jackboots, and black leather gauntlets. In his right hand he held a stick upon which he leaned heavily.

Now there was no sound but the fall of the boy's steps and the soft creaking of the leather he wore. A couple of yards from the table where Harry and the others were sitting he stopped; the dim light glinted on his heavily-embossed and studded belt. Someone cleared his throat nervously and a tumbler was knocked over on the bar where it rolled unheeded on the marble surface backwards and forward, twice, three times, and was still.

The youth spoke. 'Where's Red?' It was a simple, straightforward question, asked quietly without histrionics; the menace it achieved was supplied by the charged atmosphere into which it was dropped, and by the uneasy mutter of movement which followed. Eugene behind the bar placed himself strategically within reach of the phone. 'Now calm down, Boy,' he warned, 'don't let's have any trouble or I'll clear the place.'

'I'm calm enough,' returned the youth. 'I want a word with Red, that's all. Too much to ask? I know he's here so if he's skulking behind your apron you'd better tell him to show himself, before there *is* any trouble.'

From the far side of the room a girl panicked; heels clacked hysterically on the stone steps and a door banged. No one else moved.

Maisie whispered nervously. 'Why don't we go, too?'

'Shut up,' breathed Ob.

'I'll ring the police,' threatened Eugene.

'You do that; you just do that.'

Somebody giggled and the situation began to lose some of its tension. Harry found himself wondering whether the 'Red' in question was his cowboy-booted acquaintance of the snack bar earlier in the day. He hadn't long to wait for confirmation. Red, his two unalluring henchmen on either side of him, hunched himself out of the gloom. The atmosphere tightened up again.

Red lounged to a standstill at a wary distance from the fair boy; he straddled his short legs lazily and thrust his thumbs manfully through the belt loops of his jeans. His voice was thin and mealy.

'So?' He gazed with round-eyed insolence around the room; it should have got a laugh, it didn't—he was a bad actor. 'So? Where's the trouble?' The top of his knobbly head barely came to the other's shoulder.

The fair boy's voice was sibilant with restraint. 'My girl's in the hospital with a broken thigh-bone and a smashed-up face . . .'

Out of the corner of his eye Harry noticed Ob's hand clenching and unclenching on the table before him.

Red rocked slowly to and fro on his high heels. 'So?' he said again. 'Your girl's in the hospital, Boy? I'm sure we're all very sorry to hear that, Boy . . .'

The other, suddenly lunging out at him, grabbed him by the front of his jacket; 'I want to know exactly what you did to my bike on Wednesday night—you and your two dirty little tykes here . . .'

The two henchmen pincered themselves around and took up their positions behind him.

Red swore viciously. 'Lay off, will you? What the bleedin' hell are you talking about?'

From the bar came the *ping* of the telephone as the frightened Eugene lifted the instrument from its rest.

The grip on Red's jacket tightened and trembled. 'Two blokes saw you working it over on Wednesday night with a hacksaw —you and your two mates here . . .'

He got no further. The spotty-faced 'Mate'—the one with the Beatle haircut—kicked out suddenly at Boy's stick, which was supporting the youth's entire weight, and Boy went down heavily, dragging Red on top of him. The other henchman, the one with the permanent drip to his nose, losing no time at all, settled down professionally to the belabouring of Boy's ribs with his heavy boot. However, twice only had he found his mark before Ob's considerably larger and heavier boot had caught him fairly and squarely in the crutch and he retired from the fight hastily, holding on to himself and screaming unpleasant imprecations at his unexpected assailant.

Ob's left foot meantime had planted itself firmly on Red's right hand, in which had appeared a wicked-looking flick-knife. Ob shook his head sadly, took possession of it, and retracting the blade said mildly, 'You really are a nasty little man, aren't you? I think you'd better bugger off before you get trodden into the ground.'

Seizing Red roughly by the collar of his jacket and the back of his belt he transported him across the floor and up the stairs like a bundle of dirty laundry; when Red seized hold of one of the iron stanchions on the staircase to prevent his unceremonious exit, Ob adjusted the balance by raising his left knee pointedly into the other's stomach.

Ob kicked open the door. 'Don't come back tonight, there's a good lad,' he said quietly, and sat Red upright in an open dustbin. Turning back into the room he was faced with the spectacle of the spotty-faced Haircut doing a four-minute mile across the floor in the direction of the door with the remainder of the clientele in full cry at his heels. Whimpering with fright he hurled himself at the staircase only to come face to face with Ob, who was standing with his arms crossed at the head of it. Everybody stood still and there was a long anticipatory silence whilst the two of them stood and regarded each other with care. Remembering the treatment dispensed to his late associate Spotty-face placed a protective pair of hands over his more sensitive parts.

'I'll 'ave the pleece on you,' he quavered hoarsely.

'Good,' said Ob, 'Then you'd better go and get them, hadn't you. Allow me to open the door for you.'

He did so and Spotty-face, in spite of a couple of wary, crablike feints, departed with more alacrity than even he himself had anticipated. The dull clang of the dustbin outside denoted that its recent occupant had moved on.

The last of the three delinquents, the one with the drippy nose, still languishing from his contact with Ob's boot, was carried shoulder-high by the entire company and deposited with great ceremony in a horse-trough which happily was situated not a stone's throw away on the other side of the road.

'Thanks very much, the lot of you,' said Eugene when they returned to encounter him standing in the doorway of his establishment. 'I'm shutting up shop now, if you don't mind, so you can collect your clobber and hoppit. It's past twelve and I've had enough excitement for one night.'

'Did you ring the police?' someone asked.

'No I didn't. I never do until the blood starts to flow—gets the place a bad name.'

As Ob, with Maisie wound around his waist, was leaving a few minutes later he was buttonholed by the proprietor. 'I'll tell you something for nothing; I wouldn't be seen around for a few days if I was you. Give that Red sod a chance to cool off, otherwise he'll have your guts and I'm not kidding. He's a sod if ever there was one, so don't underestimate him just 'cos he wears fancy boots and is knee-high to a grasshopper—they're usually the worst, the little ones. There are more of 'em licking his arse than just those two squits with him tonight. So watch it, eh? And do me a favour? Keep out of here for a bit. I can't afford to keep having the place done up. Thanks all the same, you were a great help. I could do with you on the staff. Staff! That's a laugh. Cheerio then, and up your jaxey.'

When finally they found themselves out on the wet pavements listening to Eugene shooting his bolts and rattling his chains as though his life depended upon it, the rain had started again, so they settled themselves into their damp raincoats and, uncertain of their next destination, were huddling disconsolately around the base of a concrete lamp-post when Maisie in a frenzy of rustling mackintosh flung her arms around Ob's neck, kissed him full on the lips, pinched his cheek hard and cried, 'Oo, how I love this man! Will you marry me?'

Ob said, 'Why not? When?' and then blushed profusely.

Maisie's mackintosh grew quiet as her doll-blue eyes widened and her mouth fell open. 'No need to go mad,' she protested weakly.

'You asked for that,' laughed Jennifer.

'He's throwing himself at me, isn't he? You don't expect a bloke you've only just met to throw himself at you. I don't even know what his habits are like.'

Harry grinned. 'He's house-trained, if that's what you mean.'

'How do you know?'

'I live with him.'

Maisie crossed her eyes at Jennifer. 'We've got a couple of ripe old pouffes here, I must say.'

A tall figure hovered tentatively on the outskirts of their little circle. It was Boy, leaning heavily on his stick and looking extremely uncomfortable. He cleared his throat as they became aware of him and raising a thumb at Ob said gruffly, 'Just wanted to say "ta" and all that. They'd have had me if it hadn't been for you.'

Ob shrugged. 'Three into one don't go, does it?'

Jennifer said, 'You all right?'

Boy gave a slow smile. 'Couple more bruises, that's all; I'll survive.' His eyes wandered back to Ob. 'You shouldn't have got yourselves mixed up in other people's troubles—doesn't do—catch yourself carrying somebody else's can in the end if you're not careful. I'd keep an eye out for Red if I was you—he'll have a go at you for what you did tonight—and I'm not joking. Did you know him before tonight?' Ob shook his head. 'Well, you know him now and he knows you, so watch out, right?'

'Right.'

To the accompaniment of a soft whinney of delight from Maisie, Boy blinked away the rain from his long eyelashes.

'Well, it's no good standing about here getting wet, is it? I'll be getting along. Cheerio.'

Harry said, 'Come and have a drink.'

Boy hesitated. 'You don't want me busting in.'
'Suit yourself, but I needn't have asked.'
'That's right you needn't, but thanks all the same. I think I'll be getting along—get up in the morning and all that, you know. Be seeing you. Some other time, p'haps, if you're sure I won't be in the way.'
Maisie leered. 'You won't be in my way.'
Ob seized her around the neck. 'Take no notice—we keep her locked up during the day.'
Maisie watched Boy's broad, wet-leathered shoulders glint away into the darkness. 'He's beautiful—like a lovely blonde Beatle—I could go a bomb for him.'
'Just now it was me you were going for,' reminded Ob.
'It's trousers,' said Jennifer, 'She goes like that at the sight of anything in trousers.'
Maisie groaned voluptuously. 'I've never seen trousers like that before.'
Ob became lofty. 'I don't mind. It's not my fault if she's repressed.'
'You can say that again.' Maisie's blind blue eyes snapped open wide. 'And opportunity would be a fine thing too, wouldn't it?' She blinked at the other two. 'You should try dancing with him—once—just once. Have you ever danced with him?'
'No,' said Harry, 'I never have.'
'Well,' rejoined Maisie looking him straight between the eyes, 'I'm glad there's something you two haven't done together.'
'Why don't we go somewhere,' suggested Ob, 'out of the rain.'
'Like where?' asked Maisie.
'Home.'
'Whose home?'
'Mine—ours . . .'
'Where opportunity knocks, I suppose.'
Ob looked at Harry. 'What can I do with her?'
'Take her home,' said Harry.

CHAPTER SEVEN

'DIDN'T you sleep last night?' asked Ben.

'What?'

'I said, didn't you sleep last night. You don't look as if you did.'

'Why? What makes you say that then?'

'You're all dark under the eyes. My Mum says that's when you don't get enough sleep.'

The empty bottles jingled drearily behind them, the windscreen wiper developed a squeak.

'I slept all right,' lied Harry. 'I don't need a lot of sleep, as a matter of fact.'

'What time did you go to bed?'

'I don't know. What's it got to do with you?'

'Nothing.' The boy made some loud sucking noises at a couple of girls prinking through the puddles. 'Why is sex so important, do you know?'

'What?'

'You've gone deaf too.'

'Who says it is?'

'Everybody. Wherever you go you see things about it. Anyone would think you couldn't live without it.'

'I could live without it.'

'Why don't you, then? You said yesterday you had all them girls.'

'So I have.'

'Well, then . . .'

'Shut up, can't you?'

Ben hummed to himself for a bit then said, 'I bet I know one thing . . .'

'What's that?'

'I bet I know more'n you do.'

Harry pursed his lips. 'I bet you do too. You got sex on the brain.'

There was silence between them while they rattled up Station Road. A dark green Jaguar crawled behind them at five miles an hour; Harry could see the driver's sullen red face reflected in his mirror. In another thirty seconds, he thought, he'll hoot his bloody horn. Sure enough the sullen red face lived up to expectations. Harry moved sedately on to the crown of the road.

'Bloke wants to pass,' said Ben.

'Let him wait.'

'Let him pass.'

'No.'

'Why not?'

Harry suddenly looked at the boy; the brown eyes were blank. He swung the van violently to one side and the Jaguar surged past with a couple of toots on its horn. The red face smiled and raised its hand in acknowledgement.

'I know that bloke,' said Ben.

'Oh, who is he?'

'Doctor up at the hospital. Cuts people up.'

'A surgeon.'

'That's right.'

And I'm a milkman, thought Harry, getting himself into the middle of the bloody road so that doctors can't pass and get to the hospital and people die because I'm a milkman.

'What's the matter with me today?'

'I keep telling you—you haven't had enough sleep. I always get like that when I don't get enough sleep.'

Harry suddenly pulled the van into the side of the road and put the brake on. 'Look,' he said, 'why the hell do you keep talking to me like you was my father. How old are you? Thirteen. You sound like an old man of ninety, and you know it all, don't you?'

'Not all, no.'

'Oh, for crying out loud.'

'Your father isn't ninety, is he?'

Harry relaxed and grinned at him. 'No, he isn't, and I haven't got a father, anyway. He died a long time ago—before you were born.'

The boy breathed on the windscreen and drew a round head with two ears on the cloudy glass. 'You don't have to get cross.'

'I'm not cross. I'm under the weather a bit, that's all. I hate Sunday mornings, especially wet ones—and they're usually wet ones, Sunday mornings.'

'Do you get a day off?'

'Yes, Thursdays.'

'Want to come and see my sister on Thursday? I told her you was looking for a girl.'

Harry's head began to swell. 'You shouldn't have told her that.'

'Why not? You done me a good turn so I done you one.'

'Did.'

'What?'

'*Did,* not "done".'

'Ta.'

'Now you've got me talking to *you* like a father.'

After a pause the boy said, 'That's all right, I haven't got a father either.'

Harry rooted around in his pocket and produced a piece of nut milk chocolate. 'Do you want half a pint?'

'I don't mind.'

'Do you or don't you?'

'If you're going to have one.'

He reached behind the boy and fished out a couple of bottles. 'Don't throw the top away,' said Ben, 'I save them for blind dogs.'

Harry laughed. 'Sounds as if the dogs are blind.'

'They are. All you got to do is save up silver paper and bottle tops and send them in and they go to help dogs what are born blind. My sister does it at her work.'

'You've got the wrong end of the stick. It's the men who are blind—the dogs are all right; the dogs have to be trained so's they can guide the men—the men who are blind. Oh blimey, you've got me at it this morning. Look, I can't come and see your sister on Thursday.'

'Why not?'

'Because I can't, that's why not. I don't even know her, do I?'

'You never will if you don't come and see her.'

'Perhaps I don't want to know her.'

'Well, that's nice . . .'

'I didn't mean it like that. It's just that I've got a girl.'

'You met one last night, didn't you—a bird?'

'Don't call her a bird. I told you yesterday I got a lot of girls.'

'Yesterday you wanted to meet my sister, today you don't, so you must have met one last night, eh? A special one. She nice?'

'Yes.'
'What's her name?'
'Jennifer.'
'You like her, do you?'
'Course I do.'
'You don't seem very happy about it, though. You've been cross all morning. Why is that, if you like her so much?'
Harry banged down his milk bottle. 'Look, don't keep on about everything all the time. I don't know whether I'm coming or going. If you're like this at thirteen Gawd knows what you'll be like when you're thirty. Now pack it in, will you?'
'Can I ask one more question?'
'No you can't. What?'
'It's the same one. Why is sex so important? Don't go off again. I want to know, that's all. I never talk to anybody 'cept the kids at school and they don't know nothing. And when I bring it up with my sister she tells me not to be dirty. So what's dirty about it I want to know. If everybody does it—and they do—why is it so dirty?'
'Why don't you ask your mother?'
'I can't.'
'She's the right person.'
'I couldn't ask her. She'd belt me one.'
Harry shrugged. 'It's not my business. I'd get into trouble if I started talking sex to you.'
'Why, why?'
'You're too young—and I'm too old—and I'm a man, and you're a boy . . . There's funny laws.'
Ben emptied his milk bottle and set it into the tray with an expressive clang. 'That's what I mean, see? Nobody'll tell you nothing. So how do you learn about it? They don't tell you nothing about it at school.'
'Ben, listen, for Pete's sake. All I can tell you is that there's nothing dirty about it—nothing. It's people's minds that make it dirty. They've become sort of ashamed of it—don't ask me why, because I don't know—perhaps they think it's—well, sort of—animal-like. I mean if you see two dogs doing it in the middle of the road somebody'll come out and throw a bucket of water over them—you can bet your boots on that—Well, why? What's it got to do with them? Nothing!—but there you are, that's what I mean, it's got to be kept secret, and

when a thing is secret you sort of drive it underground, don't you? And it becomes a bit dodgy. But everybody does it—as you say—all the time—otherwise there wouldn't be no more people. But the real thing is, you don't do it with *anybody*. You ought to love somebody first. Anyway, that's what they say.'

'Who?'

'They. I'm not a good one to ask, see? I've been around too much. I've done it when I haven't been in love—most men do; that's where the whole thing falls down. Because we're animals first and men second, I suppose. I don't really know what I'm talking about, so don't quote me. What I'm trying to say is that—well, because I met this girl last night, I don't see how I can meet your sister on Thursday and be honest about it—if you know what I mean. I hope you do, 'cos I don't.'

On the other side of the road an elderly man in oilskins and sou'wester, with blatant disregard for the open heavens above him, was diligently bathing his car in a splurge of white detergent. Ben and Harry watched him solemnly, the silence between them lengthening into unembarrassed companionship.

Ben said at last, 'Aren't people funny? Him, I mean . . . standing out there getting drowned washing his car when it's all wet anyway.'

The man was singing *Jesus wants me for a sunbeam* quite lustily with the sort of voice one usually associates with Drake in his hammock and television advertisements for manly beer. Apart from the introductory line his knowledge of the words were sketchy to say the least, but his interpolations seemed to Harry, delving back into Sunday school memories, much funnier and a great deal more forthright than the original.

'He's probably washed his car every Sunday since he had it. He's right not to give it up just because it bloody rains. Anyway he seems to be enjoying it.'

After another pause Ben said, 'I'll tell my sister you're not interested, then.'

Harry sighed. 'I didn't say that, did I? How do I know if I'm interested or not when I haven't even met her? I'll meet her some time, I expect—no need to push it. That's eleven o'clock striking, we ought to be getting on. You're lucky, Saturdays and Sundays are half days.'

He started up the engine and was in the midst of doing all the things laid down in the Highway Code prior to taking off when he caught sight of a pale, running lady flagging him down with some urgency.

He looked at her politely as she arrived alongside wet and breathless. She was pale because she had flour on her face and her hands were covered with the preliminary stages of the Sunday Yorkshire pudding. She's run out of milk, thought Harry.

'I've run out of milk,' she panted, 'I wonder whether you could possibly let me have an extra pint.'

'One pint, madam—silver, red or gold top?'

'What?—oh, I don't mind, red. And have you got a small single cream?'

'Small single cream, madam.'

'And half of salt butter have you got?'

'Ben, double round the back and get the lady a half of salt butter. Anything else, madam?'

'What about eggs?'

'Eggs, madam, yes, six, twelve, eighteen, couple of dozen?'

'I'll have two.'

'Two eggs. And there's your half a pound of salt butter.'

The pale lady hovered for a moment, the rain drawing strange patterns on her floured face. 'You don't happen to sell Dolly Mixture, do you?'

'Madam?'

'Dolly Mixture—you know, little sweeties for the kiddies.'

'No, Madam, I'm afraid not, I'll tell you what we have got though—a nice large tin of South African apricots at one-and-ten—cost you double in the shop.'

'Yes, all right, I'll try one of those.'

'Ben, a large tin of South African apricots for the lady. That the lot, Madam?'

'I only wanted a pint of milk.'

Harry grinned at her. 'It never works out like that though, does it? There's always a little something else. Let's see now . . . one pint red top, half butter, two eggs, one small cream single, and here comes Ben Hur with your large tin of South African apricots . . .'

The pale lady seized the apricots. 'Don't trouble to add it all up now—just put it on the account. I haven't got any money on me.' And she was away threshing through the rain with her floured clown's face before Harry had even wetted the tip of his indelible pencil.

He shook his head. 'There she goes back to her Sunday dinner. They all have lives to lead and mouths to feed, don't they? The only thing is I don't remember who that one is or where she lives. Nip after her, will you, Ben, and ask her who she is, there's a good chap.'

Ben splashed after the retreating provision-laden customer while Harry heaved himself out of his seat and had a go at wiping mud off the windscreen. He caught the eye of the man in the oilskins.

'Lovely weather,' he called cheerily.

'Duck weather,' returned the hymn-singer.

Harry strolled over. 'My boy and me was wondering why you bothered to wash it on a day like this.'

The man grunted. 'Always do on a Sunday. Why should I stop for a drop of rain. I do it so as to get out of the wife's way.'

'Ah.'

'Sunday morning, you know—women—they're everywhere, under your feet, up your nose, everywhere you go. So I remove myself regardless what the weather's up to. And apart from all that the smell of greens in there is something awful.'

Harry said, 'Ah' again, and turned to go.

'You don't sell sweets, do you, by any chance?' asked the man suddenly.

'Sweets?'

'You know, jelly babies and the like.'

'All I got is a large tin of South African apricots at one-and-ten—cost you double in the shops.'

'No, that's not quite what I had in mind. I feel like something to suck, got a sweet tooth.'

'I could lend you a tin-opener.'

The man regarded Harry under heavy brows. 'What would I do with a tin-opener?'

'You could open a large tin of South African apricots.'

The man considered then shook his head. 'No, not fond of apricots—too woolly. One-and-ten's not bad, though, is it? Wife might be glad of a tin. Why do you flog apricots, you're a milkman.'

Harry shrugged. 'Search me, specials they call 'em. They shove 'em on, we flog 'em.' Ben was hovering at the van. 'Ben, fetch the gentleman a large tin of apricots.'

'That your boy?'

'Yes—Ben.'

'You don't look old enough to have a boy his age.'

'He's not mine—I mean I'm not his dad—he just helps me on the round.'

The man regarded Ben speculatively. 'Looks like a drowned rat, don't he?'

'Poor little so-and-so. They're pretty hard up I should think—his family. His clothes are falling off him and he hasn't got an overcoat or a mack to his name.'

The man was fumbling in his wallet and produced a ten shilling note. 'Here, give him this, eh? on the quiet. Make sure he spends it on something worthwhile—not records or sweets like they all do nowadays.' Ben came up with the tin. The man took it and peered at the label. 'I never knew they grew apricots in South Africa, they don't, do they?'

'I don't know,' said Harry, 'Don't they?'

'Says they do on the tin so I suppose they must. One-and-tenpence. There you are, and thank you.'

Harry met the man's eye. 'Thank *you*, sir, very much.'

Hissing through the wet streets Harry said, 'What are you going to do with the money you get on this job, Ben?'

The boy shrugged. 'I don't know—blue it, I suppose.'

'Why don't you save it up?'

'What for?'

'You could do with a mack on a day like this.'

'Mack! I can manage without a mack. Plenty of other things to spend money on.'

'Like what, for instance?'

'Well—all sorts of things. Records . . . books . . .'

'What sort of books?'

'You know—magazines, space mags, pops and things.'

'Why not save it all up and buy a mack?'

'That woman was Mrs. Pring, by the way, number forty-nine.'

'What woman?'

'With all that powder on her face.'

'Oh yes—ta.'

Bringing the van to a standstill he clambered out, filled a basket with an assorted number of pint and half-pint bottles and handed it to Ben. 'Top floor. Number seven has a large double cream every Sunday.'

'Number seven, large double cream—right.'

He watched the boy leg it lightly up the front steps of the apartment house and let his breath go with a loud hiss between his teeth. It was nothing to do with him really. If the kid wanted to throw his money away on a lot of old rubbish that was his privilege—and his money. On the other hand . . .

Harry made a note of Mrs. Pring's purchases in his book, collected a further couple of dozen bottles of milk, dumped them in a basket and tramped thoughtfully up the steps after his young assistant.

CHAPTER EIGHT

WHEN he arrived back at the flat Ob was hooked over the kitchen sink peeling a potato. Harry stood in the doorway, his wet oilskin held enquiringly in his hand.

'Can't hang this over the bath now, can I? It'll have to drip all over the floor.'

'Still raining, is it?' said Ob, avoiding the issue. 'Horrid day —didn't envy you going off this morning.' Harry stood his ground. Ob added, 'Why don't you hang it in the loo?'

Harry sighed gently and went and did just that.

Ob called to him. 'Do you want more than one spud?'

Harry came and peered over his shoulder. 'Why, is that the only one we've got?'

'There is another, but it's a bit squadgy. Thought perhaps one would do you.'

'It'll have to, won't it?' The gas oven gave a sudden scream. 'What we got?'

'Mutton, I thought, with a nice bit of mint sauce. How's that?'

Harry thought it was fairly discouraging but didn't have the heart to say so. Though Ob was no Mrs. Beeton he was half a step closer to a *cordon bleu* than Harry was.

'Want any help?'

'No.'

Harry took off his shoes, sat down and put his feet up on the bath-cover. The gas stove shrieked, the refrigerator rumbled, the rain beat heavily on the window and upstairs old Mrs. Thing's radio blared out military band music.

'You're very quiet,' said Harry after a moment.

'Me? No.'

'You are.'

'Am I?'

'Yes. For you.'

'Soup?'

'Eh?'

'Want some soup?'

'Tomato, I bet.'

'That's right.'
'Go on, then.' Harry watched his companion belabouring the tin with the opener. 'We ought to get one of those screw ones—you screw the lid off.'
'Good idea.'
Ob levered up the lid, stuck his forefinger in the soup and licked it.
'What do you do that for?'
'What?'
'Shove your finger in the soup.'
'I always do.'
'I know you always do. I was just wondering why?'
'I don't know. Make sure it's what they say it is on the label, I suppose.'
'It's a dirty habit though, isn't it?—bunging your finger in the soup like that—never know where it's been.'
'My hands are quite clean.'
'You know that, but I don't, do I?'
Ob looked mildly at his friend. 'What's up with you?'
'Why?'
'Suddenly, after all these years, you want to know why I stick my finger in the soup.'
Harry shrugged. 'I've always wanted to know. Only just got around to asking that's all. It's one of your habits—we've all got habits.'
'Like leaving the top off the toothpaste.'
'You don't do that, do you?'
'No, but you do.'
'Go on?'
'You do—always.'
'That's just forgetfulness—getting old, I suppose—little forgetful, that's all.'
Ob poured the soup into a bent saucepan and put it over a low gas. The rain slashed viciously at the window.
Harry said, 'So how did you get on last night, then?'
'Last night?'
'With Maisie—after we split up.'
Ob sniffed casually. 'I took her home.'
'All right?'
'Yes, it was all right. She's a bit . . . I quite liked her . . . bit strange, but I liked her. How about you?'

'I like her too.'

'No, I mean, Jenny, you and Jenny. Did you get on okay?'

Harry heaved himself to his feet and padded into the sitting-room to find his slippers.

'Keep an eye on that soup,' he warned as he passed the gas stove.

Ob leaned in at the door. His voice was sympathetic. 'Wasn't it no good?'

Harry slumped down in an armchair, and stared into the yellow eye of the morose seagull on the mantelpiece.

'Something happened to me last night,' he said, and when there was nothing forthcoming from Ob, added, 'When I was with her I felt suddenly all sort of—oh I don't know—mucky—I can't explain it. It was just a feeling I had, like as if I've been wrong all these years.'

'Wrong?'

'About birds—girls—there's more to it, you know, than just going to bed with them.'

Ob eyed him critically. 'You've flipped your lid over her, that's what's happened to you—that's all. Had to happen sometime, I suppose, and now it has—just when you wanted it, really, eh? Things do happen like that sometimes—just when you're ready for them—when you need 'em.'

Harry studied the hole in the toe of his right sock. 'I guess so—I s'pose so. But you'd have thought it would have cheered me up a bit wouldn't you—instead of all this.'

'It takes different people different ways. It's like finding buried treasure and knowing you've got to give it to the government.'

'What?'

'Isn't it?'

'What's the government got to do with it?'

'It was only a thought—trying to find a way of putting it. You've found something you want and instead of just taking it you feel you've got a responsibility—and in a way it makes you fed up—miserable, but after a bit it'll make you happy—I expect—p'raps when you get used to the idea. Like having a baby and knowing you can't afford it—it's nice having it but you can't get away from the fact that you've got to feed it and bring it up and send it to school and make a man out of it.'

'Ob?'

'What?'

'Don't go on about it. I'm mixed up enough already. If I listen to you much longer I'll start ordering the orange-juice. You've made your point and I know what you're talking about —or I think I do.'

An ominous subterranean gobbling sound from the kitchen indicated that the soup was about to erupt and Ob sped off in a frenzy. Harry sat for a moment in a brown stupor then donning his slippers lounged over to the kitchen door to watch. His friend was wiping tomato soup off the front of the cooker with the floorcloth. The high-pitched scream of the oven seemed to have taken on a note of personal outrage. Ob suddenly lost control of himself. 'Oh shut up!' he yelled, and banged hard on the oven door with his clenched fist. There was a moment of trembling tension from inside the oven during which anything might have happened. What did happen was that the gas went out with a loud pop.

'There,' remarked Harry, 'now you've put the gas out.'

'Good job too,' growled Ob unreasonably. 'Now we'll have roast leg of mutton garnished with coal gas—nothing I like better.'

Five minutes later, hunched patiently over fruit dishes filled with glutinous orange soup too hot to touch Harry said, 'You didn't finish about Maisie? You got on all right, did you?'

Ob considered the wall opposite for a bit then pushed out his lips reflectively. 'She's a bit of a dope, I must say.'

'Nice, though.'

'I think she was sending me up all the time, though.'

'How do you mean?'

'Having me on—stringing me along—all the old heave-ho—you know, "any old port in a storm" and all that. She seemed more interested in that Ted bloke with the bad leg than she was in me.'

'What Ted bloke?'

'The bloke in the fight—the blond piece with the stick and all that leather. I felt a bit out of it—she never stopped talking about him. He's quite a dish, I suppose, in an obvious sort of way. Tall with it, too.'

'He's not as tall as you are.'

'No, but then I'm too tall.'

'She's tall, too.'

'She's lanky.'

'She needs a tall bloke, though, doesn't she? she'd look daft with a dwarf.'

After a moment of brooding silence Ob looked across at him for the first time.

'I lumber a bit.'

'Lumber?'

'Yes. Blunder about—like a tank or something.'

Harry sighed. 'Ob, stop it. You're a bore when you begin running yourself down. In the end you'll make everyone believe it—say it enough times and they will. You're seeing her again, aren't you?'

'Yes, sure, tonight.'

'There you are, then. She liked you well enough to want to see you again.'

'I had to twist her arm.'

'Of course you did. You don't expect them to come running, do you? They're all the same. We all are. We all play hard to get.'

'I don't.'

'No, that's true, *you* don't.'

Ob took a tentative sup at his soup. 'Seems all right now —have a bash.'

'Why can't we have another flavour some time?'

'Don't you like tomato?'

'Be nice to have a change.'

'We had chicken-noodle one time—don't you remember?'

Harry sucked sceptically at his spoon. 'We've *always* had tomato.'

'You seeing Jenny tonight?'

'... er ... no not tonight.' Ob looked sideways at him but made no comment. Harry didn't have to go on but he did. 'Like I said—we all play hard to get.'

Ob shook his head. 'Aren't you funny? One minute you're saying you've flipped your lid over her, the next you're shoving her off with a barge pole. You don't make sense.'

'I didn't say I was shoving her off, did I? It's not like that at all. As a matter of fact ...' He splashed about in his soup for a moment or two then pushed it from him. 'Don't feel like it, sorry. As a matter of fact it was the other way about. I thought she was trying to shove me off. I started off all right —we get on fine ...'

'Then what happened?'

'Nothing—nothing happened—that's just what I say. I just felt she didn't want another date. So we said we'd see each other again some time, and that was it.'

Ob collected the dishes with a clatter and smacked them down loudly on the draining board. 'You're a clot, you know that, don't you?'

'Thanks very much.'

'I don't know much about anything as far as birds are concerned, but I do know what I can see with my own two eyes. When I go and meet Maisie tonight, you're coming too, see? What the hell's the matter with you? All of a sudden, for no reason at all, you lose your nerve. Blimey, with the birds that don't matter you're bouncing about in bed before you can say "knife".'

'It's got nothing to do with bed.'

'I know it hasn't. That's what makes the whole thing sound more healthy. Usually it's a slap and a tickle and a tongue sandwich and into bed like a streak of greased lightning. Now, for the first time in history you're on your best behaviour—and about time, too, if I may say so.'

'Well, don't go on about it.'

'Why shouldn't I go on about it? You're always on at me. I usually have to sit and listen to you, so now you can bloody well sit and listen to me.'

Harry grinned at him and leaned back in his chair.

'All right, then, get on with it.'

'What?'

'Get on with it.'

Ob stood with his mouth half-open and the oven-cloth poised purposefully in his hand. They stared at each other in silence for a second, then Ob said in a haughty voice, 'I've said what I have to say. You can take it or leave it.'

Whilst they dealt with the leg of mutton the subject was dropped and Harry told Ob instead about Ben and the unexpected gift of ten shillings from the man in oilskins.

'I haven't given it to him yet,' Harry said.

'Why not?'

Harry shrugged. 'He'd only waste it on junk. He had five bob from me this morning as it was—that's quite enough for a kid of his age to go chucking away on junk. No, I thought I'd hang on to the ten bob and maybe add something to it—not much —and get him something useful, something he could wear perhaps like a ... like a parka or a windcheater or something. They're quite cheap in these surplus stores—you can even get 'em with hoods—he could keep his bloody head dry. This potato's like a lump of iron.'

'I thought it would be—didn't have long enough. If we'd waited the mutton would have been burnt. It's one thing or the other with cooking. You care about this kid, don't you?'

'Ben? I don't care about him. I hardly know him. And he can look after himself better than I can, believe me. No, it's just that this bloke who gives me the ten bob tells me to see that he doesn't squander it on a lot of old rubbish. And he's quite right, too.'

Ob chewed thoughtfully for a moment then said, 'I'd give you something towards it if I had anything. But I haven't got anything.'

'Well, don't worry about it, we're not the Salvation Army. And if you had anything worth having, I'd have it, so there! Charity begins at home, and I'm "home" as far as you're concerned. Still, he's a quiet sort of kid—unlike most of 'em—it'd be nice to give him a hand of some sort. I'll have a browse round the shops, see what I can pick up. I'd get him a mack or a raincoat but he wouldn't wear it.'

'More meat?'

'No thanks,' Harry burped gently, 'I suppose there's no afters?'

'There's corn flakes and plenty of milk. I'm going to have All-Bran but you don't go for that much, do you?'

'I don't need it. I'd have thought with the amount of that stuff you put away you'd have enough ballast to sink the *Queen Mary*.'

'Roughage,' Ob corrected him.

Harry got up and stretched himself and wandered over to the door. 'Bring it in the sitting-room and we can put the telly on.' He stared for a second at the rain cascading down the window. 'Never a dull moment, is there? Roast mutton and All-Bran—and if that isn't enough for you, Sunday afternoon with the telly. The excitement's killing me.'

The evening cleared up, however, and found them lurking in the vicinity of the sandbin outside the stage door.

'You can take the blame if she doesn't want to see me,' Harry had warned Ob earlier. 'You can tell her you made me come to keep an eye on you and Maisie. You can say you didn't like leaving me on my own. You can say . . .'

'Oh, shut up,' Ob had told him with unusual and succinct determination.

The same little policeman in the big helmet loitered uneasily in the shadows of the doorway opposite. Harry eyed him with a morose belligerence. 'Why the hell can't he go and lurk somewhere else,' he grumbled to Ob. 'Hasn't he ever seen a couple of blokes waiting for a couple of birds?'

Ob raised his voice at a careful angle. 'Lily Law!'

'Shut up, for God's sake, he'll hear you.'

'Good—perhaps he'll get self-conscious and go off and watch someone else—a burglar or someone—there must be lots of 'em about on a night like this.'

Harry stared gloomily at the policeman. 'He looks bloody daft in that bloody great helmet.'

'If you can't fight wear a big hat.'

Harry groaned suddenly. 'Ob, mate, he's coming over. He must have heard you calling him names.'

Covertly watching the policeman's steady progress Ob planted his foot up on the sandbin with a hollow clang and fiddled with his turn-up. 'Perhaps,' he hissed in Harry's ear, 'he fancies me after all.'

Harry was humming a nonchalant and unrecognisable tune as the policeman hove alongside clearing an uncertain throat and crunching sand into the pavement with his large boots.

'Ah . . .' he said, '. . . er . . .'

Ob towered over him and even Harry looked down a bit.

'What?' said Ob.

The policeman peered up at him a trifle uneasily. 'Aren't you Ob Harvey?'

'Am I?'

'I'm Charlie. Charlie Bourne. You don't remember me, I bet. We used to be at school together—at Belmont. Remember?'

Ob didn't, but his face fell open in surprised and delighted recognition. 'Charlie Bourne . . . you're not!'

'I am.'

'Charlie Bourne . . . I don't believe it. Harry, this is Charlie Bourne. We used to be at school together. You've heard me talk about Charlie Bourne?'

Harry hadn't, but nodded gamely and muttering a few encouraging words shook hands heartily with the policeman. It occurred to him as he did so that he had never shaken hands with a policeman before and looked curiously at his hand as it was released as though half-expecting it to have changed colour.

Ob continued over-playing with loud confidence. 'Fancy you being a copper—funny sort of job for you to be doing, isn't it? I seem to remember you was always on the *other* side of the law at school. Keeping all right, then, are you? This is Harry, a chum of mine ... oh yes, you've just met haven't you ... What are you doing round here, Charlie, of all places?'

Charlie was not more confused than Harry. 'I live here. Always have done. Been away a couple of years but I'm back now. How are *you*, then?'

'Fine, fine.'

'Saw you both hanging around here last night, didn't I? Thought I recognised you then, but wasn't sure. What you up to, eh? Waiting for the girls, eh? Eh?'

Ob was souring off at the edges, 'That's right, waiting for the birds.'

'Aren't you married yet?'

'Married? Me? no, course not. You're not, are you?'

'Got a couple of nippers.'

'Go on.'

'Fact.'

'Well I never.'

During the short pause which followed Charlie looked thoughtfully at Harry, who nodded his head up and down like a china ornament and said, 'Good for you, Charlie.'

Charlie nodded too, his helmet bobbing in agreement but out of synchronisation. 'Well, I can't stand here talking to you characters all night. I've got a beat to pound. How about meeting up some time for a chin-wag, eh? Talk over old times together, eh? Over a pint, eh?'

Ob, still overdoing it, punched little Charlie on the shoulder and nearly capsized him. 'Yes, sure, why not, let's have a noggin some time. Well, well, fancy me knowing a copper, eh? never know, might come in useful some time—knowing you. I just can't get over you being a copper.'

'I seem to remember you were going off to do something

pretty funny too. What was it, now? Stuffing birds and things, wasn't it? That was it. Your old man had a shop. Do you still stuff birds?'

Ob eyed him warily. 'Not now, no. I've given it up. Doesn't pay much now—stuffing birds. My dad died—he was the—er—taxidermist—I wasn't no good at it really. It's not all that easy, you know, stuffing—things.'

With a sudden clatter of push-bars and the strident strains of the National Anthem they became engulfed in a seething mass of homeward-bound humanity.

Charlie yelled above the tumult. 'Give us a ring then, eh? I'm in the book under Millicent Johnson. Nice to see you. Cheerio.' And he disappeared, suddenly, as though he had dropped through a hole in the road. They gazed after him, momentarily bereft of words. The unspoken query was still there when their eyes met. Harry shrugged. 'Maybe he's Millicent Johnson during the day.'

'He's got two kids,' said Ob eschewing the whole idea. 'Well, how about that, then? Friends in high places.'

'You didn't know him from Adam, did you?'

'I don't remember ever seeing him before in my whole life.'

'That was pretty obvious, the way you overdid everything.'

'Well, he knew me, anyway—even to remembering what I did for a living.'

'Putting it the way he did, it would be difficult to forget.'

Ob tossed his head in contempt. 'He didn't even know what day it was, poor old thing. Still, I suppose they're liable to get a bit stunted in the police force. I mean, it can't be a natural sort of life now, can it? Think of all the things you wouldn't be able to do in that pointed helmet.'

There was a frenzied rustle of mackintosh and Maisie appeared with startling suddenness between them. 'Hello, 'Obby 'orse.' She struck Ob smartly on the chest then peered inquisitively at Harry. 'I'm glad *you've* turned up. She's been right fed up about you, I can tell you. What's the matter, don't you like her or something?' She laid hold of Ob's arm as though he were a fruit machine. 'Come on, Ob, we'll leave them to get on with it. She'll be out in a sec.'

As he listened to the clatter of her high heels Harry counted four of her paces to one of Ob's gangling shuffles. It's not possible, thought Harry, four to one, it's not possible. But then, *she's* not possible . . . Maisie's not possible . . . a funny couple, Ob and Maisie . . . imagine them clacking up the aisle . . . four to one . . . with the wedding march out of time like Charlie's helmet bobbing up and down out of sync . . .

Apart from a couple of stragglers the street was empty. The church clock was striking the half hour. He heaved himself up on to the sandbin and stared hopefully at the dim light burning over the stage door. The rain began again, heavy, well-aimed gouts at first developing in a few seconds into a steady monotonous downpour. He turned up his collar, muttered a rude word at the open heavens, and drummed his heels on the side of the sandbin. He felt suddenly very depressed and more alone than he could have thought possible. An ambulance roared through the town, its clamorous bell tearing the wet darkness apart.

From the far side of the stage door came the rattling of a chain and the shooting of bolts. The light went out.

Midnight had struck when he finally slid off the bin, plunged his hands deep into his pockets, hunched his shoulders and trudged off through the puddles.

CHAPTER NINE

THROUGHOUT the night and most of the following morning it rained relentlessly.

Monday is bad enough for most people whatever the weather, but a dull, cold, misty, leaden-skied, rain-soaked, spray-sodden Monday morning on the South Coast of England is calculated to freeze the blood of an oversexed Hottentot and guarantee the ultimate step in the direction of anybody's death-wish. Laughter, good works and the feeling of happy comradeship flush themselves noisily down the nearest drain and leave behind them misery, dejection, rheumatism and the overpowering desire to shrink the head of the nearest living creature, be it friend, foe, fish or fowl.

Jangling discordantly along the high street at eleven o'clock Harry wondered malevolently how Ob's head would look on the end of a pointed stick or dangling from a gas-bracket. One jaundiced glance at his room-mate that morning flat on his back in a bed that looked like a hamster's nest, snoring like a bronchial grampus, with a fatuous smirk plastered over his face, had been enough to speed Harry on his way through the ice-cold mist muttering imprecations about people in general and Ob in particular.

And as if all that wasn't enough he discovered, upon arrival at the depot, that he had forgotten to plug his van into the booster mechanism, or whatever it was—he had never understood it (Ob had explained it to him one day with an incoherence unusual even for him)—and the battery was flat and the thing wouldn't go. Everybody who earned more than he glowered at him vindictively and reminded him that this was by no means the first time this particular misfortune had overtaken him and that it might be to his advantage to see that it did not occur again. Those who earned less than he were of course delighted and gave vent to a great deal of unpolished humour and a variety of rude gestures some of which were unfamiliar even to Harry. Kicking out angrily at empty milk-cans he had splashed around to the rear of the depot to ensconce himself first in the lavatory where he had read a curious though highly debatable statement written in red pencil on the white-washed wall, and second in the driving seat of the ancient spare van which was kept serviced and in good running order for just such an emergency as that which he had precipitated.

Thus by the time he was bucketing down the high street he had 'had it' in a 'big way' and had his unfamiliar charge been capable of more than five miles an hour he would cheerfully have employed it as a lethal weapon against those pedestrians who were less quick off the mark than others. As it was even the frailest of old-age pensioners could be safely and comfortably installed on the end of the pier by the time the motor had received its initial incentive.

However, England's weather, unlike most of its other troubles, is apt to improve upon occasion, and sure enough as the clock on the town hall was preparing to launch itself into its midday rendering of *Rock of Ages,* the grey pall began to dissolve and the sun, wary with British reserve, peered through suspiciously; the town shifted, sniffed, shook itself like a wet dog and luxuriated for a few moments with an abandon incompatible with its narrow brown beaches and the hard obstinacy of its unlovely promenade.

Harry heard himself begin to whistle, which was ridiculous for a start because he never whistled, couldn't whistle—a hissing of breath between his teeth was the nearest he had ever been able to get to a whistle. Nevertheless for one auspicious moment he delivered himself of a whistle loud and clear, flat and horrible, but an unmistakable whistle, so surprising and so enjoyable that it occupied his mind on and off for the next ten minutes or so to the exclusion of most things other than an occasional ache of unhappiness centred around the non-appearance of Jennifer the night before.

That was the whole trouble really; it was nothing to do with the weather, nothing to do with Ob, nothing to do with the fact that he hadn't plugged in his bloody van, or even with the utter improbability of what he had read on the lavatory wall—it was simply and solely Jennifer. The way he had sat on that sandbin in the rain last night until past midnight waiting for her to come—hope and love in his heart—that was it: Hope and Love ... *Land of Hope and Glory* ... *Seated one Night on a Sandbin Weary and Ill at Ease* ... to the tune of the *Lost Chord.*

'All night long I sat there waiting for you, but you never came.'

So what would she say to that? 'Who asked you to sit there all night long waiting for me? I never said I'd be there, did I? Silly old fool, sitting there all night on that wet sandbin—you could have caught all manner of things sitting there on that cold wet iron . . .'

The roads were steaming under the sudden heat of the sun and Harry banged off his squeaking windscreen-wiper with an angry gesture. Why the hell hadn't Jennifer come out last night? Had she left by another exit because she had known he would be there waiting for her? What had gone wrong? What had he said to upset her? Maisie had said that she was upset? Why? Because he hadn't made another date with her?

And suddenly, by the roundabout, smiling and waving at him, she was there, trim and boyish in her scarlet raincoat and black leather boots. Her appearance was so unexpected that the van had whined past her at its full five miles an hour before he had recovered sufficiently to put his foot on the brake, which he did with such suddenness that some fat fool behind him almost ran into him and cursed him with a roundness reminiscent of the first Elizabeth.

A second later she was on the seat beside him.

'Hello.'

'Hi.'

Now, of course, he couldn't think of anything to say.

She said breathlessly, 'I wondered whether I might see you.'

'Oh?'

'You said your round took you up here.'

'Ah . . . fancy you remembering.'

'Everything all right?'

'What?'

'All right?'

'Yes.'

He edged the van into Brook Street, took the next turning and pulled up again.

'There,' he said. He looked at her. 'You staying?'

'Can I?'

'Sure, if you want to.'

He took a surreptitious peep at himself in the driving-mirror. He would have to look like the back end of a bus just at this moment, wouldn't he?

'Ha,' he said. 'Well ... there we are then ...'

She smiled. 'Sorry I waved at you like that. Nearly caused an accident, didn't I?'

'It was his fault—the bloke behind me. Shouldn't have been halfway up my exhaust pipe like that. He was too close. If I had pulled up any quicker he would have had me. You mustn't ever get too close, see, otherwise you haven't got a safe distance to pull up in ...'

She was staring at him in a way which made him suddenly speechless.

'Hello,' she said again, but this time it meant something more than just 'hello'.

He took her hand in his. 'I'm glad you're here. I waited for you a bit last night, but you didn't come. Only a little while I waited ...'

'In all that rain?'

'Did it rain?'

'You didn't say you'd be there. What a pity! I usually go out the other way because it's right next door to the bus stop. Fancy you waiting. Poor you! I'm sorry. You didn't catch cold, I hope.'

Harry snorted. 'I never catch cold. It doesn't matter; it was only that old Ob was going off to meet Maisie so I thought I'd sort of come along for the ride—sort of—on the off-chance like. It was my fault. I should have told you.'

Her hand tightened on his. 'Want me to tell *you* something?'

'What?'

'I've been waiting about up here specially to see you.'

'Go on?'

'I just wanted to see you again, make sure everything was all right. Do you mind?'

'I've been going mad sitting here, wondering ... I thought I'd done something—that you didn't like me—that ... oh, I don't know ... You're just not like any other girl I've ever had —and I'm not saying I've never had any others because I have and it's no good saying I haven't ... but you really are different —honest ... I feel as if I've known you for ages ... ages and ages ...'

The next thing they knew was that they were coming out of a long clinch.

They looked into each other's eyes for a long time.

'Your mack's all wet,' he said at last.

'So's yours.'

'And your hair . . .'

'I'd nearly given you up . . . I have to be at work at half past.'

'Half past what?'

'One.'

He looked at his watch. 'Have you had anything to eat? What about a bite of something? It's not half past twelve yet.'

'What do you usually do about eating? Where do you go?'

'I usually just have a bun or something in the van. I have a proper meal when I get home at night . . . at least . . . well, Ob manages a meal of some sort usually . . .'

'Can he cook?'

'No.'

She was smiling at him. 'Why don't you take off that terrible old oilskin and put your feet up while I go and get us some buns and sandwiches or something?'

'I'll go.'

'*I'll* go. Now take it off, it's dripping all over the place. Would you like anything special?'

He beamed at her possessively as he removed the offending garment. 'Only you.'

Suddenly she was serious again, sitting beside him quite still, her small, gentle hands quiet in her lap. 'You've already got me.' He touched one of her hands with the tips of his fingers and when she looked up at him her eyes were brimming with tears. 'I shouldn't say that. I don't want you to think I'm throwing myself at you . . .' For a second or two she was silent then, rousing herself, she said, 'I'll go and get those buns,' and was gone before he could prevent her.

There was a pain in his chest as if something were trying to get out: it hurt and constricted his breathing so he crossed his arms and gripped hard on his elbows and gradually it lessened. Why should he feel pain? Why should it hurt to find that he had flipped his lid over a girl for the first time in his life? If this was what they called being in love he wasn't sure he was going to enjoy it—not if it was going to hurt.

He had never really believed in the sort of love that was served up on the screen where it all happened to some big, bronzed, handsome nit with flaring nostrils who fought and killed, lived and died and well-nigh sacrificed his all for the privilege of walking off into the sunset with the bird you knew he was going to finish up with in the end anyway simply because her name had been the only one above the title with his. You could keep that sort of love. It was nice to watch, of course, in colour and Cine-dynamic-scope '93 but you had to keep your feet on the ground and remember that it was raining outside and there would be a queue for the bus and Ob would be waiting back at the flat with cold bangers and bread and butter. Nobody fought and died for love any more—at least milkmen and taxidermists didn't. Love to him—and he had to face it—had usually meant the arrival at an understanding with someone—the achievement of having lured the victim, suspecting or otherwise, finally to bed ... the physical act of 'making' love.

Ob was always maundering on about there being more to love than just bouncing up and down on a bed with a girl whose name you hardly knew. He was quite a bore about it one way and another and on one particular occasion Harry had reared up and faced him with open derision.

'A bloke goes and looks for a bird like he would go and look for a flat, right?'

'Wrong.'

'If he likes the furniture and the outlook, and the mod. cons. are fairly mod. and pretty con. he puts down his deposit, pays the rent and moves in. And when he gets tired and fed up with the view and things begin to get a bit worn round the edges, he gives in his notice and moves out at the end of the month.'

To which Ob had replied with his usual obstinacy that he had never heard such a load of 'old crap'. 'What if he wants to settle down, this bloke, get married to this bird and have a family?'

Harry remained patient. 'What *man* ever wants to settle down—a real man, that is, with blood and beer in his veins? It's only the birds who want to settle down—the birds who are afraid of becoming old hens with no particular perch to roost on. I'm not blaming them, far from it—who's blaming them?—it's not their fault they lose their looks quicker than we do. But that's life, isn't it—dolce vita—nothing's fair—you pays your money and you takes your pick—its' the luck of the game and all that cock. But I'll tell you this much—and this much I'll tell you for nothing—no bird's going to get her claws into me until I'm well and truly ready for it. When I make up my mind to settle down I'll be so old I won't even remember what a bird was for.'

At the time he had thought himself positively inspired; now even the hazy recollection of the conversation nauseated him. Mind you, a lot had changed since then, birds had come and birds had gone, and loneliness and frustration and a sense of incompleteness had chipped away at his armour of complacency—and he'd been exaggerating a bit, too; you had to exaggerate a little with Ob because Ob was inclined to get slushy about Love and Music and Flowers in the Spring and so forth. Ob was a star-gazer and a cloud-watcher and sometimes you couldn't get him down to earth again without being slightly revolting.

Now the situation had changed somewhat. Ob was bashing about with Maisie and being slightly revolting, whilst he, Harry, was having a go at the Hearts and Flowers.

When Jennifer returned with cheese sandwiches in a polythene bag, a couple of doughnuts and some bananas, Harry weighed anchor and steered the van in the direction of a quieter backwater he knew of. As they crawled through the traffic Jennifer laughed suddenly and pointed out a sad-looking man in a green bowler hat who was stumbling along the sidewalk with an enormous Busy Lizzie in his arms.

'My mother used to have a Busy Lizzie the size of the Albert Hall,' she told him.

'What happened to it?'

'My dad got fed up with it and planted it out in the garden and the frost got it; mum was furious.'

'Wonder she didn't divorce him.'

'She didn't have to. The same frost got poor old dad, too, I think. He died of pleurisy a few weeks later.'

Harry felt awkward. 'Sorry, I didn't know about that.'

'How could you?' she said gently.

She unbuttoned her shining mackintosh, hunched herself up in the corner and considered Harry's profile critically. He found himself reddening under the scrutiny and when finally he had drawn the van quietly to rest he switched off the motor, leaned back and looked at her enquiringly.

'Well, what was all that about?'

'All what?'

'That staring?'

'How old are you, Harry Stillwater?'

'Twenty-two.'

She smiled, sighed and took his hand. 'Aren't you old?'

PART TWO

CHAPTER TEN

Ob first became aware of his uneasiness as he was passing through the narrow tunnel—*For Pedestrian Traffic Only*—which linked the Old Town with the New.

Whilst he was not unduly sensitive with regard to atmospheres, psychic flashes and so forth, the dank mustiness and ill-lit echoing confines of the tunnel had never exactly inspired the full measure of his confidence; as a boy he had studiously avoided it, as a man he used it only when the short cut it afforded was advantageous to him. As far back as he could remember it had been known as The Tunnel, having been excavated long before subways had become fashionable. It plunged precipitously beneath the railway embankment from what was called the Old Town, where most of the new development was now going on, and climbed steeply up the far side to the New Town, which consisted mainly of the Esplanade, the Pier and the Amusement Park. The drainage system situated in the V-shaped trough of its lowest reaches was out of date, overworked and completely ineffective; on a night like the one in question the footpath would be awash.

It was past midnight and Ob, homeward-bound after having dallied too long at Maisie's front door, had chosen the tunnel route not only because it was quicker but because it afforded at least eighty yards of shelter from the lashing rain outside. The tunnel, a mere five feet wide and no more than eight feet high, smelled like a tomb and the steady monotonous dripping of water into puddles did little to banish the depression created by such an association; the sound of his footsteps was loudly disconcerting and without focus; his shadow, monstrously disproportionate, lurched and heaved before him. There were only two sources of light—naked electric bulbs—one behind him, the other ahead. Someone had just passed beneath the one ahead; the black shape bore down upon him and strangely seemed to be unaccompanied by the sound of footsteps—just the hunched figure moving silently towards him.

It was then that Ob recognised his uneasiness and found

himself listening for the approaching footfalls with an intensity which served only to magnify their absence. He trod softly and heard only the dripping of water into puddles and the sludgy gurgling of the drain.

Then came the feeling that someone was behind him and when he turned to look could see nothing but the sordid glare of the bulb in the ceiling. And all at once every instinct for self-preservation was alerted. Danger, they said, was a smell; he was now aware of that smell for the first time in his life; and with it came fear, the crawling fear of the unknown, of physical pain and the inability to be able to bear it when it came.

The dark figure was suddenly still and stood straddle-legged across the path. The confined space and the fact that it stood on the brink of the oily overflow of the drain and was reflected on its surface made it appear the size of a Colossus.

The glint of metal brought Ob to a halt. He had not needed to hear the slight scuff of sound behind him to know that his retreat was covered.

He thought quite calmly that he was about to be killed.

With a tinkle of glass the light behind him was extinguished; his shadow died abruptly. There came another sound, a moronic, soft wet giggle of anticipation.

Ob felt his knees begin to tremble and when he braced them the denim of his trousers clung to the sweat which crawled down his legs.

The straddling black silhouette moved again, still without sound, and Ob watched mesmerised as each foot was placed with meticulous precision into the oily black water. It was like the commencement of some fantastic *danse macabre* to the accompaniment of a tuneless hissing of breath from between someone's teeth—someone behind him, drawing closer . . .

Ob's brain cleared as he waited motionless listening and watching. Now there were three advancing shadows before him and, he guessed, as many behind—six to one; those were the odds you laughed about in Douglas Fairbanks' films—everybody cheered and clapped as one after the other the villains bit the dust. But now, unfortunately, it wasn't funny any more; there was no Douglas Fairbanks and no one to cheer—just he, Ob, and six unknown assailants in a dark smelly tomb thirty feet beneath a railway embankment.

He moved swiftly, putting those behind him on his left flank and placing his back against the wall. Now he could see them all, six of them, those on his left no more than a frieze of hands and faces white against the darkness; the others, more distant, still no more than black shapes. His sudden movement had frozen them all into momentary stillness; he could hear the stealthy, animal creaking of leather, and on his left with startling clarity he saw the clean bare blade of a cut-throat razor.

At that moment he acted. Kicking out viciously at the razor with his left foot he turned and threw himself down the ramp at the oncoming trio. From behind him came a cry of pain and one of them swore violently, then he was in the midst of the three, his hands clawing at wet leather, his knee hard in the stomach of the foremost. The impetus of the attack carried the other backward stumbling and lurching against his companions and spreadeagled him finally in the black water, the back of his head striking the ground with a force which almost split his skull. For a brief instant of shock Ob sprawled across the still figure, then flinging himself sideways he dived frantically at the nearest pair of legs and thrusting with his shoulder upwards hard into the man's groin he heaved himself by brute strength to his feet. Then the others were upon him.

Outnumbered as he was Ob found himself strangely calm. It was perhaps the knowledge that he couldn't win which made his movements so deliberate. He couldn't box, never had been able to, and you couldn't suddenly, overnight, taken unawares and set upon in greasy wet darkness, become heavyweight champion of the world. Anyway, who was boxing? This was the way men fought in reality, by instinct, swearing and cursing, clawing and kicking, the eyes and sex organs being the main objectives. Ob laid about him lustily like a Samson deprived of his ass's jawbone. He was licked and he knew it, but he wasn't going to let anybody else know it; step by step he was losing ground, but what the hell, the worst they could do was kill him and somehow even that didn't seem to matter any more. But now a change began to take place inside him, a dull burning glow taking the place of cool deliberation; it twisted inside his stomach and smarted like acid behind his eyes; it grew and blazed into blood-red, bludgeoning anger in the lust of which he wanted only to kill, to destroy them, to batter each one of them into the ground.

He could see them clearly now, four of them, pale, sweating, straining faces, coarse and brutal, faces which would degrade the animal kingdom; he could smell them, the sweat, the stale beery breath, wet leather and the sickly flowery perfume of cheap brilliantine. He felt the blows rained upon him, saw the weapons, the knives, the razor, the bicycle chain, but there was no pain, no hurt—just anger, blind and bloody.

Above him now glared the one remaining electric bulb and lashing out at it frantically he felt the white hot glass splinter agonizingly into the palm of his hand—that was the only moment of pain.

The unbelievable blackness which now engulfed them seemed also to close in on his assailants' senses; as blindness took them over and their quarry became invisible in the darkness, they thrashed about helplessly among themselves, and taking advantage of their momentary confusion Ob crouched low to the ground and laying about him in all directions, charged through them. But the darkness was his enemy too. With a violence which knocked the breath out of him and well-nigh dislocated his shoulder he crashed against the wall and with head spinning and lungs screaming for air floundered to the ground where he lay for what seemed like minutes on end trying to summon up enough strength to pull himself together; the only conscious thought racing and reiterating itself through his stunned mind was the urgent frantic necessity to get away before anyone thought of striking a match.

The commotion was dying down and was now little more than a shifting of feet and the harsh straining for breath; further away someone groaned monotonously. The contestants had sorted themselves out and were listening intently for any sound which would give away the whereabouts of their victim.

Using the slimy wall for support Ob managed to lever himself to his feet and edged along it cautiously; all sense of direction had gone from him, but he knew if he followed the wall . . . he felt the incline raking up beneath his feet—it would lead him to the Esplanade.

Suddenly, barely a foot away, someone spoke softly.

'Mac?'

Ob froze. It was the one with the cheap brilliantine; the sickly stench of it nauseated him.

Another voice, a little way off, said, ''Ere, I'm over 'ere—who's that? . . . Jim? . . .

'Yeah ...' Ob flattened himself against the wall. 'The bastard's still down here somewhere ... hasn't no one got a light, for Christ's sake? ...'

A hand groped at Ob's shoulder, found and seized the epaulette on his raincoat. He wrenched away from it.

The voice was ugly in triumph. 'He's here, I've got him ... he's over here ... for Christ's sake somebody ...'

Ob smashed his fist into the man's face and as somebody else struck a match began to run.

If anyone had told him ten seconds before that his life would depend on running, his answer would have been that death was preferable to having to make one more exertion—yet here he was beating his way up the echoing ramp and to hell with everyone who liked to call him a coward. 'I am a coward and proud of it ... up all the cowards! ... yellow's my favourite colour ... I like running anyway ... the Loneliness of the Long Distant Runner ... Up him, too ...'

Then he was out in the fresh air—the rain streaming and drenching down on him cold and relentless, the blood smarting in his eyes. On his left the black sea raged; before him, straight as a die, rainswept and deserted, a low railing separating it from the beach which at this point lay some fifteen feet below the level of the street, stretched the promenade.

The shock of the rain and the icy coldness of the wind slowed him up considerably and it was only seconds before he realised that one of his pursuers was snapping at his heels blaspheming and swearing at him. He knew it was useless to continue running ... turn and fight ... that was the thing ... turn and fight and you'll be a man, my son! ... silly bastard ...

He pulled up suddenly and turned; the other was so close that they cannoned into each other. Ob raised his foot and with all his remaining strength kicked hard. He could see the boy's face—he was about nineteen, black hair and heavy eyebrows—he didn't hear the scream; he saw the mouth open and the agony on the face, but the beat of the sea and the clamour in his own ears prevented him from hearing the scream. He swung back his hand, saw the bicycle chain clutched in the other's fist, seized it from him, struck out at the face, now fiendish with hate, and watched the boy stagger towards the railing; it caught him in the small of the back and turned him slowly, like a catherine wheel on a pin, in a full circle.

Now, above the sound of the sea and the clamour in his own head, he heard the scream, and the boy was gone—there was only the low railing and the black sea . . .

And once again Ob turned and ran . . .

Harry was late getting home that night, too, and when he saw the untidy figure sprawling in the rain on the front step his first thought was that the local drunk who lived only a few doors away had decided to sleep it off on the wrong doorstep.

He stirred the figure gently with his foot.

'Come on, mate, uppity, uppity—time all good pisspots were in bed.' And while he stood wondering what the hell he was going to do about it Ob opened his eyes, groaned, and was violently sick.

Harry stared at him horrified. 'For crying out loud! Ob! What the hell's up with you? What have you been up to? Are you sloshed or what?'

'Shut up for a minute, will you,' begged Ob feebly, 'and give me a hand.'

Harry squatted down beside him and thrust an arm roughly around Ob's shoulders. 'You old so-and-so, never thought I should ever see you in this state. What happened? Did she tell you it was all over and was going back to mother? . . .' Then his hand touched bare skin slimy with blood. 'You're bleeding . . . what the . . .?'

He leaned in closer and what he could see of Ob's face bereft him of further speech. Ob was crying. 'Sorry mate,' he muttered, 'Give us a hand, will you?' and passed out cold on the step.

Harry knelt there for a moment staring at him in disbelief. Then he looked up and down the street in the forlorn hope that some stupid idiot might be abroad at this time of night to give him a helping hand.

'Bloody hell,' he said to no one in particular, 'There's fifteen stone of him there, how the hell am I going to shift that lot on my own. Poor old bugger, what happened I wonder.' He shook his friend gently. 'Ob! Ob mate, wake up, I can't lift a great lump like you on my own. Hey! Ob!'

But Ob was away and made no answer. Harry considered for a moment, then fumbling for his key he straddled the recumbent body and opened the front door, then with his back to the door he stooped, grasped hold of Ob beneath the armpits and heaved. Nothing at all happened except that he lost his balance and sat abruptly on the front door mat with an alarming bump. The whole house seemed to shake. That's all we need, he thought, everybody coming to have a look at us sitting in the rain on the doorstep!

'Ob.'

He got up, braced himself and tried again. But Ob was fifteen stone when he was alive, in this state he was worth an additional five.

To make matters worse the rain increased and all Harry could do was to stand there looking at Ob lying on his back being rained on. With a sudden thought, he went inside, ferreted around in the kitchen cupboard where he found the smallest bottle of brandy that money could buy, snatched his oilskin from its hook and returning spread the garment over the sodden form of his fallen friend, and, inserting the neck of the bottle into the corner of the already slightly-open mouth —thank God!—tipped a dram or two of the liquid down Ob's throat. As he did so he wondered a trifle anxiously whether the bottle did in fact contain brandy—bottles in the kitchen cupboard were only too apt to contain beverages and poisons other than those indicated on the labels. To make sure he sniffed at it and poured a quantity of it down his own throat, and felt a lot better.

Ob spluttered and muttered a bit and stirred uneasily.

'Ob,' said Harry in his ear. 'Ob, mate, wake up will you, old darling. Just a couple of ticks. I can't get you into the bloody house. You're too heavy. Only a couple of ticks, eh ...?'

'What?' said Ob.

'Here, have a spot of brandy and turn over a bit, can you, so's I can get hold of you properly. You're like a ton weight.'

Ob gobbled at the brandy bottle until it was empty then closed his eyes with a sigh, or a groan, Harry wasn't sure which but whichever it was filled Harry with anxiety. He prodded at Ob with gentle persistence. 'Don't go off again for a minute. Let's get you inside first then you can go off for as long as you like, you poor old devil ... Come on now, upsidaisy ... lean on the doorpost, can you, a bit more—and not on me so much? ... that's right ... that's it ... lovely ... careful ... that's my old cobber .. '

Sweating and straining, with Ob in agony and Harry on the

verge of hysteria, they finally managed to get each other into the kitchen where Ob promptly passed out on the coconut-matting leaving Harry, exhausted and dripping, on his knees in the doorway.

A few deep breaths and a couple of bows in the direction of the bath and Harry roused himself sufficiently to roll Ob over on to his back, collect some lumpy cushions from the sitting-room and stuff them beneath the wet, spiky-haired head; he then sat back on his haunches and stared at the battered face of his best friend with awe.

'Jesus.' He shook his head in disbelief. 'Like a bloody steam-roller must have hit him.'

Putting a kettle of water on the gas he messed about in the so-called medicine-cabinet where they kept toilet-rolls and toothpaste and a small plastic reproduction of the Taj Mahal but a bottle of influenza mixture and a crumbling white tablet which might have been an aspirin were the only objects which could even remotely be said to have had medical associations. He went back and took another despairing look at his prostrate friend; what did you do with a face like that? He fished in his pocket, found fourpence, went into the hall and rang a disgruntled doctor who breathed heavily down the phone and demonstrated a lack of enthusiasm which in anyone other than a doctor would have been remarkable.

'Perhaps you should have rung the hospital.'

'I rang you instead.'

'The hospital might have been better.'

'He's not dying.'

'How do you know that?'

'What?'

'I'll come as soon as I can.'

'Sooner, if you can manage it.'

'I beg your pardon?'

'Granted.'

Harry hung up, said an offensive word at the telephone and then went to the lavatory where he was sick.

When the doctor had finished Ob looked like an old Egyptian mummy.

'He looks like an old Egyptian mummy,' said Harry.

The doctor, quite a nice little man whose name was Bumphrey, looked at him sternly. 'He won't last as long as an old Egyptian mummy if he goes on like this. What's he been up to, did he say?'

'Looks like he ran up against a steam-roller.'

'He should be in hospital, really—and it wasn't a steam-roller.'

'No, I didn't think it was really.'

'He's been beaten up. By whom, do you know?'

'Didn't he say anything to you at all?'

Dr. Bumphrey looked at him with tired eyes. 'I wouldn't be asking all these questions if he had, now would I?'

Harry said, 'Some people are funny, they ask questions even when they know the answers. Like I told you, he was passed out on the doorstep when I got home.'

The doctor contemplated the end of his stethoscope and blew down it experimentally. 'The police ought to be told.'

'Yes.'

'*I* ought to tell them really.'

'Ah.'

'Otherwise we'll have everybody going around being beaten up, won't we?'

'Yes.'

'Might be an idea to pass that on to him when he wakes up. I've given him an injection; he ought to feel better; stiff though, he'll be stiff for a couple of days. He's also got a lot of stitches in him.'

'How many?'

'Enough. Somebody was at him with a razor, I shouldn't wonder. Is he a fighter?'

'Pardon?'

'Does he get into fights often?'

'Never.'

'Never?'

'Once he did . . .' He stopped.

The doctor humped himself into his overcoat. 'Thought of something?'

'Like a cup of tea?'

'No thanks. I'll look in tomorrow. He'll be all right. If he's in pain when he wakes up give him a couple of these, eh?' He put a small round box on the bedside table. 'He needs quite a bit of rest.' He twinkled suddenly, and jerked his head at the sleeping form on the bed. 'That would just be an out-of-season dust-up for James Bond, wouldn't it?'

'What time tomorrow?'

'Time?'

'When will you be coming?'

The doctor raised pale eyebrows. '*I* don't know. Why? Is it difficult?'

'I've got to go to work.'

'Someone ought to be around.'

'That's what I mean.'

'He needs a bit of looking after. Couldn't you take a couple of days off?'

'Have to, I suppose. They'll like that.'

The doctor put his hat on. 'Do 'em good, whoever they are.'

'Couldn't give me a certificate, I suppose?'

'What for?'

'Doctor's certificate, saying I'm ill.'

'You're not ill.'

'I know I'm not, but if I take a couple of days off, just like that, I'll get my pay docked, won't I?'

The doctor sniffed sympathetically. 'That's life, isn't it?'

Harry handed him his bag. 'I had an idea you were going to say that.'

'Well I have to, don't I? Goodnight, see you tomorrow some time. Sorry they beat him up; he doesn't look the type—not the usual type.'

'He's not.'

'Goodnight, then.'

On the doorstep he stooped, picked something up, peered at it shortsightedly and handed it to Harry.

'I hope,' he said softly, 'that doesn't belong to him.'

It was a bicycle chain.

Harry didn't know whether to go to bed or not. He had never looked after a sick person before. In Dr. Kildare people sat up with people and took their temperatures and gave them pills every few hours and Dr. Gillespie would come in the small hours and say: 'Well done, Jim, he's pulling through.' But Dr. Bumphrey hadn't said anything about sitting up all night—he hadn't said much about anything at all if it came to that—except that he wouldn't part with a doctor's certificate . . . And what was that bit about James Bond? . . .

Harry hovered indecisively around the bed humming and

hahing and squinting at the invalid who was just beginning to slide into a gentle snore. Harry hoped fervently that there wasn't going to be a great deal of that to contend with during the night; you could hardly throw a boot at a sick man, and with all those bandages blocking his ears up it would be a waste of time asking him politely to put a sock in it.

He wandered through to the kitchen and for want of something better to do made himself a cup of Ovaltine. He thought about Jennifer and what she would say when she heard what had happened to Ob. And Maisie, what about Maisie? What would *she* say? Maybe she would come round and keep an eye on Ob—that was an idea. She didn't work during the morning and might be pleased to do a bit of Christian service for a chap. Not that there'd be a great deal of Christianity about Maisie looking after Ob. It would be much more like a sort of Pagan ritual.

How about Jennifer coming round to lend a hand? That was an even better idea. So far she hadn't set foot in the place, and though he had pointed out the house to her from the other side of the road she hadn't said anything about an urge to see his etchings and he certainly hadn't wanted to force the issue. That was the extraordinary thing about this association with Jennifer. In all other circumstances, with every other girl to date, the whole thing would have been over and done with by this time—nobody could ever say the grass grew under his feet. With him it was simply a question of giving the current bird a particular sort of sultry look and then following it up with a piece of off-hand dialogue like, 'How about it then?' or 'Do you feel like it, then?' or even 'Don't you think it's a bit chilly out here then?' It was the look which counted more than anything else, though. On one occasion he had only said, 'Eh?' and she'd said 'Ay' and as far as he could remember no other word has passed their lips for the remainder of the evening. They had probably said 'goodnight' but if they had he couldn't remember it.

But now, he thought, it was time that Jennifer was introduced into the home circle, and with Ob prostrate on a bed of pain, opportunity was knocking; indeed another opportunity of inveigling her into the family parlour was unlikely to occur in the foreseeable future. 'Will you step into the parlour?'—as the Milkman said to the Usherette.

Some parlour! Harry stared broodingly at the dresser. It was still as untidy and mucky as it had ever been.

After the Episode of the Hard-Boiled Egg the good intentions responsible for that operation being swung into motion had flagged. Nothing further had been done about anything. Ob's saw and hammer and three ounces of nails were still there —so was Harry's record.

Lounging to his feet he went over to see what the record was about. It was called *Three Coins in the Fountain,* which probably accounted for it having lain there so long. He remembered the tune and tried it over to the words, *One Hard-Boiled Egg in the Water-Butt* but it wouldn't go ... *Boiled Eggs in the Bath-Tub* went all right ... He gave the record a sharp smack against the edge of the sink but it didn't break; it said it was unbreakable on the label so Harry took the hammer and dealt it a couple of lusty blows but no great harm was done—there were two dents in it but it still looked like a record. He bent it in half like an apple turnover, folded it down the middle and hit it again with the hammer. When that failed he gave up; it was just one of those records he would never play again. Moodily he replaced it on the dresser, picked up his Ovaltine and went to have another look at Ob.

Nothing had changed. He looked fairly peaceful, Harry thought, underneath all those bandages. He also looked a bit like the Invisible Man ... if you took away the bandages there wouldn't be anyone there ... *As I was going up the stair I met a man who wasn't there ...*

In Harry's mind there was no doubt at all as to who was responsible for his friend's condition. Both Eugene, the bald-headed proprietor of *The Elbow Room,* and the beautiful blond youth in leather had warned Ob of the potential danger of the clash with Red and his two henchmen, and if that little sawn-off half-pint pot of nastiness hadn't something to do with all this then he, Harry, was a Dutchman.

Harold Van Stillwater ... Harold Still Vanwater ... Still Harold Watervan ... Gunga Din and all that ... Oh God!

He finished his Ovaltine, clambered into his pyjamas and wondered what to do about the morning. He'd ring the dairy and tell them he had the plague or Housemaid's Knee or something equally unlikely so they would believe him. There was that illness where you swelled up like an elephant—it was called Elephant-something . . . No, he wouldn't have that—they might want to come and take a picture. Then he'd go round to Maisie's place and Jennifer's place and tell them the story and they'd both come flocking and twittering with fruit and magazines and fascinating food parcels.

Ob was snoring pretty hard by this time so Harry stood over him, stared at him with intensity worthy of a warlock and willed him to be quiet. Silence fell as though someone had dropped an iron curtain. Harry, pleased and impressed, draped himself in his ancient dressing-gown and decided to sit up for a bit and keep an eye on things.

There was a small pile of dog-eared paperbacks on the stool under the television set and squatting on the floor he went through them in the hope of finding something interesting with which to while away the long watchful hours before him.

He was looking at the pictures in a book called *I Have A Theory about Men* by a dog named Philamore Brighteyes when he fell asleep.

CHAPTER ELEVEN

WAKEFULNESS returned to him grudgingly at half past four when he sat for several stupefied moments of bleary-eyed wonder trying to comprehend why he was sitting cross-legged in front of a dead television set like a petrified Yogi. When he attempted movement it was to the accompaniment of agony unsurpassed since the merry days of rack and thumb-screw —and clambering to his feet turned out to be one of those performances about which, in the years to come, he would no doubt laugh a great deal; at the present moment his sense of humour steadfastly refused to comment.

Only when the scratchings and thumpings on the bedroom wall impinged themselves upon his shaky consciousness did he realise what it was that had roused him to his present state of muscle-bound torment.

He went over and peered through the bedroom door.

Ob, twisted across the pillows, his arms twining restlessly above his head, his hands clawing and clutching at the wall-paper, was in the throes of a nightmare.

Harry tried to quieten him without waking him, holding on to his hands and cooing at him—gentle as a mother—and soon the spasms passed and the harsh breathing eased. Harry found a large silk handkerchief in a drawer and draped it carefully over the shade of the bedside lamp, noticing as he did so that Ob's bandages were wet with sweat; he swore violently beneath his breath and found himself wishing he had taken a course in First Aid instead of Bird Watching.

The rain was hurling itself in great gusts against the window; he pushed back the curtain and stared out into the blackness. Out there he could see not one single glow of light. He had the curious sensation that he and Ob were the only two people left alive in the entire world.

'Harry?'

He was at the bedside in an instant.

'Hello mate. You're all right. Go to sleep.'

Ob's eyes glinted between the bandages. 'I'm in a mess, aren't I?'

'You're all right.'

'Listen ...'

'Go to sleep.'

'... You've got to listen ...'

'The doctor told me ...'

'I think I've killed someone.'

Somewhere in Harry's stomach a knot was tied. Miles away, somewhere in that empty world, he heard the dismal wail of a ship's siren.

Ob's voice was hoarse but distinct. 'Did you hear what I said?'

'You sure?'

'Not sure, no ...'

'Who was it?'

'I don't know ... a kid—just a kid with black hair ... he was one of 'em.'

'Where was this? ... Ob? ... You still with me? Try to remember where it was. I'll go and see. Ob?'

'The Tunnel ... this end ... He went over the railing off the prom. There are rocks down there ... he went over backwards ...'

'You saw that?'

'I saw it. He must have broken his neck—or drowned—the sea was pretty high.'

'I'll go and have a look.'

'It's no good looking now—he'll be gone ... what's the time?'

'Nearly five.'

'He'll be gone by now ... no point in looking now.'

Harry took up the little pill box and extracted a couple of white tablets. 'You're going to have a couple of these and go off to sleep again, see? The doctor said so; they're to make you sleep and ease the pain. I'll get some water.'

Out in the kitchen Harry's brain whirled with desperate uneasiness at the new turn of events. Ob killing someone ... Christ, that wasn't funny. Even in self-defence that wasn't funny. What the hell had got into him? He was such a placid bloke normally, wouldn't hurt a bloody fly ...

Ob took the pills without any trouble and for a few seconds there was silence between them.

Harry said, 'There was a pack of them, was there?'

'Six.'

'They don't believe in taking chances, do they? Who? Red's mob?'

'I haven't done anything to upset anybody else.'

'Nowadays you don't *have* to do anything except walk down a dark alley on your own, that's enough for some of 'em. But no one would tangle with someone like you unless there was a reason. You didn't see Red among them?'

'No one I knew, no. There was a 'Mac' and a 'Jim'. They got me in a tunnel. God, that place's a deathtrap.'

'Shut up now, and get off to sleep for Gawd's sake; you're keeping me up.'

There was a long silence during which Harry thought Ob had finally dropped off, but suddenly he spoke again.

'Harry ...'

'What?'

'Did the doc really say I'd be okay?'

'Shaky—he said you'd be shaky for a bit, but then you'd be all right. Go to sleep.'

'I feel like I'm dying.'

'Don't worry, mate, you won't die. You're too bloody artful. Now belt up, will you?'

Ob was asleep before he had finished the sentence.

Harry wandered about the room restlessly finishing up at the window where he stared out once again into the black night. Reflected in the glass he could see the room glowing behind him, the still figure on the bed, and if he crossed his eyes slightly he was able to focus on his own face, frowning and anxious, peering dimly back at him from the darkness.

It was all much more serious than anyone had imagined—'anyone' being the doctor and himself. To have been beaten up by a gang of toughs was one thing—to have killed one of them was another ... under whatever circumstances. Ob was in trouble, big trouble, police trouble ... if he had killed that kid. But he wasn't sure—he said he hadn't been sure. He had seen the kid do a header over the railings; that didn't mean that he was lying dead on the rocks below ... not necessarily ...

Harry went and stood over his sleeping friend. The sleep seemed to be deeper and easier than before. Harry wondered whether it would be safe to leave him for a little while on his own. Ob had said that there would be no point in looking to see whether the boy was there still, but why shouldn't he be? He might have busted his arm or something and could be lying there dying of exposure—or being drowned by the high sea simply because he couldn't move. There was no reason to assume that a drop of fifteen feet or so had killed him however hard he had fallen. You could fall a couple of hundred feet and still live.

Harry arrived at a decision with a well-chosen swear word. Clambering out of his dressing-gown he kicked off his pyjamas, climbed into jeans, jersey, gumboots and oilskins, snatched up an electric torch and, taking a final look at the invalid who hadn't moved a muscle, plunged out into the filthiest night he could remember.

The gales were blowing in off the sea and appeared to be bringing most of it with them; the rain had turned to hail and the individual stones, hard as metal, lashed against his unprotected face in a ceaseless, merciless, barrage until he found himself wondering whether they would leave scars. He strapped the high collar of his oilskin up over his mouth and nose—as high as it would go—leant against the wind and set off in the direction of the sea. At the first corner he found himself clawing desperately at a lamp-post to prevent himself being hurled bodily across the road; the impact of the wind drove the breath out of him. Hanging there like a scarecrow he speculated for a couple of storm-swept moments upon the wisdom of his projected mission; if the boy weren't there he would have wasted his time and a great deal of energy; if he were he would either be dead or so badly incapacitated that Harry alone would be able to do very little to help. Nevertheless, even if that were the case, it would still be possible to ring the police or the ambulance or somebody, and Ob, at least, would be able to rest easy knowing where he stood instead of just lying there guessing.

He relinquished his hold on the lamp-post and battled on.

Everything worsened on the promenade itself where shelter and protection from the fury of the sea was down to its minimum. Each alternate street-lamp was still burning but did little to illumine anything other than a few square feet of streaming asphalt around its base. Damage to property seemed to be considerable. Harry noticed an overturned car nestled against a wrecked shelter; a metal refuse bin bowled past him at the rate of knots, bounced across the road and judging by the splintering of plate glass which followed finished up in a shop window. Tomorrow's Best Bargain ... Periodic rumbling sounds followed by staccato slithering crashes told of slates and tiles dislodged and uprooted.

Only from the insular depths of a plush seat in the cinema had he ridden the heaving decks of ocean-going vessels ploughing implacably through the paths of hurricanes, but it had never been anything like this—if acting in *The Cruel Sea* had been anything like this Jack Hawkins should have been given the O.B.E. long ago ...

Reeling from one hand-hold to another, clutching like a drowning man to the slippery iron railing which ran the full length of the Esplanade he began to believe that the ground itself was lurching and fighting to free itself of his stumbling feet. And suddenly it did; it opened up beneath him and he pitched headfirst down a steep flight of metal-edged steps and, stunned and breathless, found himself spelling out a large notice which had a dim lamp burning over it. It didn't say much—just *Ladies*. He lay there and grinned at it, not caring if the entire female population came and tramped over him in their stiletto heels—in fact, he thought, he might even enjoy it; indeed, he decided, it would be delightful—it would be a change anyway. He was sitting in a puddle, but what was a puddle after all he had been through? for a few self-indulgent moments he enjoyed the comparative peace and quiet of this unexpected haven.

They were still hurling hailstones the size of golf-balls down upon his unprotected head and in a sudden fit of thwarted fury and in the name of Suffering Mankind he laid hold of the largest stone he could find and threw it back with all the strength he could muster. And what good did it do? It bounced off one wall, ricocheted off another, and, unerring as a well-flung boomerang, struck him smartly on the head.

The four-letter expletive which exploded from his lips was not one to be heard every day within those hallowed precincts, but it echoed splendidly up and down and in and out of their subterranean depths.

'Your journey,' he declaimed sonorously, 'is not necessary. Go home. Go Home, Stillwater!'

It sounded absolutely marvellous—like singing in the bath,

not the bath in the kitchen at home, but a real bath in a marble-walled bathroom—so he said it all again lingering over the vibrant resonance of the vowels.

'Go-o-o-o H-o-o-o-me Sti-i-illwa-a-a-a-ater!'

In the midst of it all he was suddenly bathed in bright light whilst an unamused voice coming from somewhere behind its dazzling source said sourly, 'And not a bad idea at that. What do you think you're up to?'

'Pardon?' asked Harry.

'Notwithstanding which you're trespassing—in case it has escaped your notice.'

The light left his face, hovered for a significant moment on the word *Ladies* and returned to his face.

'Ah,' said Harry. He felt slightly stupid. He also became aware of a hollow thudding sound which was new, and which didn't belong to him. 'Er . . .' he said and finding his torch switched it on. The beam picked up a pair of large black boots, navy blue trousers and the dripping skirt of a very official-looking blue mackintosh. 'Ah,' he said again, 'I fell down.'

The boots came down a couple of steps and the hollow thudding grew louder. Then Harry realised what was causing it; it was the thud of hailstones on the copper's helmet.

'I think,' he lied, 'I've broken my leg.'

The constable rustled with interest inside his wet mackintosh. Here was a find indeed—a bloke with a broken leg halfway down the Ladies' Loo.

'You know you're halfway down the Ladies' Loo, don't you?'

Harry simpered. 'I *would* have to fall down the Ladies', wouldn't I?'

The constable's voice darkened. 'You sure you *fell* down?' Harry boggled at the implied suggestion and said nothing. 'If we're going to hang about for any length of time I suggest we move next door.'

'Next door?'

'To the Gents.'

Under other circumstances it might have been hilarious, but Harry had detected in the constable's tone a sinister note which drained the humour out of the situation.

Now his lie began to worry him. 'I don't know whether I can walk.'

'Well, let's have a try, shall we?'

Awkwardly they scrabbled together for a bit in the half-darkness then Harry found himself being lifted bodily to his feet.

'Well,' he muttered with a certain amount of awe, 'It seems to be all right.'

It was the policeman's turn to say 'Ah', but he managed to make it mean a lot more than just 'ah'. He leaned in close and Harry could hear him sniffing away like the *Hound of the Baskervilles.*

'I'm not drunk, if that's what you're thinking.'

The policeman said nothing, just seized hold of his arm in a grip which would have done credit to a boa-constrictor in its prime and marched him off upstairs.

Harry's uneasiness grew. What had he done? Was he under arrest? All he had done was fall down the Ladies—what was wrong with that?—it wasn't his fault. The grip on his arm was too high, it was practically dislocating his collar-bone and what with the pressure and the fact that the copper appeared to be about ten feet tall in his stockinged feet, Harry once again more or less left the ground. Arriving on the surface he did in fact leave it altogether and was prevented from returning to the pit from whence they had come only by the timely intervention of the policeman. Together they swayed dangerously among the elements clutched closely in each other's arms.

'Do you,' enquired Harry breathlessly, 'come here often?'

He thought the remark was side-splitting but had a feeling the moment he had said it that it was one which would be met with considerably less appreciation by his blue-clad friend.

He was right. 'Ha-ha,' said the policeman in a flat voice.

Locked together and inseparable they battled their way along the front for a moment or so until they came to the steps leading down to the Gents.

A few moments later in the dank, dimly-lit marbled depths they surveyed each other with interest.

The policeman was enormous; he was like a 'Thing' in an X film; he was six-feet-six if he was an inch and had a chest on him like a wardrobe. His face resembled a bland York Ham and the black eyes, which were prevented from getting together only by the timely insertion of a king-size nose were about the size of a couple of small burnt currants. He wasn't a man, he was a gorilla—useful in a fight if he was on your side —hideous if he happened to be on the other.

Which was where he was at the moment.

He grinned suddenly, groped hugely in his mack pocket, produced a battered pack of cigarettes, offered it to Harry and said by way of the understatement of the year, 'Nasty night.'

Harry didn't smoke but hadn't the courage to refuse the proffered friendship. He took a cigarette gingerly and stared at it with remote curiosity, and when an enormous flame appeared under his nose he sucked and puffed obediently at its filter tip until he was breathless.

The constable regarded him steadily over the flame as he lit one for himself. Then he removed his helmet—he had spiky hair like Ob's only blond—blond!—balanced it carefully on a washbasin, unbuttoned his mackintosh, shook it vigorously with a great clatter of sound, and folding his arms sat carefully on the edge of the basin.

'Well now,' he said conversationally, 'What's to do?'

Harry sucked at his cigarette.

'I fell down the Ladies. I was blown down. One minute I was there, the next minute I wasn't—like.'

The copper was full of sympathy. 'It's a nasty night, there's no denying that.'

There was a sudden flushing and rushing of water on all sides which went on for about thirty seconds and until it had spent itself nobody said anything. Then Harry grinned sheepishly.

'You look like you think I was up to all sorts of terrible things. I just fell down the Ladies, that's all. And I was making all that noise because it was like singing in the bath ...' He looked at the policeman's large boots, '... room. I could have hurt myself, couldn't I? ... badly ... could have ... with a fall like that ... I mean, suddenly like that without any warning ... bang ... flat on my back down the Ladies' Loo ... I didn't know it was the Ladies till I got there ... did I? if I'd known I was going to fall down I would have waited till I got next door, like—eh?'

The policeman was grinning again; Harry wasn't sure whether he cared for him grinning like that.

'What are you worrying about? I'm not going to run you in or anything like that, if that's what's worrying you.'

'Aren't you?'

'Not unless you want me to? Have you done anything you think I ought to know about?'

'What?'

'Like robbing a bank, or hitting an old lady over the head?'

'No.'

'All right then, enjoy your fag, put your feet up and have a bit of a breather. Must have been a nasty shock falling down the Ladies like that.'

'It was.'

'Bound to be. There you are, then.'

Harry hated his cigarette. He used to say at school that cigarettes were made of camel-dung and old army socks, but it wasn't until now that he realised how near the truth he appeared to have been. He crossed his eyes and peered at it with some malevolence.

'All right?' enquired the policeman.

'What? Yes . . . lovely . . . nice . . .'

The policeman drew a great gulp of smoke down into his lungs and luxuriated in it for about a minute and a half—it would have killed Harry—then he released it through every aperture his vast face afforded, nose, mouth, and—Harry was quite certain—both ears too—it poured out in all directions.

'You've no idea,' said the policeman, ignorant of his feat, 'how bloody lonely we get of a night, if you'll excuse my French.'

'Go on?'

'The unutterable dreariness of pounding a beat. Up and down, round and round, and nothing ever happening 'cepting blokes like you falling about. You didn't even have a broken leg; I could have got you to the hospital and cared about you for a bit and I would have remembered this night because it was different.'

Harry jerked his head upwards in the direction of the noises they were making in the reconstruction of the universe.

'I'd have thought all that was different enough for you.'

'It's not the worst night I've known—not by a long chalk.'

'Well you can still care about me a bit if you like.'

The policeman looked suspicious.

'What exactly do you mean by that?'

'Well . . . you know . . . here we are, smoking together—chatting—it's sort of—I was going to say "cosy" but perhaps "cosy's" not quite the right word down here—I don't suppose it's every night you come down here for a smoke . . . I mean . . .'

'Every night I come down here for a smoke . . . every night.'

'Oh,' said Harry.

The policeman puffed industriously at his cigarette and never for one moment took his small currant eyes off Harry. Harry looked around self-consciously for somewhere to sit but apart from the obvious places drew a blank, so he just stood and dripped on the tilework.

'Out late, aren't we?' It was the policeman again.

Harry looked idiotically at his watch. It said five-forty. 'Twenty-to-six,' he said.

'And who's Stillwater?'

'Stillwater? I'm Stillwater, Harry Stillwater.'

'I see.'

'Why?'

'You were telling yourself to go home down there next door. Sounds like a good idea to me. Why don't you? We don't usually find honest citizens tramping around the town at this time of the morning. Are you an honest citizen?' He was grinning again.

'As honest as the next man.'

The policeman sniffed and took another long drag at his cigarette. 'That's the trouble, you see; the obvious answer to that one is just how honest *is* the next man? In my job you get never to judge by appearances. Taking it by and large and on appearances and circumstantially only, of course, I would have every right to book you as a suspicious character.'

'I'm not suspicious.'

'You are to me.'

'Oh.'

'Loitering with intent.'

'Who was loitering?'

'You weren't going anywhere.'

'I was flat on my back . . .'

'. . . singing.'

'It was the echo made me do that. Like I said, it was like being in the bath.'

The policeman looked benign. 'Don't fight me, Mr. Stillwater, don't fight me. I'm not accusing you of anything. This is all hypothesis.'

'Is that what it is?'

'That's the trouble again, see? A policeman's helmet is like a reverend's dog-collar. Everyone seizes up. We're only human beings, you know, like everybody else. We've all got our own lives to lead—'

'We've all got different jobs, too.'

'That's what I'm saying.'

'And some jobs are not as popular as others.'

'But when we're not doing our jobs we're all just human beings, that's what I'm saying—that's *all* I'm trying to say. We've all got our private lives which have nothing to do with anybody else. You've got your private life, I've got my private life . . . of a sort . . .'

He trailed off and the little eyes clouded over for a moment and Harry thought he saw untold depths of misery hidden behind them. And suddenly he wanted to get away—not because the man was a policeman but because he was a human being like everyone else.

'You're right,' he said, 'you're right . . . yes . . . well, I suppose I'd better be getting along or you won't have any milk in the morning.'

'Pardon?'

'I'm a milkman.'

The policeman's face split open like a pumpkin into a broad sunny smile and he almost opened his arms to Harry. 'A milkman, why didn't you say so? You're going to work?'

'And I fell down the Ladies.'

'And I've held you up.'

'I enjoyed it.' Harry tramped meaningly on his cigarette, which seemed to be a cue for all the water-works to fling themselves once again into action. When it was over he held out his hand. 'See you then, eh?'

He steeled himself against the enormous fist which came out to enclose his but it was as gentle as a rabbit's foot.

'Perhaps we'll see each other again sometime,' said the policeman. 'I've enjoyed our chat.' With a magnificent portentous gesture he donned his helmet and they stood looking at each other like David and Goliath.

Harry said, 'You look seven foot tall in that thing.'

'Seven foot one to be exact.'

'Blimey,' said Harry. 'Goodnight.'

Up among the elements once again Harry wondered whether he should continue on his way or go home; Ob might be stirring and need something. On the other hand the whole episode with the policeman had taken no more than ten minutes and having come so far and through so much it seemed stupid not to press on to the bitter end.

He wondered in which direction the policeman had been heading when they had, so to speak, stumbled over each other. If—and he hoped fervently that it would not be so—but *if* he should discover a dead body on the rocks it would be better not to discover it under the beady eyes of a seven-foot policeman.

'Seven foot one . . .' said Harry aloud. 'Blimey!'

He fought his way along the front clinging like a maniac to the wet rail. The hailstones had become less lethal and in fact were in the process of turning themselves back into rain, but the wind hadn't abated in the slightest and fought furiously back at him at every step.

Eventually, after what seemed an age but was less than five minutes, the black mouth of the Tunnel loomed up ahead of him. 'This end of the Tunnel,' Ob had said. 'He went over the railings off the prom,' he had said.

Keeping a tenacious grip on the slimy iron rail Harry attempted to focus his tired smarting eyes into the well of blackness beneath him—and received in return a stinging faceful of salt water. Some distance away a break in the railing indicated a flight of steps which would lead down to the beach. Directing the beam of his torch on to the rocks below he examined as best he could with such inadequate illumination every inch of the beach, moving, as he did so, slowly and laboriously, towards the steps. One heart-stopping moment occurred when the beam picked up a black rock which looked exactly like a black body and it was several sickening seconds before he had convinced himself that it was, in fact, only a black rock.

As he clambered carefully down the steps the wind, as though possessed of a sudden personal hatred for him, tore savagely at his aching arms, wrenching at his muscles, beating the hard rain against every inch of his straining body. He wasn't caring for this part of the business one little bit—in fact he hadn't cared for one single moment of any of it—but somehow this was the worst part of it, here and now, below the level of the street in a pit of seething blackness.

There was a foot-wide ledge running about ten feet below and parallel to the promenade, and from this was another drop of about—as far as he could judge—eight feet. The boy would have fallen nearly twenty feet and if he had tipped over the railings backwards the chances were that he would have—could have—landed on the ledge on the top of his head. The consequences of such a fall made Harry's blood run cold.

By ducking beneath the handrail and clutching with his right fist at an upright stanchion he was able to straddle himself over to the ledge which was overgrown with seaweed and slippery as an ice-rink. His gumboots helped a lot! Once there he was immediately pinned against the stonework by the unbelievable impact of the wind; up top on the promenade it had somewhere else to go—down here it didn't, it just concentrated on the stonework and Harry. And it wasn't even as if its direction was constant—he soon discovered that great gusts of it would hurl themselves around him and behind him clawing at his shoulders and his arms and ankles, doing everything in their quite considerable power to dislodge him from his precarious hold. And if all that wasn't enough the sea came with it. It was like standing under a gigantic shower with all his clothes on.

Steeling himself against every eventuality that might come his way he began edging along the ledge, the beam of his torch directed into the broiling mess of sea and rocks and sand beneath him. It was a hopeless task. What the hell had he ever hoped to find? Anything which had fallen from the rail above would have been swept up and washed away within a matter of seconds and any sign of blood would have gone the same way.

Still he persisted. He wasn't a Stillwater for nothing. He strained his eyes down the narrow, rainswept beam of light until his head ached, until the swirling surge of the sea mingling with the sharp black rocks began to take on imaginary shapes of horror, and when one of these monsters leapt up and bit his hand with such violence that he almost relinquished his hold on the torch, it was time, he thought, to pack up and go home. 'Go home, Stillwater.'

It was at that precise moment that the wind suddenly decided to have it out with him once and for all; it turned on him, wrenched him from his perch, flung him down among the rocks and went off and left him wallowing in six inches of freezing sea water. For a second or two he lay breathless; he wasn't hurt, he knew that—he couldn't think why he wasn't, but he wasn't—and no thanks to them up there! Something suddenly snapped inside him. He became furiously angry. Covered from head to foot with slush and slime, one boot half on, the other completely gone, he rose fuming to his feet and stood, bareheaded and magnificent, a major prophet in a minor role, towering in his rage, epileptic in his hatred for the elements.

He raised both fists and shook them vehemently in the face of the storm. 'You bloody bastards,' he screamed at them. 'Why don't you go and hit someone your own size!' 'Bloody' wasn't the word he used and neither was 'bastards' but whatever the chosen expletives their effect was instantaneous.

For one breathless awe-inspiring moment the elements seemed to draw back upon themselves in open-mouthed astonishment to take stock of him; for about three frightful seconds there was a silence louder than a thunder-clap—you could have heard a pebble dropped into the gulf of Mexico—Harry's new-found courage ebbed away as the wind and the rain and the sea gathered themselves for the last and final onslaught ... and from above, as though the heavens had opened, a white light descended upon him ... mystic ... wonderful ...

But the eerie radiance didn't come from Heaven, and the flat distinct voice which said, 'So what have we down there, then, the dairy?' wasn't the voice of God either.

CHAPTER TWELVE

So there they were, Harry and the policeman, jammed up against each other in a phone box which seemed to be half the usual size, with nothing but a telephone between them; Harry pale, soaked to the skin with seaweed in his hair and wearing only one boot, and the policeman, seven-feet-one, huge, implacable, and smiling like a hammer-headed shark with its dinner in its sights.

It was one of those occasions when words would seem to be inadequate, appearances being enough to be getting on with.

Harry sad, wet and extremely frightened, tried vainly to come to grips with the situation. This morning—was it only this morning?—he had launched himself into a newly-awakened day—a horrible, miserable, filthy day but newly-awakened nevertheless—there had been no premonition of the tragedy which was to befall him within a few hours, no warning in *The Stars and You* section of his morning paper ... 'Finances', it had stated quite calmly, 'will take a turn for the better. If you are thinking of buying a house, now is the time to place your deposit' ... nothing about going forth into the blackest night of his life to search for a body of someone whom he didn't even know was dead—nothing about being bruised, battered and broken on the wheel of the elements ... nothing about being wedged tight in a telephone box with an oversized policeman with a smile like a hammer-headed shark ...

Over the policeman's shoulder, through the window of the box, dimly lit by the spill of light from the low-voltage bulb, Harry could just make out a poster stuck on the wall. There was a bird in a bikini sitting on a blue and white beach-ball and the caption said: *Welcome to the Sunny South Coast.*

'What was that?' asked the policeman.

'Eh?'

'You said something.'

'No. I was thinking, I expect. Sorry.'

The policeman leaned back against the glass-squared wall and looked down his nose at his captive. 'I hope you're going to say something soon, though, 'cos I'm running out of patience.'

A spark flared for a second in Harry. 'You haven't asked me anything yet,' he snapped, then the spark went out.

The policeman drew in his breath. 'All right then, how's this: What were you doing down there on the beach on a night like this, acting suspiciously?'

Harry said wearily, 'I was looking for a dead body.'

His companion eyed him for some time in speculative silence then he said politely, 'And did you find one?'

'No, it wasn't there.'

Harry felt himself seized by the front of his oilskin and lifted off the ground until his eyes were level with a blunt set of enormous yellow teeth.

'Now look . . .' began the policeman.

'It's true what I said, it wasn't there . . .'

'I'm warning you, my lad . . .'

Harry's head began to swim. 'Why don't you put me down and listen to what I've got to say. You're not even listening to me. A bloke's innocent 'til he's proved guilty . . .'

The policeman breathed heavily for a second or two then, gentle as a feather being wafted to the ground on a hot summer's afternoon anywhere but in England, he replaced Harry on his single gumboot.

'That doesn't happen to be the gospel I believe in,' he pointed out.

Harry thought at random: whenever anything important happens to me lately I always seem to lose my boots. He said aloud, 'Do you know Charlie Bourne?'

Suspicion lurked in the blackcurrant eyes. 'Charlie Bourne? You mean *our* Charlie Bourne?'

Join the Police Force and become 'One of Us.'

'I expect that's the one,' said Harry. 'Small chap—smaller than me, even . . . Well, he's a friend of a friend of mine, bloke named Ob Harvey. Well, he was beaten up tonight by a lot of toughs and he says one of 'em fell over the railing off the prom.'

'Charlie was beaten up?'

'No, Ob was beaten up—this friend of Charlie's. They went to school together.'

'And who says one of 'em fell over the railings?'

'Ob says.'

The policeman was chewing his lower lip with a certain amount of intensity. 'So who are you, then, and what have you got to do with anything?'

'I'm a friend of Ob's.'

'I see. And what were you doing down there?'

'Looking for the body.'

'And what's become of this Ob? Fled the country?'

'He's in bed with ninety-eight stitches in his face.'

The policeman paused, sighed then said, 'Oh dear. Tell us again, start from the beginning, and try to make me understand.'

So Harry did, right from the moment when they came up against Red and his couple of lovelies in *The Elbow Room,* to the moment when he found himself incarcerated in a telephone box with a policeman. And when it was over the latter was nodding monotonously like one of those china ornaments his mother had dusted year in and year out on the piano.

'You should have told me all this before, shouldn't you?'

'Yes, I expect I should have.'

'Withholding information, that is.'

'No.'

'Withholding information.'

'I'm cold,' said Harry.

'I expect you are. That's on account of your having lost one of your boots, I expect.'

'I expect so, yes.'

The policeman pulled experimentally at his nose. 'I don't quite know what I'm going to do about all this. I ought to take you along to the station and book you, but you couldn't come looking like that, that's for certain. Besides you'd catch your death of cold and then I'd get into trouble, and we can't have that, can we? So do you know what I think?'

'No. What?'

'I think . . .' He didn't say what he thought for a moment but stared out through the glass at the sea which was just beginning to be visible in the cold nasty light of another dawn. 'You didn't see nothing down there, I suppose? No signs of any body or blood or nothing like that?'

'There's nothing there, I'll swear to that.'

'You may have to. If he fell over there he'd have been swept out to sea and no mistake; he'd have been a goner in a matter of seconds. In which case your friend Ob is in a bit of a bother, I'd say, wouldn't you? I'll have to go and check up myself, I suppose, otherwise they'll say "why didn't you go and check for yourself"—you know what they are—the least little thing nowadays and they're at you wanting to know why you haven't done this and why you haven't done that. But what am I going to do about you while I'm down there risking my life?'

'There's nothing there. I'd have seen it if there was.'

The policeman looked gloomy. 'I know and I believe you, but I'll have to go and have a look; it's got to go down in the report, you see 'I went and looked and there was nothing there,' signed P.C. 149 Hearthbright. F.'

'Is that your name? Hearthbright?'

'That's right.' He looked steadily at Harry then said, 'We've almost become friends haven't we?—in a funny sort of way?'

'I suppose we have,' agreed Harry with care, 'In a funny sort of way.' There was silence for a moment then he added, 'What's the F. stand for?'

'F?'

'Hearthbright F.'

'Fred.'

'Fred.'

'Fred Hearthbright. Funny couple of names aren't they—Hearthbright and Stillwater—sounds like a family solicitors ...'

'Or one of those funny chemists where they sell health foods and things in plain jars. My other name's Harry.'

'Harry and Fred. They're plain enough, I must say.' Harry shivered suddenly and Fred Hearthbright waxed solicitous. 'You're catching your death. You'd better get off home, I think, your teeth are going like castanets. Can I trust you?'

'Trust me?'

'To go home and have a bath and not move until I come and have a word with you?'

'Course you can. Don't be daft, where else could I go except home? Where else would I want to go with only one boot?'

'Where can I get hold of this Ob character? Now there's a funny name—Ob.'

'We live at the same address.'

'Oh do you? Together, you mean?'

'Not in the way *you* mean.'

'I wasn't inferring nothing. But it's all the same to me even if you were, nothing to do with me. Good luck, I say.'

'Well, we're not. If you've got a pencil I'll give you the address.'

He peered over Hearthbright's book whilst the policeman laboriously spelt out the address and copied it down with a pencil which was no more than two inches long. When it was finished he looked down at Harry's feet. 'Wish we could do something about your boot. Shall we go down and have a look, see if we can see it?'

'We could try I suppose. Don't feel like going all that way with only one boot!'

The first thing they saw when the beam of Fred's torch swept the greying waterfront was a waterlogged gumboot. Fred was tremendously bucked and seemed happier than he had been since the commencement of their short though eventful relationship. He himself swung down into the depths and squelched about healthily in the slush, retrieved the errant boot and returned it triumphantly to its owner, who thanked him, emptied the water out of it and didn't discover the mud until his foot was well into it; it oozed glutinously over the top of the boot like uncooked Christmas pudding.

'You should have put your hand down it first,' Fred pointed out. 'It's always safer to put your hand down first.'

'Can I go home, then?'

'Why not?'

With the approach of dawn the wind had considerably abated; the rain was still drenching down but they'd got used to that. Fred leaned over the railing and strained his eyes into the gloom. He stood there for a couple of ticks like Napoleon on the *Bellerophon* then said, 'Well, there's nothing down there as far as I can see. You can witness that I looked. I can see no dead body, can you?'

'No,' said Harry not looking because he had already looked.

'Right then, off we go.'

'Where we going?'

'You're going home and I'm going back to the station where I shall put in my report and if the Sergeant says it's okay, I'll be calling round during the morning to get a proper statement from you and this Ob character. Now there's a funny name . . . Ob . . . Ob . . .'

'Short for Hobson.'

'Oh, it's H-h-h-ob?'

'No, it's not, it's Ob. *H*obson *H*arvey was too much for everybody. Right, then, I'll buzz off, eh?'

'Don't be surprised if it's not me as calls on you later. The Sarge might decide otherwise—he might smell something nice cooking and come round himself.'

'He'll be lucky if he smells anything nice cooking in our house.'

'You know what I mean. Still, I expect it'll be me. We're short just now, everyone's off with the 'flu and those of us what's left are having to work twice as hard and twice as long. Right then, be seeing you, I expect.'

Harry trudged off.

'Oi!' called Fred after he'd gone about five yards.

Harry stopped. 'What?'

'You *are* going home this time, aren't you?'

'What do you think?'

'I'm trusting you.'

Harry said, 'I'm catching the first plane to South America,' and splashed off again. After another ten yards he turned to see if Fred was still there. He was. They waved at each other companionably. He was still there after another ten yards. And another. In fact he was still there when Harry finally crossed the road and disappeared up a side street.

There was the Rock of Gibraltar, the Rock of Ages, and Fred Hearthbright . . .

Harry, submerged and steaming in a blazing hot Radox bath, pondered with morose intensity over the excesses of the past few hours. No normal person could be expected to go through what he had gone through and come out at the other end unscathed; just how scathed he was remained to be seen, but he knew quite well that he would carry the scars with him for the remainder of his days—and he didn't mean just physical scars, though they were enough to be getting on with.

He went lovingly over the physical body, studying each bruise, brooding over each abrasion, applying hot water to this one and cold water to that one. His mother had said something wise about bruises but he couldn't remember what it was. No one ever took any notice of mothers until it was too late. 'Home,' she used to say in her frequent moments of exasperation, 'is the place where you grumble most and are treated best.' It was one of those dreary old maxims which had been passed down from generation to generation and made you want to spit when it was levelled in your direction, because it was only brought out and aired when you were in the middle of a good moan about something and in no mood to listen to smug little homilies thought up by frock-coated blokes in side-boards who looked like old Whatsit in Wimpole Street . . . who was it? ... Barrett, Dad Barrett ... Charles Laughton ... Henry the Eighth. Harry had preferred Henry the Eighth. All those toffee-nosed dames with handles to their names going in for a bit of slap and tickle on the side, and old King Henry getting so fed up with it all that he had chopped their heads off, one after another, just like that. Bit drastic, Harry thought, chopping their heads off like that—no chance of saying 'sorry and all that' later on if you felt like it. Still, they did things like that in those days apparently—didn't care—life was cheap, see. Couldn't happen nowadays, of course. Life was much more expensive now—cost of living had gone up quite a bit since then. Chop a bird's head off nowadays and you'd have the rozzers round banging on the door before you even had time to wash the blood off your hands.

'So what were you doing on the night of the thirteenth?'

'I was looking for a dead body down on the beach.'

'And did you find one?'

'Yes, but it didn't have a head on it so I don't know whether it was the one I was looking for.'

'How would you recognise the one you were looking for?'

'By its head. It would have had two eyes, a nose and a mouth, which would have helped me to recognise it. And hair.'

'What colour hair?'

'Whatever you fancy, we have a fine selection ... I saw a woman with pink hair the other day.'

'Eyes, then, what colour eyes?'

'Black ... currant-bun black ... squashed flies—squashed fly cakes—used to be a ha'penny each ... more now though ... fourteen-and-six a dozen ... but thirteen to the dozen remember—a baker's dozen ...'

'Don't make me laugh.'

'Who's making you laugh? Fourteen-and-six a dozen—what's there to laugh at. I'm not trying to make you laugh. That's another thing: I'd have recognised this body by its laugh.'

'If it was a dead body it wouldn't be laughing.'

'That's what I'm saying, I didn't recognise it. It didn't have a head so it wasn't laughing. Not much to laugh about really when you come to think of it—no head. How would you like it if you didn't have a head—you wouldn't be doing much laughing either. It's not much fun you know.'

'Like rheumatism—that's not much fun, either.'

'Who said anything about rheumatism?'

'You did, but don't take any notice of me. I just like to talk while you're drowning. You carry on.'

Pause.

'Who's drowning?'

'You are. Glug-glug. I hope you're enjoying it. It doesn't happen to all of us and when it does it only happens the once. So you just lie back and try to enjoy it.'

'I will, thanks.'

Harry came to the surface with a mouthful of bathwater. He jerked himself bolt upright, ejected the bathwater and sat in trembling dismay at the thought of what so easily might have occurred.

Drowned. Dead. Harry Stillwater dead. What would he be doing dead? He hadn't done anything living yet. A lot more dirty water had to flow down that waste pipe before he was ready and willing to settle down on Cloud Nine or whatever its number was.

With self-preservation uppermost in his dazed mind he stepped out of the bath and stood shivering on the cracked brown lino, and after a cursory exploration of the bath-cover with his fingertips—splinters were always a hazard—he lowered himself carefully on to the wooden edge of it. He shook an admonishing head at himself. That's how it could happen—just like that—no warning—any time of the day or night you could wake up and find yourself dead for no reason at all.

He jerked his head back, grabbed frantically for the towel and did running on the spot for about three-quarters of a mile. He had to keep awake . . . people were depending on him . . . at least Ob was . . . but oh, mate, he couldn't ever remember having felt so tired.

He dried himself vigorously and felt better. He put the kettle on for a cup of tea and went and had a look at Ob. It was several moments before he realised that Ob was awake and regarding him steadily through the slit in the bandages.

'You're awake then?'

'Who have you got out there?'

'Eh?'

'You were talking to someone out there?'

'Me, I expect. Talking to myself, I shouldn't wonder. I'm going a bit like that lately. I've just nearly drowned myself.'

'What for?'

'I fell asleep in the bath.'

'Shows you how it can happen, doesn't it?'

'That's what I was saying.'

'What's the time?'

'Coming up to seven.'

'You're not at work.'

'No.'

'Why not?'

'I'm not going. Better not, I thought.'

'Because of me?'

'I suppose so, in a way.'

'I feel a lot better.'

'You've had a good sleep, that's why.'

'A bit stiff, though.'

'Yes, well, the doctor said you'd be a bit stiff, didn't he? and I said, "He's a big stiff already." '

He had no way of seeing whether Ob thought that was funny or not—there were no great guffaws of laughter and the bed didn't shake at all, so he left it at that. He climbed into Y-fronts and jeans and havered for a few seconds over a choice of jerseys. His mood was Vandyke Brown so he chose a Fairisle to offset it.

He then sat on the edge of the bed and told Ob what had occurred since they had last been conscious together. After the recital when Ob didn't say anything, he went and made the tea.

'I saw him go,' said Ob in a persistent tone a few minutes later when Harry was back.

'What?'

'He went over backwards, I saw him go. He must have been washed out to sea.'

'Now don't go thinking the worst. He could just as easily have got up and climbed out again.'

'He couldn't have done that.'

'How do you know?'

'He would have landed on his head, falling like that.'

'You don't *know* that.'

'I don't *know* it, no, but I don't see how it could have been otherwise. He's dead, and I killed him.'

'All right, so he's dead and you killed him, but it wasn't your fault, was it?'

'I didn't have to kill him.'

'Look, Ob, it was an accident. You didn't kill him on purpose, did you? You hit him and he fell over the railings. You didn't put the railing there, did you?'

'No, but I hit him.'

There was nothing to be gained by argument—everything Ob said was true; all Harry wanted him to do was look on the bright side however difficult that might be. In an attempt to divert him and whilst pouring out the tea Harry told him what he had seen written up on the wall in the Gents at the dairy. The bandages made it impossible to see any expression there might be on his friend's face but the ensuing silence suggested that Ob's imagination was working on it.

'How are you going to drink this?' asked Harry. 'You ought to have a straw or a glass tube or something.'

'I'll manage, if you can just help me to sit up.'

Two or three minutes later Ob said, 'It's impossible.'

'What is?'

'What was up on that wall. It couldn't be done . . . not unless . . . no, even then it couldn't be done.'

'No, well, there you are, that's what I would have thought. Still that's what it said, take it or leave it.'

'I think I'd sooner leave it.'

He winced suddenly.

'Does it hurt?' asked Harry.

'It's the hot tea. The corner of my mouth's cut, I think.'

'You *think*!'

'Chuck us over the mirror, will you?'

'No.'

'Why not?'

'What do you want to look at yourself for?'

'Give me the mirror, please.'

'No.'

'All right, then, I'll get it myself.'

When he made a movement to raise himself from the bed Harry leapt forward. 'Don't be a nit.' He picked up the hand mirror from the dressing-table, 'Go on then, have a good look, see if you like it.'

'Gawd,' said Ob after a moment. 'I look like Seti One.'

'Who's Seti One?'

'Some old mummy.'

Harry chortled rather sadly. 'That's what I thought you looked like at first—an old mummy.'

'Thanks very much.'

'But the doctor said you won't last as long as an old mummy if you go on the way you're going.'

'What did he mean by that?'

'Well, you know—fighting and that, getting yourself knocked about and carved up.'

Ob peered worriedly at himself for another long minute and what he saw did nothing to lessen his anxiety.

'You sure he said I'd be all right?' he asked at length.

'Well, he didn't say you'd be there with your leg up for the rest of your life or anything like that. I expect you'll carry the scars around with you for a bit, they didn't exactly pull their punches. You've got a stitch or two in you, remember.'

'How many?'

'I don't know. A couple or so, I expect, one or two. Old Bumphrey was sitting here with his needle and thread like he was knitting you a pair of socks.'

He suddenly yelled with laughter.

Ob looked at him steadily for a bit then said, 'I suppose it must have been funny to some people.' Harry felt ashamed and calmed himself. 'I suppose you were laughing while he was sewing me up.'

'No I wasn't, as a matter of fact. As a matter of fact I was being sick, so there.'

Harry got up, drew back the curtains and stared up at the leaden sky.

'Blimey,' he said, 'you'll never guess what.'

'What?'

'It's stopped raining.'

'We ought to go out in it, see what it's like.'

'Anything you want?'

'No.'

Harry stared at him for a couple of seconds then he said, 'I'd better go and ring up the dairy, I suppose, and tell them I'm not there.'

'I'll be all right if you want to go.'

'I don't want to go, don't be daft—I never want to go. What am I going to tell them?'

'How about the truth?'

'No, I'll tell 'em I've got the pox or something. Might get a bit of sick benefit then.'

'Don't you have to have a certificate for that?'

'What shall I say I've got? Something "suspected" might be nice—then when I go back I can say that the suspicion was unfounded. How about that?'

'You could be under observation for something.'

'Like a hole in the head.'

'You've already got that.'

'A tumour on the brain.'

'Don't joke about it.'

'Water on the knee, then.'

'Here,' said Ob, *à propos* of nothing at all, 'did you know there was a place called Pratt's Bottom?'

'Pardon?'

'Pratt's Bottom.'

'Never.'

'It's true. In Kent somewhere, I think. It was in the paper the other day. I've been meaning to tell you.'

'P'raps I could be under observation for Pratt's Bottom.'

He scraped up fourpence from various pockets dialled the dairy's number, and was put through to 'Nutty' Cobb who was a sort of foreman-cum-yesman and sang a lot of hymns on Sunday and moaned a great deal during the week; nobody's favourite man, quite a lot of people's *bête noire*. He was big, blustering and had a bright blue nose.

'Nutty Cobb's been converted,' Harry told Ob as he wandered into the bedroom a few moments later. ' "Well done, Stillwater," he said, "well done. Those friends you've got," he said, "clamp them to your heart with rings of steel. Carry on with the good work, Stillwater, and take as long as you like." He's gone bonkers, that's what, quietly bonkers when no one was looking.'

'You told them the truth, did you?'

'More or less. I didn't say you'd been roughed up or anything like that. He wouldn't have liked that. "Serve you right," he would have said. No, I said you had—I can't remember what it was now—Himblethroid Arthritis I think it was, something like that, it's pretty bad—like polio—he's going to look it up in his book, he says. You were paralysed all over I told him and had to be fed like a child.'

'Bloody old liar.'

'No, well, it's all in a good cause, isn't it? What amazes me is that he fell for it, that's what I don't understand. He hates me too. I almost feel sorry for him looking it up in his little book.'

'You'd better ring him up and tell him how to spell it.'

'I can't pronounce it, let alone spell it. I said you were under observation for it so when I go back I'll tell him they were all wrong and it was just a bad go of 'flu. I couldn't help laughing though when I was telling him how bad you were—poor old Ob.'

Ob said, 'You're doing it again, aren't you?'

'What?'

'Laughing.'

'I'm not laughing now—honest. Honest, Ob, now I'm not laughing.'

CHAPTER THIRTEEN

It was a little after ten when Fred Hearthbright and Dr. Bumphrey arrived on the doorstep at precisely the same moment.

'Morning, sir,' said Fred Hearthbright.

'Ah,' said the doctor guardedly.

'Not a very nice morning, is it?'

'No.'

It was, in fact, much nicer than it had been for some time—at least it was not raining and there was a faint indication that the low clouds might be persuaded to depart in the direction of the Spanish Plains if the prevailing winds prevailed long enough.

'You're the doctor, aren't you, sir?'

'What? Yes. Good heavens.'

'Seen you in the court, sir, giving evidence.'

'Well done.'

They both eyed a girl on a horse who happened to be trotting past at that moment. She wore a green sweater and jodhpurs and her hair was honey-coloured. They watched the gentle rhythmic sway of her body until it passed from their sight.

'What?' said the doctor.

'You're here to see a Mr. Harvey?'

'Am I?'

'I am too.'

The doctor sniffed and said a trifle vaguely, 'Good, well, they're sensible lads, aren't they, calling you in?' Fred looked unconvinced. 'Have you rung?'

'Rung, sir?'

'The bell.'

'No, sir.'

'Then don't you think we might do that, or shall we stand out here for the rest of the morning?'

The advent of the Law and Medicine on the doorstep at one fell swoop was an occurrence liable to confuse even the most positive of milkmen—it floored Harry completely for a couple of minutes until Fred Hearthbright took charge, then everything went as smooth as a game of bingo.

The doctor hummed and prodded and coo'ed at Ob, unwound yards of bandages, put on his glasses, nodded at the wounds as though they were old friends and redressed them with the unhesitant skill of the professional. 'Good,' he kept saying over and over again. 'Good . . . good . . . good, good . . .' As far as Harry was concerned it all looked anything but good; when the bandages had been stripped off and the jagged edges of the various wounds had been revealed it had been touch and go as to whether he would have to be sick again. He had kept a firm hold on himself, however, and had survived—pale and in a cold sweat—but he had survived.

Ob did not carry it off quite so well. In fact he passed out cold shortly after the doctor had begun negotiations with the bandages. The doctor glanced up at the gigantic policeman breathing heavily at his left elbow and shook his head. 'He's gone,' he said sadly. Fred understood him to mean that Ob had died, whereupon his face puckered up and became as lugubrious as a basset hound's; he had already removed his helmet, otherwise it would have been off and in the mourning position in a couple of shakes. The doctor went on, 'It's always the big chaps—big, hefty, powerful chaps like you, they can never stand it. Out like lights they are. Stick a needle in them and they're away on the morning tide. But women and little chaps—they can take anything. Most of 'em are asking questions the whole time, which I find even more infuriating.'

Harry said, 'Anybody like a cup of tea?'

Fred said, 'Good idea, can I come and help?'

Harry said no, it was all right, he could manage, but Fred came nevertheless, confiding in Harry when they had reached the kitchen that he had been feeling a bit queasy as soon as the bandages had begun to come off.

'Should have thought you'd have got used to all that,' observed Harry with a marked lack of sympathy, '—in your profession. Sit down. Give us your hat—helmet. We used to have a table but it's now a bath-cover so I'll have to hang it up behind the door.'

The spate of seemingly unconnected sentences confused

Fred, but he managed to remain unmoved and contemplated Harry busying himself with the tea things.

'Funny old world, isn't it?' he ventured after a bit.

'Eh?'

'World . . . funny . . .'

'Ah, yes . . .'

'How we met and all that.'

Harry looked at him curiously. 'You *are* here professionally, aren't you?'

'How do you mean?'

'Well, it sounds like you've just dropped in for a friendly chat. But you've still got your helmet and your armband and you're going to ask Ob a lot of questions, aren't you, and you're not really friendly at all, are you?' Fred's face proceeded to crumple itself into the basset hound character again and Harry hurried on. 'It's not you personally, of course, I don't mean that. It's just, well, you know, it's *what* you are, *what* you represent—the long arm of the law and all that. You're a copper and that's that—and I've been windy of coppers all my life.'

Fred's eyebrows rose into a hurt arch. 'Why?'

'What? Well, I don't know why, do I? How should I know why? I *always* feel windy when there's a copper around—always have done, I suppose it's because I always *think* I've done something wrong.'

Fred said cautiously, 'Are you trying to tell me something?'

'What?'

'Have you committed a crime of some sort?'

'No. What? A crime? Why? What are you looking at me like that for?'

Fred grinned suddenly, bland and expansive. 'You see? It's what I was saying earlier on. A copper's helmet's like a parson's dog-collar. Everybody starts counting his sins. Don't worry, Harry, I'm not after anybody's blood, honest.' He stopped and looked for approval and when none was forthcoming added somewhat gruffly, 'I *like* people.'

'Then why join the police force?'

'That's exactly why. It's *because* I like people that I *am* a bobby, don't you see that? I like being able to help people, tell 'em the way to places, take the kids over the crossings, direct the traffic on point duty . . .'

'You must be out of your mind!' Harry was derisive. 'You

like being a cop because you're seven foot high, because you like running people in and beating them over the bonce with a rubber truncheon; you like power.'

'You're not being fair.'

Harry pulled himself up and grinned amiably. 'I know I'm not, but I've never been able to talk like this to a policeman before.' He made the tea and set the cups and saucers out on a tray. 'You don't like it all that much though do you, really?'

Fred nodded stoutly. 'It's all right, I tell you. There's some of it I don't like, naturally, some of the red tape—most jobs are like that somewhere; apart from that it's all right. They look after you. Pension, holidays, and if you get shot while you're on the job there's a pension for your wife.'

'Well, that's a comfort. But what about what I was saying earlier on—about all the things you can't do with that helmet on?'

Fred screwed up his face into an excruciating expression of esoteric evil. 'Then you just take the helmet off,' he explained in a confidential whisper.

The doctor was standing in the doorway listening. 'I could have you both arrested for that sort of talk. I'm finished.'

'How about a cup of tea?' invited Harry.

He shook his head. 'I've got to get on.'

'How is he?'

'Night's rest has done him a power of good. He's doing fine, better than I expected. I've left most of the bandages off and strapped him up with plaster. I'll be in tomorrow. Carry on with the pills—every four hours, and keep him in bed, eh? You took the day off, then?'

'I had to, didn't I?'

'Good lad, well, keep an eye on him and if there's anything you want to know give me a tinkle.'

Fred enquired, 'I suppose I can ask him a few questions, can I?'

'Sure you can, yes, of course. He's all right. He's like an ox. What is he, an athlete or something?'

Harry snorted. 'He's a taxidermist.'

'Is that a fact?'

'An assistant one. He doesn't do it any more, though.'

'Well I never. He looks like a swimmer.'

'He's not.'

Fred looked hazy. 'What's a taxidermist?'
Harry said, 'He stuffs things.'
'Ah,' nodded Fred with understanding.
The doctor waved at them and left telling them not to bother to see him out.
Fred queried after a pause, 'What's he do now then, now he doesn't stuff things any more?'
'Nothing, he's joined the club down the road and that's where it all stands at this very moment.'
'What club's that?'
'The Labour Exchange. You *have* lived a sheltered life, haven't you?'
'I've never been out of work,' said Fred reasonably. 'You more or less look after him, then?'
'More or less. Milk and sugar?'
'Please. One and a bit. Shall we go in and see how the invalid's getting on, then I can get on with my questions.'
Over cups of tea and biscuits the three of them discussed the situation in detail. Ob told Fred everything he could remember and Fred busily copied it all down in his crumpled notebook and when it was all over snapped an elastic band around the book with a histrionic flourish of triumph.
'Well, there it is then. All we've got to do now is pick up this Red chap and we're laughing.'
Harry pointed out, 'We haven't got any proof that it was him though, have we?'
Fred looked serious, 'That's true, but if we could nab him with some of his boys maybe Ob here would recognise one or two of them.'
Ob shook his head. 'Only by their smell. The only bloke I'd recognise is the one who fell over the railings, and the only chance I'm likely to have of that will probably be in the morgue.'
Harry said, 'Even if you did pull in Red and his gang, you wouldn't have much on them, would you? What would they get for beating a bloke up? A fine? Prison for a week? It's hardly worth the trouble of knocking 'em off.'
'They could have killed him,' Fred pointed out.
'But they didn't, did they?' returned Ob. 'I think Harry's right. I'm the only one who's really in the cart if that bloke's dead. What can we prove? Nothing. I'm admitting that I knocked

the bloke over the railings, but that's all you've got. In a couple of days I'll have nothing to show for it either, except for my poor old face, and that'll be it.'

Fred pondered for a moment then asked, 'When you chucked this Red chap out of *The Elbow Room* there were plenty of witnesses, weren't there?'

'Hundreds of them, I'd say, judging by the row they were making, but I doubt whether any of 'em would come forward.'

But Fred had the bit between his teeth. 'This bloke What's-His-Name? . . . the blond chap with the limp . . . If he's got something really worthwhile on Red we might be able to put the blighter away for some time. These blokes need a lesson; there's too much of this sort of thing going on and they get away with it, what's more.'

Harry said, 'But Fred, they don't care about you—you know that—they don't give a damn about the police or prison; in fact being bunged into clink gives 'em a bit of kudos. That's the trouble, there's no way of getting back at them except by hurting them.'

'What do you mean by that?'

'What I say. Knock their teeth in, bash their faces out of shape—it's the only thing they're likely to understand.'

Fred nodded. 'And after you've done it to them they come back and do it to you, and then *you* have another go and *they* have another go—and so it goes on—you have a full scale gang war on your hands.'

Harry shrugged. 'So what's your suggestion?'

The silence which followed was depressing for all of them.

'The law,' said Fred at last, 'must take its course.'

'How?'

'By pulling in this Red character before he gets up to any more mischief. Prison's not all that much fun, you know.'

Harry looked at him for a moment with a speculative gleam in his eye. 'You our friend?'

'What?'

'You've been quite nice to me one way and another since we fell over each other last night. How about letting us have a go?' Before Fred could open his mouth to remonstrate Harry ploughed on quickly. 'If you start tramping about asking questions it's going to go right back to Red in no time at all, isn't it? They know what's going on, these blokes, especially in a small town like this, nobody's got to tell them twice. And before you know what's happened Red's skipped the place—moved on—and you've lost him. But if *we* did it, quiet like, Ob and me, and even our girl friends—they'd play, I'm sure—we might be able to get something really worthwhile. Ten to one he's on a racket of some sort. I'll bet he is. Don't you see? *We* might be able to get on to something where you couldn't.'

'I see it right enough, but it's not your job tracking down law-breakers.'

'Can you stop us?'

'I can give you a warning.'

'What's that mean?'

'If I warn you and you go ahead you'll be breaking the law.'

'You wouldn't though, would you?'

'What? Warn you?'

'Yes.'

'No,' said Fred. After a pause he went on, 'You could get yourselves into a lot of nasty trouble . . .'

'That's our lookout.'

'What about me?'

'You could help us.'

'How?'

'By taking your helmet off.'

Fred stared at them soberly. 'You don't seem to realise we've got C.I.D. blokes to do this sort of thing.'

He lumbered thoughtfully over to the window and stared glumly down into the street for a minute or two. The other two could hear him squeaking as he breathed—it was his belt that squeaked, or he was wearing corsets.

He said finally, 'You're not going to take the law into your own hands or anything silly like that, are you?'

'If you mean are we going to track the criminals down to their lair and capture them single-handed, no we're not. At least I'm not; I'm too fond of my own skin; I'm no hero, mate. All we want to do is see if we can find out anything nasty; if we do we'll come and tell you about it and your lot can do the dangerous bits.'

Fred raised his shoulders and made a face. 'All right, then, have it your own way, but remember, I haven't heard any of this.'

Harry grinned. 'Any of what? Have another cup of tea?'

'No, I think I'd better push off now. I'm not on duty any more. I've got some shopping to do. Home for me.'

'Where is home?' asked Harry and when Fred told him he followed up the query by asking whether he was married. He almost bit out his tongue when he saw once again the shadowed eyes and the hidden misery lurking in their depths.

'Yes,' said Fred in a flat voice, 'I suppose you could say I'm married.'

He heaved himself noisily into his mackintosh and stood for a moment, silent, head down, playing with the chin-strap of his helmet. Then he blinked up at them. 'There's nothing mysterious about it. She's gone a bit funny—you know—funny in the head. She's up at Mansfield. I see her every week; sometimes she knows me, sometimes she don't . . . Poor old girl . . . she's only young, too, hardly in her thirties. Just shows you, doesn't it? You never know what's round the corner. Well, I'm off.'

He paused in the doorway, shifting and awkward. 'Can I call in some time? Not officially, I don't mean—just for a chat, like . . .'

'Yes, sure, any time,' Harry told him. 'Come in any time.'

Fred nodded and settled his chin-strap more comfortably. 'Thanks,' he said. 'I'd like that.'

Harry watched the policeman move away from the house with firm, measured, regulation tread, then he returned to the bedroom where Ob, propped against the bed-head, had gone off into a brown study. When Harry clattered the cups he roused himself and said, 'Poor old basket.'

'More tea?'

'Eh?'

'Want another cup?'

'No thanks.'

Harry poured the slops into one cup, stacked the rest together on the tray, then stopped and looked soberly at Ob. 'Funny, isn't it? You see policemen every day of your life, and postmen, and dustmen, bus conductors—even milkmen—and somehow it never crosses your mind, does it, that there's anything going on behind the uniform?' He stared solemnly into the middle distance. 'But it's all happening. To all of us. Everybody. Nobody gets out of it. Everybody's got a can to carry somewhere.'

Jennifer was helping her mother make the beds when the pealing of the front door bell threw them both into the usual state of domestic confusion.

'I'll go,' said Jennifer, passing a pillow to her mother.

'No,' said Mrs. Love, passing it back, 'It may be the butcher.'

'He's been.'

'Then who can this be?'

'I'll go and find out.'

'If it's the milkman his money's on the hall-stand.'

It was the milkman, Jennifer's own personal milkman. She blushed delightedly. 'Hello.'

'Hi.'

'Is it the milkman?' called her mother from the top of the stairs.

'Yes.'

'Ask him if he's got any of his nice New Zealand butter.'

'Have you got any of your nice New Zealand butter?' smiled Jennifer. 'Come in.'

'No, I'd better not, I can't stay. I've really only come because of Ob.'

'Oh? Why? What's the matter with Ob?'

Harry told her the whole story in about forty-five seconds. When he had finished Jennifer, pale and alarmed, stared at him with disbelief.

Her mother was at the top of the stairs again.

'Come in and close the door, there's a good girl, there's a draught blowing right through the house. Who are you talking to down there?'

Jennifer pulled Harry over the threshold and closed the door firmly. 'It's Harry, Mum.'

'Harry?' Mrs. Love's head hung pendant over the bannister. 'Is that you, Harry?' Harry couldn't deny it. 'You're not at work?'

'No.'

'Are you ill?'

'No, Ob is.'

'Pardon?'

'Harry's friend,' explained Jennifer.

Mrs. Love made sympathetic noises then giggled a little and said, 'We thought it was the milkman.'

Jennifer nudged Harry and he laughed obediently, and said

he was sending away to New Zealand for some nice new-laid butter, which remark threw Mrs. Love into convulsions and she went off in stitches. He had only met the lady the day before when she had opened the door to him and had realised in no time at all that the quickest way to her heart was to keep her laughing.

Jennifer said, 'Is there anything I can do to help?'

Harry put on his twelve-year-old look. 'That's why I came round, as a matter of fact. I'm a bit out of my depth, you see, I've never had to look after anyone who's seriously ill.'

'What about Maisie? We ought to tell her. After all he really belongs to her, doesn't he?'

Harry grinned. 'I suppose he does, in a loose sort of way. Why don't we go round to her place and tell her then?'

They did and Maisie was suitably devastated. She made several urgent noises of distress at the back of her throat, blinked her eyes and then with an incredible show of agitated determination threw a pair of flat-heeled shoes, an electric torch, her mackintosh and a hot water bottle shaped like a rabbit into a brown paper carrier-bag and declared that she was ready to go to him.

It was like, thought Harry as they set off once again, the Relief of Ladysmith. Whoever she was.

'I suppose,' queried Jennifer, 'you've got no food in the house?'

'Food?'

'Men!' muttered Maisie succinctly striding blindly ahead.

Jennifer put forward the suggestion that Harry should give his front door key to Maisie, who could then proceed on her own to administer to the immediate wants of Ob, whilst she, Jennifer, and Harry occupied themselves by collecting a few necessities from the neighbouring shops. Maisie was delighted, grabbed the key and rushed off with a clatter of high heels before either of the others could point out that she was going in the wrong direction.

'She'll have to come back when she gets to the bottom,' grinned Harry, 'there's only the Synagogue and the Gasworks down there.'

They pushed a trolley around Sainsbury's and bought up about a hundredweight of foodstuffs, half of which seemed, in Harry's estimation, completely unnecessary. Sage and onion stuffing, for instance—who wanted sage and onion stuffing? And a small bottle of Hungarian paprika, and a tin of Instant Powdered Gelatine? How about that? *Instant* Powdered Gelatine. He couldn't imagine what you did with gelatine in the first place, whether it was instant or whether it took a bit longer. A disturbing note was struck when, having nonchalantly placed a cellophaned bundle of buns in the trolley for his own consumption, he watched it removed and replaced on the shelf by Jennifer, who informed him that not only were they a waste of money but buns were bad for him anyway.

The shopping took less than ten minutes—to pay for it they stood in a queue for thirty-five.

Pausing momentarily outside Millett's Stores to resettle the enormous bags they'd given him at Sainsbury's he bethought himself of the windcheater he had decided to buy for Ben. They browsed around happily among tents and rubber boots and fur-lined jackets until he found what he was looking for —a dark green, zipped and hooded anorak which cost seventeen shillings and sixpence and was cheap at the price.

When they returned to the street the sun was shining.

'Hooray,' cheered Harry with heavy irony.

'Why?'

'The sun's out.'

When they reached the house and pressed the bell there was no reply.

'Now what?' grumbled Harry impatiently. 'Maisie must be here by this time surely.' He prodded the bell-push again with his thumb.

'I wonder,' queried Jennifer with a far-away look in her eye, 'whether she's got herself lost. It would be just like her; she was certainly going the right way about it when we last saw her.'

They stared at each other solemnly. Harry said, 'If I go on ringing old Ob might take it into his head to open the door himself, and we don't want that, do we?'

They wandered around to the side of the house and discovered that the bedroom window was open. They studied it in silence. It would be simply a question of balancing for a moment or two on an iron-spiked railing, reaching up and seizing hold of a projecting overflow pipe, and, allowing the pipe to take the entire weight of the body, fall forward, throw the legs over a basement area which was, by conservative estimate, no more than ten feet deep, and thus clutching with the feet to a fat water pipe which oozed up the wall and passed within a couple of feet of the bedroom window, effect an entrance.

Or they could go away and find a ladder.

'Can you manage it?' enquired Jennifer, not considering the ladder for a single moment.

He was hanging on the overflow pipe when the onlookers began to assemble, several of whom immediately proffered advice and suggestions as to what his next move should be. Tetchily Jennifer told them to shut up and pleaded with Harry not to mind, give it up and come down, all of which was a lot easier said than done. So Harry hung on like a bat, ignored everybody and flayed around desperately with his feet fumbling for a fat water pipe. The next few moments were straight out of a nightmare; he closed his eyes and prayed, clutched, gripped, climbed and slithered, all to the accompaniment of cries of encouragement and groans of despair from those gathered below.

When he finally disappeared from their sight head first through the bedroom window the little band of supporters, warmed by his achievement, raised a ragged cheer on his behalf; each, however, went on his way a little saddened and disappointed that Harry hadn't slipped and fallen down the area, or better still, impaled himself on the railing-spikes.

Meanwhile up in the bedroom Ob, plastered and drowsy, accepted the unorthodox advent of his friend with a certain amount of calm resignation. He eyed the breathless and bedraggled figure slumped on the floor by the window and said, 'Someone's just been ringing the bell.'

'It was me,' groaned Harry. 'I had to get in through the window.'

'You could have hurt yourself. Then we'd both have been in bed.'

'Maisie's got my key.'

'Maisie?'

'She must have got lost.'

'Where's she gone?'

'She's supposed to be on her way round here.' Ob brightened considerably and began to sit up and take a bit more notice. 'We gave her the key an hour ago.'

'Who's we?'

'Jennifer and me—she's downstairs.'

'She's not,' said Jennifer from the doorway, 'she's up here.' Harry's jaw dropped and she shrugged her shoulders. 'I just turned the handle and walked in. Perhaps it was open all the time. I brought up one of the bags and put it into the kitchen. I couldn't carry both. Hello Ob. Sorry to hear about all this. Poor you. You do look a sight. I'm going to cook you a nice lunch—I hope.'

Harry had just deposited the second bag of supplies on the kitchen bath-cover when the front door bell rang and continued to ring until he had covered the necessary distance to answer it. Maisie all but collapsed into his arms.

'So what happened to you, then,' he enquired mildly trying to fend her off.

'Don't talk to me,' she mumbled in a strangled voice. 'Don't ever talk to me again. I've been everywhere. My feet! I've been on the go ever since I last saw you. Avenue Road, I've been to.'

'This is Avenue *Street*.'

She eyed him coldly. '*Now* he tells me. Do you know where Avenue Road is? It's the last road before you come to green fields. And do you know who lives at Number hundred-and-thirty-nine Avenue Road?'

'No. Who?'

'A sex maniac, that's who.'

She pushed past him and stumbled blindly up the stairs.

'I thought you liked sex maniacs.'

'Not when they're bald and seventy-five I don't.' She stopped suddenly and turned on him. 'I don't even know why I knocked. I knew I must be wrong. It didn't even look like this house. Why did I knock, I wonder?'

'P'raps you just hoped an unmarried sailor lived there.'

Her pale blue eyes narrowed. 'You are rotten, Harry Stillwater. Rotten, that's what you are.' She turned and continued her upward passage.

Harry said, 'So what happened to the key?'

'What key?'

'The one I gave you for the front door.'

On the landing she stopped again. 'You did didn't you? That's right. I remember you doing that. Here it is, in my pocket.' She let out a strange hooting sound. 'Oo-er, aren't I daft? I could have let myself in.'

'That was the idea.'

'Aren't I daft?' She peered around her. 'Well, where is he?'

'In bed, of course.'

'Lovely!'

She burst into the bedroom, pulled up and stared soberly at Ob propped up in his bed. At the sound of her approach he had hastily rearranged his hair but it had done very little for him.

She said slowly and wonderingly, 'Oh, mate, poor old you, who knitted *your* face and dropped a stitch? Hi Jen, what about all this, then? All those randy blokes with their tongues hanging out for us and we have to get lumbered with this lot. We ought to have our heads examined.'

On tottering heels she weaved uncertainly across the room and kissed Ob loudly on the cheek.

'Oh,' said Ob.

Maisie squinted over her shoulder at Jennifer. '"Oh!" he says when I kiss him.'

'You kissed me on a bruise,' Ob explained.

And suddenly Maisie was crying and holding on to his hand hard. 'Ah! poor old Obby 'orse, don't worry,' she sobbed, 'you'll be lovely again.'

Jennifer pushed Harry out into the kitchen.

'We'd better get on with the lunch,' she said, 'Maisie and I still have to go to work this afternoon remember.'

She began delving into one of the bags of provisions.

'What are we going to have?'

She smiled round at him brightly. 'I thought sausages and mash would be nice and quick. All right?'

Harry tried desperately not to allow his face to fall too far. 'Smashing,' he said.

CHAPTER FOURTEEN

HARRY discovered, a little to his surprise, that there existed a world of difference between sausages and mash prepared by the fair young hands of Jennifer, and bangers and spuds as knocked together by the square, heavy, do-it-yourself fists of Ob.

With an entrancement usually to be observed in the adult male only on demolition sites and in toyshops at Christmas time he watched the entire process with round, fascinated eyes, following her everywhere, treading on her heels, peering over her shoulder, handing her forks, putting away things she hadn't finished with and producing others she didn't need. All of which she endured for some considerable time with a forbearance unusual in females immersed in even the simplest of culinary projects; but when finally, on her way to the gas cooker, she met him face to face, she put down her saucepan, took him firmly by the arm and led him to a chair.

'You,' she told him gently, 'are in my way.'

And that was it. That was the moment—the moment of decision—the point of no return. 'You,' she had said, 'are in my way.' His head swam. 'You, Harry Stillwater, are in my—Jennifer Love's—way.' There was nothing more to be said. Here was the only girl with whom he would ever willingly share his pay-packet. Up the aisle with her—fast—'Do you, Harold Stanley Stillwater, take this lovely young creature, you lucky dog, to be your one and only wife? . . .' Yes! Yes, yes, yes, before she has the chance to cast any more of her bread on the waters—if that's what it meant.

He smiled smugly to himself at his newly arrived-at determination.

'What's so funny?' She swept the hair from her eyes with her forearm.

'You.'

'Oh? What have I done?'

'Nothing,' he grinned '. . . yet.'

She came and stood in front of him and calmly stared him

down. 'I know exactly what you're thinking,' she told him. 'You're terrible.'

He caught her hand. 'All right, then, what's the answer, if you're so clever?'

She was confused for a moment and to cover it she took his hand in hers and smoothed the back of it gently with her fingers. 'I'm busy, let me go, otherwise nothing will be ready in time.'

She went back to the sink, turned away from him and began slicing potatoes.

He said, 'You really did know, didn't you?'

'What was in your mind?' She nodded.

He got up and stood behind her placing his hands on her shoulders. The smell of her hair and the soft scent of her skin seemed to stir in him memories of a past he knew he'd never known.

'It's just as if I've known you all my life.'

Her hands were still and he felt the almost imperceptible pressure of her body as it ceded slightly to his.

'We haven't known each other for a week yet.'

'I know.' His hands slid over her shoulders and down. He felt the firm gentleness of her breasts in his palms and sensed rather than heard the catch in her breath as she yielded her body closer to his. 'But somehow it doesn't seem to matter, does it?'

His lips touched her ear and her cheek and the scent of her hair and skin became almost overpowering.

Her mouth turned towards his. 'No,' she whispered breathlessly, their lips brushing together, 'it doesn't, does it?'

Then she placed her hands on his and gently released them. 'Go and sit down now—please—be a good boy . . .'

Later when they were all sitting around Ob's bed balancing plates of sausages and mash on their knees Maisie made a pronouncement.

'Jen, I'm not going in this afternoon.'

'What?'

'Old Ben can go and Hur on his own for a change—he won't miss me. It's about time I took a couple of days off—they owe it to me. You can make some excuse to old Chubby-Chops for me, can't you? Tell him I've fused the bulb in my torch or something.' She went off into a shriek of merriment.

Jennifer looked soberly at Harry. 'I knew this was coming.'

Harry grinned. 'You can tell old Chubby-Chops, whoever he is, that she's suffering from Pratt's Bottom.'

Maisie nearly fell off her chair. 'What's that?'

'A place in Kent,' Ob informed her. 'Are you going to stay with me all the afternoon? Is that what you mean?'

'Well,' said Maisie darkly, 'someone's got to look after you, I suppose.'

'What about me!' asked Harry, 'what am *I* going to do with myself all afternoon? I'm not hanging around here, I'm telling you, I know when I'm not wanted.'

'You can come to the pictures with me,' suggested Jennifer with a promptitude which indicated premeditation.

'But . . .'

'You could always find a seat at the back.'

'Or even two . . .' Harry was beginning to show his teeth like a happy barracuda, but she took him up on it.

'You needn't look like that either. I'll have other things to do than look after you. I just thought it would be nice to have you there, that's all, but you'll have to behave yourself otherwise I won't let you come.'

Ob allowed his face to crumple into an excruciating grin which hurt him more than it did anyone else. 'It'll be like returning to the scene of the crime, won't it?'

'Except for one thing,' said Harry.

'What's that?'

'I'm not putting those bloody boots on again—not for anybody.'

Ob gave him a wily wink. 'This time,' he said, 'you don't have to, do you?'

Ben Hur made less sense the second time than it had the first.

The sound of a step, the flash of a torch, a whisper, the crisp rustle of a uniformed skirt—each was sufficient in itself to turn his head until his neck ached, and narrow his eyes until they smarted with peering into the smoky gloom. Once when an usherette came and stood beside him in the aisle he removed the torch playfully from her grasp, took her hand in his and squeezed it gently desisting only when an unfamiliar voice breathed huskily in his ear, 'You've got the wrong one, dear';

its owner gave his hand a suggestive squeeze, retrieved her torch and faded into the surrounding murk. They never met again.

Other better planned, though equally titillating experiences occurred at odd intervals during the course of the afternoon which served to keep him on the alert and banish all hope of his ever being able to follow the perfectly straightforward plot of the epic unfolding itself upon the vast screen. On one occasion a cool set of soft fingertips explored the short hairs at the back of his neck and when he reached up to capture the hand to which they belonged it wasn't there; later a disembodied voice pitched so low that it reached his ears alone whispered, 'Who's my favourite milkman?' Then there was the gentle pressure of a hand on his shoulder accompanied by a long sigh, and finally, in the middle of a long speech by a very old emperor of Ancient Rome, a frozen Choc-Ice fell into his lap with a faint plop.

It was like a journey through the Tunnel of Love with a spirit-guide for a companion.

When the interval came she was standing in the aisle by his side as if she had been there the entire time.

'You're a devil,' he informed her.

'Did you like the ice?'

'I feel like a kept man.'

She grinned mischievously. 'If you move up one for the second half I'll come and sit next to you.'

'If you do you'll be taking your life in your hands.'

'I'll have to keep an eye open for the manager.'

'Chubby-Chops?'

She smiled and looked guiltily around the half-empty theatre. 'He's called Chubby-Chops because he's the thinnest man in the world. He's like a skeleton. Anyway, if I disappear suddenly you'll know he's on the prowl.'

'What did you tell him about Maisie?'

'I said she had a bilious attack.'

'She's had an attack all right, but it's not bilious. I wonder how they're getting on, those two?'

'They're all right, don't you worry.'

They were in fact getting along quite well.

Maisie, voluptuously recumbent alongside the prostrate and

captive Ob, was relating the story of her life in a monotonous sing-song voice which was threatening to plunge her listener into the arms of Morpheus at any moment. Only by dint of interposing an occasional 'well I never' or an odd 'really?' was it possible for him to remain even slightly conscious, and it was not until she began to tickle the palm of his hand that the imminent danger of his drifting off to help knit up the ravelled sleeve of care was averted. An innocent enough action, tickling the palm of a chap's hand, and one which will be found to be unrecorded in the *Annals of Therapeutic Remedies through the Ages,* but it does wonders for the odd gland or two. The male animal is liable to react in a variety of different ways. In Ob's particular case it started by giving him the giggles and ended by making him breathe a little more heavily.

'You laughing?' demanded Maisie breaking off in the middle of an abortive love affair she was having with a tall scoutmaster who had just turned out to be the leader of the local Band of Hope as well. 'You're laughing.'

'No, I'm not, honest. Go on.'

'No, you're laughing.'

'You were tickling my hand that's all . . . no, don't stop . . . I like it.'

'You're not ticklish are you?' her hand rose, clawlike, and hung poised over his stomach.

'Don't for God's sake,' he whispered staring in panic at the swaying hand as if it were a King Cobra, 'I'll bust my stitches.'

Her hand dropped and enclosed his once more.

'I wouldn't do that to you—not yet—later I will, when you're better, but not now.' She moved closer to him and felt the warmth of his body against hers. 'When you're better there's lots of things I'm going to do to you,' she promised.

Their lips were very close.

He said softly, 'I don't know as I'm going to be able to wait until I'm better.'

'You're going to have to, Daddy-o,' she said quietly and touched his bruised lips with hers. The warm, intimate smell of him stirred the unknown in her. The brashness of 'sex' and 'boys' and 'all that jazz' seemed to uncoil itself and lay exposed for what it was; her head lay back quietly on the pillow beside his; in her mind crawled the uneasy suspicion that the swiftly and arrogantly assimilated facts of life might not prove equal to the fact of loving.

Ob was watching her curiously.

He smiled as their eyes met. 'Like an angel passing overhead.'

As she returned his look the thought was with her that never in the whole of her life had she felt more alone.

'Didn't feel like an angel to me,' she said soberly. 'Felt like someone walking over my grave.'

At the end of the performance Jennifer waylaid him at the top exit.

'I've only got half an hour before the next showing but if you like to wait in the café next door we can have a cup of tea together. I've got to clear up here first.'

'Clear up what?'

She grinned at him. 'Chap last week lost his boots, believe it or not.'

The café was pretty full, the atmosphere steamy and overladen with smoke; Harry shouldered his way a couple of times around the place before he discovered a pair of vacant stools tucked away in a forgotten corner by the bar. He spread his raincoat over one of them, clambered on to the other, ordered a strong tea and a cheesecake and settled down to watch with fascinated eyes a gallon and a half of orange juice bubbling busily in a large glass container six inches from the end of his nose.

'Hi,' said a voice at his elbow.

It was Boy, tall, blond and leathered from head to foot.

'Hi,' said Harry.

'Thought it was you,' Boy looked around uncertainly, 'You alone?'

Harry removed his coat from the other stool. 'My girl's on her way, but you can park here 'til she comes if you like.'

It was more of a challenge than an invitation and expressed Harry's doubts as to whether such a move could be accomplished without irreparable damage to the skin-tight, black leather jeans the youth was wearing. Boy flung a careless leg over the stool however and mounted it as though it were a motor-cycle. Harry stared with admiration at the intact gleaming trousers.

'You look great,' he said, 'All that leather.'
Boy grinned and winked. 'My bird's kinky for it.'
'She'd have to be. Want something?'
'I'll have a Coke.'
When the bottle arrived and Boy had blown a couple of times down the straw to make the stuff fizzy he said, 'Heard about your buddy.'
'Oh? How?'
'Things get around. How is he?'
'He'll live.'
Boy sucked industriously at the straw then said, 'Knew they'd get around to it. Said they would, didn't I? He's a right sod, that one. Red, I mean. So what happened then?'
Harry told him, leaving the bit about the boy falling over the railings to the end.
Boy shook his head. 'He didn't kill anyone, you take my word for it. If he had you'd have heard about it by this time. It wouldn't be like Red to keep a thing like that to himself. The word would have got round to the cops somehow and they'd have picked your mate up by now.'
'They know about it; all they've wanted so far is a statement which Ob's given them.' He told Boy about Fred Hearthbright and the blond youth pulled an amused face.
'I know old Fred. As cops go he's quite a nice old bugger.' He became serious again. 'So what gives, then?' Harry raised his eyebrows questioningly. 'About Red, what's the form? Is your mate gunning for him?'
Harry gave an inward sigh. Lurid visions of blood and bruises and flaying bicycle chains tramped monotonously before his mind's eye.
Just then Jennifer arrived and was plainly delighted to see the handsome youth. As her eyes lingered over Boy's sartorial excesses Harry wondered whether she too was 'kinky' for leather. He could see himself clambering self-consciously into scarlet leather pyjamas and hastily put the thought from him. Jennifer refused to allow Boy to give her his stool and balanced herself instead precariously on the edge of Harry's—which was all right for Harry because he had to put a couple of arms around her to keep her there. When she was settled and seen to as far as refreshment was concerned, Boy lit a cigarette and went on a bit about Red and his associates.

'He's got a racket of some sort—him and half a dozen other blokes over Oakhaven way—at least I think he has. I don't know what it is and up to last week I didn't care either. But things have a way of changing, don't they? I care a lot now.' He expelled a carefully-considered smoke ring and watched it intently as it disintegrated. 'Red's a bastard, in the best possible way as well as the worst. His father was an American G.I. on his way through to Normandy and his mother was a tart. How do I know? Because he told me. He tells everybody. Nothing wrong in that I suppose—lots of people's mothers have been tarts—it's better than pretending his mum was a duchess and his old man the Commander of the First Airborne Division—at least I suppose it is—no, it's the *way* he talks about it, and about them too. He hasn't got much to thank either of them for, God knows, but . . .' He broke off and stared blankly at the end of his cigarette. He shrugged. 'What do I care? What's it got to do with me? He's had to live with it, not me, but sometimes a bloke like that makes you want to throw up. "The world owes me a living 'cos my old woman was a whore"—you know what I mean.'

Harry stared solemnly into the orange depths of the bubbling fruit juice in front of him. A tangled web of thought was responsible for his next remark. 'Your leg's better now, is it?'

Unconsciously Boy touched his right knee and massaged it gently for a moment or two with a sexy creaking of leather. 'Yes, sure, it's okay. I was lucky. I knew it was coming.' His face grew suddenly dark. 'It wasn't good for Con, though.'

'Con?'

'My girl. She was smashed up pretty bad. She won't ever look the same.'

Jennifer said, 'Why did it happen?'

There was a smouldering anger in Boy's eyes as he looked for a moment in her direction as if not seeing her. 'Why?'

'Yes, why?'

The anger subsided a little and he said factually, 'Last Wednesday night I told one of his lovelies to take his hands off my girl.'

'Was that all?' asked Harry.

Boy's eyebrows arched. 'Wars have started for less.'

'So he fixed your bike?'

'He fixed my bike. I didn't find out about it till a lot later, not till Saturday morning, as a matter of fact, when it was all over. One of the blokes at work and his mate caught them at it, the three of them, but of course no one thought to tell me anything about it until it was too late. Typical, isn't it?'

'What happened?' asked Jennifer.

Boy stubbed his cigarette into an ashtray with a succession of vicious jabs. 'The bike fell apart, that's what happened, at fifty miles an hour. They'd only sawn through the front fork, that's all.'

There was a long silence then Jennifer said softly, 'You *were* lucky.'

The edge to Boy's voice was as potentially lethal as the blade of a razor. 'I doubt whether Con would agree to that. She will never be the same. *I* only bashed my leg, but she won't ever look the same. I felt it coming, see? The handlebars began to fold right in towards me. I yelled at her to jump but I don't suppose she could hear. I slammed on the brakes but—well—fifty on wet roads with a broken front fork . . . you know? It was just lucky that there was nothing coming up behind.'

He suddenly swore violently and crudely, 'I'll kill the bastard, that's what I'll do when I get my hands on him, I'll kill him.'

Harry said after a moment, 'Killing him won't do much good, will it? Won't help Con and it certainly won't put you up in the charts. Can you prove they sawed your bike up?'

'How the hell can you prove that sort of thing? A couple of blokes saw them messing about with the thing—they *said* with a hacksaw—but you can hardly expect Red and his lot to admit it, can you?'

'Not unless we can make them—in front of the beak.'

They watched Boy turning it over in his mind and what they saw was fairly unpromising. With brooding eyes he followed every movement of the youth behind the counter concocting a sickly-looking milk-shake and when the whole process had been completed and the long glass consigned to an unusually tall girl in an uncompromising hat and three-inch jet ear pendants, he suddenly sucked in his breath between his teeth with a loud hissing sound and said, 'Not quite the same thing, is it?'

'As what?'

'As doing it ourselves.'

'Roughing 'em up, you mean?'

'Bashing their bloody heads in.'

Harry sighed. 'I was saying that very same thing only this morning.'

'But?'

Harry thought about Fred and said, 'What good will it do—bashing their heads in?'

'It'll give *me* a whole lot of satisfaction,' retorted Boy tartly.

Jennifer suddenly grew angry. 'Isn't that just like men all over! You never learn anything, do you? The only two things that matter to any of you are sex and bashing other people's heads in; and they're supposed to make you big, brave and masculine. If only there were a few more so-called cowards among you the world might be a better place to live in!'

'Like me, you mean?' asked Harry.

'Yes, like you. But who's ever likely to listen to a woman? Nobody!'

Harry gave her the biggest squeeze to date and was about to tell her that he was listening in spite of what everybody else might be doing when Boy said somewhat surprisingly, 'All right, so you've made your point.' He looked at Harry. 'What about your mate? What does he think about it?'

'Ob? He's never been one to go out looking for trouble. Nobody's suggesting that we just sit around on our cans and do nothing. You said just now that you thought he had a racket of some sort going. All right, then, let's find out all the lurid details, ferret around for a bit, and when we're ready we could get his business busted up, so that when he comes out of clink he won't have anything to go back to. That makes a whole lot more sense to me than just giving him a bloody nose, though we might even get round to that, given a bit of luck and opportunity. What d'you think?'

Boy stared at them both for a second or two then smiled slowly. 'Sounds all right to me. It'll be like working with the law, won't it? You, me and Fred Hearthbright. That'll be a turn-up for the books, I must say. Still, I'll go along with it; so long as we nail him in the end I don't really care how we do it. Personally I'd like to do him with a meat-axe, but my licence to kill has expired.'

They all laughed.

'Thank God,' said Harry, 'for that.'

CHAPTER FIFTEEN

LYING in bed the following morning, listening to the intermittent gusts of rain beating against the window and the various inarticulate noises issuing from the slumbering Ob, Harry was congratulating himself upon not having to turn out and deliver cold milk bottles to the thirsting population when it suddenly occurred to him that being Saturday morning Ben would be standing at the corner of Watermill Street waiting for him.

He groaned heavily, rolled over and peered at the clock. If he left in five minutes he would just about catch Ben before the boy got himself drenched to the skin. He couldn't rely on Griffiths, his stand-in, to pick up Ben—even if the latter flagged him down and explained the situation, Griffiths might already have got himself a boy to help.

Crawling dismally out of bed, he hit his right knee a couple of times with his clenched fist to bring some life into it, and hobbled into the kitchen, only realising upon arrival at the sink that there was no time to shave or make a pot of tea or do anything at all other than clamber into his clothes and leave.

'Where you going?' enquired Ob who had come to with Harry's mumbling groans grumbling in his ears.

'Ben, I'd forgotten about Ben. He'll be waiting. I must go and send him off.'

'Won't he realise you're not coming?'

'Only when he's wet through. I can't let him hang about like that. He'll catch his death.'

'Don't forget to take him his present.'

Harry said, 'How do you feel this morning?'

'Much better. I'm going to get up today.'

'Who said?'

'I did.'

'You wait till the doctor comes. I haven't got any time to make any tea—sorry—but I won't be long. Hang on, will you?'

'Maisie will make some.'

'When's she coming?'

'Early, she said.'

Harry looked at him slyly. 'Why doesn't she move in?'

'I'd like that,' said Ob.

Ben was there, water dripping from his nose and chin, his black hair plastered wetly over his forehead.

Harry was cross. 'Why the hell don't you stand in a doorway—shelter somewhere, for God's sake? You'll catch pneumonia.'

'Who cares?' shrugged Ben.

'I care, that's who. Silly idiot standing there getting drenched.'

'Lay off, will you?'

'What?'

'What's up with you?'

'Nothing. Nothing's up. Let's go and have a coffee or something in the caff. Okay? Get you warmed up a bit.'

Ben looked mystified when Harry took him roughly by the hand and plunged off up a side street.

Later when they were drying off in the café over some hot coffee and dripping toast Harry explained the whole thing to Ben, who said after a long pause, 'You needn't have bothered about me; I'd have been all right.'

'You wouldn't have been all right at all. You'd have waited there until you were washed away and then gone off thinking I'd let you down.'

Ben looked at him curiously. 'It wouldn't be the first time I've been let down.'

'It would be the first time *I'd* let you down,' returned Harry tartly. 'Now, shut up and listen to me. The other day a bloke gave me some money to buy you a present—don't ask me why—he just took a fancy to you, I suppose. Anyway, what I've done is to buy you a windcheater thing. And you're to wear it, see? In this sort of weather you need it. So there it is and I don't want any arguments about it.'

He pushed the parcelled anorak across the table at Ben who regarded it suspiciously. 'Funny thing to do, isn't it? Giving money away like that? To someone you don't know.'

'Yes, very funny, I agree, but that's how it happened—just like that—and that's the truth.'

'*You* did it.'

'I didn't do it. I'll take you to the bloke who did if you don't believe me. Now get on with it, will you, and see if the ruddy thing fits. If it doesn't I'll have to take it back and change it.'

Almost reluctantly Ben unwrapped the parcel and stared at the garment. Its newness gave it a crisp, expensive look.

'Smashing,' he said quietly. 'Looks smashing.'

'Try it on.'

The boy looked around a little self-consciously but of the few early morning customers in the café none was interested in anything other than his own newspaper and his own gloom. Ben slipped the anorak over his sodden jersey and stood up to fasten the zip. His hands slid into the pockets then out again to smooth the creases in the material then back into the pockets. There was a mirror on the wall opposite and he caught sight of his reflection and stared at it for a second, then dropping his eyes he plumped down into his seat again.

After that there was a silence which threatened to be interminable.

'More coffee?' asked Harry when he could bear it no longer.

Ben shook his head and then said, 'Can I have another bit of toast?'

When he had ordered it Harry said, 'I'll have to be getting on in a minute; the doctor will be arriving to see Ob and I'll have to be there to let him in.'

'Funny name, "Ob", isn't it?'

'Yes, isn't it.'

'Is he bad, then? I mean with being beaten up?'

'He'll be all right, but you have to look after him, don't you?'

'Yes, sure . . . so what happened, then?'

Harry stared at a sticker on the steamy window which said, HOT DOG 6d.—but with all the letters round the wrong way. The man behind the counter shouted at him and waved a plate of toast in his direction, and having collected it along with another cup of coffee for himself he rejoined Ben and said, 'It was a gang . . . you know . . . Rocker types . . . they'd got it in for Ob and got him down in the Tunnel. Know the Tunnel?'

Ben nodded in a worldly way as though most of his life had been spent fighting evil influences down in the Tunnel.

'I'll have a gang one day,' he said confidently.

'I hope not.'

'Why not?'

'Gangs are for cowards. You're not a coward, are you?'

'Who says they're for cowards?'

'I do. They're for people who haven't got the guts to fight

their own battles; so they have to surround themselves with a lot of lousy layabouts and smarmy yesmen that they can bully and order about. On their own they wouldn't have the courage to say "boo" to a goose. Like Red—sawn-off little runt—he's only about two inches taller than you are—he's a right so-and-so, I can tell you. He'd run screaming home to mummy if anybody really started in on him.'

'Red Brody d'you mean?'

'Eh?'

'You talking about Red Brody?'

Harry shrugged. 'I don't know. Don't know what his other name is.'

'Nasty little bloke with red hair and cowboy boots?'

'That's the one. You know him?'

'Know him!' The boy made an uncomplimentary noise through a mouthful of toast. 'He's the bloke what's been giving my sister the run-around. I told you about that, didn't I?'

'You told me she wasn't keen on whoever it was she was going around with.'

'She can't stand the sight of him. I can't neither, if it comes to that. One of the reasons I'd like to have a gang is so I could have a go at his lot, and do him while I'm about it.'

Harry stared with awe at the youthful champion across the table. 'What's he done to your sister?'

'I haven't asked, but knowing my sister I can have a good guess. She hates him. Last time she saw him she clobbered him over the head with her umbrella. I don't know what it did to his head but she busted her umbrella.'

Harry was staring at him thoughtfully. 'You don't happen to know where he lives, do you?'

Ben made a face. 'Search me, but Betty will know. Why?' The light of battle glinted in his large brown eyes. 'You going to have him?'

'I just want to know where he lives. What a bloodthirsty little tyke you are, aren't you?'

'You got to be nowadays—otherwise you go under, and that's not going to happen to me, I'm telling you. My mum says you don't get nothing for free in this world—you've got to fight for it.'

Harry looked at him and felt helpless. 'I know what she means, but I'm not sure that you do. Still, there it is. Could you ask Betty for the address?'

'Why not ask her yourself?'

'Can't you ask her, for God's sake? She's your sister. She doesn't want a complete stranger bothering her.'

Ben leered at him. 'You don't know my sister. She won't mind, honest she won't, I keep telling you that. You might even get to like her.'

'And I keep telling you, I'm fixed up. So stop selling her, will you? You're like a—'

'Like a what?'

'Never mind.'

'A pimp? Is that what you mean?'

Harry felt his jaw drop. 'You young kids! The things you get hold of nowadays. I'd have had the hide tanned off me if I'd said a word like that when I was your age.'

'You never knew it at my age.'

'You're dead right I didn't, and what's more I hardly know it now—I don't want to know it.'

Ben was staring solemnly at his plate. 'Well, don't go on about it. You don't half go on about things, don't you?'

Harry said the one word, 'Well!' as expressively as he could. After another moment the boy said, 'I only meant it as a joke.'

'Ha, ha,' said Harry roughly.

'As a joke, that's all. You get all upset about nothing. I didn't want to upset you. Lot of people I'd like to upset, but not you . . .'

'All right, all right, forget it . . .' Harry finished his coffee. 'I just don't go for kids of your age saying things like that when you haven't even started to know what they're about—and I don't care how much you *think* you know. Live it first and then perhaps you'll begin to understand, and when you do you won't like it much, believe me. All right?'

His anger seemed suddenly unreasonable, though what he had said he believed in. He stole a look at Ben. The boy's face was white and set and he was staring through the steamy window with bright unseeing eyes. Harry gave a mental shrug. It was true, what he had said; if he said he was sorry now the kid would think that he was retracting everything. Oh, bloody hell! Kids!

The café proprietor behind the bar was staring at them with mild curiosity and when he met Harry's eye he raised his shoulders expressively and made a sympathetic face. He was thinking the same. Kids!

Ben said in a low voice, 'Will you come and see Betty then and ask her?' His tone was conciliatory.

Harry said quickly, 'Yes, sure, all right, I'll come and see her. When?'

'Now, if you want to. She'll be at home now.' Their differences were forgotten. Now there was a shyness in Ben's eyes as he went on, 'I'm not trying to sell her, honest I'm not. She's got a mind of her own, anyway—I'm the last one she'd take any notice of. Come on—you might just as well . . .'

'Isn't it a bit early?'

'Early? You're joking. My mum has to be out at six. If we're not up by then we don't get no breakfast. She works up at the Town Hall. She's a cleaner there. Coming, then?'

Harry stared at him for a long amused moment then sighed. 'All right then, pest. But I can't stay long; I've got to get back for the doctor. Okay?'

'Okay,' said Ben.

The house was a two-up-and-two-downer tucked away in an insalubrious cul-de-sac almost lost amidst the confused straggle of the Old Town. Over the wall which formed the dead-end loomed the black bricked ugliness of one of the two breweries which the town boasted; the harsh bitter smell of yeast and hops hung over the neighbourhood like an invisible smoke-screen.

'That's the brewery you can smell,' explained Ben with a certain air of propriety.

Harry wrinkled his nose. 'Does it always smell like that?'

'Not always, but it does most of the time. You get used to it when you live here. You get used to most things in the end, don't you?'

Harry gave the boy a sidelong glance, struck once again by the flash of maturity which seemed momentarily to darken the young face.

'Not much of a dump, is it?' Ben went on, stopping before a narrow front door from which the paint had blistered and peeled long ago. 'I was born here, so it's home.' He turned the handle and went in saying as he did so, 'Mind the step.'

The warning came too late. Harry, not expecting the step,

shallow though it was—no more than four inches—had dropped down it as though he was falling down a lift shaft. The floor shuddered and the dark little room in which he found himself trembled and tinkled with the reverberation.

'Most people fall down it,' said Ben unperturbed. 'You get used to it and forget about it. This is the front room. We don't ever use it, full of Mum's old junk mostly—she calls it the parlour—we call it the junk room—lot of old ornaments and plants and pictures of her wedding. I never had a dad, did I tell you? Come through here, this is the kitchen.'

The kitchen was a little brighter though not much; through the upper half of the sash-window—the lower half had been covered with varnished semi-transparent paper bearing a nasty pattern of green and red diamonds—Harry could see the black roof of the brewery wet and dreary against the grey sky. The room itself proffered little, if any, comfort. An enormous square table littered with the remnants of the morning's breakfast sat in the middle of it, flanked on three of its sides by four brown varnished kitchen chairs. The fourth side faced a huge old-fashioned kitchen range gleaming dully beneath its countless layers of assiduously applied grate-blacking; within the polished iron fender stood an oil-heater which smoked relentlessly. Against the remaining walls were cluttered the usual pieces of furniture including a treadle sewing-machine and a smart shining television set; on the walls themselves hung a picture showing King George VI in Naval uniform with Queen Elizabeth the Queen Mother, and beneath it a wartime portrait of Winston Churchill. Other pictures ranged from a frightful blue and yellow painting of the Pyramids with the Sheikh of Araby or somebody like that in the foreground to a colourful flowerprint culled from the pages of a woman's magazine.

Harry stood in the narrow doorway feeling very depressed.

'Sometimes,' said Ben, 'it's so dark we have to have the light on all day. I don't like the winter, do you?'

'No,' said Harry.

'Betty's upstairs I expect, I'll go and tell her.'

He disappeared through a door which led into a tiny hall from which arose an impossibly steep flight of stairs. Harry heard him clumping about overhead and the low murmur of voices reached his ears. He opened another door and found himself in a minute scullery with cupboards and gas stove, a sink and another table taking up most of the room. From this a glass-panelled door led into the backyard, an arid patch of wet mud with a dustbin and a broken pram covered with a shredded groundsheet. The smell from the brewery was overpowering.

Harry returned to the kitchen as Ben reappeared at the foot of the stairs.

'She's coming. She's put out 'cos she's still got her pins in. She looks like a barbed wire entanglement. Never know how she sleeps in 'em myself, they must kill her. Shall I make a pot of tea?'

'Eh?'

'Tea, shall I make some?'

'Not for me, thanks very much, no . . . You sure she doesn't mind?'

'Why should she?' Ben obviously didn't care.

'I'd be put out too if I had my head full of pins and someone came visiting without warning.'

'You'd look jolly daft with all them pins in your hair.'

'You know what I mean. Why don't I come back later?'

'She'll be down in a couple of ticks.'

Ben went out into the little scullery, stood on a chair and peered at himself in a spotty mirror. He pulled the hood of his new anorak over his head and drew it tight with the drawstring. He giggled, 'I look like one of the Seven Dwarfs—Happy.'

'Dopey, more like,' said Harry. 'It's a good fit, that, isn't it? You just see that you wear it.'

'I'll probably go to bed in it,' said Ben seriously. He looked at Harry. 'It's about the nicest thing I've ever had. Thanks, Harry.'

'I keep telling you,' said Harry, 'It's got nothing to do with me, it was this bloke . . .'

'Betty thought it was smashing too.'

There was a sudden crash over their heads and a lurid swearword swept down the stairs with the cutting edge of a butcher's cleaver.

Ben said calmly, 'That's Betty falling over. She's always falling over. Never looks where she's going.'

When Betty finally arrived and stood challengingly in the doorway the whole thing, thought Harry, had been mightily worth waiting for. Beneath the heavy black fringe which swallowed up her eyebrows and threatened also to dispose of her eyes, and within the shapeless sacklike confection of pink sailcloth hung about with several strands of brightly-coloured glass beads, there lurked an attractive, slimly-built nineteen-sixty-five edition of Young Womanhood; from the top of her glossy black head to the toes of her glossy black Wellingtons she was all woman, and Harry self-consciously checked himself in the middle of a loud gulp; he wished he could have seen her eyes properly and even perhaps a glimpse of her eyebrows and forehead; he would have liked a clear picture of the slim waist and the gentle swelling of her bustline which he knew, in an agony of masculine frustration, must be there; he would also have preferred to admire the shapely turn of her bare ankles rather than the uniform strictness of the stiff black rubber of her boots. But all this was denied him—'sufficient unto the day' as the saying goes . . . and it was enough!

'You fell over up there, didn't you?' said Ben tactlessly.

'Yes, I did,' said Betty watching Harry closely to find out what he thought of her, 'Mum left her hot water bottle in the middle of the floor. Hello, you must be Harry.'

She managed to say the latter phrase as though Harry were the last person she expected to see at that particular moment. Harry nodded and grunted out something about how nice it was to see her—at last—and prevented himself, in time, from adding that it would be nice to see even more of her, out of the sack dress and Wellingtons preferably, with her hair spread seductively and slightly disarrayed perhaps over a pillow.

He swallowed loudly, added an inarticulate 'Ha' to which Betty replied, 'Pardon?' and then there followed, inevitably, a short pause.

She shimmied deliberately into the room, disposed herself with elaborate care on a hard kitchen chair, crossed her legs with only the faintest suspicion of a squeak from her Wellingtons, then said, 'Ben was showing me his new windcheater; it's lovely; it was nice of you to buy it for him.'

Her voice, he guessed, was pitched a fraction higher than it should be and she spoke with the thinly-veiled self-consciousness of Eliza Doolittle having finally 'got it'. Neither of these vocal idiosyncrasies had anything to do with the full-blooded roar of the soldier's oath which had so recently assailed his ears when she had fallen over her mother's hot water bottle upstairs, but, if this realisation exposed in her a certain capacity of misrepresentation, it did nothing at all to diminish her in his sight.

She leaned back languorously and bared a sharp set of small white teeth at him and he felt his mouth go dry and the blood in his ears started to beat out the old war dance. He heard himself telling her that buying the windcheater for Ben was nothing, nothing at all, and was not in the least surprised to find that his thoughts were slotted into an entirely different channel which was concerning itself with matters of interest other than masculine windcheaters.

'Would you like a cup of coffee?' she asked.

It's not a cup of coffee I'd like, he thought desperately to himself. 'No, I don't think so, thanks,' he said aloud. 'I'm sorry to have disturbed you really, but it was Ben who said I might . . .'

A door shut quietly behind him and with alarm he realised that he was alone with her.

'Why don't you sit down?'

'er . . .' said Harry, and sat on the chair beside her. She was wearing a perfume of some sort which at this time in the morning was tearing him to tatters—bad enough at night when you were prepared for that sort of thing but, oh God, at half past nine in the morning . . . He would have welcomed death at that moment—if he could have taken her with him.

He stared at her stupidly for a moment then said, 'You're quite a girl.'

She leaned closer to him. 'Am I?'

'I'm—er—engaged—actually . . .'

She was so close that he had to cross his eyes to see her properly. 'Pity,' she said, 'Isn't that a pity? I could go for you in a big way—really big . . .'

'Oh?' One of her hands was on his thigh. '. . . er . . . Betty . . .'

'What?'

'Ben . . .'

'What about him?' Her voice was no more than a whisper and it was the sort of whisper with which Josephine might have prevented Waterloo. She was unbuttoning his raincoat.

'He might come back.'

'He won't.' Now it was his shirt.

'Stoppit, Betty . . .'

He felt her cool fingers against his skin. Her nails bit lightly into his flesh.

'Why? Don't you like it?'

'You know damn well I do.'

'What's the matter, then?' She was suddenly kneeling in front of him, pressed between his knees, her body close against his, her head thrown back, her lips slightly parted; he could see the tip of her tongue against her teeth. His hand trembled as he pushed the black hair up and away from the cool whiteness of her forehead. He stared at the gentle arching of her brows. Her eyes were closed.

As his mouth moved slowly down to hers she sensed its approach and strained upwards to meet it. The kiss began gently and ended in a kind of madness. In the midst of it he saw very clearly the face of Jennifer; it was entirely without expression and had a pale deadness about it. After a second or two it receded and was gone.

He felt Betty's nails clawing at his back and in a sudden spasm of pain he released her and stared down into the hot brown eyes.

There were only two courses open to him—to take her or discard her—and he knew himself too well to be in any doubt as to which of the two he would choose.

'Well?' she said softly when she felt that they had stared at each other long enough.

'Where can we go?'

For a second longer she looked searchingly into his eyes then rising unsteadily to her feet she pulled him up roughly by the waistband of his trousers, 'Come on.'

Upstairs, sprawled on her unmade bed beside the unmade bed of her mother, they made love to each other, lustful, greedy and selfish love, and when it was over Harry, still and spent, felt only revulsion for himself. For her he found an unexpected tenderness and understanding; reaching out to her he held her close to him rather than allow her to sense his loathing for what had occurred. Now her body was limp, now her hair was spread in disarray on the pillow beside him; what he had willed had happened and there was nothing but weariness and hatred in him.

'You hate me, don't you?' She was staring up at him, her eyes cool now, soft and full of anxiety. She seemed younger.

'Of course not,' he said in all truth. 'Of course I don't. I don't like myself much but I don't hate you. Why should I hate you?'

'Don't take it out of yourself. It was nothing to do with you. It was my fault.' Her eyes suddenly filled with tears. 'It's always the same.'

'What is?'

'With men, it's always the same, and so easy.'

'Easy?'

'To make a man do what you want. I don't seem to be able to stop it. It's a sort of—I don't know—it's a sort of illness I suppose.' She smiled with such bitterness that Harry found himself unable for a moment to look at her. 'They've got a word for people like me somewhere in the dictionary—I can't even pronounce it and I don't want to either.' She put up her hand and ran her fingers gently through his hair. 'It's not your fault, Harry, don't blame yourself, really . . . I'm glad it happened; I'm only sorry it's upset you. I think you're lovely—honest, honest I do, and I'm not kidding.'

He put his hand over her mouth. 'Shut up, will you?' he told her softly. 'I wanted it to happen, too. It wasn't only you—how could it be? First moment I saw you standing in the doorway looking at me like that I wanted it to happen. I don't ever remember wanting a girl as much as I wanted you. If it hadn't happened now it would have happened later and I'm glad it did. Like I said before, you're quite a girl.'

She took his hand. 'What about your own girl?'

'What about her?'

'Will you have to tell her?'

His mind became blank; now when he tried he found it impossible to picture Jennifer. 'I don't know. I'll have to think. I'll have to walk it off a bit and think.'

'What's her name?'

'What?'

'Her name?'

'Does it matter what her name is?'

The rain beat against the curtained window; he was naked and cold and when his lips touched hers for a brief moment there was nothing but sadness between them. But she smiled up at him nevertheless and touched his chin lightly with her finger-tips.

'You never even bothered to shave, did you?'

For over an hour he had stood at the rail at the end of the Pier watching the endless procession of black-green waves rearing their wind-torn heads, to bear them proudly for a brief moment or two then crash them relentlessly against the iron and concrete pylons beneath his feet.

Long ago the rain had penetrated his thin showerproof, soaked through his jacket and shirt so that his bare skin shrank from their clammy contact; from thighs to ankles his wet jeans clung to him like a shroud; his shoes were soggy and water-logged. But he remained oblivious to bodily discomfort.

At the entrance to the pier where he had paid his sixpence over an hour ago the officer at the turnstile peered at him, ever more curious, through field-glasses. There was an anxious twitch at the corner of the man's mouth as he studied the lonely figure; in his mind he was turning over a possible plan of action should the figure by any chance disappear suddenly from his view. One thing he was certain about: there would be no foolhardly attempts at life-saving on his part—not in this sea; if the fool wanted to chuck himself off the end of the pier that was his privilege; still, you couldn't just stand about and calmly watch a fellow human being take his life without picking up a telephone or bunging a life-belt over the side in case the chap suddenly decided he wanted to change his mind. He eyed the telephone at his elbow for a moment and then thought disconsolately of the solitary sixpence which lay in the cardboard box beside the handle of the turnstile. It was nearly two o'clock, he had been open since ten and all he had to show for it was one solitary sixpence. He slipped off one of his shoes and watched the steam rise from his stockinged foot as he held it suspended over the one-bar electric fire which glowed redly beneath the pay-desk. With a sigh he picked up the glasses, scrubbed with his gloved hand at the steamy window and stared once again at the lone figure at the end of the pier.

Harry's teeth chattered with the cold. The hands which gripped the rail in front of him were blue and wet and without feeling. The rain beat down on his bare head, streamed into his eyes, down his cheeks and neck and seeped finally into his already sodden clothes. None of it disturbed or worried him. It was the hideous ache within him that really hurt—as though he had swallowed great gulps of emptiness which nothing could displace.

His lips felt dry and it was a shock when he licked them to find that they were running with water. What had he done with Betty that he had not done a dozen times before with a dozen other girls—what was wrong with it? *He* was unmarried, *she* was unmarried, it was an ordinary, natural, healthy masculine way to behave . . .

The officer at the entrance to the Pier lowered his glasses with an odd sense of relief as the lonely figure turned away from the rail and began trudging slowly towards him.

There had been something on that bloke's mind he thought, but any danger there might have been seemed to have passed.

Halfway along the Pier was a glazed shelter beneath which stood several machines 'for Amusement only'. Harry groped in his pocket and found half a dozen pennies. He spun a bright silver ball around a steel spiral and was more surprised than the ball was when it disappeared down a hole and delivered him a clattering bonus of threepence in the metal cup below. He lost it immediately by trying again three times. He then turned his attention to a fortune-telling machine; the dark face of a papier-mâché gypsy woman stared at him searchingly from behind the glass; her gold earrings trembled slightly as he inserted his penny. The card said: *You are of a happy disposition. Members of the opposite sex should love you—if they do not you alone are to blame. You must try harder. Your lucky day is Saturday.*

'Balls,' he said aloud and tried again.

You are too contented. Look around yourself a bit more. Romance looms on your horizon. Don't discard it because you think it can offer you nothing. Your lucky day is Monday.

The dark gypsy face mocked at him behind the glass. 'You,' he said aloud, 'are a liar and a cheat. I want my twopence back' and he gave the machine a lusty blow with his fist. The earrings shook and bounced alarmingly.

'Oi,' said a voice behind him. A man in a soggy peaked

cap and a donkey jacket stood looking at him. 'What are you up to?'

'I was banging it.'

'Why?' He didn't care 'why' but it was his duty to ask.

Harry said, 'First of all it tells me my lucky day is Saturday, then it's not Saturday at all, but Monday.'

The man sniffed. 'What do you expect for a penny? It's only a penny.'

'Twopence,' said Harry.

'Well, don't bang her; that won't do her no good.' He peered around at nothing in particular, then said, 'You going to be here long?'

'Why?'

The man looked crestfallen. 'I've been here since ten o'clock and you've been my only customer and I thought as how if you were going home I might shut up shop and go home myself. Who wants to go on the pier on a day like this?'

Harry looked at him with new interest. 'Is it your pier?'

'What do you mean, is it my pier?'

'I mean it doesn't belong to you, does it?'

'Course it doesn't.'

'Only you're saying you're going home and shutting up shop just like it was yours.'

'It belongs to the Council. They all do—piers. I wouldn't give you twopence for it myself. What would I want with the bloody thing? Look at it. What good is it? What does it do? Doesn't go anywhere. I've been here for over twenty years and it hasn't been anywhere yet.' He squinted at Harry more closely. 'You all right now, then?'

'What?'

The man raised his soggy cap and scratched noisily at his sparse wiry hair. 'Thought you wasn't feeling very well earlier on. Seen you standing down at the end there—for hours—I was worried about you for a bit. Never know with blokes nowadays. You look all right, like you've got your head screwed on the right way, but like I say, you never know. I tell you one thing, though, if you don't go home and get out of them clothes you're going to catch your death. Mark my words. You're soaked through.'

'I don't mind the wet.'

They began walking together towards the exit.

'I don't either,' said the man. 'So long as I'm dressed for it I quite like it. It's the wife who minds. She'd have forty fits if I arrived home in that state. You married?'

'No.'

'Just as well. If I was you I'd go straight home and hop into a nice mustard bath—that's what I would do if I was you. You can't be too careful, eh?'

Harry nodded. 'You're right. I'll do that. Thanks.'

They parted at the turnstiles and the man in the soggy cap watched Harry as he loitered at the edge of the pavement for a bus to pass. The bus threw up a wall of water as the wheels churned through the flooded gutter. Harry looked down at his white and completely useless raincoat—black mud now splattered the front of it. With a wry smile on his lips he looked back at the man at the turnstiles and showed him the damage done to the raincoat. The man in the soggy cap raised his hands and shook his head in silent sympathy.

CHAPTER SIXTEEN

OUTSIDE the bedroom door Harry hovered anxiously for a moment or two, listening intently for any sounds of animation from within. All seemed to be as silent as the grave. He turned the handle quietly and stuck his head into the room. Ob's bed was empty and, even more surprising, Harry thought, tidier than he could ever remember having seen it before. It was as though Ob had died and moved on leaving only a memory behind. Then he heard the clink of a teacup and put his hand around the edge of the door. On the floor before the glowing gas fire, propped against an armchair and buttressed by several cushions, imbibing tea and bread and butter, reclined Ob. He hadn't died at all but lay there regarding his friend intently over the rim of his teacup.

'And good evening to you,' said he with an attempt at sarcasm which fell very flat.

Harry edged into the room and rocked a little desolately on the fringe of the threadbare carpet. 'You're up,' he observed. 'You've got up.' Ob just went on staring at him sombrely. 'Did the doctor say you could get up?'

'Dear God,' said Ob quietly.

'Are you better?'

'What in blue blazes has been happening to you? You look like something the cat's brought in. You're covered with muck.'

'I'm all right.'

Ob's cup clattered angrily in its saucer. 'They haven't been having a go at you, too, have they?'

Harry shook his head. 'I've just been on the wander, that's all.'

'On the wander? On a day like this? What happened? Your girl friend's been hanging around all morning like a cat on hot bricks.' Harry opened his mouth to say something but Ob galloped on. 'It's all right, you're safe. I told her you'd probably decided to go to work. She's gone now—they both have—Maisie as well.'

'Thank God for that.'

'What?'
'I went and stood on the Pier.'
'Bully for you.'
'The bloke there thought I was going to knock myself off.'
'You didn't, though?'
'No, I didn't.' He fumbled with icy fingers at the buttons of his ruined raincoat. Ob, with the aid of an anguished face or two, began struggling to his feet. 'What are you going to do?' demanded Harry.
'Help. Now, shut up. Get out of those clothes and into a hot bath.'
He pushed past Harry and disappeared abruptly in the direction of the kitchen and whilst he muttered and clattered his way noisily about the bath his companion came and stood forlornly over the sink and began wringing out his raincoat.
'You're really feeling better, are you?' asked Harry.
'Old Dr. Thing said I could go back to work on Monday.'
'That's a laugh.'
'He only put me to bed in case I got an attack of the shakes or shudders or something.'
'You look a bit better, I must say.'
'Which is more than I can say for you. You seem to be making a habit of it, don't you?'
'What?'
'Getting yourself drenched.'
Harry became suddenly and vigorously animated; he flung his wet coat over the seat of a chair with a violent soggy slap. 'It's this bloody, bloody, bloody awful climate. What a flaming country this is to live in. You get the sun for a quarter of a flaming hour and then the bloody rain for twenty-bloody-three-and-threequarters. What's the matter with it? What have we done to deserve it, that's what I'd like to know? It was never like this when I was a boy. It's that damn' bomb, that's what it is. It's not only this country it's the whole damn' world —and the people who live in it—they're even worse than the weather ...'
'Shut up.'
'Letting off their bloody bombs all over the bloody place. No wonder it bloody rains!'
'Shut up.'

'I'd bloody rain too if I was the bloody weather.'

'Harry.'

'What?'

'Shut up. Your bath is running and if you don't strip off and get into it . . . Right?'

'Right.'

When, at last, Harry was safely ensconced in the bath, Ob lowered one of the cover-flaps, parked a loaded tray and himself on top of it, poured out a couple of steaming hot cups of tea and for several silent moments sat in mournful contemplation of his friend. Harry lay back with his eyes closed not caring about anything in particular other than a wish, perhaps, that it was still yesterday.

'Tea,' Ob reminded him when he felt the silence had gone on long enough.

'I've really caught something this time,' said Harry, shivering slightly in spite of the heat of the bath.

'The pox, I shouldn't wonder.'

'Don't joke about it.'

'What on earth possessed you?'

Harry peered morosely for a moment into his cup then said, 'I told you Ben had a sister, didn't I?'

'Ben? Who's Ben?'

'You know, the boy . . .'

'*Your* boy—oh yes, with the anorak, you mean?' He stopped suddenly, as illumination descended upon him with the force of the clanging lid of a psychic pressure-cooker. As understanding slowly dawned his jaw began to drop. At last he said, 'You didn't?' Harry stared ahead for a moment in silent misery, then put his cup on the tray. 'So I went for a walk after—on the Pier. I thought it might help.'

'And it didn't.'

'No, it didn't.' Harry gave an impatient splash. 'I don't belong to her, you know.'

'Who?'

'Jennifer. I don't belong to her. If a chap wants to go off and sew a few wild oats he's got every right to go off and do it. That's what I say.'

'Wild oats! That's a laugh, too!'

'Whose side are you on?'

Ob threw his hands in the air which gave him a jab of pain

under one of his armpits. 'What's she like, this bird, for God's sake, that you have to go and do your nut with her?'

Harry said soberly. 'She's a nice kid.'

'She sounds like it.'

'No, she is, honest. She's a bit of a nympho, but even a nympho's not much good on her own. And there was I, weak as water, and there was she . . .'

'Strong as an ox! What did you want to go and do it for just when things were working out with you and Jen?'

'I don't have to tell her though, do I?'

'That's up to you, mate, but if I know anything about Jennifer she won't have to be told.'

'What do you mean by that?'

'They know about these things, women do, nobody has to tell 'em. It's what they laughingly call their intuition. They know what's going on a darn sight better than you do. When there's a woman around the best thing to do is keep your mind a blank, I'm telling you.'

'And you should know.'

Ob ignored the sarcasm. 'The moment she sees you she'll know—it'll stick out a mile—unless you're a very much better actor than I think you are—and even I don't think you're a very good one.'

'You're a fat lot of help, I must say,' grumbled Harry, 'especially when I only did it for you.'

Ob almost fell off the bath with dismay. 'You what?'

'I only went to see her to get Red's address—for you!'

Ob snorted. 'Where was it? Tattooed on her navel? Don't give me that!' He paused, frowning suddenly. 'Red? What's he got to do with anything?'

Harry told him what he had to do with it but his friend appeared to derive little comfort from the revelation; he still waved his arms about in an alarming manner and tossed his head up and down like an aggravated shire-horse. 'I must say, the thought of Red climbing all over her would have been enough to put me off her for life—let alone anything else.'

'It's all right for you, little Miss Prim, you've never been in a situation like that. Blimey, this time last week I didn't even know Jennifer; I hadn't even lost my bloody boots, this time last week. Why should she suddenly be standing there demanding that I don't go around with anyone else? Eh? Tell me that if you can.'

'It's your beastly conscience that's got you into a lather about it, not hers. It's you that goes walking in the rain on the Pier when it's all over, not anybody else. Stupid old fool. You know as well as I do that you've either got to stop sleeping around with other birds or pack it in with Jennifer. It's not a very difficult thing to make up your mind about, I'd have thought, but you might see it differently.'

If he could have flounced off the edge of the bath without hurting himself he would have done so; as it was he rose with a certain amount of dignity and picking up the tray dumped it on the draining board with a loud thump. Harry lay in the bath watching him drearily.

'You're being an old so-and-so, you know that, don't you?'

Ob stood for a second with his back to Harry and when he turned the atmosphere had changed considerably. 'You know I'm on your side, always will be, but that means being on Jennifer's side, too, doesn't it? She's the best thing that's ever happened to you and I'm not going to stand by and watch you mess it all up.'

'Do you think I ought to tell her?'

Ob sighed heavily. 'How do I know? Wait 'til you see her and play it off the cuff. I certainly wouldn't go barging in all set for the great confession.' He grinned. 'Play it cool, as they say, and play it for laughs, for God's sake. Nobody ever got anywhere with a load of old misery on his shoulders.'

Neither of them said anything further for quite a time. Ob clattered about with the tea things at the sink whilst Harry lay glooming in the bath going over the events of the past week. Everything seemed so untidy, loose ends straggling away into an uncertain future, beginnings with no conclusions.

'It's been quite a week,' he observed at last, 'one way and another.'

Ob grunted. 'You can say that again.'

Harry stared thoughtfully at his spiky head. 'How is it going with you and Maisie?'

'She frightens the life out of me, but she's all right. She's quite a nut in her own small way, but I go for her, you know?'

Harry gave a martyred sigh. 'I know.'

Ob squinted round at him. 'Now don't get all down in the

mouth about it. Everything's going to be all right, you'll see. These things happen—they have to, otherwise you never know where you are. If you don't test a thing you never know how much it's worth, do you?'

He put down his drying-up cloth and regarded his friend with gentle compassion. 'I think you understand women even less than I do. She's not expecting you to be either a martyr or a paragon. If it's a saint she's after she's going to be dead unlucky. All she wants is someone to be fond of, however weak or strong he is or however much of a nit he is. And that someone, at the moment, happens to be you.'

'So what if she's after a paragon, then?'

'She'll be unlucky there, too.'

'What's a paragon?'

Ob grinned. 'I'm a paragon.'

'Bung us over the towel, will you, I'm getting out of this bloody coffin.'

Later when he was huddled in front of the fire in the sitting-room, shivering a bit, notwithstanding the fact that he was warmly cocooned in the eiderdown from his bed, Ob asked him about his gleanings with regard to Red.

'There's not much. So far as Betty knows he's up to the armpits in the car racket—stolen cars and what-nottery. I wouldn't say he was the big shot or anything like that—from what she said it sounds to me as if he was carrying out orders. He certainly collects a regular pay packet from someone. And apparently he's always driving around in important-looking cars.'

'That doesn't sound like him at all.'

'Not as we now him it doesn't, in the leather jacket and boots. But then we don't know him much, do we? She was pretty vague too, I must say, for someone who had kept company with him for quite a time.'

'Was this before, or after?'

'After, if you must know. What's that got to do with it?'

'I think everything's a lot more truthful after than before, don't you?'

Harry shot him a sidelong glance. 'Someone ought to stuff *you* when you die and shove you in the Natural History Museum.' After a pause he went on, 'So what do we do about it all? I've got his address—he lives over in Oakhaven behind where the Fun Fair is—between the Fun Fair and the Railway Bridge.'

'Alone?'

'Well, officially he does, but more often than not he has a moll with him. That was one of the reasons he packed it in with Betty, according to her. He wanted her to share his wigwam with him but she didn't go for it much. I think the best thing we can do is pass it on to Boy and see what he's got in mind. So long as he doesn't go barging off on his own. He'll land himself in even more trouble if he does. They've always got to do it themselves, haven't they? An eye for an eye and a tooth for a tooth. Whoever said that ought to have had his head examined.'

'Moses said it, didn't he?'

'Then he ought to have known better.'

'Well, he did have all those terrible old Israelites round his neck. No one could blame him if he went off the rails every now and again.'

'God did.'

'What? went off the rails?'

'No, blamed him.'

'God would! Poor old Moses! Fancy wandering about for forty years with that lot trailing after him.'

'We know where to get hold of Boy, do we?'

'He said he would be in Fat Doris's caff most evenings. I don't know how we're going to go about it, though. What do we do? Set up a sort of watch committee on him, I suppose—on Red, I mean—see where he goes and what he does.'

Ob sat for a moment or two staring at the gas fire. 'It all seems daft to me, you now,' he said at last.

'Why?'

'As far as I'm concerned the whole blasted thing's over and done with. I hit him, he hit me back, so we're quits. I don't hold it against him. I can't stand his guts, but why the hell should I want to wear them for garters? The best thing we can do is to let Fred get on with it. It's his job, not ours.'

Harry made a face but didn't say anything. He agreed with it all. But theory, unfortunately, wasn't practice. Humankind, it seemed to him, was born to bear grudges and harbour malice and wage war and if you didn't hitch a ride on the delivery van you'd find yourself in no time at all on the receiving end, which was a fairly unrewarding end to be.

Ob was going on. 'I could quote the Bible at you again if you like.'
'What's up with you all of a sudden? You seen the light or something?'
'Vengeance,' boomed Ob in the rumbling overtones of an Old Testament prophet, 'is mine, saith the Lord.'
'And by the time he hands it out everyone's dead and buried,' retorted Harry truculantly, 'which seems a fat lot of good to me. I suppose that was old Moses again?'
'I expect so.' They exchanged gloomy looks. 'There we are, then.'
'Yes,' agreed Harry with caution. 'As you say ... there we are.'
From behind the muffled murmur of traffic arose the clamour of a fire engine, distant at first but growing swiftly to a frenzied fury of sound, to fall away with equal swiftness into a slurring series of diminuendos until it held no more threat than the jangle of sleigh-bells.
'Fire,' said Ob ambling idly to the window. 'Someone's lit a fire.' Hopefully he peered out into the growing dusk for a minute or two then turned back into the room. 'Can't see anything ... not even a glow in the sky. Funny. Never seen a fire in my life ... lot of fire engines but never a fire. You ever seen a fire?'
'... er ...' said Harry.
'Neither have I.'

As Ob's strength and feeling of well-being grew in him Harry's slid slowly downhill, until on the day when Ob stood in front of the mirror and smiled broadly at himself without feeling any ill-effects from the stitches which still kept his face together, Harry, peering later into the same mirror with aching bloodshot eyes, took a long frightened look at the colour of his tongue and retired forthwith to bed.
'I've got it,' he told his friend.
'What do you think it is?' was Ob's anxious enquiry.
''Flu,' Dr. Bumphrey told them with no dramatic pretensions. 'It's just the 'flu. It's going around. Stay in bed, keep warm, and you'll be up and about in no time.'
'I've had the 'flu before,' croaked Harry from the bed.
'So?'

N

'It never felt like this. You sure it's only the 'flu.'

Bumphrey smiled in a slightly superior manner. 'I wouldn't underestimate the 'flu if I were you. In 1918, in London alone, it killed off over a thousand people a week.'

'That,' said Harry, 'makes me feel a whole lot better.'

'Mind you, that was the Spanish variety.'

'What's this then?'

'The one you've got?'

'Yes.'

The doctor looked thoughtful. 'It's the one that's going about.'

'No one's died of it?' asked Ob.

'Not yet.'

'But we know who's going to be the first, don't we?' groaned Harry.

In due course—very swift due course—Jennifer came and ministered to him, held his head and his hand and crooned over him with soothing commiseration. Almost the first thing she made him do was change his pyjamas in front of the fire, and she certainly didn't bother to look the other way while she was helping him into a fresh pair. Though this event didn't concern him at the time, the memory of it the following day caused his temperature to edge up a notch or two. The argument he used in her defence was that had she subscribed to the usual books of etiquette and relieved him of her support he would no doubt have fallen over, hit his head on the fender and died, whereupon she would have been arrested and charged, the way they do, with negligence.

She made no mention of the Saturday morning escapade and Harry didn't feel like bringing it up.

There was, however, something about Maisie's behaviour which made him wonder whether she had stumbled over the truth; Ob would never have told her, of course—upon Ob's loyalty he would have staked his life—but there was a sinister, probing curiosity about the way in which she prodded him with a long, sadistic finger and peered at him through the lush fringe of her false eyelashes and said, 'huh-huh' in a tone which didn't mean 'huh-huh' at all but something entirely different—something like, 'So what about Saturday morning, then? It won't be any good you coming to *me* for sympathy when the whole thing blows up in your face, because you won't get it. I only hope Jennifer knows what's she's doing, that's all, and wakes up to what's going on right under her nose before she does anything she'll be sorry for . . .' Nevertheless when he collapsed and retired to his sick bed she made the usual clucking noises and delivered the traditional bunch of grapes—which she demolished in less than a quarter of an hour—but then, alarmingly, just sat on the end of the bed and stared at him long and fixedly with a pale blue eye which would have made Argus look old-fashioned.

'Does she know?' he demanded of Ob in a hastily-snatched moment when the girls had retired into the kitchen.

'About what?'

'Me and Betty.'

'Maisie?'

'Yes.'

'No.'

'You sure?'

'Of course I'm sure.'

'You haven't told her?'

'What do you take me for?'

'It's the way she keeps looking at me.'

'She always looks like that.'

On the evening of the second day of the 'flu Fred Hearthbright came in and sat, huge and comforting, in the old wicker chair which creaked with alarm beneath his enormous bulk, and beamed at Harry in a fatherly fashion, shaking his head with sympathy, saying 'Well, well, well . . .' and adding that had he known of Harry's indisposition he would have baked him a cake. It was his evening off and in a loud check sports jacket and a waffly pair of grey flannels he was, for a moment or two, completely unrecognisable. You could still see he was a policeman, of course, but in civilian disguise he looked more like a sartorially-retarded Chief Superintednent of the C.I.D.

Harry was delighted to see him and they sat and talked about the war and gardening and what a clever animal the beaver was, the latter topic leading quite naturally to the great new dam at Abu Simbel which brought them back, via Egyptian monuments and antiquities, to Ob's sarcophagus in the kitchen which housed the bath. After which, utterly exhausted and not a little confused, Harry fell asleep and when he awoke Fred had gone.

On his way to the police station the following morning Fred

dropped in a pound of apples and half a dozen bananas—four of which Maisie devoured before leaving for the afternoon shift at the cinema.

That night and subsequently, Ob, in an effort to relieve the boredom and monotony of the sick-room, began to read aloud to him—a detective novel called *The Nose on my Face* which became so twisted and complicated that neither of them had the slightest idea of what it was all about, and Harry, who invariably fell asleep within ten minutes of the commencement of each session—Ob not being the most dynamic performer when it came to reading aloud—had the feeling that the author, aided and abetted by his publisher, had deliberately written three different novels and bound them together in order to test the perspicacity of his reader.

On the fourth and final day of the 'flu—as such—he surrounded himself with cushions and eiderdowns, sat up primly in bed and received his visitors in much the same manner as Queen Elizabeth the First might have given audience to the ambassadors of France and Spain had she been confined to her bed with influenza, or whatever dire disease they had instead of influenza in those insanitary days.

Now that he was becoming more conscious of his immediate surroundings he was amazed to mark the improvement that had occurred in Ob with regard to the wounds and bruises the latter had received during his unpleasant experience of barely a week ago. Apart from his battered face there was little to remind one of the severe manhandling he had undergone. The doctor was amazed too and appeared slightly resentful that his patient had reacted so favourably to his Hippocratic ministrations. 'There's nothing you can do with a chap like that,' he confided gloomily to Harry that morning when Harry's mouth was full of thermometer, 'except stitch him up and leave him to get on with it. Fantastic constitution that. Funny, him being a taxidermist; would never have thought that—not in a month of Sundays . . . never . . . If you were all like him there'd be no need of us doctors. We'd all be able to get on with the things we really like doing.'

'Like what?' Harry inquired when the thermometer had been removed.

'What?'

'The things you really like doing.'

Dr. Bumphrey looked at him vaguely for a moment, forgetting, as he did so, to examine the thermometer. 'Horses,' he said, 'I like horses. Big chestnuts ...' He shook the thermometer, still without looking at it, and replaced it carefully in its little metal container.

Harry grinned. 'I'm better, am I?'

'You ever been in the saddle?' asked the doctor solemnly.

'Never, no.'

Bumphrey sucked in his breath and shook his head reminiscently. 'Nothing like it ... the living power, the muscle, the sinew ... nothing like it in the whole world.' He tossed his head a little effeminately. 'I rode with the hounds once, years ago ... down in Surrey ... a meet down there ... what? ... Yes, you're better. You can get up if you want to, but keep warm. I shouldn't go out for a day or so if I were you—not while this stinking weather lasts ... All right?'

He went off saddened by his memories.

'I wish,' said Jennifer that afternoon as she relentlessly belaboured his pillows behind him, 'I didn't have to go back to work.' She had rushed over in her half-hour's break to see how things were going.

'So do I,' returned Harry fervently.

'I wish I didn't have to go to work at all.'

'So do I.'

'I hate work.'

'So do I.'

She stopped beating the pillows and regarded him steadily. 'Well, one of us will have to go to work, we can't live on air, so it's no use saying "So do I" like that. I only hope you're going to be able to earn enough money on your own to keep me in the luxury to which I'm accustomed.'

Harry said, 'I'm going to have to keep you, am I?' She suddenly dropped her head and blushed furiously. 'You're blushing.'

'I'm not.'

'You are.'

'You shouldn't take any notice.'

'Why not?'

She buried her face in the pillow beside him. 'Because,' she said in a muffled voice.

Neither of them said anything for a time but their hands intertwined and became so tightly clasped that it was almost painful.

'Jen.'

'What?'

'You know I love you, don't you?' She half lifted her head and looked at him with one eye, then she placed her forehead against his lips. 'Did you hear what I said?'

'Yes.'

'*Do* you know?'

'Yes, I think so.' She became so still that it was almost as if she had forgotten to breathe. There was a yearning within her which seemed to turn her blood to water and check the beating of her pulses.

'You still with me?'

She nodded in silence.

The pause before his next words was unbearable and when they came there was such love and warmth and need behind them that the tears sprang to her eyes.

'Marry me, Jen, will you . . . please?'

She threw her arms around him and cried on his chest. He held her closely to him for a moment or two then complained, 'You're making me all wet,' at which she fumbled for the handkerchief in the breast pocket of his pyjamas and dried her eyes with spasmodic dabs, still not looking at him and still without saying anything.

He kissed the top of her head gently. 'I'll get the 'flu again if you go on like that.'

She undid the top button of his pyjama jacket, mopped at his perfectly dry chest then kissed it and buttoned him up again. Lifting her head she looked into his eyes and touched his lips fleetingly with hers.

'Oh Harry . . .'

'What does that mean?'

'Just "oh Harry" . . .' She traced his upper lip with her finger. 'I just don't understand why I love you so much.'

Now it was his turn to stop breathing. He stared at her wonderingly. 'You said it . . .'

'Yes . . . and meant it . . .' There was a mischievous quirk at the corner of her mouth. 'I never thought I should ever fall in love with a milkman.'

'Milkmen,' Harry told her, 'are the salt of the earth.'

'How was I to know that until you told me?'

He took her head between his hands and after a second said, 'You going to marry me, then?'

She smiled through the remainder of her tears. 'I suppose so ... I'll have to ... You'll be a nuisance if I don't.' He folded her possessively into his arms.

'There are so many things you don't know about me yet. Not nice things ... you ought to know about them I suppose before you go any further ...' The proximity of confession brought a sudden constriction to his throat.

She pressed her cheek hard against his. 'If they're over and done with, I don't want to know. If they happen tomorrow we'll talk about it then ... but not now ... don't let's even think about them now. It'll only spoil everything.' She looked into his eyes. 'From this moment I love you as I've never loved anyone in my whole life before. That's enough for me ... for one day ...'

In self-defence Harry lowered his eyes. 'I'd have thought that would have been enough for anyone,' he whispered, '... for ever.'

CHAPTER SEVENTEEN

A COUPLE of days later Dr. Bumphrey came and unstitched Ob's face and everybody sat about and admired it from various angles vociferating the while upon the result.

Ob surveyed himself critically in a hand mirror and grunted his satisfaction. 'Not too bad . . . not nearly as bad as I thought it would be.' He held the mirror close to his eye and peered into it like a half-blind philatelist. 'What about all those little holes?'

'What little holes?' demanded the doctor stopping what he was doing with some asperity.

'Those little holes,' Ob told him, pointing them out.

'They're the holes made by the stitches. If you're going to have stitches you've got to have holes to put them in. Being a taxidermist I'd have thought you'd have known that.'

'But they'll go though, won't they?'

The doctor regarded him with patience. 'Of course they'll go —eventually.'

'This one,' Ob pointed out, laying a cautious finger along the worst scar which sprawled lividly across his right cheek, 'looks like a plum tree.'

'A plum tree?' queried the doctor eyeing an equally mystified Harry.

'The holes,' explained Ob, 'are the plums . . .'

'. . . and the scar-tissue is the tree. Yes . . . I see . . . well, we always try to please—even in the little things . . .'

When the doctor had gone the four of them—Jennifer and Maisie had come over to watch the operation—gathered around the bath and partook of a dainty luncheon which the girls had knocked together from a few old onions, some tomatoes and half a pound of cheese.

Ob kept the mirror by his side and took a quick peep at himself every now and again.

'Won't get any better if you keep staring at it,' Maisie informed him in a flat voice.

Ob held the glass at arm's length, half-closed his eyes and

peered into it through his lashes. 'They could be sabre-scars, couldn't they?'

'They could be, but they're not.'

Ob looked at Harry and jerked his head in Maisie's direction. 'My friend,' he said.

'Well,' the disillusionist went on, 'what's the good of fooling yourself. It just looks like you got into a rough-house and didn't get out fast enough. What's wrong with that?'

Harry nodded wisely. 'It happens to all of us.'

Maisie darted him a quick look. 'I haven't noticed it happening to you, Harry Stillwater.'

'No, well, it's my mind that gets battered, not my body.'

Maisie sniffed. 'What mind?'

She looked like someone's least-favourite maiden aunt.

'Maise,' said Ob.

'What?'

'Shut up.'

'Well . . .' It was a long drawn-out sound of justification.

'You always going to be like this?'

'Like what?'

'Rude.'

Maisie's jaw dropped. 'Rude! Me! Well, I like that. The truth is what I'm telling you.'

Jennifer spoke for the first time. 'P'raps people don't always want to hear the truth.'

Maisie tossed her head and swept a superior blue-eyed look over the heads of the males present. 'If you mean who I think you mean, who can blame them? They're all the same.'

'Who are?' asked Ob knowing full well.

'Men, of course,' supplied Jennifer.

'Deceivers,' said Maisie.

Jennifer gave a theatrical sigh. 'She's off.'

'You'll listen to me one day, Jennifer Love, when you're alone and desolate—when *he's* gone off and left you—' she levelled a bony finger at Harry, '—you mark my words.'

'I love you, too,' Ob remarked in a bored sort of tone.

'Ah,' crooned Maisie, fluttering her eyelashes and going off suddenly and enthusiastically on a completely different tack. 'Isn't that nice? I don't include *you* when I talk about "men" like that.'

'What am *I*, then?'

'Mine!' screamed Maisie joyously grabbing with a predatory claw at his hand which at that moment happened to be bearing a loaded fork in the direction of his open mouth. The result was a forkful of cheese, onion and tomato on the wall opposite and they watched fascinated as it slid down slowly to within an inch of the bath-cover when Harry adroitly fielded it with a piece of bread.

'Oh, well caught sir,' cried Ob and then fell abruptly silent as he disappeared into Maisie's arms.

Harry looked at Jennifer. 'Take to the hills,' he said. 'It's an orgy.' He was not displeased at the sudden unexpected turn of events. The coupling of the words 'men' and 'deceivers' and 'truth' had begun to undermine his peace of mind, and though Jennifer had appeared momentarily as witness for the defence he was not foolhardy enough to believe that she would for ever remain on that side of the court. Girls-Together-Week must eventually dawn and when it did it would be *Woodman, Spare That Tree* and every man for himself.

The four of them walked over to the cinema together and having seen the girls safely into the arms of *Ben Hur* the two men loitered for a moment or two around the sandbin, looking at it fondly, patting it and knowing perfectly well that in forty years' time, when a couple of sets of grandchildren would be hanging on their every word, they would tell them how granny had been wooed and won on a sandbin.

'Wonder whatever became of Millicent Johnson,' said Ob suddenly.

'Who's Millicent Johnson?'

'Charlie Bourne. He never rang, did he?'

'You never rang him.'

'No.'

'You should some time.'

'Yes.'

They stood on the corner and looked up and down the street.

'It's not raining,' Harry said.

'No.'

'What shall we do, then?'

There was a pause during which various unspoken suggestions perambulated through their minds and a lady motorist, thinking they were waiting to cross the road, pulled up and waved at them.

'That bird's waving at us,' said Ob waving back.

'Bit old for a bird,' returned Harry also waving.

'She wants something.'

'You, perhaps. Why don't you go and ask her?'

So Ob sauntered over to her and stuck his head in her window.

'Can I help?'

The lady, an indeterminate female all over, looked confused and stalled her engine. 'I was waving you over.'

'Ah ... sorry madam ... we were just standing ... not going over ... just looking ... sorry ...'

'I thought you wished to cross.'

'Hold on a minute, will you?' He went back to Harry. 'She would like it,' he said, 'if we crossed over.' He took Harry's arm and together, bowing a little and raising their hands, they moved sedately in front of the small car which housed a now beaming lady who, in acknowledging their breeding with a gracious hand, did far too much with her feet, the net result being that her car left the tarmac with the determination of a jet aircraft, missed by a hairsbreadth a small unhealthy-looking child clutching an empty birdcage who had also decided to take advantage of the temporary lull, and hurtled out of sight in full throttle.

'You all right, mate?' enquired Ob as the child sped into a new and completely fortuitous phase of life.

The youngster's head wobbled expressively on his shoulders. 'Women drivers!' he spat and marched importantly into a pet shop.

They stood on the kerb and watched him wonderingly. 'So how old do you think he is, then?' asked Harry.

'Six, I should think—not a day older.'

It was their turn to wobble their heads at each other.

Ob pointed suddenly at a blue bus with *Oakhaven* on the front of it. 'Let us,' he said, 'get on a bus ...'

'All right, then. Let's do that.'

'Have you noticed,' asked Ob, clutching at the seat opposite as they lurched precipitously along the coast road, 'how much bumpier the blue buses are than the red ones, or even the orange ones, if it comes to that?'

'No,' said Harry, not caring.

'They are ... much ... it's the springs.'

'Oh?'

'Older buses, of course, than the others.'

'That would explain it, then.'

'Yes . . . older . . .'

Without slackening its speed the bus bounced healthily over a level-crossing and only by the swift marshalling of their reflexes did they avoid putting their heads through the roof.

'Why?' asked Harry determined to ignore the whole thing, 'are we going to Oakhaven?'

'To have a look, I thought . . . a snoop . . .' Ob's uneasiness showed only in the way in which his head slewed round until his eye caught sight of the emergency handle at the back of the bus. 'Then we can tell Boy about it tonight, perhaps . . . eh? . . . if you feel like it. Feel like it tonight? Going to the caff, I mean . . . if he's there . . .'

'Why not?'

Ob brooded for a second. 'That is,' he added as an appendage, 'if we come out of this lot alive.'

Harry made no answer. Ob glanced at him. 'You all right?'

'Me? Yes. Why?'

'I just thought . . .'

'What?'

'Quiet . . .'

'Me?'

'. . . all of a sudden . . .'

'No. Am I?'

'I thought so . . .'

'No . . .'

After which exchange they both fell silent, their attempts at speech having been therapeutic rather than a need for communication.

A lamp-post rocketed past.

For Those in Peril on a Bus . . . chanted Harry to himself at odd intervals, his heart full of fear . . . Death was at the wheel . . . that little old skeleton in a black hood was sitting up front —out there on the driving seat . . . 'Room for one more inside,' the coachman had invited, leaning down from his high perch on the coffined hearse . . .

Upon being disgorged at the terminus a little gaggle of shaken passengers, including Ob and Harry, stood in respectful and thankful silence for two minutes as they watched the blue bus sway perilously out of their orbit at an angle of seventy degrees. One man, a tall, bearded figure who wore his hat on his chest in the position of prayer, shook his other fist at the departing vehicle and said a few words in a foreign language. A Black Magician perhaps, thought Harry, muttering an incantation or two over the bus driver in an effort to change him back into whatever he had been before he became a bus driver.

'Running late, I suppose,' suggested a mild, middle-aged lady.

'Nobody,' declaimed her companion, an actor with an eyeglass, 'could be that late.'

Miraculously, the sun was shining and the sea sparkled with light. Harry took a deep breath of ozone and coughed himself into contortions. Ob studied him anxiously but said nothing.

On the beach a large, perspiring man, cowering beneath a raincoat, was removing his trousers. Several people, including a policeman, slowed up to watch, but when the man finally allowing the raincoat to drop from his shoulders, revealed himself to be no more than a large pink-and-white blancmange-type businessman braced into an impossible pair of egg-coloured briefs intent upon what the English are pleased to call a 'dip', the little assembly dispersed in good order.

'I thought,' said Ob in a disappointed voice, 'there was going to be a moment of drama then.'

Harry tersely informed him that he, personally, had had enough drama for one afternoon and if it was all right with everyone else he, personally, was going to buy himself a large hot, strong cup of tea.

Like a couple of private-eyes without portfolios they lurked in a phone box and peered across the road at the house where Red lived.

Ob grunted. 'Not much, is it?'

'Ordinary,' agreed Harry.

It was no more than one of a long dreary row of red villa-type dwellings set behind pocket-handkerchief front gardens which, in the palmy days before the war-cabinet had seen fit to requisition fancy ironwork for conversion into less fancy battleships, had probably boasted a flower or two, even a rose tree, most certainly a plot of grass; but now, deprived of gates and railings, exposed to the gang warfare of the local children, open to the passing whim of every wandering dog and battered into submission by the weekly tramping of dustmen's boots and the tense trudging of tired tradesmen all too quick to discover that the shortest distance between two front doors was certainly not the three sides of a rectangle, the gardens had long since given up their pretensions along with their flowers and rose bushes and were now repositories for rusting mangles and anything with wheels which had ceased to function.

Number 57 differed from the others inasmuch as it boasted in its 'garden' a bust of William Shakespeare wearing a sou'-wester—at least that's who it looked like—but someone had snapped off his nose, rouged his cheeks and added a pair of horn-rimmed spectacles, to say nothing of a rude word, which doubtless would have warmed the cockles of the old bard's heart, scrawled in lipstick across his forehead—so it could have been anyone wearing a sou'wester; the latter article was ancient, discarded, made of oilskin and a product of the twentieth century.

'Vandals!' muttered Ob crossly, in whose mind there lingered no doubt as to the stonework's identity.

'Eh?'

'In the garden. Bill Shakespeare. Look what they've done to him.'

Harry regarded the bust without sympathy. 'After what he did to me in school he had it coming to him.' He pushed up his voice a notch or two and proceeded to declaim in an odd sing-song, 'O Mary, go and call the cattle home, And call the cattle home, And call the cattle home, Across the sands of Dee . . .'

Ob stared at him with curiosity. 'What's that got to do with it?'

'Shakespeare,' Harry told him, really believing it.

'My Aunt Fanny,' said Ob rudely.

'It is, too.'

'It's not, neither. Where does it come from, then? What play?'

'*Mary, Queen of Scots,*' replied Harry promptly.

The answer shook Ob for a moment and he stared narrowly at his companion with a doubt the size of a mustard-seed rattling away at the back of his head. The situation was saved by Harry saying, 'There's a man out there . . .'

'What?'

'Wants to make a phone call. He's standing around looking at his pennies.'

'He'll be lucky,' said Ob and grabbing at the instrument launched himself into a series of unconnected phrases and an unrehearsed selection of hideous grimaces which even Harry had never seen before.

'We can't stay here all day,' the latter pointed out. 'It's not *our* box. Why don't we go and walk around for a bit? I don't know why we came in here in the first place.'

'To case the joint,' Ob told him with a professional snap of his lips. 'If we keep standing around on the pavement and he happens to take a look out of his window and sees us he says to himself, "Ho, ho," he says, "what are those two up to? I'll have to be on my guard."'

'Ho, ho,' said Harry. 'You're a twit. Let's go, I'm suffocating.'

Ob hung up the instrument and pressed Button B; nothing came out, so when the waiting man surged up full of hope Ob shook his head sadly at him and told him the whole thing was out of order. The man's face fell.

'You can try though,' said Harry feeling sorry for him, 'but we even lost our money.'

They tramped off down the road giggling like a couple of schoolgirls.

It was almost a week before anyone caught so much as a glimpse of Red Brody. He seemed to have disappeared from the face of the earth. Harry and Ob found themselves at odd intervals loitering unobtrusively opposite the sou'-westered bust of Shakespeare, but nobody went in or came out of Number 57—nobody at all, not a moll or a mother or even a lodger. Nobody. Boy did the rounds of the cafés and pubs and coffee bars, occasionally caught sight of one or two of Red's mob, but found that a respectful distance was being observed between them; if he attempted to reduce that distance they somehow managed to fade into the background before he could approach them. It was really only Boy's persistence which kept the thing going at all. Harry and Ob became bored stiff with the whole affair.

Harry even drifted back to work for want of something better to do. He found himself well received by Mr. Cobb in whose estimation he had definitely risen and who mentioned in passing that though he had searched the medical books in his immediate orbit he had been unable to track down *Himblethroid Arthritis*. No, well, Harry had explained carefully, it had turned out not to be exactly an arthritic condition, but more of a sort of facial stroke—it had gone up into his friend's face and left him with funny sorts of scars. The doctors had been mystified too.

It was two days later when he was chuntering down Brook Street on the crown of the road, as usual, with irate traffic piling up behind him, that he noticed the large dove-grey Bentley reflected in his mirror—at least it was a registering of the Bentley's passenger rather than the car itself that persuaded him to push his van even more into the middle of the street. The reflection of the sky in the windscreen of the large car made it difficult for him to swear to the identity of the red-headed man in the passenger seat and that being the case there was only one way to find out for certain.

He reached over for his shiny-peaked cap and rammed it heavily over his ears like an idiot; then he stalled his engine and brought the vehicle to a sudden stop. Everyone else came to a sudden stop too—most of them on a sixpence—and the drivers, never very happy in their work, expressed exasperation for a moment or two on their horns. The Bentley's horn sounded like the *Queen Mary* leaving port. Having made certain that the oncoming traffic was thick and fast and that a large meat van, unloading sides of beef, was obstructing the nearside, Harry stuck out a hand and waved everybody on, which was not only ridiculous but caused a new outburst of concern from those behind to say nothing of several succinct unpleasantries. A schoolboy sped past on a bicycle but anything wider in the beam than he would have been hard put to it to make a successful passage. Harry clambered out of his cabin, stood for a second in the middle of the road, and stared thoughtfully at his van. Then he hit it hard with the flat of his hand, kicked it on the fender, turned to the waiting traffic, raised a pair of lumpy shoulders in a Latin gesture and waited . . . for two seconds . . .

Three resigned men, including Red Brody, climbed from their cars and, while Harry steered carefully around the meat van, laid their combined weight behind the van and pushed.

Harry rolled his eyes and delivered a torrent of theatrical

thanks; two of the men grunted and departed; Red Brody lingered for an amiable moment and said, 'Why don't you ... keep your ... van out of the middle of the ... road,' to which Harry replied, 'And the same to you,' and retired hastily to the comparative safety of his cabin. For a pregnant flick of time Red eyed him ungraciously then, mercifully for Harry, was recalled to the *Queen Mary* by a long blast on her siren.

Harry, sweating slightly, lay back in his seat and watched the lean grey shape flow past. The driver was smooth and dark-haired with a trim moustache, a cigar and a smart grey suit, and in no way to be confused with a chauffeur. There was something about the way the man sat and fondled the controls, and leaned and lounged and hooded his eyes which said, 'Have Car—Will Travel ... if it please *Me*.'

So thought Harry, depressed, Mack the Knife's in town once more. Here we go.

A small policeman stuck a large helmet into the cabin. 'You all right?'

'Hello, Charlie.'

'Eh?'

'Don't expect you remember me. Harry Stillwater? Friend of Ob's. Ob Harvey? Outside the pictures waiting for the birds?'

Charlie Bourne looked happy. 'Course I remember. How goes it? Everything all right here?'

Harry shrugged. 'I expect so. Bloody thing packed up all of a sudden right in the middle of the road—stalled—she's always doing it. Sorry if I upset the traffic.'

'You couldn't upset it more than it is.' He watched Harry pressing switches and turning knobs. 'They're electric these things, aren't they?'

'I suppose so. Don't ask me; we plug 'em in every night, I know that—if we remember. Coming up to see us sometime, then? Said you might.'

Charlie nodded. 'I'd like to sometime ... have a pint or so.' He paused and thought for a moment balancing himself on the balls of his little feet. 'Didn't I hear? ... Wasn't he bashed about some time back? Ob, I mean? Didn't someone have a go at him? Who told me now? Somebody told me ...'

'Fred, I expect ... your Fred Hearthbright.' He reminded Charlie of the salient facts. The little policeman nodded again. 'I remember. He thought he'd knocked someone over the

o

railings, didn't he? Well, he didn't, so far as we know . . . Well, I mean, he did, obviously he did because he saw him go, but what I mean is that there haven't been no repercussions of any sort—so far . . .'

'Like dead bodies, you mean?'

'Well, complaints and the like. Apparently he didn't even know who was responsible either, did he? Which is a pity. Like to nail some of them yobs. They get too much of it their own way. Well,' he looked up and down the street. 'I suppose you'd better be on the move or you'll never get the baby bathed—me neither. Have I got your phone number?'

'I don't know, have you?' Harry parted with his number which Charlie copied into his book, while passers-by looked apprehensively at Harry and wondered what he'd done.

'I'm in the book,' said Charlie.

'Under Millicent Johnson.'

'That's right; fancy you remembering. Millicent Johnson. Poor old girl. She had the place before us. She was in the R.S.P.C.A. Got bitten by a dog and passed over.'

'Go on?'

'Fact. Shows you, doesn't it?'

'Sure does.'

''Bye then. Regards to Ob.' He paused and nodded his head in the direction of the van's works. 'Does it go now, then?'

The motor whined. Harry raised a thumb at the little policeman and pulled out into the traffic.

When he got home that evening Fred was there chin-wagging with Ob. They both shut up like clams when Harry walked in.

'Hi,' said Harry.

'Ugh,' returned Ob.

'Glad to see you up and about,' said Fred getting up and shaking him heartily by the hand.

'And at work, what's more,' added Harry giving Ob the benefit of a glance laden with significance. 'Anything?' He meant was there anything doing down at the Labour Exchange; Ob knew exactly what he meant.

'No,' said Ob. 'Nothing.'

Harry said, 'Saw your mate today, Fred—Charlie Bourne—Number 99.'

'Millicent Johnson?' asked Ob.

'Don't joke about poor Millicent. She was eaten by a dog.'

They explained to Fred who Millicent Johnson was and Harry enlarged upon what had happened to the real Millicent Johnson which saddened them a little.

Then Harry said, 'Fred . . .'

'Yes, Harry,' said Fred.

'How's the stolen car racket going in this part of the world?'

Fred shot him a cautious look. 'Funny you should ask.'

'Why?'

'The Super was on about it this very morning.'

'Was he laughing?'

Fred looked very unhappy. 'He was just standing there blaming us. It's not our fault. These blokes are clever . . .' He broke off and pinned his tiny eyes on Harry's chin. 'I know what's on your mind, but it's bigger than him, you know.'

'Red Brody?' Fred nodded. 'Your super thinks it's a big thing, does he?'

'He does since his own car was swiped.'

'Go on?'

'Right under his nose. Nice Riley, red and white, in the square on a parking meter.'

Ob said, 'There's been a lot of it going on, has there?'

'More than I'm allowed to say. We know it must be organised because most of the vehicles aren't recovered.'

'Which means what?'

Fred made a face. 'New spray job, new numbers, the lot. Probably new log books and all. The cars that go aren't beaten-up jobs—they're usually pretty new—lower the mileage, the better the price.'

'What about the second-hand dealers? Have you checked on them?'

Fred thought for a moment. 'You see, they wouldn't be flogging them in this part of the world, would they? Stands to reason. You pinch a car down here, do her out in different colours, put new number plates on her and then take her up North to sell her—West, East—anywhere but here.'

Harry put in, 'But you're all organised for that sort of racket, aren't you? The police force, I mean. You don't all just work in your own little area. You must have some sort of connection with the other cop-shops up North and in Wales and so on . . . surely?'

'Course we do. But so many factors come into it. It's not all that easy. How long do they keep a car on ice, for instance, before they try to sell it? How honest is the man who buys it? Is he a dealer or is he private?'

He stopped and peered curiously at Harry. 'Why are you going on about this? You on to something?'

Harry shook his head. 'Everybody says Red's on a cushy racket, so why shouldn't it be a big racket run by big blokes who own big Bentleys?'

'Like who?'

'Like the bloke I saw him with this morning.'

There was a pause and Fred's eyes became smaller. 'In a big Bentley?'

'That's right. Beautiful long grey lovely Bentley.'

What was its number?'

'Number?'

Fred stared at him levelly. 'You don't mean to say you didn't get the number.'

Harry returned the stare sadly and shook his head. 'There you are,' he said. 'We need professional help.'

'So that you can go and break open a few heads.'

Harry was patient. 'We've been all over this, Fred. Stand on the side-lines with your helmet under your arm if you like and don't put it on 'til the whistle blows. I'll tell you this, if you're not along to see that things are done properly you really will have blood on your hands, and Boy Thing's the one that's going to spill it—I'm telling you.'

'Who is this Boy Thing? I don't know him.'

'That's not going to stop him laying into Red. He says he won't, but he will if he gets half a chance. You mark my words. Why don't you stop being stuffy just because you're in the bloody police force and be an ordinary chap like us. Be on our side.'

'I am on your side.'

'Prove it, then.'

CHAPTER EIGHTEEN

For good measure Fred brought Charlie Bourne in on it—probably in self-defence—and, under the beady, yellow eye of the imperturbable seagull on the mantelpiece a Council of War Extraordinary, presided over by Fred, took place in the sitting-room.

Harry, Jennifer, Ob and Maisie, Boy (whose surname turned out to be Blue), Charlie and Fred were present, the latter two in civilian clothes, Charlie looking like an off-duty croupier of the twenties. Actually it was not a particularly extraordinary council, firstly because there was not much of an extraordinary nature to council about and secondly because as the evening wore on the two girls found it increasingly difficult to concentrate. They were inclined to take a dim view of this method of spending their one-night-a-week-off.

So they sat around and drank beer and ate omelettes until an early hour and, though a *modus operandi* of sorts had been decided upon, most of them had forgotten what it was by the time the meeting broke up. In fact Charlie, who revealed himself to have no mean capacity for beer and less for carrying it with dignity, rang up the following morning with a delicate enquiry as to whether any significant decisions had been reached. 'It's unlike me,' he explained shakily, 'but I don't seem to be able to recall much of what went on at all. I was probably very tired.'

'Sloshed is the word,' Ob told him.

'Ah . . . yes, that too. I was all right though, wasn't I?'

'In what way?'

'Apart from being sloshed. I—er—behaved all right?'

'You sang a fair bit.'

'I'm inclined to do that. What?'

'Pardon?'

'What did I sing?'

'Gilbert and Sullivan mostly . . . and then there was *Drink to Me Only* and *Show Me the Way to Go Home* among quite a few others.'

There was a pause until Charlie enquired tentatively, 'I didn't by any chance render a ballad about a sailor and the Duchess of Mevagissey, did I?'

'Not that I can remember. How does it go?'

'I wouldn't like to have sung that—not in mixed company with the girls there.'

'It's choice, is it?'

'I can never remember it when I'm sober, but my wife didn't care for it when I sang it to her once.'

Ob told him about the motions carried during the meeting and the axes that were ground and the arguments which had ensued and Charlie hung up, still with a headache but less confused.

The decision to carry the war into the enemy's camp, which is what it had all been about, was a boring one for most people since, in the first place, not many of them were particularly interested and in the second place no one had the faintest idea where the enemy's camp was to be located. Number 57, they had unanimously decided, though being the lair of Red Brody was unlikely to be the headquarters of a profitable car-stealing organisation—if, in fact, one existed.

The difficulty they were up against was that none of them knew exactly what they were up against. The idea of breaking Red and his mob and putting them out of business was an admirable one, to be nourished and led carefully through an uncertain period of gestation, but what the business was and where it was to be found were two ingredients which threatened it with still-birth. Only Boy Blue had fought their apathy; he had beaten it out in a relentless rhythm on the arm of his chair, slopping his beer in the process, he had raised his voice in a moving plea recalling to their minds the helpless Con lying prostrate in hospital never to look the same again as long as she lived, he had flung a dramatic finger at the ugly scars scrawled across Ob's disfigured face; as a law-abiding and tax-paying citizen—though in point of fact he was neither—he had even challenged the police force, in the redoubtable persons of Fred and Charlie, to search their consciences, if there was room for them beneath those 'terrible pointed helmets', and then say: 'Nothing can be done.'

He had lain back breathing heavily for a moment or two then with a great effort raised a leather-clad arm. 'You can't,' he intoned in the voice of one about to be guillotined, 'not do nothing about it,' and dropped off to sleep.

After that it had been the turn of the others to lie back and breathe heavily, which they did for several minutes, Maisie watching the sprawled sleeping figure with an avid lust in her eye. 'He's so lovely,' she sighed dreamily and then turned on Ob who had been on the point of nodding off himself, 'Why can't *you* be lovely like him?'

The result of Boy's oratorical rarity was that it carried the girls away, which of course meant that Harry and Ob were obliged to go along too, leaving the police force to tag behind or sever connections—whichever course was dictated to them by the esoteric thumpings under their helmets. The vote was unanimous, and it was then that the girls went out into the kitchen and prepared the omelettes.

Now that Red had returned from wherever he had been they experienced little difficulty in keeping an eye on him; he had made no secret of his comings and goings and went and came with monotonous regularity to the most boring places. Bars, clubs, dives, cafés, billiard saloons and fun palaces—all were included in his sphere of movement within the first two days.

The watchers managed to sort themselves out into a sort of rota whereby Red remained under someone's surveillance during the entire period that he was away from Number 57; even Fred and Charlie had been persuaded to volunteer their help between spells of duty and of course in heavy disguise.

If Red was in a racket of any kind he would sooner or later have to get on with it, and if he were on somebody's pay-roll the chances were that eventually he would gravitate towards that someone in order to sign on the dotted line. That was the theory, but for the first two days it just sat up on its hind legs and appeared determined to disprove Euclid himself.

The first day the shiftless Red did nothing at all but wander from bar to café, from café to billiard saloon, lolling, lounging, spitting and scratching his tight-jeaned bottom. During that day his shadows consisted of Ob for three hours, Charlie and Fred two each, Boy for three and when Harry finished work in the late afternoon he and Ob took over the evening shift.

Ob was jaded and grumpy and not the best of companions,

but when Red disappeared down the red-lit entrance-pit of a strip-club things seemed to take a turn for the better.

'We'll have to go in, too, won't we?'

'It'll be expensive,' Harry mentioned.

'Ah,' said Ob.

The place was called the *Hot Spot* and announced in fiery letters a 'searing' cabaret entitled *Nudes of a Feather*. They stood outside for a couple of seconds peering short-sightedly at curling photographs of various birds in and out of several sets of unexpected and peculiar garments.

Neither of them had ever actually been into one of these establishments and both felt an uneasy stirring of anticipation as with heavy masculine step they loped down the steep, uncarpeted stairs towards a red velvet curtain behind which the *forte* part of a piano was being pulverised by a pair of inexpert fists which could only be wearing boxing-gloves.

No, said the young lady in an alarming, low-slung confection of black velvet, who sat dispiritedly beneath a red lamp which made the narrow compartment she occupied look like a photographer's dark-room, it was not necessary for them to be members but they would naturally have to pay the special entrance fee for non-members which of course would entitle them to honorary membership for that particular night only.

'How much?' demanded Harry.

'Four pounds, please.' The young lady's 's' was sibilant.

'Pardon?' That was Ob rearing in dismay.

The young lady raised a cold eye and a white lip in his direction and toyed tantalisingly with the plunge of her dress with the tip of a silver-taloned finger. 'Two pounds each, sir.' The sibilant 's' hissed at them like a white cobra guarding the entrance to Nefertiti's tomb.

Parting with four crisp notes Harry felt inconsolable, blamed Ob for the whole sordid business and knew perfectly well that nothing which was likely to occur behind that red velvet curtain was going to be worth four smackers.

They plunged down three steps, through the velvet curtain, and stumbled down a further two. They stood still with apprehension and allowed the place to hit them, which it did, with the smell of cheap scent and disinfectant, tobacco smoke, carbolic soap, and, most prevalent of all, male sweat.

'Just like home,' groaned Ob.

Nobody came to help them find four pounds' worth of seating accommodation so they waited patiently until their eyes became a trifle more accustomed to the gloom then edged their way in behind a table near the wall. A glowing red spot of light on a small platform at the far end of the room was, for the moment, unoccupied. From the next table they came under the close scrutiny of a heavy woman dressed in tweeds and a moustache; she flashed a set of gold teeth at her companion, a frail frightened English Rose who cowered before the onslaught, and muttered something derogatory about the newcomers.

'I'll bash her bloody gold teeth down her gullet,' promised Ob grittily.

There were a couple of handclaps, two or three pounding chords on the invisible piano, and the red spot on the platform became occupied by a lady in long gloves, long boots, a scarlet mask and three strategically-placed tassels.

So the entertainment commenced and the evening dragged along with it—one of unutterable boredom and unmitigated puerility which unfortunately had to be experienced to be believed. Two rashly-ordered whiskies set Harry back twenty shillings, he therefore switched to beers which cost three shillings each; when a sinewy Italianate girl came over and perched herself uninvited at their table and ordered a champagne-cocktail, Ob suggested to her convincingly that she should 'beat it'.

Three tables away Red sat alone and stared ahead of him with stony eyes. Nobody approached him, no one spoke to him—even the little hostesses who lurched from table to table ordering champagne-cocktails at fifteen shillings a go seemed to make a point of avoiding him, and it soon became apparent that this assiduous disregard was the result of an accepted familiarity rather than a deliberate attempt at the cold-shoulder. With the waitresses who brought him unordered and certainly unspecified drinks in obedience to his lifted hand he exchanged neither words nor money.

'He hasn't paid for a bloody thing yet,' observed Harry. 'It's all been on the house. Everybody else gets lumbered with the open palm on delivery but not him. What do you make of that?'

'Friendies with the owner.'

'Right. And whoever owns it must make quite a packet. I wouldn't say his expenses are high, would you, but there's a fair amount of the old mazooma going in the opposite direction at this very moment.' At that moment Red, burrowing in his pockets, discovered an empty cigarette packet and snapping his fingers at a passing floozy bearing a sales-tray around her neck helped himself to a fresh packet without so much as a by-your-leave or thank you or here's-ten-bob-keep-the-change. 'There, did you see, even cigarettes are for free. Friends in low places all right.'

The only time Red woke up and took a bit more notice of what was going on around him was when a dusky-hued female with a fair amount of Eastern promise came and performed a belly-dance not two feet from the end of his nose; she wore an Oriental bangle and a glass jewel inserted into her navel. With slow insidious sensuality she rolled and coiled and undulated in front of him whilst he stared hypnotised at the glass jewel in her navel. Harry wondered whether it was telling him anything. He remembered seeing a television play where the jewel in a dancer's navel transmitted radio signals to enemy submarines lurking in the Channel. He watched Red's little pig eyes and decided that if anything was being transmitted he was doing a damn good job of keeping it to himself.

'Oh mate,' said Ob, suddenly holding his head, 'I could have done without this tonight.'

'Headache?'

'I used to giggle about this sort of thing when I was at school.'

Shortly after the belly-dancer's final convolution Red lurched unsteadily to his feet and set a shaky course for the Gents which was called '*Chaps*'.

'Get after him,' muttered Ob in an urgent hiss.

Harry shot him a startled look. '*You* get after him.'

'Don't be a nit. He knows me. Suppose there's a way out through there?—suppose it's the way to the manager's office . . .'

'Funny place to put the manager's office.'

Unwillingly Harry clambered to his feet and leaning low over Ob breathed as many beer fumes as he could muster into his friend's face. 'If I'm not back in three minutes . . .'

'I'll run a mile,' finished Ob unsympathetically.

'What you don't seem to realise,' pressed Harry, 'is that he knows me, too. I met him in Fat Doris's caff that Saturday, remember? And what's more he could easily have picked me out at *The Elbow Room* that night too ...' The heavy lady in tweeds was craning in their direction, ears flapping. Harry stopped and looked at her. 'Can I help you?' he asked coldly.

She flashed a gold smile at him. 'Oh dear, I do so wish you could.' Her rumbling masculine overtones were unperturbed. 'These things are sent to try us, aren't they? It's an uphill battle all the way, there's no doubt about that. What's your name?'

'Mary,' snarled Harry and set his helm for *Chaps*.

As he pushed the door Red was on the other side pulling. They came face to face. Though Red's eyes were glazed and bloodshot a glimmer of recognition glinted its way into his consciousness.

'Flash.'

'Red,' said Harry, deciding to bluff it out. But he didn't have to.

'How goes it, Flash?'

'Beaut, Red, beaut! You?'

'Dandy, dandy. See you, Flash.'

Harry stood up against a wall for a dazed moment in the dark interior of *Chaps* and then sallied forth once again into the bright lights.

Ob was on his feet. 'He's gone.' He turned to the heavy lady. 'Good night, Arthur,' he said.

'Good night dear. Good night, Mary, and good luck.' Once again she was in danger of losing her teeth.

'Jesus,' exploded Harry as they emerged into the clean air. 'Arthur!'

'That's her name, so she told me,' said Ob. '"Call me Arthur" she said when you'd gone. "She's sweet, isn't she—" "Who?" I said. "Mary" she said—meaning you.'

Harry's fists clenched. 'I'll go and bash her bloody teeth in.'

Ob laid a restraining hand on his coat collar. 'Later. He's just gone round the corner.'

'Who has?'

'Who do you think?'

They sauntered slowly around the corner into a narrow alley which sported the so-called Artist's Entrance of the *Hot Spot* —at least it *had* been called the Artist's Entrance but a skilful felt-tipped pen had been at work and it was now called 'Tart's' Entrance.

Red and the Belly-Dancer were doing a quiet bit of snogging on the pavement, so Harry and Ob faded into the shadows until it was over.

'Fab,' Red was saying in a frothy voice as they passed the concealed watchers. 'Fab bod you've got. I could watch it all night.'

'And probably will too,' groaned Ob as if in pain.

Harry stared after the retreating pair. 'Perhaps that bit of glass in her belly-button gave off signals after all.'

'What shall we do now?' asked Ob, as if he hadn't been giving the orders all evening.

'I'll give you three guesses what *they're* going to do,' Harry invited, 'and one what I'm going to do. What are you going to do?'

'Come with you.'

'Good.' He sucked his teeth ruminatively. 'Let's go and make ourselves a nice healthy cup of Ovaltine.'

Ob wavered. 'Shall we go and bash old Arthur on the bonce first?'

'No,' said Harry, taking him firmly by the arm. 'Home.'

The events of the following day with regard to the progress of Red Brody were conceived upon much the same unimaginative lines as those of its predecessor. With true professional zeal Fred and Charlie insisted upon keeping a log book—(a pattern, explained the former, might reveal itself)—the perusal of which offered about as much excitement as an account of the sex-life of plankton captive in a plastic bucket of tap-water. The police force was undisturbed, pointing out that the major part of every investigation consisted of dull, footslogging routine, for which the only prizes were blisters, flat feet and an irate nature—not quite the impression conveyed by the average detective story.

That evening found Harry and Ob cowering in the darkest corner of a 'queer' club where the Gents was called '*Buoys*' and the waiters, dressed as sailors, were called 'Miss'. Since neither of them had particularly gone in for a study of homosexuality but had learned to accept and understand it as something which could happen to other people, they found it now not a little disturbing to realise that a fair amount of girlish gossip was being indulged in with reference to themselves. Eyes ogled and hips swayed and various hissing invitations were levelled at them.

With a dispassionate eye Ob regarded two enormous males lounging at the bar who looked as though they might be lorry drivers or stevedores—tough, blue-jowled, bicepped and heavily masculine.

'You wouldn't believe it, would you, not if you didn't see it with your own eyes.'

Harry said, 'Perhaps they're detectives like us.'

Ob made a rude noise.

As on the previous evening, Red Brody sat alone knocking back whiskies for which he didn't pay; this time, however, they noticed that he was keeping an eye on his watch.

'Waiting for someone,' opined Harry. 'Got an appointment, perhaps.'

In this club, mercifully, there was no cabaret so everybody just sat and whispered at one another, and there were covert glances and sighs and an inordinate amount of giggling.

The hideousness of the evening reached its climax when Arthur, with her girl friend in her wake, plodded in and pounced joyfully upon Harry and Ob as though the desire for their companionship was the one thing which had kept her going since the previous night.

'Can Winnie and me sit here, darlings? Hello, *Mary* dear, and how are *we* this evening? How *lovely* to run into you both again. I was only saying to Winnie this morning how *funny* it was that we hadn't seen *either* of you before. One gets so *bored* with the *old* crowd, and my *dears,* in *this* place *they—are—* the absolute bottoms, if you *know* what I mean.'

'Have a drink?' suggested Ob, looking sideways at Harry, because it was Harry who happened to have the money.

'Lovely, Bloody Mary's both of us . . .' She banged Harry on the chest and giggled. 'Pardon me for taking your name in vain.'

Harry would have dearly loved to bang her on the chest, too, but old-fashioned scruples about banging even half-ladies on the chest prevailed, so he smirked sourly instead and looked around for a waiter.

'There's Edna,' cried Arthur. 'Call *her* over. She's the tops.'

She raised her voice and bawled 'Edna!' in a stout baritone and a gentle-looking sailor with hurt brown eyes and a sensitive mouth shimmied over to the table. Arthur gave her order gruffly and Edna went off. '*Isn't* she a poppet? Much the nicest of them *all* in this *den* of iniquity.' She frowned at Winnie, who had done nothing at all, and inquired of them both. 'Have you been here before?'

At that moment Red Brody got up and went into 'Buoys'. Ob looked meaningly at Harry. Harry shook his head. Ob said in a sepulchral whisper. 'Don't be a nit. He might give us the slip that way.'

Arthur's great head loomed between them, 'Who are you after, dearies, which one?'

Harry could have clumped her one on her great fat ear, which was no more than three inches away from his right eye. He glared at Ob, pondering for a moment on the possibility of biting off the lobe of Arthur's ear, then lurched to his feet.

It was very nearly a repeat performance. Red was combing his sparse coarse hair when Harry pushed his way into 'Buoys' and they peered blindly at each other in the spotty mirror. Red turned slowly and with comb poised continued his staring with narrowed eyes.

'Flash again ... well, well, well ...' A tinge of suspicion coloured his tone.

Harry managed to pitch his voice into a high squeak of surprise, 'Red ... hi!' then diving into the one and only cubicle he hastily bolted the door.

Beneath the door he watched the pair of feet, pointed cowboy boots with high heels ...

'Flash ...'

'Red?'

The voice was thin. 'You following me, Flash?'

Harry swallowed. 'Me?'

'Who else?'

'Why would I be doing that, Red?'

'You tell me, Flash.'

'No, Red, don't be a nut. Of course I'm not. Couple of nights running we just happen to be in the same dives that's all.'

'Like a coincidence?'

'That's it—like a coincidence.'

There was a pause.

'Funny, though.'

'Yes, funny.'

Harry sat down gingerly and stared miserably at the nasty pair of boots under the door. Attack was his only means of defence.

'Red? You still there?' Still there! The boots had taken root.

'Yes, Flash, I'm still here.'

'Have a drink with me, Red, I'd like that.'

Another pause then he heard the zip of Red's leather jacket.

'No, ta, Flash, I got to go. 'Nother time, eh, Flash?'

'Right, Red, look forward to that. Tara.'

Red burped loudly. 'Tara, Flash.'

The boots gritted away and Harry nearly cried with relief as he heard the compressed air hiss of the closing door. He didn't have to examine his brow to know that it was damp.

'I hate,' he said to himself, 'bloody Ob!'

When he finally released himself from the cubicle it was still with the fear that Red might be lying in wait for him. He was alone. He glared accusingly at himself in the mirror. 'Coward,' he said.

Ob was on his feet when he got back to the table and Arthur was complaining about everybody wanting to go the moment she arrived.

'I'm fed up,' muttered Harry darkly as they stumbled out into the rain. 'Fed bloody up! I nearly lost my life down there, do you know that, and if you know it, do you bloody care? Not on your Nelly you don't! Every time I go into one of those places it's like going over the top. "You following me, Flash?" he says and you only have to hear him say it to know he's got a bicycle chain wrapped round his ruddy mitt.'

'Who's Flash?'

'What?'

'Flash. Who's Flash?'

'He calls me Flash.'

'Why?'

Ob's hand on his forearm prevented his reply. Red was standing under a lamp waiting to cross the road.

'Be careful, for God's sake,' muttered Harry. 'He's getting suspicious—he thought I was following him.'

It was still only about half past ten and the traffic was pretty heavy—they managed to lurch and leap between oncoming vehicles as they followed their quarry across the road.

'Why does he call you Flash?'

'How the hell do I know.'

'Perhaps he thinks you're someone else?'

'No, he thinks I'm me. He always calls me Flash.'

Red paused for a moment lighting a cigarette, and Harry and Ob fell over each other into a shop doorway when he suddenly turned and looked in their direction.

'I can't stand this,' grumbled Harry, glaring at a large glass bottle of pink boiled sweets in the shop window.

At the clock tower Red came to a final standstill and took up the stance of someone waiting. The clock boomed out the half hour. Harry and Ob lurked in the doorway of Boots the Chemist, which afforded a great deal more shelter than did the clock tower.

'He's getting wet,' said Ob.

'Good, I hope he bloody drowns.'

And suddenly Charlie was there beside them in glistening cape and dripping helmet with a lighted torch in his hand.

'Hello,' greeted Harry. 'Don't we have more than two coppers in our police force? This isn't your beat, is it?'

Charlie nodded. 'I come up there, round here and down there into Havelock Street. What's doing? You working or just on the prowl?'

Ob nodded at Red over the road. 'Sir is waiting at the clock tower.'

Charlie switched his light out and cowered back into the shadows.

'What's been happening tonight—anything?'

'Do you know *The Happy Hunting Ground*?' asked Ob.

'The queer club?'

'That's what's been happening tonight.'

'Blimey,' said Charlie, 'I had to go there once—it's quite a dump, isn't it?'

'Who did *you* go as,' asked Ob, 'Millicent Johnson?'

Charlie snorted with amusement. 'Poor old Millicent. Don't be unkind about her. No, we did a raid on it one night, picked up a bloke who was flogging purple hearts and things, but I don't think we actually got what we were after, whatever that was, don't ask me what it was 'cos I don't know—ours but to do and die, you know.'

'I know,' said Harry miserably and with feeling.

He suddenly caught sight of a long grey Bentley moving slowly in their direction.

'That's it, there it is,' he cried excitedly. 'That's the Bentley and the bloke behind the wheel's the same one. I bet he's picking Red up.'

Sure enough, the Bentley slowed down as it approached the clock tower situated in the middle of a traffic roundabout.

Ob groaned. 'Now what? If he gets in that we've lost him.'

'Get a cab,' said the professional Charlie. 'Got some money?' He dived in his pocket and fished out a pound note. 'Here, that'll help. Sorry I can't come. Grab a cab and tail them.' Harry took the money. 'If you get into any trouble call the cop-shop, right? Our one, Queen's Road, okay?'

They were across the road and standing on the island by the time the Bentley pulled away smoothly from the kerb with Red lounging back beside the driver. Ob waved frantically at a taxi-cab which lurched towards them with all the frenzy of the mills of God.

Ob wrenched open the door. 'Follow that car,' he yelled, indicating the departing Bentley with a wild gesture as he leapt into the cab's interior. Harry leapt in after him, slammed the door and they waited expectantly. The taxi-driver pushed down his little glass panel and looked at them—he was a lugubrious man with a cloth cap and long moustache, and had a dead cigarette stuck on his lower lip.

'Which car?'

Ob knelt passionately on the floor in front of the glass panel. 'That one, the big grey one.'

'The Rolls, you mean?'

'Bentley.'

'I 'ope you're joking. Follow a Bentley in this! You couldn't keep up with a push-bike in this thing.'

The long grey Bentley was fast disappearing into the mêlée of traffic.

Harry joined Ob on the floor. 'Try, will you? Double fare if you keep it in sight.'

'This is police business,' said Ob with a flash of inspiration.

'Get away,' said the man, revving up his engine and releasing his clutch with a jerk which sent the two of them on their backs. 'You're not cops, are you?'

'I didn't say we were,' spluttered Ob, 'We're Foreign Office.'

Harry's jaw dropped, and the cabby's foot fell on to the accelerator. 'My Gawd,' he said, 'spies, eh? Whacko! 'ere we go then.'

He crouched over the wheel and the old cab seemed suddenly to take wing, threading its way through the traffic with the deadly precision of a homing missile.

The driver leaned back against the glass and spoke through the corner of his mouth. 'Who's up front there, then? Goldfinger?'

'His name's Schmidt,' Ob told him.

''Un, eh? Bosche? They never learn, do they? And you're the Men from Auntie, are you?' That made him yell with laughter. His long sad moustache seemed to curl up the other way and become possessed with a madness unexperienced since that memorable day when he had lobbed a hand-grenade on to the nose of a Messerschmidt 109 from the beaches of Dunkirk.

It soon became plain that the Bentley was heading out towards Oakhaven and, luckily for them, was taking her time about it. Once the main part of the traffic had been left behind there was no difficulty in keeping her in sight, she hummed along at about forty-five whilst the rattling old cab behind champed and snorted like an armour-plated war-horse.

'My name's 'Arry,' yelled the driver.

'So's mine,' said Harry.

'Go on? Any idea where we're off to?'

Ob joined in. 'Probably only going to Oakhaven. When he pulls up go on past him and round the next corner if it's not too far. Otherwise give him about fifty yards. Okay?'

'You're the guv,' cried 'Arry. 'Is he dangerous?'

'Very.'

'Gun?'

'What?'

'Will 'e 'ave a gun?'

Ob and Harry looked at each other. Harry said, 'He's got one of those cyanide guns.'

'Gawd!' said 'Arry and leaned over his wheel.

Ob muttered, 'What's a cyanide gun?'

'I don't know. Shoots cyanide, I suppose.'

As they approached Oakhaven the Bentley swung away from the sea-front and plunged into the network of smaller streets all of which led to the centre of the little suburb where the fairground was situated, and it was at the rear entrance of this that the Bentley finally came to rest. 'Arry roared past the stationary vehicle, swept adroitly around the next corner, and drew up with a clatter.

The clock said eight-and-sixpence. Harry pressed Charlie's pound note into the driver's hand, who sat spent and panting over his wheel and said, 'Can you hang on for a bit? We might want to go back.'

'We *will* want to go back,' affirmed Ob.

'Can't I help?' asked 'Arry. 'I'm 'andy with me dukes.'

Harry put a firm hand on his arm. 'Keep out of it if you value your life.'

They doubled back to the corner to find that the Bentley was nowhere in sight; moving cautiously to the locked gate of the Fun Fair they could see the glare of its headlights threading its way between the kiosks and roundabouts.

As if all this was second nature to them the two moved forward examining the surrounding fence for a possible break. It was not much of a fence and soon they came to a point where a couple of the iron stanchions had been bent apart leaving enough room for the admittance of one average-sized child. Harry was horrified as he saw Ob seize hold of one of the stanchions, take the strain, grit his teeth and pull. The iron just bent. Then he did the same to the other.

'Blimey,' murmured Harry in awe, 'Can I have a go?'

He did and nothing happened, but the gap was already large enough to admit them. They moved quietly. There was no way of telling whether there was a nightwatchman on duty or even a savage dog or two on the prowl. The strange, tarpaulined shapes of the usual fairground amenities loomed up above and around them. A monotonous creaking and groaning came from the direction of the swings where one of the boats, having come adrift, swung to and fro in the high wind. The canvas roof of a shooting-booth flapped loudly against its supporting spars. With the high scream of the wind and the continuous sludge and beat of the rain it needed little imagination to create the illusion of being aboard a sailing vessel on the high seas.

The light from the nearby street-lamps was sufficient for them to pick their way with little difficulty but greater care through the complicated maze of ropes and spars and stalls and unexpected hazards like painted barrels full of wooden balls for coconut-shies, tent-pegs, and waist-high signposts indicating the direction to be taken for various public services and the like.

Away to their right a torch flashed and a voice shouted. Another answered and someone laughed.

'Watchman,' hissed Ob.

The glow of the Bentley's headlamps led them through a creaking collection of silent caravans, none of which seemed to be occupied. They skirted the large roundabout and though it was draped about with tarpaulin were able to catch a glimpse now and again of the magnificent prancing horses gleaming in their magical colours and blazing brasswork. On each side of the tarpaulin was painted the words *Morton's Amusements.*

The sudden revving of the Bentley's engine brought them to a halt and all at once the lights were doused. Doors banged, feet crunched over stones, then there was silence. They strained their ears through the battering of the elements to catch any further sound of human origin, but none came.

It took them less than a minute to locate the big grey limousine reclining aristocratically under a canvas awning. Ducking beneath the shelter they stood for a second or two, half deafened by rain beating on the canvas, and peered through the dripping fringe of water.

Immediately ahead of them and facing the car's radiator was a green-painted door with *Private* painted on it. There seemed to be nowhere else in the immediate vicinity where their quarry could have gone. They looked at each other, nodded and moved off. Their feet encountered pebbles and they froze as the crunching sound seemed to tear the night apart. However, nobody else's night appeared to have been affected and after a couple of moments of tense immobility they started off again.

The door was firmly locked; the brass disc of a yale-lock gleamed in the dim light. Ob made a peculiar sign with his head which Harry didn't understand but he fell in behind and followed his companion as he edged his way around the small brick building keeping carefully to the narrow verge of grass which clung to its walls. Together they pressed their faces up against a dark window and waited until their eyes prepared something for them to look at. When eventually it arrived it was no more than a dynamo looming, still and silent, in the darkness.

Ob leaned in to Harry. 'Their private power-house. They must need it with all this lot.'

Harry nodded. He understood that; what he didn't understand was why Red and his companion should have gone to visit a dynamo and even if they had, where had they got to now?

'Who wants to go and sit with a dead dynamo?' he enquired.

Ob repeating the gesture with his head which Harry was now interpreting as 'Follow me' and led the way along the wall to the farther end of the little building. They could see now that it backed on to another, larger structure with which it presumably had communication and which, after a careful circuit of the entire block, revealed itself to be a sturdily-constructed rectangular building of light-coloured brick against three walls of which were backed various small booths housing such innocuous sideshows as hoop-la, shove-ha'penny, fortune-telling and so on. The building itself, according to a faded painted notice-board nailed to its only door, purported to contain facilities for maintenance work, but if any maintenance work had gone on there during recent weeks it was certainly not with the active assistance of that door—several months, if not years, had elapsed since a key had been turned in the rusted padlock with which it was secured. Ob squinted closely at the padlock, shook it gently and appeared, for a second, to be listening to it.

'Is it ticking?' asked Harry.

Ob shook his head. 'Never bust that in a month of Sundays.'

He stood back and surveyed the building with frustrated eyes. Harry had noticed the top few rungs of an iron ladder glinting at the far end of the wall, and he was hoping that Ob wouldn't. His hopes were dashed when Ob touched his arm, pointed to the ladder and moved along the wall towards it.

The foot of the ladder was set at the rear of a photographic booth which announced that it would give you three prints for one shilling. *Developed and printed by Professional Photographer on the premises,* it boasted. *Come in for a Sitting—*

Have it done Now and Make the Family Laugh. Thank you very much, thought Harry, take my picture and make the family laugh!

Inside the booth the darkness was complete.

'We can't stamp around in the dark,' complained Harry, 'We'll knock everything over.'

'Got any matches?'

'You know I don't smoke.'

Ob thought, then said slowly, 'If they print their photographs on the spot they must have a dark-room, yes?'

'So?'

'And if there's a dark-room the chances are there might be a torch somewhere around.'

'Why?' enquired Harry sarcastically. 'So that they can find the light switch?'

At that moment his groping hands touched a solid door set in the lath and plaster wall. 'There's a door here. Hang on, don't go away. It might be the dark-room. I'll see if there's a light.'

He ducked through the door, closed it and explored the wall for a light switch. Next moment he was almost blinded by the dim red glow of a photographer's lamp. Ob had been right. It was a dark-room.

Harry pondered for a moment over the peculiar collection of drying prints hung with pegs on to a clothes line; there were grinning, toothy children, and self-conscious adults all looking as though they had been photographed by surprise at the London Airport. Harry's heart felt heavy for them as his eyes wandered around the tiny red claustrophobic cubicle. Sitting almost immediately beneath the red lamp was a hefty, rubber-cased Ever Ready torch.

He grabbed it and returning to Ob, who hadn't moved a muscle since his disappearance, pushed the torch into his hand.

Ob was startled. 'What's that?'

'What does it feel like?'

'There you are,' said Ob, 'told you so, didn't I?'

A few seconds later they were clambering up on to the roof. It was a flat, sunken affair of cracked concrete with a square skylight in the centre. They gravitated towards this and squatting on either side of it peered gloomily into Stygian blackness.

'If there's anything going on down there they're making a

damn good job of keeping it to themselves,' grumbled Harry always ready to give up. 'It couldn't be darker, could it?'

Ob's voice sounded a trifle irate. 'Well, they couldn't just have disappeared into thin air, could they?'

'Oh, I don't know,' Harry growled unhelpfully.

'Gather round,' said Ob. 'I'm going to risk the torch.' He cupped the business end of the big torch in his hands and directed the beam down through the grimy glass.

Maintenance work, the board had said, and maintenance work was what to all intents and purposes had obviously gone on there. Two long benches littered with mechanical odds and ends stretched the full length of two of its walls. Immediately beneath them a horse from the roundabout lay on its side with a broken leg, beside it a model car of the type to be seen on small children's merry-go-rounds; there were wheels and cogs and axles and staves and spars, painted canvases, booth walls, broken wooden chairs, pots of paint, buckets—all of them slimed over with a thick layer of dust and filth. It was all of the past. As the padlock on the door had suggested, the place was abandoned. Decay and disintegration was everywhere ... and yet ... at one end was a fairly clean strip of carpet. And there was a door, and that door communicated with the small power-house—it had to, there was nothing on the other side of that wall *but* the power-house—and the strip of narrow, fairly clean carpet ran from the door to the head of what looked like a spiral staircase.

Ob doused the light.

'They're underneath this place,' he said, an edge of excitement to his voice. 'That's where they are, underneath. Did you see that spiral staircase? They go through the power-house, through that other door and down the staircase. How about that?'

After a moment Harry said, 'I've proved it tonight, Ob, I've proved it.'

'Proved what?'

'That I'm a coward. I don't want to go any further, Ob, if it's all the same to you. I sat in that lavatory and sweated blood until he had gone. I thought then that I was a coward, now I know.'

'What the hell are you talking about?'

'About me being a coward.'

'Until who had gone?'

'Red—in the lavatory.'

Ob was heaving strenuously at the cover of the skylight. 'This isn't properly fastened. We could get down there and have a closer look at everything.'

It was just as though he hadn't even been listening.

Harry sent up a belated prayer and decided to leave it at that. There wouldn't be anything worse than death ... except, of course, slow death. There was that beam of blue light which burnt through toughened steel in *Goldfinger* and nearly burnt through James Bond too! That was pretty nasty and something he wouldn't care to have to face. Still, perhaps Red and his cronies wouldn't have one of those—they probably came expensive. But little cages of hungry rats which fitted over your face weren't very expensive. Anyone could afford a little cage and a couple of rats ...

'What?' he asked as Ob said something.

'Give us a hand, I said. What's up with you? Are you still with me?'

'Are you quite sure,' asked Harry as a last stand, 'that you know what we're doing?'

'You *have* got the wind up, haven't you?'

'Yes, I have, haven't you?'

'Course I have.'

'Why don't we go home, then?'

'Just now! When everything's beginning to pay off?'

'We could ring up the cop-shop and tell old Fred or someone. They could come over in their helmets and arrest everybody and there wouldn't be any nastiness. How do you know what they might do to us if they caught us? Nobody would miss us. Nobody even knows we're here.'

'The taxi-driver does.'

'That's another thing, ticking away out there. It'll cost the earth and I haven't got the earth to spare.'

'Shut up.'

'Charming. Come on, then. I'm cold.'

'Yellow, you mean.'

'That's right, yellow, but at least I'm still alive.'

'We've got to go through with this.' He broke off with a warning hiss. 'Look!'

A glow of light was manifesting itself in the corner of the

building where they had noted the staircase. They flattened themselves against the roof and watched.

The light grew brighter and presently resolved itself into a hurricane lamp which had been adapted to battery power. It was carried by Red Brody. The man preceding him was the grey-suited, sleek-moustached driver of the Bentley. Reaching the head of the staircase they stood for a couple of seconds, their shadows, huge and black, lurching over the walls of the dilapidated building. The watchers could hear the low murmur of voices without being able to discern anything that was said. They moved finally to the door where the man in grey, with a hand on the latch, looked pointedly at the lamp in Red's hand. Red placed it on the floor and extinguished it. The muffled click of a latch, a momentary silence, then the dull thud of a closing door; the crunch of feet on gravel, slamming car-doors and suddenly the whole landscape was illuminated as the Bentley's huge headlamps came into play. Safe though they were on the roof, Harry and Ob pressed themselves into the cracked concrete.

The big car's engine burst into life, roared for a moment then settled down to a gentle, dreamy purr. They crawled to the edge of the roof and peered over. The long fingers of light probed out across the broken ground swinging slowly and steadily across the entire length of the amusement park; the gravel crunched closely beneath the wheels as the long grey shape slid back the way she had come.

'I wouldn't mind that old heap,' muttered Ob in Harry's ear.

Out of the darkness came the figure of a man in shining oilskins and stood for a second in the beam of the headlights; the car drew alongside him, a few words were exchanged, then the figure moved again into the light, opened the gates and waved the driver through. The red rearlamps flicked twice, dimmed, flicked again and then followed the long streams of silver light into the darkness.

The two watchers heard the slam of the gates and watched the faint blur of moving shadow as the man in oilskins moved towards them for a moment and then was swallowed up in the surrounding blackness.

'Bloody nightwatchman,' grunted Ob.

'Let's go home,' said Harry.

'Pipe down,' Ob told him.

By dint of hanging for a suspended moment and swinging his legs a couple of times, Ob was able to pitch himself in the general direction of a lumpy-looking mattress they had located by torchlight from the skylight. The cloud of dust which greeted his falling body would have done a North American Indian smoke-signaller proud. It billowed with a great bound of new-found freedom up the bright beam of torchlight held in Harry's hand, and Harry, starting back to avoid its onslaught, stuck his elbow through a pane of glass. The splinters showered Ob below.

'Oi!' protested Ob.

'You all right?'

'Stop messing about. Lower yourself slowly and put your feet on my shoulders. Okay? And lets have the torch.'

Harry said, 'You sure you want me down there? I could stay up here and keep watch.'

'Torch,' said Ob not listening again.

A few seconds later Harry was balancing on Ob's shoulders like an inebriated circus performer, and after an energetic series of intimate embraces found himself breathless on floor level again beside his stalwart companion. He swore violently into the darkness.

'What's up?'

'This'll end in tears, I know it will.'

The beam of the torch picked up the hurricane lamp which Red had deposited just inside the door. Moving towards it, Ob turned the latch of the door, poked his head through and saw the looming bulk of the dynamo silhouetted against the lighter rectangle of the window.

'The stars are out,' he told Harry inconsequentially as he re-closed the door and picked up the hurricane lamp. 'Didn't even notice it had stopped raining, did you?'

Harry didn't care.

With Ob in the lead they moved cautiously to the head of the staircase. Ob paused and strained his ears for the slightest sound; from below came the faintest hum of an electric motor. The sort of hum that Goldfinger's blue-beam machine might have made.

'What's that humming?' demanded Harry fearfully.

'How do *I* know? Why don't we go and find out!' He pushed the torch into Harry's hand and the latter felt a little better as his fingers closed around the heavy, bludgeoning weight. 'Don't switch it on 'til we're certain there's no one down there,' warned Ob. 'I've got the other lamp. Okay? And don't fall over.'

They negotiated the slippery iron staircase with care, keeping to its outer perimeter where the foothold was greater. Harry had counted twenty-two steps, when Ob hissed and froze in an alarming manner. His hand had encountered a door covered with a rough material—baize probably—and after groping around for a moment found the handle, and turned it gently. The door moved easily inwards. Ob explored the ground with the toe of his right foot—there was another step inside the door and another, then he was on level ground.

The heat in which they found themselves was stifling, coming to it as they did from the raw cold air outside; apart from the steady hum which had grown in intensity the origin of which, they guessed, was an electric heater of some kind, there was no other sound. For two whole minutes they stood just inside the door, waiting and listening; the darkness crowded in upon them; there seemed to be no windows to relieve or soften its density.

'Shall I have a look with the torch?' asked Harry when he felt they had stood there long enough.

'Keep it down, though,' muttered Ob. 'Just in case.'

The first object to be revealed by the cautious beam of light filtering between Harry's pink fingers was one of those model dogs with nodding heads which people who can't drive display in the rear windows of their family saloons; its head moved gently to and fro in the intense heat, and the eyes glowed mysteriously in the bright light. It stood on a large desk littered with papers and documents, rubber stamps, ink bottles, pens and pencils, and a couple of white china cups half full of cold tea.

Since no one had leapt out of the shadows at the sudden projection of their beam of light, Ob took his courage in both hands and switched on the hurricane lamp. The green-baize covered door swung to behind them with a gentle hiss.

They were in the long underground workshop, half as long again as the one above, but unlike the latter a veritable hive of interrupted industry. Highly polished and obviously cherished tools and instruments glinted from wall-racks; cylinders of compressed air in silent rows, trolleys loaded with bottles, cans and paint tins, great drums of oil, an enormous variety of wheels, hub-caps and spare parts, one would think, for every make of car on the market; and in the centre of the floor, like a star exhibit, raised on the hydraulic lift of an inspection-pit, stood a gleaming olive-green Jaguar.

Harry and Ob exchanged looks. 'Well,' said Harry, 'that's it, isn't it? Red's racket. New cars for old.'

There were three other cars in the workshop, each of which were undergoing or had undergone paint-jobs. One of them, a sleek Continental, had just been completed, and a battery of four electric driers strategically placed around it played streams of air upon its newly-sprayed panels.

Each of the cars, they noticed, was rendered ostensibly untraceable by its absence of registration plates, but judging by a nearby pile of these all of them would soon receive counties of origin and index numbers other than those with which they had been originally recorded.

'Very nice,' murmured Ob, 'Nice set-up, eh?' Wandering to the desk he pored for a moment over some of the papers, squinted closely at a couple of the rubber stamps, and then with a curious finger slid open the top right-hand drawer. Harry came over and looked. A pile of log books met their eyes.

'*Very* nice,' said Ob again, pocketing half a dozen of the books. He picked up a couple of the stamps. 'Which do you want?—L.C.C. or Surrey County Council? They're all here. There's also quite a selection of insurance companies represented.' Harry looked at him questioningly. 'We've got to take Fred something otherwise the old so-and-so will never believe us—you know him.'

He took a random handful of papers and stuffed them into an inside pocket.

Harry said, 'How do they get down here? The cars, I mean? Where's the entrance?'

'Up the other end, I suppose. Let's go and have a look.'

They slowly traversed the shop, taking in other points of interest as they went. There was little doubt that this was an extremely efficient and profitably run business. A nice sideline for someone like Mr. Morton who owned and ran an amusement park and fun for the kiddies in his spare time. With those steam-organs blasting away on the surface and the coming and going of hundreds of people—especially during the season—not to mention hundreds of cars, it was, as Ob had termed it, a very nice set-up with little chance of detection unless someone really set out to find it. As someone had.

At the far end of the workshop the floor sloped up to a steep ramp at the head of which stood two massive strongly-barred wooden doors. In the lower half of one of them a wicket was cut. Ob switched off his lamp and had a go at the yale lock, but the door wouldn't yield. Harry held his torch close to it. 'There's a mortice lock, too. You need two keys to open it.'

Ob said, 'Let's get out of here, see what the other side of this door's like and then call it a night, shall we?'

'With pleasure,' said Harry.

They retraced their steps and with a final look round left the overheated workshop and mounted the spiral staircase.

'We had one of these at school,' said Ob.

'One of what?'

'These staircases. We used to spit down the middle on to the girls' heads.'

'I bet they enjoyed that,' said Harry.

Leaving the hurricane lamp where they had found it they had let themselves into the little power-house when Ob said, 'What about that skylight? We'd better close it. Don't want them getting suspicious before we're ready.'

Harry opened the green door marked 'private' and peeped out into the now-clear, starlit night. Nothing stirred. They slipped through and keeping close to the wall as before, retraced their steps to the iron ladder. Ob hissed something to Harry and disappeared like an Indian doing the rope-trick. Harry heard, a few seconds later, a dull thud as the skylight was closed; he also heard a soft tinkle of glass as more of the pane he had broken was dislodged.

He stared uneasily over his shoulder, wondering where the man in oilskins had got to. Fine nightwatchman he had turned out to be. Thank God.

A huge shape descended from the sky and stood amiably at his elbow. 'All done,' said Ob, 'now just a peek at that door and then we're off.'

The door was brilliant. It was painted to represent one of the more startling events of the Garden of Eden and was designed to whet the sensual appetite and in exchange for the nominal deposit of one shilling plunge you and your 'intended' into the exotic shrieking mysteries of the Tunnel of Love.

It took ten minutes of scratching and peering in the dim starlight before they finally located the little inset wicket complete with its yale and mortice locks.

'There we are, then,' said Ob.

'Don't let's hang about,' said Harry.

'Don't you think you ought to put that torch back?'

'Oh God! Aren't we ever going to get out of this bloody dump?'

'Ullo,' said a deep voice two yards ahead of them, 'and what do you think you two are up to?'

A bright light blazed in their faces. Harry's first instinct was to throw his skirts over his head and run, his second to brazen it out.

'Thank God!' he said with greater thankfulness than he felt. 'Is that a policeman?'

'No, it's not a policeman.'

'Who is it then?'

'Doesn't matter who *I* am, who are *you*, that's what I want to know, and what the 'ell are you doing here?'

'Where?' said Ob. 'That's what *we* want to know. Where the hell are we? We crawled through a fence thinking we were crossing to the railway and find ourselves in a bloody madhouse. What is this place?'

The voice hesitated. 'Don't you know?'

'If we did we wouldn't be asking, would we?' growled Harry tetchily. 'What is it? A fun fair or something? Wish to God you was a cop, at least he'd know where we were.'

The voice was convinced. 'I know where you are all right, but where are you trying to get to?'

'The station,' said Ob. 'The railway station. Some nit told us there was a short cut if we climbed through a fence; it went straight to the embankment, he said, and then we just had to follow the railway line and bingo! there it was! and here we are instead.'

The light dropped from their faces. They heard and now saw the gleaming oilskins. 'I'm the nightwatchman of this place—It's Oakhaven Amusement Park you've got yourself into—lucky I didn't have Flo with me tonight or you'd have been for it.'

'Flo?'

'My Alsatian. She's a bit under the weather tonight so I left her at 'ome, but any other night and she'd have torn an 'ole in your trousers.'

'Ah, well,' said Harry, 'I'm glad she's off sick, in that case. Do you know where the station is?'

'Course I know; you're not far from it. I'll take you down to the gate and let you out properly. You oughtn't to go nipping through fences, you know. This is private property. Dangerous.'

He led the way, talking all the time, telling them about his dog, Flo, and his wife, Gertrude, and when they came to the gate unlocked it gave them a great stream of complicated directions to which neither of them listened and sped them on their way.

Harry slipped him five shillings in return for his kindness.

They waved to him as they turned the corner.

The taxi was still there, 'Arry fast asleep at the wheel.

They nudged him into wakefulness. 'Gawd,' he muttered, clambering unwillingly from his heavy slumbers. 'I'd given you up for dead.'

'Nice way of mourning for us, falling asleep,' said Harry.

'Ah well, it's been a long day, you know, been on since eight this morning. Where now? Whitehall?'

Harry gave their address and they sat back in the dark interior of the rollicking vehicle.

Ob said, 'I enjoyed that.'

Harry peered wonderingly at his shadowy profile. 'What?' he queried.

'That,' said Ob, and fell asleep.

CHAPTER NINETEEN

WHEN Harry came in from work the following evening Fred was there again crouched in secret conference with Ob on the sofa. He loitered in the doorway. 'Don't let me interrupt anything.'

'You're not.'

'How's tricks?' asked Fred.

'Fine.'

He went into the kitchen to hang up his coat and when he returned to the sitting-room everything stopped again.

'Anything wrong with me?' he demanded huffily.

'What?'

'You're talking about me, aren't you?'

'Why should we be talking about you?' asked Ob.

'That's what I want to know. If I've got B.O. or the plague or something I think I've got a right to know, don't you? You give me the dead needle, both of you. Who wants a beer, then?'

Everybody wanted a beer and when a few moments later he returned with three cans on a tin tray he said cheerily, 'How about last night then, eh Fred? I suppose Fat Face here has told you all about it?'

Fred moved his head up and down a couple of times with caution.

'What's that mean?'

'What?'

'Your head going up and down like that.'

Fred pursed his lips as though he were going to kiss someone then said, 'You managed to do a fine old bit of trespassing between you, didn't you? Not to mention breaking and entering and a spot of petty larceny thrown in. Cheers.'

'Petty larceny? ... Bung Ho! ... Who did that? Petty larceny?'

'You did.' Fred balanced a heavy Ever Ready torch in his enormous hand and looked steadily at Harry with eyes the size of pin-heads.

Harry said, 'Well, I must say, you're not exactly rolling in the aisle with laughter, are you? We risked our lives last night, Ob and me, for you.'

'For me?'

'The community at large—that includes you.'

After a pause Fred said, 'Even *we* aren't allowed to go barging in like that without warrants and things.'

Ob said, 'Don't take any notice of him, Harry. He's got to go through all this official bumph first otherwise we might run away with the idea that he approves of our methods. Which he does. Don't you, Fred?'

'Of course I do. As Fred Hearthbright, of course I do.'

Harry sighed with relief. 'Well, that's all right then, you had me worried for a moment then. So what's going to happen?'

'Working on information received from an unknown source we'll eventually get out a search warrant and tear that place apart.'

'Eventually?'

'Eventually.'

'What about Red Brody?'

Fred shrugged and looked gloomy. 'There's nothing on him.'

'Nothing on him! We saw him go into that bloody place.'

'But is he involved?'

'Of course he's involved.'

'Prove it.'

Harry stared at him. 'What's the matter with you, Fred?'

'Nothing's the matter with me. But before you start pressing charges against someone you've got to make pretty certain that there is enough evidence to make those charges stick. Right?'

Harry exchanged a look with Ob and shook his head helplessly. 'I don't understand it.'

Fred went on, 'It's always best to go slow in these sort of cases—wiser—don't you see that? Then you can gather all the loose ends together before you pounce, otherwise what happens? Half the bastards get away—do a bunk. The bloke who runs that workshop, for instance.'

'Morton.'

'If that's who it is, yes, Morton. Now he could be no more than a fence, a receiver of stolen goods, who just changes the goods a bit and then resells them. Don't misunderstand me, he's still guilty of a serious offence, but so is the bloke who originally does the pinching. But, if the one who does the pinching is in the regular employ of the one who does the receiving—even on a sort of commission basis—then we have the beginning of an organisation, which I'm dead certain we've got here, and when you're dealing with an organisation you're dealing with a brain, the sort of brain which has already conceived at least one escape hatch long before it's needed—*if ever* it's needed—and could probably pack up and be out of the country before we've even had a chance to fill up the forms. These blokes have good lawyers on their side, you know, they know all the loopholes. When we go in we don't want just half of 'em, we want all of 'em, with all the loopholes tight shut. It's like fishing, I suppose—keep quiet, don't disturb the water, and eventually the one you're after will come along—or so they tell me.'

'I stuffed an eight-pound trout once,' Ob said reminiscently.

'You do see what I'm getting at, don't you?' Fred persisted, ignoring the interruption. 'You've given us something to work on—a lot to work on, I'm not belittling it—and when eventually we've got them in the bag it's you two we'll have to thank for it. But I believe in fighting organisation *with* organisation, that's why I'm in the Force, I suppose.'

'Have another drink?' said Harry.

There was a long pause, during which each supped moodily at his beer. Finally Harry said, 'In the pictures and all the books I've read there's always a big climax when the crooks are rounded up by the hero—usually a photographer or a newspaperman—and the police only turn up when it's all over.'

Fred made a hideous face. 'That's books, isn't it, and pictures? Not real life. Even you two stopped being average law-abiding citizens when you started clambering about on roofs and breaking into workshops. Milkmen don't usually do that sort of thing, you know.'

'You telling me. That's what makes life so bloody dull, I suppose. Nothing ever happens.'

'Life *is* bloody dull for most people. Dull and expensive. That's why so many of 'em turn to crime—it's exciting, pays the bills and gives you a decent bit over so that you can buy up all the nice things you've ever wanted. The only trouble is you're not always there to enjoy them.'

Ob raised his glass. 'To crime,' he said.
'Crime,' said Fred and swallowed the remainder of his beer.

Later that night Harry was walking Jennifer home by the most circuitous route he could think of. Under a lamp-post she paused and looked up into his face. The light seemed to turn the hazel of her eyes to gold; he felt the pulse at the base of his throat quicken as he stared down at her, then the mischief of her smile and her tiny ears sticking out at right-angles through the urchin cut made her look like a pert elf. He folded her closely in his arms and kissed her.

'Love you,' she said as he released her. She put her head against his chest and added, 'I wish it didn't always sound so sloppy and old-fashioned. It isn't meant to be. But it's been ruined, rather.'

'What has?'

'The word "love". It doesn't mean anything any more—at least it doesn't mean what I want it to mean.'

They crossed the road and walked by tacit consent towards the Promenade. There they stopped, leaned over the rail and stared at the dark sea, glittering, cold and mysterious, in the starlight. In silence they listened to its steady rhythm, the incessant beat of the waves on the foreshore and the long sighing susurration of their retreat.

'You can almost hear it breathing, can't you?' said Jennifer. 'I've always thought of the sea as being alive.'

Their cheeks were touching. 'When will you marry me?' asked Harry.

The sea breathed three times before she answered. 'Are you sure you really want to marry me . . . *really,* I mean . . .'

He took her hand and put it against his mouth. 'You know how I feel about you.' They stood for a long time in silence, close in body and in mind, then he said, 'I feel like you do when I'm talking about it . . . phoney—a lot of words that don't seem to mean anything. It's all been said before, I suppose . . .'

Some distance away, along the beach somewhere, a girl was laughing; it was coarse, harsh laughter and because of its ugliness drew them closer together.

'When's your birthday?' asked Jennifer.

'June.'

'June the what?'

'The ninth.'
'It's a nice month, June.'
The sea fell away, the undertow rustling and swirling and hissing into silence. Jennifer said quietly, 'If you really want me you can have me for a birthday present.'

Boy Blue was far from pleased when he heard about the decision which had been reached with regard to Red and his racket. He lounged against the bar and glared moodily into his glass of beer.

'It's bloody daft,' he grumbled. 'I don't get it. We go to all this trouble to find out what he's up to and now we know we're not supposed to do anything about it. Doesn't make sense.'

Ob, with little hope of convincing him, pointed out that probably the police knew what they were doing.

Boy drained his glass and wiped his mouth with the back of his hand. 'The cops can go to hell as far as I'm concerned. For me, if anyone wants to know, I'm still out for Red's blood.'

'You agreed to play it this way,' Ob reminded him.

'I said I'd go along, I didn't say how far.'

'Then why the hell didn't you lay into Red before, when you were keeping an eye on him during the last couple of days, for instance? What stopped you?'

'Nobody said there wasn't going to be a showdown in the end. Old Fred and Charlie and their mob will go clumping in there with their great big flat feet and their helmets and gloves on and everybody will be lined up against the wall and marched out to the Black Maria as though they were going on a bloody Sunday School treat. You're joking, aren't you? Don't you even want to spoil that bastard's hair-do? After what him and his lot did to you? For crying out loud! Haven't you looked in the mirror lately?'

Ob stared at him for a moment in silence then sighed and ordered more beer.

It was Saturday lunchtime and the bar was crowded and noisy and the loud-mouths were out in force bestowing upon unwilling ears their unsolicited opinions about the afternoon's scheduled sport.

Since it had been possible the day before to do no more than slip a note through Boy's letter-box informing him that they had run Red Brody to earth, that for the time being therefore the hunt was off, and that further explanations would be available from Ob at the bar of *The Grapevine* on Saturday at midday, this was the first Boy had heard of the actual details of Thursday night's exploits at the Amusement Park.

Ob said carefully, 'I know how you feel about Con, we all do. If it was Maisie I'd feel the same way. That's why it's so difficult to argue with you. We're all in this together, Harry and you and me, I'm not denying that, but you yourself said when we first met, if you remember, that it wasn't a good idea to get mixed up in other people's troubles. Well, we got mixed up, we've all fought each other's battles, but how long is it going on for? That's what I want to know? If we can get Red Brody bunged away in the nick for a couple of years then that's it so far as me and Harry's concerned. Why the hell should you run the risk of getting your head bashed in, not to mention the chance of joining Red behind bars? Let the cops do it. It's all set now.'

But Boy had already stopped listening; he finished his drink, set down his glass, and zipped up his leather jacket.

'What are you going to do?' asked Ob.

'I'll tell you what I'm going to do,' returned Boy in a thin voice. 'I'm going to round up one or two of the lads and I'm going after Red Brody, and to hell with you, to hell with Harry and to hell with the bloody police force. Okay?'

'You're a nut.'

'Okay, so I'm a nut. I started this war and I'm going to finish it. It may satisfy you to see Red and his mob behind bars but it doesn't satisfy me, see?'

Ob lost his temper. 'You won't be satisfied until he's been beaten to a pulp, will you?'

Boy's blue eyes were cold and expressionless. 'I won't be satisfied 'til he's dead,' he said quietly, 'Okay?'

CHAPTER TWENTY

THE stuffed seagull on the mantelpiece had a note stuck in its beak. *Little Boy Blue,* it said in taxidermist's copperplate, *has blown his top and if Red Brody's not careful he's going to run out of blood. Thought I'd go along. If you want to come you know where I am—on the roundabouts! I'm not* with *him, by the way, I'm* after *him. Fred and Charlie both on duty so no help there. If you do come I would suggest a heavy disguise—you never know who might be watching and recognising. I'm wearing a hat!!! Come for the ride. O!*

'Nit!' said Harry aloud staring solemnly into the seagull's yellow eye. 'He'll get himself killed in the end and that'll be that.'

He trudged out to the refrigerator, helped himself to a cold sausage and a glass of milk and wandered unhappily back into the sitting-room where he read Ob's note again.

What the hell was he trying to do on his own? What could even two of them do against Red and a mob like his? And what was all this bit about a heavy disguise? What hat was Ob wearing? 'Didn't even know he had a hat,' he muttered to himself. That old cap perhaps that he'd argued off the head of a guy one fifth of November and had finally purchased for the price of a Little Demon. It was a frightful thing in red and black checks and Ob had worn it happily back that evening looking like nothing on earth, since when Harry had neither seen nor heard of it and had presumed it lost or consigned to the dustbin. If there was one thing designed to make Ob conspicuous it was that cap and Harry hoped fervently that there were other hats.

He moved to the window, pushing up the lower sash and squatted uncomfortably on the ledge. It was a cold brittle afternoon, bright with pale sunshine, with the slightest promise of spring in the clear air; there were a few clouds about but they didn't look like rain clouds, which was something to be grateful for; if it didn't rain for the next three months it would be too soon.

He swallowed his milk and slammed down the window. He would have to show willing even though it was the last thing he wanted to do. Ob's battles were Harry's, after all—a comfortable and heroic platitude and one that stuck leaden soles on to his boots. What a disastrous doctrine involvement was—why couldn't you get on with your own life without having to worry about what the other fellow was up to? The real trouble lay in the fact that the other fellow was worrying about what *you* were up to, and if you attempted to tell him to mind his own business—even in the nicest possible way—that was it—the fat was in the fire—after that you just *had* to worry about what he was up to otherwise he would slip one over on you when you were least expecting it . . . It was a jungle . . . a jungle . . .

He put his head under the tap, burped to himself and felt a little better. 'Life,' he chanted morosely, 'was just a Bowl of Cherries.' He dried and combed his hair, stood for a moment in the front of the mirror making experimental Quasimodo faces in the hope of hitting on one for a disguise, then remembered the brown velour hat he had bought four years previously and never worn. It was in the cupboard under the sink—had always been there—and he tried it on. 'You look like a pouffe,' he told himself and returned the hat to the cupboard under the sink. Then he remembered the large pair of sunglasses he had purchased full of hope at the beginning of last summer. He ran them to earth in an empty Lux packet along with seven discarded toothbrushes. He placed them experimentally on his nose; the kitchen went dark; moved to the sitting-room where there were two windows and used the mirror in there. They added a certain air of mystery and placed him in a higher salary bracket, but apart from that they were unimpressive.

'Right,' he said, 'off we go.'

Pulling on his damaged raincoat he stalked unwillingly to the front door, where he hesitated for a moment or two thinking of all the things he would rather be doing than stalking unwillingly to the front door. Behind his dark glasses the passage was as black as night. He slipped them down his nose, stared at the front door then, with a succinct and quite loud four-letter word rising unexpectedly to his lips, found the necessary impetus to cross the threshold.

Bumping jauntily on his way to Oakhaven in a blue bus he pondered over the absence of Ben that morning—and the previous Saturday morning, to say nothing of the intervening Sunday. In fact the boy hadn't turned up since Harry had demonstrated his instability with his sister. Not that it hadn't been a considerable relief to have been out of reach of that all-knowing, thirteen-year-old scrutiny with the inbuilt cynicism of an octogenarian, but to Harry it seemed a pity that an irresponsible act of his should prevent the lad from attending a job which he had so obviously enjoyed. In view of that precocious maturity it would seem odd if mere embarrassment had kept him away. Maybe it was contempt, or Betty herself might have gone to work on him and persuaded him not to come. Whatever the reason, Ben's absence had saddened him, for in some inexplicable, if not utterly maddening, way he had become quite attached to the boy. Still, there was nothing to be gained by brooding about it. Short of tramping up to Ben's front door and asking him to come back there was little he could do.

It being out of season, the Amusement Park, as such, was functioning only upon a very limited basis; the roundabouts, switchback, cakewalk, the Wall of Death and the majority of the main attractions were still and silent behind their shrouds of heavy tarpaulin; only the swings, Dodgems, miniature railway and the sideshows appeared to be working with any degree of success whilst the various booths in which countless slot-machines clicked and rattled, whined and thudded were patronised best of all by milling crowds of youths and girls raucous and brash in their Saturday afternoon enjoyment.

Harry, incognito behind his glasses, pressed steadily through the jostling groups searching for a glimpse of Ob in a hat.

A youth in leather jacket and jeans lounged unobtrusively against a lamp-post; his vacant eyes followed Harry with a studied lack of curiosity. Ten yards further on Harry hesitated before a Try-Your-Strength machine and flicked a backward glance the way he had come. Another boy similarly attired had joined the first; their heads were together but there seemed to be no ulterior significance in their meeting. Harry moved on.

Through a crackling system of amplifiers wired to posts and buildings pop-music was being relayed; the static was louder than the music, but the beat came through and here and there a frustrated dancer jerked and pulsated with the uneasy rhythm of an awkwardly-manipulated puppet.

For a minute or two he stood watching the Dodgems as they bounced and bumped into each other to the accompaniment of screams and shouts from those behind the wheels; he was half tempted to have a go himself; he had always enjoyed the idea of driving deliberately into things at full speed, though he had done nothing about it since he was nine years old when he had pointed his small lethal pedal-car at a fat boy on a pair of roller-skates; he had damaged the fat boy quite splendidly but had unfortunately removed his own front teeth in the process.

He was reliving the experience voluptuously in his mind's eye when there was a sudden loud 'Psssttt!' in his right ear.

Refusing to be startled, he turned his head quite slowly and stared unmoved at Ob who was standing wreathed in smiles at his elbow.

'You look quite frightful,' he said with calm deliberation.

And it was true. Even in the uncharted stretches of Ob's own adoring mother's imagination it would have required on her part no mean mendacity for her to have laid her hand firmly on her bosom and say, 'That hat suits you, Ob.' No hat could ever have suited Ob, but if a nation-wide competition could have been promoted wherein, from a comprehensive selection of every hat known to man, it was necessary to choose the one that best suited Hobson Harvey, this black and red check acorn-cap would surely have come last.

'I had a feeling,' went on Harry, 'that was the hat you meant. I'd hoped you'd bunged that away years ago.'

'I've never even worn it 'til now.'

'Now is not the time to start, believe me.'

'It's disguise, that all.'

'First of all,' sniffed Harry, 'it makes everybody turn and look at you twice, and secondly, as far as disguise is concerned, you look exactly like Ob Harvey in a funny hat. I think you've gone off your nut. So, what happened? Anything? Nothing? Why you can't leave all this alone I'll never know. You'll get yourself killed in the end if you go on like this, you know that, don't you? Why don't you pack it in, go home and mind your own business . . .'

'Harry . . .'

'What?'

'Can I say something?'

'What's stopping you?'

'The clans are gathering.'

'It sounds like the White Heather Club,' snarled Harry. There was a shuddering impact as a Dodgem car struck the barrier and bounced off two feet away from them. They clutched at the rail. 'Let's get out of here.'

'I like your glasses,' admired Ob, unperturbed by Harry's ill temper. 'They're just the job. You look like Harry Stillwater in a pair of dark glasses.' Harry grinned in spite of himself. Ob caught his arm and steered him between a couple of stalls. 'I want to show you something.' Coming to a halt in front of the shooting gallery Ob turned his back on it and stared ostentatiously at a laughing crowd of sailors leaning precipitously from the top platform of a tower called *The Spiral Slide*. 'Don't look now,' he said in a low voice, 'but the bloke in charge of the shooting gallery behind us is the bloke I knocked over the railing.'

Harry swivelled round like a Dalek and took in the dark young man with one swift glance. 'Thank God for that,' he grunted with relief. 'You're sure of it?'

'I don't have to smell his hair-oil to be certain. That's a face I'll never forget. He's the one they called Jim, I think. Now listen, and this is the interesting thing: I've recognised three of those blokes who had a go at me, and they're all working on the stalls here. Eh? see what I mean?'

'One big happy family?'

'Like you said.'

As they strolled off again two girls nudged each other and giggled about Ob's headgear. 'Wish you'd get rid of that bloody hat,' grumbled Harry.

'Hold on,' said Ob and suddenly went away disappearing behind a stall selling candy floss. He came back just as suddenly. 'Lend us one and six, will you?'

'What for?' queried Harry burrowing in his pocket.

'Because I haven't got enough,' Ob told him and sped off again.

When he returned the second time he was wearing a Mexican Bandit hat with a fringe of silken balls bobbing around the brim. Harry stared at him aghast.

Ob raised a hand. 'Before you say anything, just look round and see how many birds and blokes are wearing them. They're practically gear in these places. Three bob, not bad, eh? Why don't you get one?'

Harry didn't trust himself with an answer but asked instead, 'So what's with Boy Blue? Why all the panic?'

Ob told him about the way Boy had received the tidings of recent events and how he had decided to collect 'some of the lads' and hie off to Oakhaven to settle accounts with Red once and for all.

'You told him about this place, did you?'

'Of course I did. I didn't expect it to blow up in my face. He said he was going to play it our way, didn't he?—I told him everything—about the skylight and all. He knows the way in —the lot.'

'He said this afternoon, did he?'

'He's here already, don't worry. I've seen him a couple of times. And the lads are collecting too . . . his lads.'

'He hasn't got a mob, has he?'

'No, but a buddy of his has—bloke by the name of Alf Martin—they call themselves the Skyriders— bikes and gear and that, you know. Pretty tough crowd by all accounts and according to him just dying to have a round or two with Red Brody and his pals.'

Harry stared at him blankly through his dark glasses. 'How the hell do you know all this?'

'I asked him. When he dropped his bombshell and got up to go I squeezed as much as I could out of him. I pretended we'd go over on his side after all and join the happy throng. Then I tried ringing the cop-shop. Fred and Charlie are both on duty at the football matches—special Saturday afternoon duty—but they'll be off when the games are over; we'll ring again if things look like they're going to get ugly here.'

'Why didn't you tell the sergeant at the desk? He'd have sent some blokes along.'

'Not to Oakhaven, he wouldn't, they've got their own lot here. They can't go trampling over somebody else's property. Anyway, they haven't got blokes to spare. There aren't enough of 'em to go round as it is. And I didn't tell the Sarge anything in case Fred and Charlie got let in for any trouble. After all, they've been acting unofficially, haven't they? They'll both be at the shop at about five, so I thought we'd ring through then, okay?'

Harry fell on to a green park bench and hunched his shoulders in a disgruntled huddle. Ob collapsed by his side and pulled his large hat over his eyes. They were silent for several minutes, idly watching the passers-by and occupied with their own thoughts, wondering among other things what the hell they could do on their own if anything broke in the way of trouble.

'Any sign of Red?' asked Harry at last.

'No.'

'Or the Bentley?'

'No.'

Harry brooded for a bit then said, 'I suppose we don't really know whether they're coming at all, do we?'

'Well, I don't. And neither does Boy. He says they'll show up sooner or later, so presumably he's going to keep an eye on the place until they do.'

'But it could be a fortnight.'

'It could also be tonight.'

Harry glanced at him sourly. 'Do you know what you look like in that bloody hat? Sandeman's Port.'

Ob shrugged good-naturedly. 'If you can't fight, wear a big hat,' he said with a smirk. He suddenly kicked his friend painfully on the shin. 'Over there,' he muttered out of the corner of his mouth, 'by the red caravan—there's a couple of 'em.'

Harry saw them. One of them, with his back towards them, had *Skyrider II* painted in white letters across the shoulders of his leather jacket. Harry shook his head nervously. 'This is going to be a full-scale gang war if we're not careful.'

As he spoke two other youths joined the lounging couple, *Skyriders IV* and *VII*. 'Blimey! they've all got numbers. Let's scout around,' urged Harry. 'I feel safer on my feet; I can run faster.'

They made a slow circuit of the entire Amusement Park but saw nothing of Boy Blue; they saw someone called *Skyrider I* whom they presumed to be Alf Martin himself and who impressed neither of them either in stature—he was not much taller than Red Brody—or in appearance; his greasy black hair was shoulder-length and was surmounted by a leather cap with gold braid around its peak; he moved with the muscle-bound stiffness of the self-appointed superman. 'The big boys,' observed Harry, 'are all little blokes.'

'Which just goes to show,' nodded Ob, 'as my friend Freud would say.' He nodded in the direction of a stall which contained a large revolving dartboard at which a couple of girls threw darts and hoped for prizes. 'Remember him?'

In charge of the proceedings was Red's spotty-faced henchman with the Beatle haircut; and straddling a chair watching the girls with his back half-turned to Harry and Ob was the other one with the thinning hair and the permanent drip on his nose. Ob said, 'Dare you to go and offer him a handkerchief.'

'Why don't we go and have a cup of something somewhere?' asked Harry *à propos* of nothing at all.

'Wonder if that means that Red's somewhere in the offing?'

'It's all deadly quiet at the moment,' persisted Harry. 'It's only just gone half past four. We can't expect Fred or Charlie much before half past five, can we?'

Ob bent a quirked smile in his direction. 'I don't think they know that.'

'Who don't?'

'Boy and Red. They might not wait for Fred and Charlie. Come on then, ten minutes can't hurt. There's a built-in caff up the other end. If anything blows up we'll soon know.'

Keeping a sharp look-out for any sign of either of the two protagonists, they slowly retraced their steps. They passed close to the Tunnel of Love and Ob expressed his desire to loiter in the vicinity of the large double doors which led down into the underground workshop, but there was a tight little group of hard-looking nuts also loitering in front of them, the inference being that they were to dissuade others from doing likewise. To Ob their presence was a tacit indication that work was in progress in the workshop, but Harry was not impressed by the assumption.

'They're probably always there,' he pointed out, stirring a cup of strong tea, 'just in case someone like you gets curious.'

'Didn't you hear a sort of rumbling going on from down there?'

'No, I didn't, and neither did you; if you had you would have said so at the time. I didn't hear a thing and I just hope there's no one there. And I hope too that bloody Red Brody doesn't turn up. At least it would give Fred and Charlie a chance to line things up properly before you and Red and Little Boy Blue get yourselves killed.'

'And you.'

Harry snorted with contempt. 'Not me, mate, count me out. The moment trouble starts I'm off like a bomb to the nearest police station screaming for help. I've got things to think about other than private vendettas between a lot of teenage thugs.'

'Like what?'

'Like Jennifer, for instance.'

Harry couldn't see his friend's face beneath the bobbing fringe of his large hat but his words made the right impression, for when he spoke again Ob's voice was subdued. 'You're right there . . . you've got to think about her . . .'

'Did I tell you we'd fixed a date?'

'No! . . . for the wedding, you mean?'

'Ninth of June.'

'Your birthday.'

'That's right, yes . . . it was her idea.'

Ob played with the spoon in the sugar-basin. 'Nice that . . . I'm glad . . . I'll have to think about a wedding present then, won't I?' After a further pause he added, 'Then there's Maisie, too.'

Harry finished his tea and placed his cup firmly in the saucer with an air of finality. 'Why don't we go, then—now—while the going's good?'

The fringe on Ob's hat shook vigorously. 'You go, I can't.'

'Why not?'

'Because I can't, that's why not.'

'There's no reason for you to stay.'

Ob raised his head and for the first time Harry saw his eyes clearly; they were dark and troubled. 'There is a reason . . . somewhere . . . I don't think I really know what it is, but it's there just the same.' He dropped his eyes abruptly. 'If you want to go you mustn't let me stop you—you've got a mind of your own, after all; I'm not in charge of this operation. Go on. I'd hate to feel I was responsible for you getting hurt . . .'

Harry stared wretchedly at his fingernails for some moments then said, 'I can't go. I'm a nut with a hole in my head but I can't go either.'

'Why not, for God's sake?'

Harry looked at him abruptly. 'Because of you, I suppose,' he said ungraciously. 'I can't think why else. At least I'll be around to pick the pieces up. I'm warning you though, if I get roughed up, if there's one drop of my blood on me when it's all over I'll never let you forget it . . . never . . . you great hulking bow-legged ape!'

There was a short silence between them stemmed from embarrassment then Ob said, 'We'd better be getting back, then.'

They had been in the little café for no more than ten minutes and it would seem incredible therefore that the atmosphere could have changed as much as it had during such a short period of time. But it was true. Not only had the pale sun dropped below the roofs of the surrounding buildings, leaving the Park in a chill blue valley of shadow, but the wind had freshened considerably, whipping up scurrying clouds of dust and grit and snatching at the loose, unroped corners of tarpaulins which flapped and snapped back upon themselves with the sharpness and insistence of a circus whip. But the change was not confined simply to the outward manifestations of an unsympathetic climate; it was more subtle, incalculable. It had to do with tension. If the Amusement Park had been conceived as a huge clockwork toy then someone had just given the key a couple of turns. With the shadows had come an unnatural quivering of the senses; premonitory uneasiness stalked and skirmished with the restless wind. Even the brash laughter from the fast thinning crowds seemed subdued, and though the amplifiers crackled with static no music came from them.

Harry and Ob stood in silence for a moment on the steps of the café, the sense of foreboding heavy on them. A fluttering, windswept newspaper wrapped itself around Ob's ankles with a sharp sucking sound and, as he stopped to dislodge it, curled itself outwards like the sail of a galleon and cavorted unsteadily out of sight.

Ob said, 'I remember my father saying once that paper and leaves being blown down an empty street in the early morning were like the souls of the people who had died during the night.'

Harry glanced at him nervously. 'Thank you,' he said, 'for those few kind and encouraging words.'

'Just telling you what he said.'

They turned up their collars, thrust their hands deeply

into their coat-pockets and moved off. Harry had discarded his dark glasses long ago, but Ob still retained his large hat rammed firmly down to within half an inch of his eyebrows.

Harry's stomach felt empty and his solar-plexus had become the aching centre of his very being; the palms of his hands were sticky and the skin on his face taut and cold. When they turned a corner and came suddenly upon an inoffensive couple locked closely in each other's arms his heart seemed to rise and hit the roof of his mouth like the indicator ringing the bell on the Try-Your-Strength machine. It was still up there jangling at his nerves when a black-leathered figure appeared almost magically in their path.

'Is that you?' queried Boy, peering cautiously beneath the wide brim of Ob's hat. He nodded a greeting to Harry. 'Been looking for you everywhere. Glad you turned up after all. The kite's going up any minute now. Red's on his way.'

Ob said quickly, 'How d'you know that?'

'Alf said.'

'How does he know?'

'There's not much Alf doesn't know when he puts his mind to it.'

Ob trod gently on Harry's foot as he asked, 'So what's going to happen?'

'Do you know *If You Gotta Go, Go Now*?'

'Eh?'

'You know Manfred Mann?'

'Who?'

'You don't even know what I'm talking about, do you?'

'Start again, then.'

Boy sighed deeply and treated them both to a steady look of condescension. 'It's a number—a pop number well up in the charts and it's sung by a bloke—a group—called Manfred Mann. Right?'

'What's it called again—*If You Gotta Go* . . .?'

'. . . *Go Now*. Now, when that's played over the loudspeakers it'll mean that Red and his buddy—who is old man Morton himself, by the way—have arrived, see? When we hear it we all start edging in a bit. Alf's got his lads staked out around the workshop, which is where we hope Red will be heading. But nobody's to start anything until Red's inside, right?'

Ob said, 'How does this thing go? *If You Gotta Go* . . .'

'Er ...' said Boy and screwing up his right eye thoughtfully he beat the air a couple of times with a black-gloved hand and came in with a sexy-sounding light baritone:

'If you've gotta go, go now
Or else you gotta stay all night ...'

'Cor luv'ly!' exclaimed one of a brace of bleached-headed harlots aged about seventeen who happened to be passing at that moment. 'I fancy 'im, don't you, Lil? ... dig all that luv'ly levver too ...'

Lil made a hoarse grunting sound reminiscent of a pig farm.

Regarding them for a cool moment as they loitered to a standstill of invitation Boy delivered himself of two words which had an immediate effect upon them, for not only did they obey them with alacrity but they went off setting them to music and rendering them in an excruciating series of unintentional accidentals.

Boy turned back to his two companions. 'You've got that, then, have you? When you hear it on the Tannoy, move. Okay? Alf goes in through the skylight with some of his mob and I go in right after Red with the rest of 'em. You two had better come with me.' He stopped and squinted up at Ob with sudden curiosity. 'What are you wearing that terrible hat for?'

Harry asked, 'How many of you altogether?'

'With Alf and me thirteen—plus you two, fifteen. That ought to be enough.'

Ob said dryly, 'I thought you were only out for Red's blood.'

Boy turned on him, 'It was you who wanted to bust up his racket, not me.'

'Nobody said anything about tearing the ruddy place apart.'

Boy stared at them in sullen silence for a moment then said, 'Tell me something, you two.' All friendship had ebbed from his voice. 'Are you with me or against me?'

Above the soft whine of the wind Harry thought he could hear the striking of the church clock; he looked quickly at his watch.

Ob was saying, 'This time tomorrow you're going to be in hospital or in clink, you know that, don't you? If you want to tangle with Red tangle with him for God's sake, but do it on your own—call off the mob.'

R

'I tried that once, remember? Who interfered?'

'I interfered because it was three to one. Now it's fifteen to one and I hope it makes you happy.'

For a long moment Boy's cold blue eyes stared at Ob, then they shifted to Harry and back again to Ob. 'Right,' he said at last. 'Now I know where I stand, don't I?' He bared his sharp white teeth at them. 'There's one thing I'd like *you* to know, though . . . Just keep out of my way, that's all—both of you.'

Turning abruptly on his heel he strode away.

The lights were beginning to come on, their brightness serving only to deepen the shadows. The wind was really cold now and they shivered beneath their thin raincoats.

Harry said, 'I'm going to ring Fred on the offchance, I think. He ought to be back by now. It's nearly five. We've got to do something, Ob mate, we can't just stand about.'

Ob stood thoughtfully, his face beneath the brim of his hat in heavy shadow; there was no sign that he had heard Harry. His eyes suddenly glittered. 'There *is* something we could do.' Harry waited. 'Listen, the balloon's not going up 'til when?'

' 'Til Red gets here.'

'So we've got to stop him from getting here, haven't we?'

'What?'

'Stop Red from getting here.'

'How we going to do that?'

Ob was already moving off in the direction of the rear gates of the Park. 'I don't know how we're going to do it, but we're going to have a damn good try. We've got to go out and stop him before him and his buddy drive through that ruddy gate.'

'We don't even know if he's coming through that ruddy gate,' protested Harry, trotting breathlessly at his side. 'He might come through the other ruddy gate.'

'We've got to risk that, haven't we? Unless you like to take one gate while I take the other.'

'No,' said Harry, 'don't let's split up, for God's sake. I'll go straight home if we do.'

'All right then.' He was moving with a speed of which even Harry had never suspected he was capable. 'Come on, hurry up.'

'I'm running already,' panted Harry.

At the gates they elbowed their way roughly through the

thickening crowd and a few moments later were out on the open road.

Ob was speaking. 'We've got to assume that they'll come from the same direction as they came the other night. That's the only thing we can do. If we're wrong, that's that.'

Harry's voice rose. 'How are we going to stop 'em? Chuck ourselves under the wheels of that ruddy great Bentley?'

'Don't ask daft questions, I don't know any more'n you do,' retorted Ob tartly. In profile he looked as though he were on the London to Brighton walk. Harry was fairly galloping along by this time.

'You do know you're still wearing that hat?' he snarled by way of diversion.

'There's a telephone box,' Ob told him. 'You go and ring Fred and tell him what's happening; let him decide what to do about the locals here. Tell him we'll hold Red off as long as we can to give them a chance to get here. I'll go on—the further we can get away from this place the better it'll be. When you've done you're phoning come on after me.' He paused and added significantly. 'I might need some help. Got fourpence?'

Harry fell into the telephone box, snatched up the instrument and fumbled fourpence out of his pocket. He stared through the window at Ob's fast-receding figure. London to Brighton in a Mexican hat!

He jabbed at Button A. 'George? Harry Stillwater.' George was the station sergeant; they were all good friends. 'Is Fred back? Fred Hearthbright.'

'Hello, Harry, how are you, then? Yes, Fred's back—came in five minutes ago. You want to talk to him, then?'

No, you silly old nit, I don't want to talk to him. 'If he's there,' he said aloud.

He peered out of the window. Ob had disappeared. The orange street-lamps were beginning to glow a little brighter—everything was beginning to look thoroughly nasty as they always did under those lights.

'Hullo, Harry.'

'Fred, listen.' He gabbled away for a breathless minute, putting Fred in possession of the facts, coloured a little by his own over-exuberant panic. Fred sounded terribly slow at the other end and kept saying 'I see, Harry' and once even asked which gate of the Park was the one through which they had just passed—the North or the South.

'It's a gate,' shrieked Harry desperately, 'I don't know where it bloody is. It's the back gate. How long will it take you to get here? Is Charlie there too, couldn't he come as well? The more the merrier. And do you think I ought to ring the local cop-shop and get some of them in?'

'Harry . . .'

'Ob thought it might be a good idea to let the local police know . . .'

'Harry . . .'

'Fred? Yes Fred? You there?'

'Relax, Harry, we're on our way. Leave it all to us. Just you sit back and relax.'

Harry went off into an unnerving paroxysm of laughter.

'Where are you, Harry?'

'What?'

'At this moment, where are you?'

'In a phone box.'

'Yes, I know that, but where?'

'How'd I know? On the road somewhere, in a phone box. I feel sick.'

Fred's voice took on a sternness. 'Don't give way, boy. And stop laughing, d'you hear? Harry?'

'Fred?'

'That's better. See you soon. Goodbye and stop worrying.'

'Who's worrying.'

'You are.'

'Yes, well . . .'

'Right. Goodbye.'

'Tara.'

Harry pushed open the door and hung half in and half out of the box for a second or two like a broken butterfly then, pulling himself together, he pressed Button B hopefully and floundered off down the road leaving the phone box ticking like a time-bomb.

Ob had meantime covered a further half mile, walking more slowly now, his entire concentration centred upon the desultory stream of traffic moving towards him. He had formulated no plan as to what method he would adopt to bring the Bentley to a halt should it suddenly appear before him. He could stand in the middle of the road and wave at it, or, as Harry had peevishly suggested, throw himself beneath its wheels; he could hurl himself over its aristocratic radiator and smile winningly through the windscreen at its startled driver, or hang about a set of traffic lights hoping that the red would do his job for him, in which event he would simply open the door and step inside without even a 'by-your-leave'—to finish up, no doubt, on his back in the gutter with a broken neck.

When finally he came upon the Bentley it was to discover that a benevolent Fate had stepped in and was arranging things to suit herself and Ob rather than *Skyriders I to XII*. The long grey car was suffering the indignity of a jack under its rear axle and whilst a sleek Mr. Morton leaned negligently against a nearby wall smoking a long thin cigar, a sweating, bad-tempered Red Brody was changing the wheel.

Ob stepped into a bus shelter to consider his next move. Though the 'flat' had postponed the war for a short time the moment that spare wheel was fitted it would be battle-stations again for one and all.

A bus lumbered up and came to rest amicably at Ob's elbow. Ob and its conductor eyed each other without much interest, then the conductor raised a pale inquiring eyebrow. Ob shook his head. The conductor gave Ob's hat a baffled look, said 'Viva!' dispiritedly and placed a grimy thumb on his bell. Ob felt sorry for him as the bus rolled away, empty as a drum.

His brain seemed to have taken the night off; nothing was occurring to him. He stood in the bus shelter and watched Red Brody change the wheel and wondered unhappily *why* his brain seemed to have taken the night off. If he had a gun he could have shot one of them—or even both of them—that would delay them somewhat. Peering down the road through the bobbing fringe of his hat he hoped for a glimpse of a hurrying Harry who might be more forthcoming in the way of ideas but he could see no one who remotely resembled him.

His brain heaved a tired sigh. 'Why don't you remove the wheel?' it suggested.

'What wheel?'

'The spare wheel of course, idiot.'

Ob leaned out of the bus shelter and surveyed the crippled Bentley for several moments. 'Because,' he answered at length, 'the spare wheel is already in place, that's why.'

'Then you'll have to think of something else, won't you?'
'Like what?'
'Ignition key.'
'Ignition key?'
'Ignition key. It would be the work of a moment to remove the ignition key—then the car wouldn't go, would it?'
'Neither would I after that. They'd kill me.'
'Only if they see you do it.'
'What?'
'Oh God.'
'Perhaps the key's not there.'
'You won't know if you don't go and look, will you?'
Ob leaned out of the bus shelter and took a further review of the situation. One thing was certain—if he didn't act fairly fast the wheel would be fixed and everything would start moving again. The ignition key was quite an idea—if it worked!
With a sudden determined gesture he thrust back his hat so that it dangled down from his neck by the long noose-like chin-strap and set off across the road. Opposite the Bentley he lingered for a brief moment in a darkened doorway whilst his plan crystallised itself. It being the rear nearside wheel which was giving trouble the car was jacked up so that its floor sloped downwards towards the centre of the road. From where Ob stood he could just see the head of the sleek Mr. Morton above its gleaming roof; Red, on his hands and knees on the edge of the pavement wrestling with the wheel, was invisible.
He hesitated only until a slow-moving Oakhaven-bound bus rumbled abreast of him and using it as a screen struck off into the road like a cross-channel swimmer leaving Dover; by the time the bus had dawdled to Ob's recently-vacated shelter he was crouched watchfully alongside the driver's door of the Bentley. He felt as though he had suddenly acquired a duodenal ulcer and his head throbbed with the rise in blood pressure, but apart from that he simply wished he was dead. Raising his head cautiously he peered through the window. He could see nothing of either Morton or Red. His eyes dropped to the dashboard. A small bunch of keys hung there, trembling slightly with the motion set up by Red's exertions.
A passing car flashed its headlights at him and sounded its horn as it sped past; the noise brought a muffled oath from Red.

Ob's hand crept up to the door handle and slowly depressed it; a well-oiled click froze him once again into immobility and the short hairs at the back of his neck reared in obedience to the scent of danger. Red swore again and there came a swift sharp altercation between him and the elegant Mr. Morton—evidently little love was being lost between them; apart from that there was no indication that either of them had heard the click of the lock. Because of the cant of the car the door swung suddenly down under its own weight and only a lightning reaction from Ob prevented it thudding into the tarmac; slowly he eased it down until its lower corner rested gently on the road. Another car screamed past, this time leaving behind it a hurtled imprecation from its driver. And little wonder, thought Ob in a panic—a car on its side with its door wide open and an idiot kneeling in front of it in the middle of the road—no wonder!

Deftly and noiselessly he removed the keys from the ignition. 'God!' he thought as the sweat dripped down his collar, 'what a way to earn a living.'

He was squatting there wondering whether or not he should close the door and how he would undertake the dash back to safety without Morton becoming aware of him when it was borne home to him that neither of these questions were going to be in need of an immediate answer. The grey suede shoes which had appeared noiselessly beside him must have been quite expensive—only somebody who could afford a beautifully-cut pair of trousers similar to those which rested upon their insteps would be able to afford their soft snug luxury—somebody who owned fun fairs and drove Bentleys and ran rackets; someone whose name, at a guess, was Morton.

The blood drained from everywhere as he blinked up blankly into Morton's eyes.

There was no welcoming smile in those eyes, nor was there anything in the face to suggest that the forthcoming interview was going to be anything other than strained. The books say that time stands still on such occasions. Ob found somewhat to his surprise, that the books were right. Nothing happened for about twenty-four hours except that he became conscious that a muscle at the right corner of his mouth was no longer in control; its lack of moral fibre was causing that particular side of his mouth to slide upward so that to all intents and purposes—to the casual observer at least—he was indulging in a lop-sided grin. Which was not the case at all. If he could have thought of anything likely to induce in him the luxury of a lop-sided grin he would have thought of it. But there was nothing. All was desolation and the Valley of the Shadow stretched endlessly before him.

Morton's eyes were black. Hard. Like jet.

His voice was soft. Smooth. Like his hands, one of which rested lightly on the door.

'Can I help you?' was his first remark, which under the circumstances, thought Ob, was a fairly inefficacious effort and could be answered with equal inefficacy by a reply such as, 'yes, you could help me to my feet if you would be so kind'. But Ob didn't make it. He squatted unhappily in the shadow of the car whilst other cars, in a world which had ceased to concern him, roared and screamed past within a foot of his heels. This, he thought, is going to get worse before it gets better. A reckoning is at hand and it won't surprise me in the slightest bit if the next voice I hear is the voice of God. It wasn't, however; it was the voice of Red Brody, one as far removed from God as Dan was from Beersheba—and, by conservative estimate, further still.

'You talking to me?' he grunted ungraciously from the far side of the car.

'Get up,' invited the smooth Mr. Morton gently.

Ob got up. The keys clutched tightly in his hand. Nothing—nothing would make him relinquish them.

Death would, of course . .

Ob towered above Mr. Morton but Mr. Morton asked nevertheless, 'What, little man, are you up to?'

When you were only five feet eight and your adversary well over six feet only money could make you talk like that.

Ob looked calmer and more aggressive than he felt. 'Nothing.'

It was a peculiarly fatuous conversation they were having, he decided.

Morton held out one of his smooth hands. 'I'll have those keys, if you don't mind.'

Ob felt them bite painfully into the palm of his hand. 'But I do mind.'

Later on, when he got out of all this—*if* he got out of all this—he would doubtless be able to think of some splendidly withering retorts worthy of the situation, funny ones probably which would make the corners of Morton's soft mouth twitch with merriment suppressed with difficulty, and an unwilling admiration would blossom between them—a bond of understanding such as invariably exist between detective and his own personal arch-criminal ... But just at the moment they wouldn't come, those witty remarks ... he could only think of 'But I do mind'—so he said it. It had no impact whatsoever and there was no merry fleeting twitch at the corners of Morton's mouth.

'The keys,' insisted Morton.

'Over my dead body,' said Ob rashly and could have bitten out his tongue.

Morton sighed, smiled a thin smile and delivered himself of the best line so far: 'I'm sure we could arrange that too, if you insist. Red!' the word spat from between those smooth lips like the bullet out of a gun. Ob began a rapid reassessment of him.

'What is it?' The querulous Red was too short to see over the top of the Bentley so he came rollicking around the rear and closed up behind Ob. 'What's going on?'

Slowly Ob turned and stared down at him.

Red's mouth fell open. 'You again!'

'You know him?' Morton asked.

Red snarled. 'He's the one we had to take care of in the Tunnel. 'Member me telling you about him? Nearly did for Jim over the railings. What's he doing here?'

'For some reason best known to himself he has just removed the keys from the car. Persuade him to put them back, will you? "Over his dead body" he said, but try not to take him too literally.'

Ob stared contemptuously at the top of Red's head and said with quiet malevolence, 'Just try, mate, that's all, just you try.'

With no hope of success Red squared up to him nevertheless, and held out a hand. 'Hand 'em over, you!'

Ob smiled at him benevolently. 'You tight-bottomed, undersized, copper-knobbed twit!'

Standing between the two of them he contemplated the possibility of a couple of simultaneous knock-out broadsides and was still toying with the idea when he became aware of an approaching Harry hurrying towards them. The unguarded moment was enough for Red to take a lunge at him. The blow caught him in the solar-plexus, which was where it had been intended to catch him, but though he doubled up for a split second, his solar-plexus was sturdier than his assailant had hoped. He raised his right fist and thumped it down hard on the top of Red's head and following it through with a well-placed left hook, was delighted to see Red take off in a vertical direction as though suddenly equipped with jet propulsion. The car behind them swayed dangerously on its jack and gave off a mournful clang as Red draped himself heavily over the boot.

'Well done,' said Ob and turning to Morton in order to pass on one or two things which had occurred to him now that the tension had somewhat eased, found himself looking at a small, flat automatic pistol which, in its turn, was staring him steadily in the eye.

'The keys,' repeated Mr. Morton.

The gun was ridiculous—it was a toy—no more lethal-looking than David's sling! The lop-sided grin was there again as he gazed at it in disbelief. 'Is that a real one, then?' There was a hole at the end which was bigger than the hole in the end of a water-pistol, so it wasn't a water-pistol. Morton made no reply except to lower the hole until it was pointing at Ob's chest. This was nonsense! It was Saturday night in Oakhaven—they were standing in the middle of the road; it wasn't exactly the High Street but there were quite a number of people milling about if you cared to look for them, not to mention a considerable amount of traffic . . . and there was this gun pointing at his chest . . .

He cleared his throat. 'Have you got a licence for that?' He didn't give a damn whether Morton had a licence for it—all he cared about was whether Morton could shoot with it.

His eyes drifted over Morton's shoulder. Harry Stillwater seemed to have been erased. It was as if he had never been there. Behind him came a muttering groan of pain as Red began pulling himself together, which was disappointing because Ob thought he had hit him harder than that.

'The keys,' repeated Morton monotonously.

'You're a nut,' Ob informed him, 'Waving a thing like that about in front of everybody . . . you wouldn't use it . . . you wouldn't dare, not with everybody looking . . .'

Morton didn't even bother to see whether everybody *was*

looking; he simply looked academic. 'Why not? It makes very little noise and would certainly not be heard over the traffic. Now let's be sensible, shall we? I don't know who you are nor what you are—nor do I care—I simply want my car keys. Fight out your sordid battles with the delectable Red if you must, but let's not make this situation more farcical than it has already become.'

'If you shoot me,' said Ob playing for time and peering frantically through the gloom for a glimpse of Harry, 'I shall scream.'

Morton gave a confident smile. 'I doubt it,' he said with well-bred derision.

'You wouldn't kill me, you couldn't, not with your bloody great car lying alongside you couldn't. You couldn't go any place—not on three wheels.'

A flicker of something passed over the other's face. He shot a quick glance at Red, who was over-acting his return to consciousness. 'Have you nearly finished?' he spat.

Red fixed Ob with a bleary eye and muttered some incoherencies but Morton cut him short with an oath and told him to shut up and get on with it, at which he stumbled out of sight behind the car and vented his spleen upon inanimate objects which clanged back at him.

With affected nonchalance Ob began to stroll towards the pavement.

'I wouldn't move if I were you,' warned Morton.

'Oh, go and get stuffed,' returned Ob. 'I'm fed up with standing about in the middle of the road.' He had also noticed a couple of people approaching scarcely ten yards away—a man and his wife, he guessed.

'Excuse me,' he said to them as they faltered to a standstill before him. 'This—er—gentleman is threatening to kill me. I wonder if you would be so good as to inform the next policeman you happen to bump into.'

The couple were dumbfounded and stared at him with blank frightened eyes. The woman found her voice first—they always do. 'What are you talking about?' she asked, although she had heard and understood every word.

'This man,' repeated Ob turning towards Morton, who had meantime pocketed the gun and was leaning against the car smiling like someone's favourite uncle, 'has got a gun in his pocket which is pointing straight at me at this very moment and if you don't do something to help me he's going to kill me ... he says ...'

'Oh yes?' said the woman, staring pointedly at Ob's fancy-dress hat, which was peeping incongruously over his shoulder. 'Well, well, fancy that now ... poor you ... Come on, Albert.'

The man called Albert squared his shoulders and said in a throaty beer-drinker's voice, 'People like you ought to be put in prison—a menace to the public I say. I've a good mind to call a policeman.'

'Which is exactly what I am asking you to do, you bald-headed nit!' The woman gave a little whinney of protest and Ob turned on her too. 'You too, you old faggot, go and fetch a policeman, see if I care—prove you're a decent law-abiding citizen for once—just for a giggle.'

The woman's mouth opened and shut several times but no sound issued therefrom until with a tremendous effort she managed to whisper in a quivering undertone, 'Albert!'

Albert was no help but simply caught her hastily by the midriff muttering, 'Come on, let's get out of here—he's bloody mad ... mad, that's what you are, ruddy mad ... you ought to be locked up ... locked up, I say ...' His voice grew more strident as the distance increased between them; the two of them raced off as though the dogs of war were at their heels.

Mr. Morton leaned back and laughed softly and leaned so hard that the heavy car juddered and shook on its jack and Red started away from the rear wheel in a panic. Ob chose that moment to leap forward to take Morton off his guard but the gun was quicker than he was.

'The keys,' said Morton coldly.

And suddenly over Morton's shoulder was Harry, holding up both his hands like a fielder waiting in the slips for the catch upon which the chances of his being selected for a trip to Australia will depend. Over Morton's sleek head flew the keys and into Harry's hands.

'Oh well caught, that man!' yelled Ob.

Morton turned and Ob kicked out viciously at his hand. As the gun went spinning into the air, Ob lunged for it, missed it, and knocked it neatly into the waiting fist of Red Brody.

Red Brody smiled evilly as he levelled the gun at Ob. 'I'm quite good at the catching, too, aren't I?'

Ob advanced on him, hoping fervently that Harry was keeping Morton busy behind him. 'You wouldn't have the guts, you nasty little runt, you wouldn't have the guts. Go on, kill me, I dare you . . .'

Red, backing, lowered the muzzle of the gun until it was pointing ominously at Ob's stomach. 'Who said anything about killing,' he snarled. The muzzle of the gun slipped even lower. 'A nice bit of maiming would suit me.'

Ob suddenly reared like an angry bull and moved so fast that even Red didn't see him coming. What struck Red most of all was a thunderbolt delivered with the omnipotence of Jove himself, loud, crushing and full of coloured light. He went down as though pole-axed. The gun skittered across the pavement and Ob skittered after it, but Harry was already there fielding it with an adroit foot. He picked it up calmly, winked at his friend and placed it carefully in his pocket. Morton had given up the fight long since—except to wring and massage his injured hand—he hadn't really moved since Ob's boot had made contact with it; he was shaking a little, not from fright, but from pain and from the cold which was inclined to creep up on you if you should happen to stop fighting and running about. He regarded the two victors with little expression in his hard black eyes.

'Who are you two? What the hell's all this about?'

Ob replaced his large hat carefully on his head and studied Morton solemnly through the fringe of vibrating silken balls. 'You're Mr. Morton, aren't you?'

'So?'

'You should thank us. We've saved you from worse than death.'

Morton looked frustrated. 'What are you talking about? You're a couple of maniacs. That man was right—you ought to be locked up.'

'No,' smiled Ob shaking his bobbles as he cocked an ear in the direction of an approaching police-car. 'You're the one who's going to be locked up.'

The raucous clanging bell seemed to ride up on the wind. Harry stood in the middle of the road and flapped his raincoat at it.

No less than three curious onlookers were lingering on the pavement; Ob regarded them sourly as the police-car drew up with a shriek. 'I thought people were always supposed to stop and watch a fight. I thought crowds collected from nowhere. That's what all the books say.'

With mayoral dignity Fred Heartbright stepped from the car, placed his helmet impressively on his head—he was too tall to wear it in the car—and stared sternly at everybody. Charlie followed with less dignity but with his helmet already on. Another policeman of the flat, peaked-cap variety, extricated himself from the front passenger seat and doubled energetically around the back of the car on to the pavement; the driver just wound down his window and settled back to enjoy the fun.

Ob's cheery 'Hello, Fred,' was greeted by a wooden stare.

'Hello, Charlie,' said Harry, but Charlie made a face which was difficult to decipher and looked up at the towering Fred as though he, Fred, were his, Charlie's, adopted father.

Fred soon had the whole thing under control; he was a born leader, was Fred. He scooped the unconscious Red from the greasy pavement and bundled him up in his arms as though he were a baby, though it would be true to say that had Red indeed been a baby and had chosen that moment to open his eyes to encounter the expression on Fred's face he would doubtless have done his best to crawl screaming back into his mother's womb. Fred frowned severely at Ob, with no great ceremony dumped the sprawl of arms and legs in the back seat of the police-car, indicating as he did so that Morton should join it. Morton, quietly fuming, demanded to be informed upon what charge he was to be held, at which Fred bared his teeth and looked engagingly at Ob and Harry who had been standing about feeling not a little *de trop*. Harry, with a flash of well-timed inspiration, produced the automatic from his pocket.

'He was waving this thing under our noses,' he mentioned.

Fred's eyes gleamed beneath his heavily frowning brows; he took the gun in his huge fist and regarded it for a silent moment, tiny and glinting on his enormous palm, then he raised it to his nose, sniffed at it with professional curiosity and finally clicked out the magazine thrusting the latter into his pocket. 'Ah,' he said thoughtfully, peering steadfastly at Morton. 'You were waving this thing under their noses . . . Right?'

'I would like to register a complaint against this man,' Morton told him indicating Ob looming in the background. 'He stole the keys to my car ...'

'A fully-loaded, lethal weapon ...' murmured Fred. 'Do you have a licence for this weapon, sir?'

'Of course I have. Don't be an idiot.'

'Sir?'

'I'm sorry, I'm a little distrait.'

Fred nodded slowly. 'And well you might be. Threatening with an offensive weapon should be enough to ensure that your journey won't be wasted. But apart from that there are several other small things of interest which we shall be glad to reveal to you at an opportune moment. If you please, sir ...'

He was magnificent. The phrases rolled off his tongue like thick honey. Morton could do nothing other than obey his invitation.

The flat-capped policeman got in beside him and Fred leaned down and spoke a word or two in the driver's ear. The latter nodded, started up his engine, raised a hand, and without really looking where he was going made a devastating U turn and made off at breakneck speed the way he had come.

With his hands behind his back Fred stared at the retreating flashing blue light. He looked like Wotan in the last act of *Die Walküre* saying goodbye to his favourite daughter ... except that he was a good deal more silent about it. When finally he looked at Ob it was more in sadness than in anger.

'You pinched his keys?'

'Yes.'

'Why?'

'We had to stop him, didn't we?'

'Why?'

'Didn't Harry tell you on the phone?'

'Tell me again.'

So Ob told him again, this time in more detail and making a great deal more sense than it had made in Harry's garbled pidgin English over the telephone. Fred remained immovable until the whole story was told, then looked at Harry. 'Keys?' He held out his hand and Harry dropped them into it.

Charlie had meantime been dickering with the car and when they turned their attention to it once again it was to find that he was in the act of removing the jack from beneath its rear axle.

‘We’d better be getting off, then,’ said Fred.

‘Where?’ asked Charlie.

‘How about the Amusement Park? We might as well check that everything’s all quiet there, and after we’ve done that we could all go home, I reckon, not before time.’

He climbed importantly into the driver’s seat, removed his helmet and presented it to Harry who sat beside him. Harry tried it on for size to find that it swallowed up most of his personality. He grinned sheepishly as he met Fred’s quiet gaze. ‘Too big,’ he said.

Fred was a good driver and looked magnificent behind the wheel of the big car. Ob, uneasy in the back seat, leaned forward tentatively. ‘If you drive into the Amusement Park in this thing you know what’ll happen, don’t you?’

‘What?’

‘All hell will be let loose. They’ll attack us. They’ll think we’re Red and his boss.’

‘They’ll have a surprise, then, won’t they? Not to worry. The Oakhaven police are standing by and if there’s any trouble there’ll be plenty of them to deal with it.’ He paused for a moment and added, ‘I do wish you hadn’t got yourself mixed up in all this. It’s not going to look too good, you know.’

Ob said impatiently, ‘If we hadn’t stopped those two on the road they’d have been lynched at the Fair Ground. Was it our fault that Boy took the whole thing into his own hands? He wasn’t going to wait, you know. You can’t blame him.’

‘I can.’

‘You’re just being rotten.’

‘I’m not being rotten,’ Fred sounded hurt. ‘I just wish you hadn’t got mixed up in it, that’s all.’

Further altercation was prevented by his application of the brakes as he swung the car through the gate of the Amusement Park.

‘Fasten your safety-belts,’ he advised.

By this time the place appeared to be fairly deserted, for though it was hardly six o’clock the majority of its clientele had drifted away to the warmth of their fires and the doubtful pleasure of Saturday night with television.

Slowly the big car purred and threaded its way through the colourful jumble of caravans and stalls, the powerful headlights picking up an occasional glimpse of a staring white face. The silence inside and out became tense and deadly—only the crunch of the heavy wheels and the occasional gust of wind buffeting at the windows disturbed it.

The lights had picked up the green-painted door of the little power-house when all at once the amplifiers blared with sound, hideously loud and distorted.

'Gawd,' muttered Ob beneath his breath.

If you gotta go, go now, screamed the loudspeakers, *or else you gotta stay all night . . .*

Black and gleaming in shining leather, still and dramatic in the blazing glare of the headlights, stood Boy. To his right and to his left, shoulder to shoulder, were other figures similarly dressed, equally menacing in their stillness. Harry glanced out of the side window. They were there too; and on the other side. Behind too. He felt slightly sick.

'I hope,' he muttered fearfully, 'everybody's going to understand.'

As the car slid to a smooth standstill the circle of leather-jacketed youths moved in slowly, step by step. It was like watching a 'with-it' ballet.

'Hold on to your hats,' warned Fred softly. 'Do everything gently and softly and it'll be all right.'

'We hope,' prayed Charlie, fiddling with the strap of his helmet.

Fred opened the door, put on his helmet and stepped out into the light.

The encroaching circle swayed and became immobile. Somebody swore in a soft, hoarse voice.

'Evening all,' said the imperturbable Fred. 'I wouldn't try anything if I were you, Boy Blue. Morton and Brody are under arrest and so will you be, too, and all your mates, if you so much as raise one little finger. I suggest you all—all of you—pack up and go home.'

Boy's bright blue eyes stared blindly in the blaze of light but as Ob moved in alongside Fred they flickered with contempt. 'You bloody copper's nark,' he sneered.

Ob took a short step forward but found himself clamped in the vice-like clutch of Fred's stalwart right hand. 'Break it up, I said, break it up and get off home—all of you.'

The tight ring of Boy's supporters wavered with uncertainty; a number of spectators were gathering, among them several members of Red Brody's little band of brothers, who taking in the situation with one swift professional glance, began now to amuse themselves by flinging derogatory and derisive remarks and suggestions at the discomfited *Skyriders.*

As the tension began to mount all the lights went out.

For a brief blinded moment everyone stood stunned by the unexpected descent of darkness, then, above the din of the amplifiers, came a single ear-piercing, bloodcurdling shriek like the scream of a banshee, which was the signal for utter and complete chaos. With a roar the whole world seemed suddenly to go mad. Everybody grappled with everybody else, yelling and shouting, fists and feet flaying, friend or foe, what did it matter? It was a glorious Saturday night in Oakhaven and there was nothing else to do, anyway . . .

But alas for the diehards, it was over before it had even begun. The milling, struggling, screaming mob became gradually aware of a circle of flashing lights closing in upon it, then there were policemen everywhere with lusty, restless truncheons and glaring torches, silent and determined, encroaching on the trouble centre with the ruthless relentlessness of an army of marauding ants.

There was little or no resistance from the contending forces. The fun had gone out of it. The bogies were in. There was not much to be gained by kicking a cop in the groin or knocking his helmet off when he could see who was doing it . . . so melt into the landscape, disappear while the disappearing's good, fade, man, fade . . .

Somebody yelled with laughter and the banshee voice cried, 'Take to the hills!' and except for the screaming cacophony of the loudspeakers the tumult and the shouting died almost as quickly as it had begun . . .

A uniformed Inspector of Police approached the huddled, battered group by the Bentley and flashed an inquisitive torch over it.

'Constable Hearthbright?'

'Sir,' Fred saluted briskly.

'Your sergeant informed us of the possibility of trouble here tonight and said you were responsible for the tip-off. Well done. I shall be interested to hear further details at a later date, in the meantime thank you . . . and, er . . .' the beam of his torch wandered down to Charlie smiling underneath his large slightly crooked-helmet '... you, too ... er ... Bourne ... is that right?'

'Yes sir. 318, sir.'

'Very good ... good work ... good work ...' The torch beam hovered for an uncertain moment over Harry and Ob. 'Who have we here? Who are these two? '

'They're with us, sir,' Fred told him with haste. 'Goodies, sir, on our side.'

'Ha,' said the Inspector. 'Goodies, eh?' He peered more closely at Ob and said with some embarrassment, 'Pretty hat ... pretty ...'

Then the lights came on again and some invisible soul clobbered the pick-up on the gramophone so that the needle slithered hysterically across the record. The music came to an abrupt and slurring end.

Harry blinked around in the stunning brightly-lit silence which erupted over them. Nobody but policemen. Nine hundred and ninety-nine policemen and not a human being within sight.

Funny how it had all not happened.

Ob, too, was a trifle disconcerted. He gazed around at the sea of blue uniforms waiting to take off. Even Boy had gone. 'Well,' he grumbled, 'that was a bit of a let-down, I must say. In all the books ...'

'Oh to bloody hell,' cried Harry tetchily, 'with all the blasted books!'

CHAPTER TWENTY-ONE

So that, more or less, was that.

Repercussions of Saturday Night at the Fun Fair proved to be almost endless and dragged on for several weeks. Statements and questions, questions and answers, innumerable invitations to the local police station until they were as well known there as Cabinet Ministers or Members of the Royal Family; hot strong tea with the sergeant at the desk, George, to be followed by police interviews perched uncomfortably on high-backed wooden chairs with the C.I.D. The chairs were two of four other pieces of furniture in the Detectives' Room and one of them boasted a considerable amount of rock-hard chewing gum stuck around the underside of its seat. After the interviews more glutinous tea with George, who seemed never too busy to welcome them with smiling jaws and brewing pot. One could not fail to notice, however, that everybody was received with an equal show of joy, even though a great many of his visitors turned out to be hard-bitten criminals, so not unnaturally Harry found himself tempering his reciprocation of George's friendship with a certain amount of reserve. But one day George included with the tea an enormous, still-warm doughnut full of raspberry jam, at which proof of goodwill even Harry capitulated.

After some weeks all seemed to get ironed out, though how it came about to everybody's satisfaction was something neither of them could even begin to conceive; to the mind of the simple layman the affair was what police-circles are pleased to term 'an open and shut case', but to the local police who enjoyed it immensely it was more of a revolving door—everybody could have a go—and did—rode around a couple of times, reviewed certain aspects of it, then got off and let someone else take over.

Ob appeared in court and gave evidence, which was quite a giggle for Harry, Jennifer and Maisie, all of whom took the day off to go and have a look. In spite of the fact that he fell up the steps leading into the witness box and cracked his head on the brass rail, Ob cut a splendid figure and they felt quite proud to know him. He was much too big for the box, or so they thought until Fred Hearthbright took his place.

Beneath their plodding patient exterior the C.I.D. had been extremely busy and had uncovered a great number of facts and figures unsuspected by Harry and Ob with regard to Morton's stolen car racket as well as a profitable insurance swindle which had been in full swing for several years.

The latter offence proved to be the important one as far as the police were concerned and the whole thing was transferred to the Old Bailey where Ob was not asked to appear. No less than six people were convicted and Morton himself was directed to withdraw from society for eight years.

With regard to Red, a year was the utmost that anyone could pin on him, which while it was a disappointment to Ob and Harry was a knife in the back for Boy Blue, who retired behind a malevolent blue-eyed exterior and sat down to wait—presumably for a year!

Harry and Ob came out of it very well and there was a short period during which Harry found himself wondering whether perhaps the Queen might present him with an O.B.E. or something equally gratifying for services rendered, but since nobody wrote to him from Buckingham Palace or Number 10 he simply accepted the inevitable and settled down to remain a philosophical nonentity for the rest of his life.

Ob and Fred became closer and more secretive as the investigation into Morton's misdemeanours progressed and there were even a couple of days when Ob was incarcerated in the police station, invisible to his friends, for six or seven hours on end. Harry wondered whether he had been arrested and demanded satisfaction of the smiling George who was drawing ladies' hats on his blotting paper with a well-chewed pencil.

'Nonsense,' said George, scandalised. 'Ob? Arrested? Nonsense.'

'Well, where is he then?'

'Who?'

'Ob. Where is he? Don't tell me you haven't got him locked up somewhere. He's been here since nine o'clock this morning, and hasn't been seen or heard of since. I want to know where he is. If he's being held for something I'd like to know what it is because whatever it is I've done it too and by rights you ought to arrest me, too.'

'Nonsense,' smiled George. 'Have another cup of char.'

'I don't want another cup of char. I want to know where my buddy is.'

George stared at him with moistening eyes. 'It's good to listen to you, do you know that? All my life I've been dealing with the seamy side one way and another and, you know, the thing that never fails to move me is loyalty. Even among criminals there's loyalty. Did you know that? "Honour among thieves" they call it . . .'

Harry swallowed. 'Thieves? What's he done, for God's sake?'

'Who?'

'Ob. He's not a thief. Ob's not a thief.'

'Who said he was? You're misunderstanding me again, Harry boy. I was simply saying that I was affected by loyalty, which is what you've got for your buddy . . . and I admire it . . . a little more loyalty in the world today and the world would be a far, far better place for people like you and me to live in, you know that?'

Harry groaned and gave up.

And when Ob got home that night there was a withdrawn secretive look behind his eyes and he had a paper-backed book wrapped up in *The Evening News* which was called *The Criminal Law* by F. T. Giles. Harry stared at the picture of a judge and a policeman on the cover and felt his throat go dry. What had Ob done?

'Read any good books lately?' he asked later when they were indulging in a pot of tea during advertisements on the television.

'What's that mean?' asked Ob.

'Books. I noticed you had a book when you came in. I was just wondering . . .'

Ob shook his head. 'I haven't read it.'

'What's it called?' The advertisements were over and the second act of the play was beginning. Ob became immersed.

'Eh?' demanded Harry truculantly.

'What?'

'What's the name of it?'

'What?'

'Your book—the one you brought in—what's it about?'

Ob flicked an impatient look at him. 'I keep telling you I haven't read it yet. Belt up, can't you, and watch the play. Thought you were enjoying it.'

The Criminal Law! What could it mean? Harry stared at Ob's flickering profile in the darkened room. There was something up, he knew that perfectly well, but you'd never guess what it was by looking at Ob's profile. It gave about as much information as a walled-up railway bridge.

'Ob . . .'

'What?'

'More tea?'

'Why not?'

The following day he talked to Jennifer about his worries. She smiled at him and shook her head with philosophic confidence. 'If it's anything you ought to know he'd tell you about it. Perhaps he doesn't want to tell you.'

'Why not?'

'I don't know.'

'He always tells me everything.'

'How do you know?'

'He always does. I know he always does. He hasn't got anybody else to tell.'

'He has now.'

'Who?'

'Maisie.'

Harry stared at her searchingly. 'Has she said anything?'

'No.'

'Sure?'

'Of course I'm sure.'

Harry brooded. 'He tells Fred Hearthbright things, too.'

Jennifer laughed and changed the subject. 'Mum wants you to come to tea this afternoon.'

'Is she still all right?'

'All right?'

'About us, I mean. She hasn't taken a scunner against me or anything?'

'Why should she?'

Harry grunted. 'People do,' he muttered darkly.

The next day was his day off and in spite of vigorous protests from Jennifer he drew out some money and, clutched closely to each other, they set out on a search for an engagement ring.

'I should have given you one weeks ago,' said Harry. 'It's only that things seemed to get on top of us. Where shall we go?'

'I don't want an engagement ring; you can't afford it.'

'Where?'

'There's Corbett and Handley's in the High Street.'

Outside the jeweller's window they lingered for a moment studying an emerald necklace solitary and shimmering on pale blue velvet; it cost £435. It glinted at them invitingly.

'I'll get you two of those,' promised Harry, kissing her with sudden passion on the forehead.

A little gold-painted plaque on the counter announced that they were dealing with a Mr. Prior, a small, bespectacled, Dickensian character with gentle, blue-veined hands and stooping back. Impeccable was the word for Mr. Prior. His smile was warmly avuncular as he greeted them.

'An engagement ring for the young lady?' he said in a voice dry as autumn leaves. It was more statement than enquiry.

They looked at each other and grinned sheepishly.

'Not too expensive,' said Jennifer.

Their experience with Mr. Prior was one which they were to remember for the rest of their lives . . . his gentleness, patience and complete absorption with their humble requirements; his obvious affection for their youth, the deep pleasure he derived from their reactions as he produced tray after tray of his softly-glowing merchandise. He took her left hand gently in his as though it were of Dresden, placing ring after ring upon her third finger with delicate care.

Once, looking over his spectacles, his pale eyes smiled sadly at Harry.

'Nothing,' he said, 'is quite so beautiful as the well-shaped human hand; the most perfect diamond in the world is unworthy of it.' He made it sound as though he were talking of Jennifer's hand.

When at last Jennifer had made her choice—a solitaire diamond in a filigree setting—Mr. Prior beamed his satisfaction and bowed over her decision as though she had selected his most valuable exhibit.

'The perfect choice, if you will allow me to say so, and one which I am certain you will never regret.' And he made that sound as though he were talking, not of an engagement ring, but of a husband. Harry hung his head in respectful silence.

As he held open the door for them Mr. Prior slipped a small package into Jennifer's hand. 'This is our wedding present to you both—with the compliments of Corbett and Handley. May I wish you both lifelong happiness.'

On the busy pavement outside they clung to each other, disconcerted and a little regretful at having to exchange the quiet grace and gentility of the little Victorian backwater for the brashness of their own age.

'Will you be happy with me, do you think?' asked Harry suddenly disturbed.

Her hand tightened on his. 'If you're nice to me, yes.'

'God, I hope it will be all right.'

She smiled up at him. 'Cold feet?'

'No, but I think I'm just beginning to realise what we're doing. "Lifelong happiness," he said. It's a long time, isn't it, for two people always to be happy.'

'We won't be happy all the time. No two people ever are; it would be terrible if they were. I expect we'll both cause each other a lot of unhappiness, people who really love each other always do—because they can hurt more than other people can.'

They went into a café and sat over some coffee.

Jennifer said with a twinkle in her eye, 'Did you know that Maisie and Ob are thinking about it, too?'

'About what?'

'About getting married.'

'Never.'

'Honestly.'

'What are they going to live on, air?'

'Same as we're going to live on, I suppose—love.'

'But Ob hasn't even got a job, and it doesn't look as if he's ever going to get one either. Maisie hasn't got any money, has she?'

'If she has she's never told me anything about it.'

'They really fancy each other, do they?'

'She's soft about him.'

'They'll be good for each other.'

They stared in entranced silence at Jennifer's engagement ring glowing on her finger. 'It's beautiful,' she whispered, '... quite beautiful.'

'Shall we look at the old boy's present?'

It was a set of small silver teaspoons in a black leather case lined with pale blue silk. They stared at them for a long time.

'Our first wedding present,' said Harry, 'and from a complete stranger.'

Jennifer touched the spoons gently. 'I've heard about jewellers giving presents to customers who buy wedding rings and things but I thought they would be only for posh customers. Perhaps he shouldn't have done it for us.'

His hand closed on hers. 'You're the poshest customer he's ever had in his shop and he knew it.'

He walked with her to the cinema and they stood for a moment or two hand in hand at the stage door.

'I see *Ben Hur*'s coming off,' he said.

'Yes.'

'It's been on a long time.'

'Three months.'

He looked down at her fondly. 'He'll never know what he did for me.'

The sun was bright and the sea sparkling with gaiety as he strolled homeward along the promenade. An itinerant photographer walked backwards in front of him took his photograph and thrust a ticket into his hand. 'Nice, sir, nice. Ready on Thursday.'

Without thinking Harry crumpled the ticket and threw it into a litter bin. 'Charming, I must say!' muttered the photographer behind him.

He thought deeply about Ob and Maisie and the chances of their getting married coupled with the remote possibility of Ob finding some suitable employment the income from which might aid and abet those chances.

It was going to be pretty tough even for Jennifer and himself, but for Ob and Maisie . . . He sighed and let himself in the front door. Poor old Ob . . . what would become of him now he and Jennifer were going to get married . . .

In the sitting-room a policeman was standing staring fixedly out of the window; he loomed large and black and his figure added further despondency to Harry's cheerless mood.

'Hello,' said Harry wearily for whom policemen in his sitting-room was becoming a daily occurrence. 'What do you want, then?'

'I wonder, sir,' said the policeman in a hoarse voice, 'whether you'd mind stepping over here for one moment.'

'What?' said Harry and went. He stared blankly out of the window. There was nothing to see out there except a street, and people, shops, traffic and a man with a barrow selling ice-cream. 'I don't see anything,' he grumbled, staring at the policeman. 'What's up?'

His jaw dropped.

'Hullo, Harry,' said Ob, solemn and red-faced beneath the helmet.

Harry gaped.

'You're not going to laugh, are you, Harry?' asked Ob, his face puckered with anxiety.

Harry moved slowly backwards, found a chair with the back of his knees and lowered himself carefully into it.

'I just thought . . .' said Ob and stopped.

'What,' asked Harry in an awe-stricken whisper, 'have you done?'

'What does it look like?'

Harry's head waved to and fro like corn in the wind. 'You must be joking.'

'No, I'm not . . . honest . . .'

The man with the ice-cream barrow was ringing a bell and shouting about the excellence of his ice-cream. Harry continued to stare transfixed at the enormous blue-clad Ob. Ob grinned sheepishly.

'What do you think, then?'

'Think?'

'About me being a copper?'

Harry struggled out of the chair and walked back to the window, his eyes never leaving Ob. 'I feel,' he said slowly, 'like as if you'd gone over to the other side.'

'Over the other side—me?'

'Well, haven't you? I mean you're one of Them now, aren't you?'

'I'm not any different from what I've always been.' He slowly removed the helmet and ran his fingers through his spiky black hair. 'Well, I thought, I've got to get a job, I thought. Who was interested in giving me one? No one. It was Fred gave me this idea. He's nice, old Fred, I like him . . .'

Harry's brain began to click little things into place.

'Are you going to like it?' he demanded somewhat petulantly. 'Running poor blokes in, spying on them, having your helmet knocked off in the football crowds. You'll have to go to football matches ... Oh mate! What *have* you done?'

Ob stood at ease on the hearthrug, his hands clasped behind his back.

'I've been over all that with Fred and in my own mind, too, and it's going to be all right, Harry, all right. I think it'll be quite good when I get used to it all. The helmet feels a bit unbalanced just at the moment, but I expect I'll even get used to that in time. Eh?'

Harry leaned back on the window. He said aggressively, 'You're going to marry Maisie, I hear?'

Startled, Ob said, 'Why, do you mind?'

'How's she going to take it—you being a rozzer—she's not going to care for it one little bit you know, Maisie isn't. I can just see her as a bogey's wife ...'

'There's no need to keep calling us names, you know. Maisie's all right. She says it's okay with her, so sucks to you.'

There was a moment's silence then Harry grinned. 'Well, you could knock me down ... P.C. ... what's your number?'

'Haven't got one yet. I've got to go down to Folkestone for about thirteen weeks' training, then I'll probably be coming back here on the beat and that. I've only just got the uniform, see, so I thought I'd just slip into it—give you a bit of a start like ...'

'Blimey, you certainly did that all right. I still can't believe it. I still think you're a nut ... however, you've decided to do it, so bloody good luck, I say. You might have told me what was going on, though, I've been thinking the most terrible things about you.'

'I thought you might laugh.'

'Laugh? Why should I laugh?'

'I don't know. You laugh sometimes for no reason at all—at the most extraordinary things. I just thought I'd get the whole thing fixed up properly before I told you.'

He strode awkwardly over to the sideboard and produced a couple of minute bottles of Babycham. 'Why don't we have a drink then, eh? As a sort of good luck thing? Celebration ... like launching me ... I name this ship P.C. Hobson Harvey like ...'

After that they both laughed for about ten minutes.

On the night before the wedding the four of them sat quietly in the sitting-room thinking about tomorrow and this and that. The night was hot and the windows were open ... they could hear the distant surging restlessness of the sea.

'Incidentally,' said Harry *à propos* of nothing. 'Ben came back on Sunday.'

'Oh?' said someone.

'There he was, just standing on the corner as if nothing had ever happened.'

'What did happen?' asked Jennifer.

Harry stared at Ob's profile. 'Nothing. It was just that he stopped turning up—for some reason ... nice kid .. I'm glad he's come back ...'

The silence lengthened then Ob said, 'Do you think you two are going to be comfortable here ... without me?'

Jennifer grinned. 'We'll manage. There are one or two things I want to do to the place.'

'One of them, I hope,' put in Maisie belabouring a cushion, 'being these ruddy cushions.' She suddenly held her hand limply and shook it as if in pain. 'What have you got in this thing? There's a lump of iron in here. What is it?' She felt the cushion and listened to it carefully.

Ob said, 'They're just filled with old junk. I don't believe in spending a lot of money on all those feather fillings and the like.'

Maisie was already pulling Ob's primitive tacking apart. They watched her with interest. From the interior of the cushion she produced an ancient sweater full of holes and covered with paint stains, a couple of ragged shirts, a pair of underpants, a tie, a piece of blanket, and half a loaf of bread, bright blue and hard as a bullet. Maisie held the bread before her blind eyes and stared at it with wonder.

'Bread,' she said, 'in a cushion. Half a loaf of stale bread.'

'It wasn't stale when I put it there otherwise I'd have noticed it. It's all ballast, anyway. It must have got mixed up with the other things.'

'Men!' exclaimed Maisie. She stared intently at Ob. 'I think I must be raving mad having you move in with me. It'll end in tears, I know it will!'

Ob grinned. 'I bet you haven't even got any cushions.'

'I have too, you know I have . . .'

'Shut up,' said Ob and seizing her in a masterful embrace pulled her close to him.

Jennifer and Harry sat silently staring through the open window. The moon sailed high and free in a deep velvet sky. It was like a jewel in the window of a jeweller's shop—bright and gleaming on soft blue velvet—Jennifer looked at her ring and raised it to her lips.

There was a long contented sigh from Maisie on the couch as she came up for air. 'Oh dear . . .' she murmured, 'You can't help laughing, though, can you?'